BOY MEETS BODY

COLLECTED NOVELLAS, VOLUME TWO

LOVERS AND OTHER STRANGERS

Recovering from a near-fatal accident, artist Finn Barret returns to Seal Island in Maine to rest and recuperate. But Seal Island is haunted with memories: some sweet, some sad. Three years ago Finn found his lover in the arms of Fitch, Finn's twin brother. Since that day, Finn has seen neither Conlan nor Fitch. In fact, no one has seen Fitch. Did Fitch run away as everyone believes? Or did he meet a more sinister fate? To put the past to rest—and see if there's any chance of a future with Con—Finn must discover the truth. But the deeper he digs, the more reason he has to fear Con is the only one who knows what truly happened to Fitch...

GHOST OF A CHANCE

Over a century ago, Illusionist David Berkeley committed suicide in his mansion by the sea, thus dooming his restless spirit to wander forever. Or so the local legend goes... Professor Rhys Davies, a part-time parapsychologist, is writing a book on California hauntings, and he believes the crumbling ruins of Berkeley House will make a terrific chapter—if he can gain access to the house and grounds. The only obstacle is brooding cop and self-appointed caretaker, Sam Devlin. As obstacles go, Devlin is a big one.

A VINTAGE AFFAIR

Somewhere in the cobwebbed cellar of the decrepit antebellum mansion known as Ballineen are the legendary Lee bottles—and Austin Gillespie is there to find them. What he discovers is the dashing and disturbing Jeff Brady.

BLOOD RED BUTTERFLY

Despite falling in love with aloof manga artist Kai Tashiro, Homicide Detective Ryo Miller is determined to break the alibi Kai is supplying his murderous boyfriend—even if it means breaking Kai with it.

Boy Meets Body

COLLECTED NOVELLAS, VOLUME TWO

Josh Lanyon

VELLICHOR BOOKS

An imprint of JustJoshin Publishing, Inc.

BOY MEETS BODY
Collected Novellas, Volume II

ISBN: 978-1-945802-58-4
Printed in the United States of America

JustJoshin Publishing, Inc.
3053 Rancho Vista Blvd.
Suite 116
Palmdale, CA 93551
www.joshlanyon.com

This is a work of fiction. Any resemblance to persons living or dead is entirely coincidental.

BOY MEETS BODY
COLLECTED NOVELLAS, VOLUME TWO

LOVERS AND OTHER STRANGERS

*I like pushing readers to consider and explore the
boundaries of transgression and forgiveness. Interestingly,
I've found that readers involved in healthy, ongoing
real-life romantic relationships are best able to deal with
the extreme emotional challenges some of my characters
dish out in the course of a story. I'm not sure that's a
coincidence. I think romance novels can actually teach us
quite a bit about ourselves.*

CHAPTER ONE

If he had been painting the scene before him, he would have used only four colors: Permanent Rose alkyd for the pink streaks in the fading sunset and the reflections in the water; Dioxazine Purple alkyd for the shadows lengthening on the creamy sand, the crevices of the rocks, the glint and gleam of water, the edges of the pier; Cadmium Yellow alkyd to blaze from windows, for the dimples in the sand, to limn the rocks, to gild the tips of scrubby, windblown grass, more reflections in the water; Indigo oil for the tumbling waves, for the indistinct forms of the buildings beyond, for the swift coming night.

For the first time in weeks, Finn felt the desire to take a palette knife and mix color, to pick up a brush and try to capture what he saw. For the first time in weeks, he felt a flicker of something close to interest, to emotion.

Maybe it was the salt air, maybe it was the cold—the briny wind whipping off the ocean stung his face—maybe it was the smell of wood smoke with all the warm memories it conjured. Or the cries of the gulls, the slap of the waves, the mingled fragrance of pipe smoke and car exhaust as he waited in the old station wagon for Hiram to carry his bags from the dock. Maybe it was all these things.

But it was the color he felt most intensely. Luminous color seeping into his consciousness, the hues and values, the shadows and lights, the dull tones, the vibrant—he was waking up. It was not a comfortable process, and Finn huddled deeper into his leather jacket.

Hiram strode to the car and threw Finn's bags in the back. Coming around to the front, he climbed in behind the wheel. Starting the engine, he glanced briefly at Finn as he backed the car, narrowly missing a leaning tower of stacked lobster traps.

"Guess it looks pretty different after all this time?"

Seal Island didn't look different at all in the purple dusk, but Finn said, "Three years is a long time."

"Ay-yup," Hiram said. "Your uncle Thomas is going to be happy as a clam at high tide to see you."

Finn's smile twisted. Everyone was being very kind. Especially considering what a pain in the ass he was to show up with almost no warning.

The station wagon crunched its way slowly over sand and shale, past the shadowy buildings and boats, the faded, peeling signs.

"'Course Thomas is in France right now. Some art show or another."

Finn murmured something. He didn't need to say anything. Hiram was happy to fill in all the blanks. There were a lot of blanks after so long.

"Martha's arthritis is giving her heck. Well, we're all gettin' older. Mr. Peabody's gone now. Pneumonia. Last month. Miz Landy took over the general store."

The car reached the surfaced road that ran around the island—smoother in some places than others. By now the amethyst dusk was falling back before the onslaught of night. Finn felt tension growing inside, his stomach knotting up with his fists. It was irrational. Irritating. Fear of the dark? At his age? It was cold, though—bitingly. After a short battle with himself, he reached for the rough plaid car blanket that smelled of a million journeys and spread it over his left leg, which had started aching.

"Not used to the cold anymore," he muttered, but Hiram took no notice, still palavering about people and things Finn had stopped caring about—tried to stop caring about—a long time ago. Ay-yup, what a pleasant surprise—shock, translated Finn—it had been to hear from Finn. Martha had been in a twitter ever since she got his message. And what a surprise Thomas had waiting for him when he got home. What a surprise it was going to be for everyone.

Finn almost asked then. But it was too much effort, and he wasn't sure even now he could take the answer, so he smiled politely and stared out the window as though he had newly arrived from another planet, which was pretty much how it felt.

Stands of pine trees rose stark and sharp against the dusk as the car climbed slowly, winding up through the rolling hills. The pines looked black against the lowering sky, but that was an illusion. He'd start with a sketch, using a No. 0 watercolor brush. For the sky and water, he'd use a blend of Cadmium Yellow Medium, Cadmium Red Light, and Titanium White. For the upper sky, he'd choose French Ultramarine, Dioxazine Purple, and more Titanium White...

White. He had a sudden flashback of blazing white walls and the sun bouncing off pale sand—too much light, and a brightness that hurt the eyes. The white beneath a silent gull's wingspan, the white of the craggy clouds, the white of the tiny wildflowers growing beside the white speckled stone walls.

The lighthouse was on the other side of the island. No need to see it at all if he didn't choose to—and why the hell would he ever want to see it again?

Hiram was saying, "Miz Estelle won first prize at Union Fair for her wild blueberry sour cream cake."

Finn felt an unexpected twinge of hunger. "I still remember those cinnamon-sugar biscuits she used to make."

The old man nodded in heartfelt agreement.

The car turned off the main road and ground its way up the steep last stretch. The house was called The Birches. One of those charming turn-of-the-century, ten-bedroom "cottages," it stood in a grove of white birches overlooking Otter Cove. Green lawns swept down to the rocks at the water's edge, ancient, gently tilting pines framed sunsets so beautiful they made the heart ache. In the failing light, the house looked eerily untouched by time.

Hiram pulled up in front of the long porch. Lights shone welcomingly from several downstairs windows.

"Ain't no place like home," he said, and Finn made a sound in his throat that was supposed to be humor but wasn't.

Hiram got out of the car. The front door of the house flew open, and Martha came bustling down the shell-strewn path as Finn climbed carefully out of the station wagon. Tears glittered on Martha's wrinkled cheeks, and she hugged him tight, pulling him to her ample bosom like he was a child again.

"Look at you, you young rascal!"

Finn didn't have to do much more than smile and permit himself to be hugged again; Martha was doing all the talking—although afterward he had no idea of anything she'd said. He was literally overwhelmed with memories and unwelcome emotion.

Hiram went to get the bags, and Finn was being urged inside the house to warmth and comfort—the prodigal returned. By then he was exhausted. He should have brought the cane; he was hobbling badly, not used to walking any distance yet, and the plane flight and boat ride not helping any. Maybe he was more crocked up than he wanted to admit—he was certainly in more pain.

The house smelled familiar. It smelled of baking and wood fire—and the invariable ghostly hint of oil paint, although it had been decades since anyone in the house painted with oils. It smelled like his childhood: safe and warm and loved. He stared curiously as he was hustled past a familiar painted chest, wing chairs upholstered in pale gray roses, white bookcases, well-remembered paintings. It felt odd to see these things again—like he was visiting a museum.

Ushered into the kitchen, he was ensconced in the old rocker and ordered to stay put near the enormous gas stove where Martha had cooked breakfast, lunch, and dinner for the Barrets for the past thirty years. That suited him fine. Gave him a chance to catch his breath and get control of himself.

Martha and Hiram conferred outside briefly—he could imagine how *that* went—and then Martha was inside the kitchen and chattering a mile a minute, banging pots and pans around to relieve her feelings.

Finn eyed her curiously from the perspective of his years away. She was in her late sixties now, a small, very plump woman with silky white hair—it had been white since her early thirties—and soft dark eyes. Something about her had always reminded him of a dove, though doves were fairly stupid birds and Martha was a far-from-stupid woman.

"Now that you've been living in New York, I suppose you won't be happy with fiddleheads and potatoes anymore? It'll be fancy curries and nouveau cuisine you're used to, I reckon."

Finn laughed—he lived on peanut butter sandwiches half the time— and said, "I haven't had a decent bowl of chowdah since I left here."

She stopped chattering then, coming to him, putting her hands on either side of his head. She turned his face to the light, examining him closely. The only damage that showed was the one scar—still healing—on his temple. What didn't show was the horrific long gash from his hip to the middle of his calf. Torn muscles, damaged nerves, but oddly no broken bones. He had been left with one hell of an ugly seam down his leg, but he knew how lucky he had been. And aside from the scars, he was going to be as good as new eventually. That was why he had to stop dwelling on the might-have-beens. The close call didn't matter because he was going to be all right—as soon as the headaches stopped.

Martha was staring into his eyes as though trying to read his mind. He blinked up at her, and her eyes filled with tears again. She kissed him— something he couldn't remember her doing since he had been very small. She was clearly horrified at herself. Not as horrified as he was, though— not that she had kissed him, but that he had been so moved, his throat closed and he had to look away.

It was only for an instant. Nothing more than the aftermath of the accident—and probably his meds. It did something to you, nearly dying. And dying sometimes felt like the least of it.

"Your uncle Thomas will be here tonight," she said.

That snapped him out of his self-consciousness. "Uncle Tom? I thought…"

"Why, I phoned him the minute I heard from you," Martha said a little defiantly—because Finn had expressly told her not to bother Thomas. "Of course he'd want to know! Of course he's coming home. And while I'm thinking of it, that friend of yours phoned up. Mr. Ryder. He's coming day after tomorrow."

The funny thing about the spell the island cast, the silken weave of childhood memories, was that he'd already forgotten he'd asked Paul to come along and lend moral support. Now he wondered why. Paul was going to be a fish out of water here, and Finn was going to have to expend energy he didn't have in trying to keep him amused. Paul took a lot of amusing.

He brooded over this while Martha rattled cheerfully on, finally surfacing to hear her say, "…Barnaby Purdon retired from school teaching."

"Do he and Uncle Tom still get together to play checkers once a week?"

"Every Wednesday when your uncle is here. What else? Oh, Miss Minton took first place at Union Fair for her wild blueberry sour cream cake."

"I heard that. Is she still taking painting lessons from Uncle Tom?"

"No. No, she gave up on that idea. Your uncle Tom doesn't teach anymore, you know. Too busy judging art shows and writing his books."

She brought him a mug of coffee. Finn took the yellow cup, sipping cautiously. It was boiling hot, but creamy and sweet—the way he had liked it when he was a kid. Creamy and sweet—and spiked with something.

"What's in this?" he asked. "I'm on pain pills, you know." In fact, he urgently needed medicating. His back was beginning to ache—his leg never quite stopped—and his head was starting up again despite the muted light and warmth.

"A little something to warm your bones," Martha told him. "It won't do you any harm. Might put a little color in your face."

Finn raised his brows but kept drinking. It was good. Martha's version of an Irish coffee perhaps. All at once he was so tired he thought he might fall asleep at the fireside wrapped like an ancient granny in these cedar-scented blankets. Martha chattered comfortably on about this and that person, the changes he would soon see in the island—and of course, in Martha's view, none of the changes were for the better.

He smiled to himself and sipped his coffee.

His smiled faded as she said, "Mr. Carlyle has a new book coming out."

She was not looking at him, which was just as well since he couldn't think of anything to say.

"He's not here now. He was in England for six months doing research for the one he's writing now. It's supposed to be a murder mystery about the princes in the Tower. And then he went on a book tour for the last one. It's hard to keep 'em all straight. I don't expect we'll see him back till next month sometime."

That was a relief. More than he wanted to concede. "I'll be long gone by then." His voice came out flat.

Martha still didn't look at him. "Well…that's all right so long as you don't take three years to visit again."

She spoke cheerfully, but he could hear the strain and knew that he had to make the effort. For his own sake, if nothing else. Had to prove that he could say it and not…well, what? That he had moved past it. That it was over and done with, chapter closed. Not forgiven, not forgotten…but old history. Con should appreciate that.

So he said, "How's Fitch?"

And after a funny little pause, Martha said, as though the name were unfamiliar to her, "Fitch?"

"Is he...?" He tried to make his voice light, but he was never good at that kind of thing. Fitch was the old pro at games and deceiving. "Are he and Con... Did they... Are they still together?"

"Fitch and...Mr. Carlyle?" She said it almost wonderingly.

Finn remembered belatedly that this was a small island, a backwoods sort of place really, and that while a romantic relationship between two men might be silently tolerated and civilly ignored, it was never going to be openly acknowledged and condoned. But his nerves were on edge, he was tired and much more raw than he had realized; he simply blurted out, "Or did he split?"

Martha said, "Didn't Fitch come to you in New York?"

"Come to me?" That made him blink. What a funny idea—but maybe not so funny because Fitch wouldn't see what he had done wrong, would he? He would expect to be forgiven as he always was by his—his words— *better half.*

"Didn't Fitch follow you to New York?" asked Martha again, and she was staring at him hard now, as though only realizing that something was very wrong. But Fitch had always been her favorite. Fitch was everyone's favorite for all he shocked and appalled people with his outrageous—but God, yes, funny—antics. The things he did and said. It was impossible not to love Fitch.

Even when you hated him.

Finn said, "He didn't follow me to New York."

Had that been Fitch's intention? Had better sense prevailed? It must have hurt Fitch too; he must have felt the same persistent ache that was almost physical pain, the pain of being cut off from your other half. A phantom pain, like losing a limb. It had never happened to them before: a break so deep, so wide, there was no bridging it. Oh, they had fought, fallen out—what brothers didn't quarrel? Finn had always forgiven Fitch because…he loved him. And he couldn't do without him. Until he could.

Until Con.

Because there was no forgiving that. Con had been different.

Not that Con wasn't every bit as much to blame.

But then Finn hadn't forgiven Con either. Never would.

Anyway, it was a long time ago. He was never going to see Con again. So what did it matter? As for seeing Fitch…he had always accepted that Fitch knew how seriously he had transgressed because he hadn't followed his twin to New York.

And that was just as well because as lonely as he had been, there was no forgiveness in Finn.

Not then. Maybe not ever. Something had died in Finn that summer. That last day of summer.

But now he sat in the kitchen of the house he had grown up in, the home he had shared for twenty-three years with his twin. Slowly, he worked it out, tried to absorb what it meant. He said, "Fitch isn't here?"

And Martha shook her head slowly, her bright, birdlike eyes wide.

Reading her expression, Finn smiled reassurance because it seemed ridiculous—like they were talking at cross purposes and they would soon realize what the other actually meant. In a moment they would laugh as the misunderstanding was straightened out. "You mean no one's seen him since…?"

"No."

"No?" He took it in slowly, absorbing it much like the heat soaking into his chilled body or the alcohol wending its way through his blood-stream—a gradual realization that he was warm and tipsy and…alone in the world.

He said carefully, "No one has seen or spoken to Fitch in three years?"

"No." And Martha looked…frightened. It was her fear that woke Finn to the belated realization that his twin brother was missing.

"Come here, Huckleberry," Con murmured. His pale hair was wet and dripping from their swim, his bare brown skin shining in the sun. His dark eyes laughed into Finn's, and his mouth—covering Finn's—was sweet with the taste of the berries. His skin smelled like the sun and clean sweat and deep water.

From overhead came a burst of laughter—

A hand on Finn's shoulder woke him. He jerked, opened his eyes, and his uncle Thomas was gazing down at him. Uncle Tom was smiling, but his eyes were grave.

"Welcome home, Finn."

"Hi," Finn said. It was probably a little anticlimactic after three years, but he was fogged from sleep, disoriented to suddenly find himself in the kitchen at The Birches. He straightened, wiped his eyes with the heel of his hand. "I must have fallen asleep."

Martha chuckled, although her voice had that strained note again. "Sleep is exactly what you need!"

"Sounds good to me," Uncle Thomas said wearily. He was tall and very thin with the bony features and red-brown hair that distinguished the Barrets from the rest of the small population of Seal Island. Now in his sixties, he was going silver at the temples, which perfectly suited his image as an esteemed art critic.

"I didn't intend for you to be dragged home from Paris," Finn apologized.

His uncle was looking at him as though he were speaking a foreign language. Translation having failed, Uncle Thomas said, "Martha told me about your accident. Said you insisted you didn't want anyone there at the hospital. You're all right?"

"A few bumps and bruises."

"Well, you're staying here till you're back on your feet."

Finn chuckled. "I'm on my feet now." Or he would be if he could unfold from this rocker without landing on his face.

"You know what I mean." Uncle Thomas said it firmly; that was the polite fiction they had all played. That Uncle Thomas was actually in charge. He had been, at best, an absentminded guardian, but he was fond of them in his own way, and Finn and Fitch had certainly never lacked for anything growing up. Well, possibly attention. But then they had always had each other, so nothing else really mattered.

"Yes," Finn said. "Thank you."

"This is your home," Martha said sharply. Both men looked at her, having forgotten for a second that she was in the room, and she blushed. But she said stubbornly, "It's not right, you and Fitch gone all these years and never coming back for so much as a visit."

"Now, Martha," Uncle Thomas said in his easy way. "He's here now." To Finn he said, "It's too late for talk tonight. We'll catch up in the morning. Did you need some help getting to bed?"

"I'm okay. Is it really that late?" Finn looked automatically for the old wall clock, shaped like a ship's wheel, but it was gone, replaced by an efficient and modern titanium square.

"Nearly midnight," Uncle Thomas said. "I meant to be here much earlier, but my flight was delayed."

Nearly midnight? Could that be right? Could he really have been sleeping for over six hours? "Hell. You really shouldn't have dropped everything to come home for this." Finn was growing more awkward by the minute. "I didn't mean to disrupt everyone's life. I just…"

Just needed time to rest and recover. Time to come to terms with how close he had been to dying. To losing everything. Time to regain his strength and natural optimism; he was still astonishingly, aggravatingly *weak*. In fact, as he forced himself up out of the comfortable rocker, he was made painfully aware of how feeble he still was.

"Nonsense," Uncle Thomas and Martha both said—and then looked at each other.

Martha said, "But you've neither of you had any supper."

"I ate on the flight," Uncle Thomas said, which happily distracted her while Finn stood swaying, biting his lip against the myriad aches and pangs and throbs.

Uncle Thomas said with unexpected determination, "I think I'll give you a hand upstairs anyway."

Finn nodded. No point pretending he didn't need it. Uncle Thomas wrapped a strong arm around his waist, and Finn hung on to him as Martha bade them good night.

"I'm stiff from sitting so long." Finn explained as they passed slowly through the hall with its lilac sprig wallpaper. "I really am fine now."

"Of course you are. You'll be working again in no time."

Ah. Of course. In this house, the work was paramount. Well, it was to Finn too.

They crossed the dining room with the long formal table and harp-backed chairs where they had all eaten dinner when his grandfather was alive, across the back hallway, and then up the narrow staircase with the gleaming banisters Finn recalled sliding down as a child. Or was it Fitch who had slid down the banisters and Finn who watched? Sometimes it was hard to separate Fitch's adventures from his own memories.

Uncle Thomas's voice jarred him out of his preoccupation. "Martha said your friend was killed in the accident."

Finn nodded tightly.

"Was he... Was your friend...?"

Uncle Thomas floundered awkwardly, and Finn said, "He was a friend, that's all. A good friend. He yanked the wheel at the last minute so that his side of the car took the worst of it."

The stairs seemed to take forever. Finn could have cried in gratitude by the time they reached the upper landing—then the final leg to his old room, the room that had been his since his teens. Fitch's room was on the other side of the adjoining black-and-white checked bath.

There was no sign of Finn's bags, but his pajama bottoms and robe were laid across the foot of the dark wood sleigh bed. He bit back a tired smile. Martha would have unpacked while he slept downstairs. There was no privacy in this house. Lucky thing Finn had no secrets. Not anymore.

Uncle Thomas helped him undress. It was embarrassing, but Finn really was exhausted beyond action now. With his uncle's help, he pulled on knit sleep pants—and though the older man said nothing, Finn saw his face tighten up at the terrifying scar down the left side of Finn's body. One inch more and Finn would have died with Tristan.

"You won't be warm enough like that," Uncle Thomas said. "You've forgotten how cold the winters are here. I'll get you one of my pajama tops."

He was gone down the hallway, and Finn sat looking around the room. Once again he had that weird sensation of looking at an exhibit in a museum. Books and model ships... He stared at the framed photographs on the bookshelves: pictures of himself and Fitch sailing and climbing and fishing and swimming. A skinny eleven-year-old Fitch's arm looped around his neck in a friendly choke hold, himself giving the eighteen-year-old Fitch an impromptu piggyback. People said they couldn't be told apart, but Finn never had to wonder who was who in the pictures—not even in the earliest photographs of them.

Uncle Thomas returned with a striped flannel pajama shirt, and Finn shrugged into it, did up the buttons.

"Is it true Fitch left the island when I did?" he asked, eyes on the buttonholes.

"Yes."

"And no one's heard of him since?"

"I don't think that's so surprising," Uncle Thomas said grimly. Finn wasn't exactly sure what he meant. Surely no one knew the full story of what had happened that day? But he was too tired to question.

He crawled into bed, rediscovering the pleasure of clean flannel sheets that smelled faintly of the crisp ocean breeze. Stretching out gingerly, his spine seemed to unkink like a Slinky. He was astonished when his uncle shook the folds out of the quilt at the foot of the bed and spread it over him.

"Good night," he said politely, wondering if he was about to be tucked in and kissed.

He was spared that much. The bedside lamp went out, and his uncle said quietly, "Good night, Finn. I'm glad you've come home." He went out. The door closed silently behind him, shutting Finn into the darkness.

His heart began to pound, turning over sickly in his chest. Finn waited, sweat breaking out along his hairline as he listened. Through the dormer windows, he could see the mutable darkness that was the sea; stars glittered on the waves, pinpoints of light.

No need for panic. There was plenty of light. Moonlight, starlight, reflected light...

His uncle's footsteps died away down the hallway. Finn sat up and turned on the lamp.

He relaxed, let out a long breath. In the mellow glow, the books and toys of his childhood looked very old, very fragile.

He stared at the photos of his cheekily grinning twin and whispered, "Where are you, Fitch?"

CHAPTER TWO

They had grown up on the island; the Barret Boys, people called them. Their grandfather was Holloway Barret, the famous artist. His lush illustrations, reminiscent of an earlier period, livened up all kinds of dry history tomes and sappy children's stories. Their mother was Pamela Barret, whose elegant watercolors hung in galleries and private collections all around the world. But here on Seal Island off the coast of Maine, they were simply the Barrets, and Finn and Fitch were the Barret Boys. Sometimes Those Damned Barret Boys. But they were good kids mostly, and it was a tightly knit community, and they had grown up safe and sheltered.

For a time it looked as though the Barret drive for success had skipped a generation. Fitch had been expelled from college after one too many pranks, and Finn had flunked out. In Finn's case, it was homesickness as much as anything else. That, and desperation to paint—really paint—not spend his life talking about painting or studying how others did it. At twenty, he had returned to the island in disgrace, for the first time experiencing what it felt like to disappoint the people you love. A feeling Fitch was well acquainted with and had learned, mostly, to laugh off.

He had certainly laughed off Finn's guilt. Finn had done exactly what he wanted; why feel guilty? And if he felt truly bad about it, he could always go to Grandy, who would pull a few strings and get Finn admitted to another brand-name college where he could excel at listening politely to people who had never painted a real dab in their lives tell the people with talent what to do. Well, Finn didn't feel *that* bad about it, and Fitch had laughed at him again.

Grandy had been less amused. Finishing university was about discipline and learning your craft and respect—it was nothing to do with talent. It was already obvious Finn was the keeper of the flame for his generation of Barrets. Even when he had been quite young, messing around in his mother's studio, he had heard the adults quietly appraising him and agreeing; Finn had "the gift." No, Finn had failed by leaving school, and Fitch was equally to blame for encouraging him.

The fact that Grandy had never gone to college was irrelevant.

And how the hell dare Fitch disparage art critics and art teachers when his uncle Thomas was one of the same, and a damned fine one!

Never mind that Fitch had been practically quoting Grandy verbatim.

That had led to one of Fitch and Grandy's famous blowups, which ended with Fitch leaving the island yet again. He was gone for nine months that time—only returning when their mother lay dying.

Finn, quietly accepting that he was in disgrace, returned to his painting and blissfully lost himself in the work. He politely ignored everyone's disappointment and disapproval—it only lasted a week or two had he even been aware of it. He was pretty much unaware of everyone and everything but the work. That was the summer he had finally given himself over to painting.

He had missed Fitch, of course, but he had missed Fitch in college too, and Fitch did periodically disappear when he and Grandy butted heads. No one antagonized Grandy like Fitch, and yet the old man adored him—when he wasn't calling for his head on a palette. But then everyone adored Fitch. Finn did. Their mother had postponed her painful dying that long summer in order to spend as much time as possible with her eldest.

But that first spring—the spring after Finn had bailed out of college— was the happiest of his life. He felt that he had at last come into his own; he was consumed with painting, with "making up for lost time," which (had he known it) amused the adults around him no end. He ate, drank, and slept painting. It was all he thought about, all he wanted.

For years it was all he wanted. And then Conlan Carlyle came home.

Conlan Carlyle, the writer—the writer of dry and dusty histories that, as Fitch had once said, could have used Grandy's illustrations to perk them up. Con Carlyle was by way of being a neighbor although his folks were "summer folk," wealthy New Yorkers who summered in their elegant and enormous "cottage" on the island. Con hadn't any time for the Barret Boys, being so much older and busy with his own friends—female and otherwise…

So many remembrances; it could have been memory lane down which Finn was making his painstaking way rather than the path that led from The Birches to Gull Point. It was the morning after his arrival on Seal Island. He had borrowed his grandfather's old walking stick, a maple cane with a nickel-silver wolf-head handle, and he was suffering the fresh air and sunshine so beloved by physicians everywhere. The fact that it was fucking *freezing* skipped everyone's notice. There were thin layers of ice over the puddles in the path as he hobbled slowly past the black fir spinneys and meadows turning gold and red in the late autumn.

Automatically, his eye began isolating colors into the paints he would use…Raw Sienna, Old Holland Yellow, Indian Red, Burnt Umber, Burnt Sienna, Cadmium Orange…

He didn't want to remember how things used to be, but it was impossible here with the salt scent of the ocean, the chill spice of pines, the taint of wood smoke—funny how fragrance brought it all back.

He passed Estelle Minton's house. Yellow shingles and red brick, red roses behind a white picket fence. The roses Estelle had been in the process of planting three years ago were now tall—if wind-tattered. At this time of year, her beloved garden was not at its best. Smoke rose cozily from the chimney. Finn half expected Estelle to wave him down—rarely did anyone slip past her front window without being spotted—but if she saw him, she did not come out to say hello, and Finn walked on, dogged by memory.

"You're Finn," Con had said. "The Barret boy." As though there were only one Barret boy.

He was twenty-three that spring, and he had met Con—literally bumped into him—walking into the Curtis Memorial Library. He had gone to the mainland to pick up art supplies and a couple of Ross MacDonald mysteries for Grandy. His thoughts had been a million miles away; he'd spent days trying to paint the fishing fleet's sunset return but couldn't get it right—and he had walked right into the tall man coming out the west entrance.

At the time he had thought the collision was his own fault, but now he realized Con had been nearly as distracted as he was. It was Con who had reached out to steady him, hands warm on Finn's arms.

"Whoa! All right?" he'd said, and he was smiling, a cynical twist of his lips as though this was exactly the kind of behavior he expected from the natives. And then his brown-black gaze had seemed to sharpen. "You're...Finn. The Barret boy."

Finn recognized him immediately, although it had been at least two years since he'd seen Con Carlyle. All the same, he was genuinely surprised. People—strangers—had trouble telling them apart, and when had Con Carlyle been anything but a stranger, for all that they'd summered on the same island for twenty-three years?

"Yeah. How did you know?" he'd asked.

Con had smiled again—and the smile was a revelation. Finn had never seen Conlan genuinely smile. Oh, maybe a polite grimace when someone—often Fitch—was acting more like an idiot than usual; Fitch had always had a little bit of a thing about Con Carlyle.

Con had grinned that devastatingly attractive grin and raised his elegant eyebrows. "How could I *not* know you? You've been stealing my blueberries and swimming in my cove for the last twenty years."

"Twenty-three, but who's counting?"

He was so very attractive—pale hair, a lean, ascetic face, sable eyes lighting with unexpected laughter. It was like one of those paintings of old saints suddenly coming to life, suddenly animated and vivid.

"But maybe I'm Fitch," Finn had suggested.

And Con had said, "You're not Fitch."

The funny part was that at the time Finn had imagined it was a compliment.

But he didn't want to remember these things. What was the point of sinking down into quaggy, regretful thoughts? If he was going to dredge all that up, better to focus on the hurt, the anger, the betrayal. But why think of it at all? It was a long time ago, and he had more important things to worry about.

Like…the fact that he had walked too far from the house. That was his impatience getting the better of him, but to hell with "not rushing things." What did that mean? You could only rest for so long. And what on earth did peace and quiet have to do with anything? It wasn't as though he lived in a box beneath a freeway underpass. This whole idea of being sent away to recover his health was so fucking Victorian.

Even more irritating was the fact that the only place he had been able to think of going to recuperate was Seal Island. What had he been thinking? But at the time—or perhaps it was due to too much pain medication—he had yearned for home like the homesick college kid he had once been. And of course the doctors thought Seal Island was a terrific idea. The fresh salt air, the sunshine, the long, quiet nights—everyone cheerfully ignorant of how goddamned cold it was, and how…painful and tiring to face the memories you had been running from for so long.

At least he didn't have to face anything more than the ghosts. Con was safely on his book tour, and Fitch…

That was strange about Fitch.

All these months…years without word. That wasn't like Fitch. Even when he had clashed with Grandy the last time, he had stayed in touch with Finn. Granted, he couldn't very well stay in touch with Finn this time.

Still…

The spark of uneasiness Finn had felt on initially hearing that Fitch was missing had kindled into quiet worry. Three years was a very long time to disappear without a word. And Fitch had never been one to hold a grudge—nor had Fitch any reason to hold a grudge since he had come out the winner that time.

Finn became aware that with his thoughts running elsewhere, his feet had followed the familiar path to the cottage by Bell Woods. The cottage was on the edge of the old Carlyle estate; Con worked there most days, safely out of reach of his devoted family. There was no phone at the cottage—or at least there had not been a phone three years ago.

For a time Finn stood, leaning on Grandy's cane, studying the white shingles and black shutters, the brick chimney and neglected garden. He felt surprisingly little. It was only a building, after all, and the memories existed independently of the architecture.

Lost in these thoughts, he noticed too late the door to the cottage swinging open. Con stepped outside. "Finn," he said.

There was an alarming moment when Finn thought his mind had snapped, that he was rolling and sliding off the edge of sanity, and then he realized that he was not imagining things. Con was striding down the path toward him.

Too late to flee even if could manage it without looking like the loser in a three-legged race. So he held his ground, clenching his grandfather's walking stick, as Con reached him.

"Finn," Con said again, and he sounded out of breath.

He had not changed much in three years. Tall and lithe, his hair was still ash-blond, straight, and fine as silk, but he wore it a little longer now. His eyes were a shade of brown-black that Finn had never managed to determine; he remembered reading in one of the books his grandfather had illustrated about a pirate with "sparkling black-cherry eyes," and he'd always thought that perfectly described Con's eyes—although the wicked laughing eyes were at odds with a face as elegantly and distantly beautiful as the saint in a Renaissance painting. But there were faint little lines now around Con's mouth and eyes, a tightness to his features. He looked tired, like he'd run too long and too far and had still not found what he was looking for.

Idiotically, the only thing Finn could think to say was, "I didn't know you were back."

"I got back last night."

Good Lord. They should have held out for a group rate given the amount of traffic to the island yesterday.

"Oh. Well…nice to see you." Finn turned to go, leaning heavily on the cane.

"Wait." Con jerked out, "Can you…come inside for a minute?"

"Not today." Finn kept moving, crablike, trying to escape. "I've got to get back."

"Finn—" Con came alongside him.

In his slow-motion panic, his foot turned on a stone, and Con reached out to steady him. Every nerve in Finn's body flinched away from his touch. He'd thought he was over it, but the feel of Con's hand—the warm weight through his sweater—warned him otherwise. Bewilderingly, it was as though no time had passed at all, all his emotions were boiling right there at the surface.

"Jesus, Finn, you're white to your lips. You should never have walked so far. Come in out of the cold for a few minutes." Con looked—Finn didn't think it was an expression he could capture on canvas. It surely wasn't an expression he remembered ever seeing before on Con's face.

"Please," Con said.

It was something in the way he said "please." Not a word Con had ever used a lot. Certainly not with Finn. As he stared at him, Finn was suddenly and utterly exhausted—light-headed with it. It was borne in on him how very far he had walked—and what a bad idea that had been. His head began that slow, ominous pound. He allowed himself to be led inside the cottage.

It was blessedly dim and warm inside. A fire crackled welcomingly in the fireplace, classical music was playing softly, the wooden blinds stirred in the draft finding a way through the window casement. A stack of printed pages sat neatly beside a desktop and printer. It hadn't changed.

Finn dropped down on the long leather sofa, put a hand over his eyes. Con hovered.

"I can't believe you're here."

Finn looked at him and failed to think of anything intelligent to say. He agreed, though. Quite fucking unbelievable that he was here.

"Can I get you anything?"

"Ouch. No." Finn shifted gingerly. Dropped the cane.

Con retrieved the cane and propped it within Finn's reach. Con straightened, and Finn realized he was staring at the bones of Finn's knees poking at his Levi's, at his wrists, which still looked too thin for the rolled cuffs of his sweater.

"I heard about your accident," Con said. "Are you… You're all right now?"

"I'm fine." He looked away.

"Relax, Finn. You look like you're going to fly up the chimney any second."

Finn's mouth curled. He didn't fly so well these days.

"Sit back," Con was urging, and Finn cautiously lifted his leg onto the sofa. Easing back, he sighed relief. Yeah, whatever made Con doubt he was in great shape?

He became aware that Con still hovered over him. He looked up warily. Con asked, "Do you have anything you can take?"

"Huh?"

"For the pain."

"Oh." Finn grimaced. "This isn't that bad. Anyway, I don't like taking that crap. It makes me dopey."

"So? I'll run you back. Go ahead and take the stuff." Con strode out of the room. From the kitchen, Finn heard water running, the sound of ice cube trays cracking open.

He closed his eyes, trying not to give in to the hot, throbbing poker of pain jamming into the base of his skull. Overexertion, that's all it was. Maybe there was something to that not-rushing thing.

"Here, Finn."

His eyes flew open. He hadn't heard Con return, but he stood over the couch with a glass of water.

Finn inched up against the cushions, found his pills, palmed two, and reached for the glass.

He handed the water back to Con, who set it aside and pulled up a footstool.

"Finn...I've been waiting three years to talk to you."

Goddamn. If that wasn't just like Con. After three years, it was all about getting off his chest whatever it was he'd forgotten to say the last time.

"Oh, man. Please don't." Finn shut his eyes, leaning back. He really did not have the strength to deal with this now. Why the hell had he walked down this way? Why the hell hadn't someone warned him Con was back?

Con's voice dropped. "I know what you're thinking."

"Yeah?" He grinned faintly at that.

"Please hear me out."

"I can't exactly run away."

Silence.

Finn opened his eyes. Con looked as though he were in more pain than Finn. Meeting Finn's gaze, he said, "I've thought about that day a million times."

A million times? Why, in three years, that would be nine hundred times a day. Impressive. Finn said, "Forget it. Ancient history."

Silence. Anger began to bubble up inside Finn. Why did Con have to start this up again? It was over. Done. Why couldn't they preserve a polite fiction…like neither of them remembered or cared? What the hell did Con want from him?

But Con plowed on. "To this day I don't know why… I don't understand how I let it happen. I didn't want that. I didn't want him." His voice sank so low, Finn hardly recognized it.

He said wearily, "We both know what it was, and it *doesn't matter*. Forget it."

"I *can't* forget it. Not a day goes by that I don't remember what a fool I was."

Finn said irritably, "Well, you need to forget it. It was three years ago. What's the point of bringing this up now? It's over."

"It's not over for me."

Finn stared at him, torn between shock and outrage. His heart was starting to slug his ribs like an angry prizefighter preparing for a match.

"What are you talking about?" He pushed up on an elbow and realized he was already starting to feel the effects of the pills. "You're not going to pretend— This is such bullshit. Do you need me to say I forgive you? Fine. I forgive you, Con. I chalked it up to a learning experience."

Maybe that was a cheap shot. Con swallowed hard. "Finn. God." He scrubbed his face with his hands. "You hate me, don't you?"

"Not at all."

He heard his tone: polite. Con heard it too.

"I was afraid you would feel like this if I didn't—" His jaw worked. "But you were so...adamant. I thought...give him time to cool down. I tried writing..."

Finn had received the letters—he'd tossed them.

The medication was kicking in big-time, the sofa beginning to glide in slow, lazy swoops. Finn dropped back in the cushions. All at once he felt quite relaxed. He felt like being candid. Why not? What did he have to lose? Nothing. "I don't know why it mattered so much, Con. I know how Fitch is, and I always knew it wasn't anything more than a summer romance for you—"

"Finn."

"You made it pretty clear, really." He smiled faintly at unfocused memory. "You were scrupulous about never saying you loved me or anything, so I don't know why I feel the way...the way I did... Maybe I was embarrassed because it meant so much to *me*—"

Con kissed him, his mouth covering Finn's, warm and insistent. Finn was too narcotized to do more than murmur a vague protest. Con released him immediately.

"I'm sorry. Damn it to hell. I'm sorry, Finn."

"Me too," he said woozily. "Love to chat. Have to...sleep now..."

He thought Con answered that, but by then Finn was whirling away into a comfortable blankness.

When he woke, it was to a complete absence of light.

Panic gripped him, and he threw out a hand for the lamp beside his bed, but there was only empty space. Instead of sheets, there was a giving stiffness beneath him—leather. At the same instant he realized he was dressed, although his shoes were missing, and that he was tangled in some kind of afghan. Desperately, he struggled up, saying, "Turn on the light!"

Even as Finn absorbed that the room was not in complete darkness— embers burned molten orange in a grate, and platinum moonlight filtered through slats of the blinds—a darker shadow detached itself from the sable nothingness.

A light snapped on.

Bright, inarguable light, golden warmth turning the room from a threatening unknown to a collection of comfortable old furniture and familiar paintings, one of them his own.

Con was crossing to him, saying, "I'm sorry. I thought you would sleep better with it off."

Finn scrabbled to collect himself. Between the dark and Con, it was a rocky awakening. He tried to hide that moment of naked fear, pushing into the corner of the sofa and raking a hand through his hair.

"I didn't know where I was." He tried to say it casually; his heart still racing and bounding like a deer in terror. Given the way Con was looking at him, he wasn't sure how successful he was. "You shouldn't have let me sleep so long."

Con ignored that. "Are you feeling all right?"

"Fine."

"You're quite sure?" Con was frowning, studying him.

"I'm sure." Actually, now that the unreasoning alarm was receding, he realized that he had slept well, and the nap had refreshed him. His head had stopped hurting, and his back was about as pain free as it got these days. Self-consciously, he smothered a yawn under Con's searching gaze. "What time is it?"

"After five."

"Oh, hell. Martha is going to think I fell off a cliff." He glanced around the cottage. "You haven't—"

"Installed a phone? No." Con liked being incommunicado when he was working, and that was the purpose of the cottage—although they had used it for other things once upon a time.

Better not to think of that now.

"You still don't carry a cell phone?"

"I'm morally and ethically opposed to cell phones." Con was smiling, but Finn knew he wasn't entirely kidding.

"I left mine in Manhattan." Then, "What?" he asked edgily as Con continued to stare at him.

"You can't know. It's…to see you sitting there again. To hear your voice. You don't know how long I've—"

"Don't."

Con nodded tightly. After an awkward pause, he said, "I'll run you back now if you like."

"I like." He reached for his cane. Con slipped a hand under his elbow, giving him a lift to his feet.

Finn appreciated the no-fuss tact of that, but he resented needing help. Where Con was concerned, he was a mess of contradictory feelings. He freed his arm, not rudely but pointedly enough that Con's face tightened.

Saying nothing, he helped Finn into his jacket again, the juggle of cane and flapping sleeves, and then Finn was doing up his jacket and Con was going to the cottage door.

He walked out of the cottage ahead of Finn, feet crunching on the shell-strewn path, a small, angry sound. It was a relief to Finn to realize that he didn't care that Con was upset. Time had been he would have been racking his brains for what he'd done, how to fix it, whether it was going to end between them. He could even spare a small twisted smile now for that insecure boy.

Con opened the Land Rover door and stood back. This was the tricky part, climbing up into the seat while hanging on to both his cane and dignity. Finn knew Con wouldn't offer help unless he asked for it.

He requested gruffly, "Will you give me a hand up?" and knew Con felt like a bastard for forcing the request.

Con took the cane from Finn's hand, set it aside. Finn turned nervously, not sure what to expect, and then Con slipped one arm around his waist, half lifting him into the seat without any apparent effort. Unnecessary and startling, but certainly efficient. Finn flicked him a quick, uncertain look, but Con's face gave nothing away.

He handed Finn his cane; then Con shut the door and walked around to his side of the vehicle. Finn buckled himself in; his heart was beating fast, and he knew it had something to do with being in Con's arms again for those brief heartbeats.

Con started the engine. Neither of them looked at the other or spoke as the Land Rover bounced over the potholes and rocks. Out of the corner of Finn's eye, he could see Con's profile, grim as that on an ancient and imperial coin. Like an emperor of ancient Rome with a rebellious senate on his hands.

They hit a bigger hole in the road, and the truck came down hard. Finn must have caught his breath because Con glanced his way.

"Sorry. Does it give you a lot of trouble?"

"What's that?" he managed to ask calmly.

"Your leg. What do the doctors say?"

"It's fine. Mostly. I'm supposed to exercise it regularly. Which is why I walked too far today." In case Con thought he had deliberately strolled down memory lane.

Silence.

They passed Gull Point. Across the bay, Finn could see the ghostly white tower of the old lighthouse. He looked away.

Con said slowly, "Or is it driving in general? Is it still difficult getting in a car?"

Funny that Con would understand that. Finn didn't have to answer; one sharp look had confirmed Con's guess. His foot eased off the gas, and Finn relaxed his white-knuckle grip on the armrest as they slowed to a sedate jog.

After another mile or so, Con questioned, "Do you remember anything about the accident?"

"I remember thinking *oh, shit* as the truck plowed into us." He added wryly, "Famous last words." Finn glanced at Con and was startled at how green he looked in the lights from the dashboard.

The rest of the short drive to The Birches passed without further discussion, which was a relief to Finn.

Con parked in the shell-shaped drive in front of the long porch and opened his door.

"You don't have to get out," Finn started quickly, but Con ignored him, coming round to his side.

He opened Finn's door, waiting in silence as Finn fumbled with the seat belt. Yanking it open at last, Finn reached to steady himself on the handrest. Con took his other arm, ignoring the exasperated look Finn threw him.

"Can I see you again?" Con asked as Finn clambered awkwardly out of the Land Rover and grabbed for his cane.

"I'm sure we'll run into each other."

"That's not what I meant."

"I know." It was hard to look away from the pain in Con's dark eyes.

"I still care for you, Finn."

Finn's hand was clutching the cane so tightly his fingers hurt.

"I want to make things right."

Finn bent his head. Took a deep breath. "I'm sorry," he said and met Con's gaze. "I don't feel the same."

Con stared at him, then nodded curtly.

Finn waited politely as Con got back into the Rover and reversed in a smooth, neat arc.

That had been easy enough. The only problem was, he thought, watching the taillights as Con drove away—he knew he hadn't told Con the truth.

CHAPTER THREE

They had not spoken of Fitch. Not even said his name. Later, sitting at dinner with Uncle Thomas, that seemed strange.

The whole day—the whole trip so far—had a strange dreamlike quality to it. Maybe that wasn't surprising given the meds he was taking and the fact that he'd spent a good part of the afternoon napping on Con's sofa. What had he dreamed there? He couldn't recall, but he had slept deeply and well. Better than he could remember sleeping for a very long time.

He'd had to tell Martha, of course—she had been giving him an earful about vanishing without a word, listing in Martha fashion all the terrible things that she had imagined happening to him. He'd stopped her at falling off the ledge at Gull Point.

"I didn't go to the point. I walked down to Con's cottage."

Martha had fallen silent, eyeing him a little doubtfully. "That's too far for you to walk yet," she scolded feebly.

"Con's back," Finn told her. "I spoke to him. In fact…"

She waited, and he could see the worry in her eyes.

He said, "It's not a big deal. I overdid it walking down there, and he let me rest on his sofa. That's what took so long."

"Is…everything all right?"

Finn's smile was rueful. "It's okay. He said his piece. I said mine. We're never going to be pals again."

He was surprised when she turned away from him and began rolling out dough on the lightly floured breadboard. Without turning to face him, she said, "We're not so backward as you might think, Finn. We still get the newspapers and now days we get satellite TV and the Internet. We've heard of gay people all the way out here, and we're not all as closed-minded as you might have been telling yourself these three years."

Finn couldn't think of anything to say.

Martha, still not looking at him, said, "It wasn't ever any secret that you and Fitch were a little bit different, and I was glad when it turned out how you felt that young Mr. Carlyle was a little bit that way too."

The rolling pin made a comfortable and familiar thump on the board as she rolled with ferocious energy.

"I know something happened with Fitch to spoil it. I don't know what, but you both left the island—Fitch that very day and you the next. And Mr. Carlyle went around looking like a thundercloud for a few weeks, and then he left too."

Thump. Roll. Thump.

"I don't know what happened, and I guess it's none of my business—"

"I didn't think you'd *want* to know," Finn managed, finally.

"I don't! That is, I don't want to know about anyone's personal business like that. But I don't want you feeling like you have to go around pretending or telling me lies. It's your own business who you're…you're sweet on. No one here ever thought any the worse of you or Fitch for that. And if that's why you've been staying away all this time…"

Thump. Roll. Thump.

Finn cleared his throat. At last he said, "It wasn't anything to do with that. At least…I don't know. Maybe it was a little. But the main reason was I couldn't be around Fitch or Con anymore. That's all."

Martha stopped rolling. "Do you think that's why Fitch went away?"

Finn said astringently, "Fitch had everything he wanted. I don't know why he went away."

* * * * *

Later, thinking of that conversation while he and Uncle Thomas ate beef pot pie at the long dining room table, he asked, "Did Fitch say anything to anyone when he left that day?"

"What day?" Uncle Thomas asked, preoccupied, glancing over a review of the book he'd written on practical art criticism.

"The summer I went away. Fitch had left the day before."

Uncle Thomas looked into the past and said, "I wasn't here. I'd gone to Portland. I was flying to San Francisco."

"But you came home that evening," Finn said. "I remember your car was parked in the drive when I got back that night."

He remembered because he had been grateful that there was no sign of his uncle when he'd let himself into the house and begun packing.

There had been no sign of anyone.

Mostly he had feared an encounter with Fitch, and when there had been no sign of him—no light beneath his door—Finn had guessed that Fitch was waiting in the cottage for Con. Because despite all Con had said—even if it was all true—Fitch would see things differently.

Fitch always did see things differently.

"I don't remember," Uncle Thomas said. He looked thoughtful now, but not unduly concerned. "I think my flight was canceled. Or maybe... Was I giving a guest lecture? Something happened, I remember, and I didn't need to fly out after all until later in the week."

Finn had not talked to anyone that night. He had packed his things, and he had left the following morning. You couldn't really run away at twenty-three, but that had been what it felt like. He said, "Martha had gone to Harpswell. Her sister was ill."

Uncle Thomas nodded, considering, and then he went back to eating his supper.

Finn ate slowly. The food was good. He mostly didn't think about food, and he was surprised to find he was hungry. But as he swallowed the last bites of golden, flaky pastry, he couldn't help thinking that there was something strangely apathetic in everyone's reaction—lack of reaction—to Fitch's disappearance.

Disappearance.

Because that's what it was. Fitch had disappeared. He had fallen off the face of the earth. And no one had noticed.

Even now no one seemed to be noticing—even when Finn was pointing it out.

"I've been thinking," he began, and Uncle Thomas reluctantly refocused on him. "I think maybe something happened to Fitch."

There. It was out.

"Happened to him?" Uncle Thomas sounded doubtful, eyeing Finn over the tops of his reading glasses.

"When he left the island the last time." That sounded too portentous. "When he left three years ago."

His uncle waited politely.

"It's not only that he never contacted me, he never contacted anyone that I know of. We traveled in the same circles."

"Fitch wasn't an artist." It was said bluntly, dismissingly. Considering that tone, Finn understood that maybe Fitch hadn't been everyone's favorite. Perhaps some of those careless jabs about teachers and critics had found their mark and left their wounds. Or perhaps the jabs had been in retaliation to a perceived rejection?

Finn said, "He wasn't a painter, but he still traveled in art circles. We knew all the same people, shared a lot of the same friends." They went to the same shows, the same bars, knew the same people—the Manhattan art scene was a small one, especially in the rarefied stratosphere the Barrets traveled in.

Uncle Thomas said slowly, clearly treading with the greatest care, "It's possible he'd have tried to stay out of your way."

"More than possible. At first." Finn's smile was crooked. "But Fitch, being Fitch, would have got over it, and he'd have expected me to do the same. He'd have arranged to bump into me at some public gathering I couldn't escape from."

Uncle Thomas looked unconvinced. "Maybe he knew this time was… different."

Finn absorbed the fact that his uncle seemed to be well versed regarding his relationship with Con—including the sordid end of it. Not only was Uncle Thomas aware of it, it didn't appear to have unduly shocked him. Granted, he'd had three years to get over the shock.

"Maybe," Finn agreed. "I never talked to anyone about what happened, yet no one ever mentioned him to me—other than to ask how he was or what he was doing."

Uncle Thomas still didn't seem to get it.

Finn tried to articulate his uneasy instinct. It was difficult because until he struggled to put it into words, he wasn't sure himself what was bothering him so much. "Fitch couldn't have made it to Manhattan because no one ever mentioned him again unless it was to ask me how he was doing. Someone would have said something in passing. He wasn't—isn't—somebody you could ignore very easily."

Wasn't? He listened to the echo of that word in something very like alarm. *Wasn't?*

"Perhaps he thought it would be wiser starting over elsewhere."

"I guess that's the way it could have happened," Finn said slowly, unconvinced. "It's just that he was a creature of habit."

"Bad habits," Uncle Thomas said grimly, and that seemed to be the end of that conversation.

* * * * *

Upstairs in his room much later that night, Finn found himself going through his old books looking for something to read, something nonnarcotic to put him asleep, turning to the comfort of vaguely recalled childhood favorites. He was flipping through Verne's *Mysterious Island*—mostly studying his grandfather's illustrations—when a snapshot fell out of the yellowed pages.

Con at age twenty or so. A reluctant smile curved Finn's mouth as he appraised the shy arrogance of the boy staring directly into the camera lens. Bold, dark eyes watched from beneath the soft blond forelock. Elegant bone structure: a hard jaw, a proud nose, but an unexpectedly sensitive mouth. They had called him The Prince. He called them—when he deigned to notice them at all (eleven years was a big gap at that age) the Gruesome Twosome. Which pleased them inordinately.

Finn and Fitch had always pretended to not think much of him, and Fitch had gone out of his way to be frankly offensive on more than one occasion, but the fact was, they both had frightful crushes on Con. Granted, he was very good-looking, like the prince in a fairy tale or a romance novel—a living, breathing embodiment of the kind of man their grandfather had painted into his illustrations. In fact, looking back, Finn realized that Grandy had probably used a few earlier models of Carlyles for inspiration. Well, why not? Those dark and luminous eyes, the noble brows and arrogant noses and stubborn chins—and those mouths...oh, those beautiful mouths.

Studying the old photo, it surprised Finn that he had never wanted to paint Con. Or had he wanted to but never dared ask? It was difficult to say. He had been so terrifyingly, overwhelmingly in love with Con. Terrifying because he knew even then it could not possibly last, so he had simply snatched at every day, every moment with Con as though it were his last.

But now, looking at the photographed face, he was sorry he had not painted him. Sorry he had not captured the play of light and shadows on that beautiful young face. Once again he felt the yearning to start work again. When he felt a little stronger. Because, as much as he wanted to tackle the work once more, he was afraid. Afraid because it had nearly been lost to him—and maybe it was supposed to be lost.

Maybe it wasn't coming back.

Paul arrived in time for lunch the following day, Tuesday. Finn drove down to the wharf with Hiram, and while the old man piled Paul's suitcases—way too many suitcases for a four-day stay—into the station wagon, Finn trailed uncomfortably after Paul, who wanted to see "the village."

"It's not really a *village* village," Finn tried to explain while Paul tripped along from general store to post office to pub.

"If it has a pub and a post office, it's a village," Paul said, shoving open the green door of Wylie's Tavern. "Let's get a drink. I'm *parched*."

"We should probably get up to the house. Martha will be waiting with lunch."

"No *way* am I getting into a car with my tummy feeling the way it feels now," Paul warned, heading for one of the battered wooden booths against the wall.

A couple of fisherman types turned from the bar to give him a long look. Finn felt color rushing to his face and was irritated. Paul was a flamboyant personality, true, but that flamboyance had never bothered Finn in Manhattan. He hadn't thought about it twice. But here on Seal Island... Paul's high, light voice, the white silk scarf, the broad gestures...Paul suddenly seemed like someone in a play. A play debuting on a night Finn would have preferred to stay home.

"There's no waitress," Finn told him. "If you want a drink, you have to get it yourself from the bar."

Paul raised his pale eyebrows and eyed the fishermen who had gone back to nursing their beers. He raised his eyebrows lasciviously, and it was all Finn could do not to groan.

"What'll you have?" Paul asked, and Finn shook his head.

"I'm on pain meds."

"Anything good?" Paul threw over his shoulder before sashaying over to the bar. Finn could hear him ordering from across the room. Paul spoke to the fishermen, who answered politely, looked at each other meaningfully, then glanced back at Finn. They left shortly after, and Paul carried over two bottles of Allagash White, setting one in front of Finn.

"You haven't changed," Finn said. "You're still a lousy listener."

"One drink won't kill you."

"Why does everyone keep trying to pour alcohol down my throat?"

"Because if you were any more uptight...well, actually that's hard to imagine."

"Thanks!"

Paul fastened his mouth daintily over the lip of the bottle and guzzled. Finn watched him, but the exasperation was slowly giving way to affection. He'd stayed with Paul when he first left the island, and they'd become close friends. Not least because Paul, as one of Fitch's ex-lovers, wasn't about to push Finn to reconcile or forgive and forget. The only thing he ever pushed Finn on was letting him handle his work. Paul was an art dealer—a very successful one.

Paul set the bottle on the table. "How's Fitch?" he asked, seeming to read Finn's mind.

"I don't know. He's not here."

Paul arched his eyebrows. He was very tall, very thin, with white blond hair cut in a bob, and a pale, bony, mobile face. "Where is he?"

"That's the funny thing. No one seems to know."

"What's that mean?"

"Simply that. No one knows where he is." Finn added reluctantly, "It seems like he vanished after he left the island the last time."

"Three years ago?"

Finn nodded.

"After you caught him and...what's-his-face in the lighthouse?"

Finn scowled, nodding.

"How...extraordinary."

"I don't know." It was extraordinary, though. And not in a good way.

"Maybe he killed himself out of guilt," Paul said cheerfully. "Chucked himself out of the lighthouse. It would be the first decent thing he did."

"No," Finn said, ignoring 90 percent of that comment. "He left voluntarily. He took his suitcases. As it was, he was only staying for the summer."

Paul watched him with his cool, bright eyes. "Then why did you say he vanished?"

"Because..." Finn hesitated. "Well, let me ask you this. When was the last time *you* saw him? I mean, saw him at all. Even from a distance."

Paul leaned back in the booth, squinting thoughtfully into his memories. "It's been a couple of years, I guess."

"Three years, I bet."

Paul's eyes met his. Neither of them said anything.

Finn said finally, "The only time anyone ever mentions Fitch to me is to ask how he is or what he's been up to. In three years, I can't remember a single person telling me they'd seen or spoken to him."

"Gadzooks."

The door to the tavern opened, and Hiram walked in. "Do you boys want me to come back and get you later, or did you want to come up to the house now?" His gaze rested on Paul without particular pleasure.

"What do you want to do?" Finn asked Paul, resigned.

"Home, James!" Paul rose, gathering up the two beer bottles and sauntering out. Finn sighed, and Hiram glanced his way.

"Don't know what Martha is going to think of *that*," he remarked.

Finn rose, steadying himself with the silver-topped walking stick. His mind was still on the conversation with Paul, and he said, "Hy, three years ago, when Fitch left the island...did you give him a ride down to the wharf?"

"Drove himself," Hiram said. "He left the station wagon here, and I had to walk down to get it. Don't you remember?"

No. Finn did not remember. He had been preoccupied with his own problems that morning. He had packed the night before and had wanted to leave at first light. In his memory that was what had taken place. Granted, both Hiram and Martha were early risers, so Hiram could have hiked down to the wharf at dawn and had the station wagon back at The Birches by the time Finn had appeared, bags in hand.

Hiram was already turning away, and Finn followed him out of the tavern. As they made their way down the boardwalk in Paul's wake, the door to the general store opened and a woman stepped out.

She nodded in passing to Hiram, nodded at Finn, and then her hazel eyes widened. "Finn Barret," she exclaimed. "I'd heard you were coming home."

Coming home. Not how Finn had chosen to think of it, but it was true that when he had been lying in the hospital, Seal Island, not his Manhattan loft, was the place he had longed for. Longed for quite desperately.

"How've you been, Miss Minton?" he asked, shifting his cane to shake hands.

"Miss Minton!" She snorted. "You're very formal these days, Finn."

Estelle Minton was a cousin of the Carlyles. She had their fair coloring and elegant bone structure, although she somehow appeared more rawboned and faded than her relations. But then Miss Minton was both a little older and not as comfortably off as the Carlyles. She supplemented her savings by supplying baked goods to the island general store—and making wedding cakes for mainlanders. Her wedding cakes were quite well-known in Harpswell and beyond.

For a second Finn couldn't think what she meant about being formal, but then he remembered that Fitch had always called her "Minty." Finn had generally tried to avoid the social dilemma by not calling her anything.

Without waiting for his response, Miss Minton went on, "How are you? Still pretty crocked up, I reckon. We heard about your accident."

Miss Minton always spoke in the plural—the royal "we," Uncle Thomas called it. Fitch had joked that Miss Minton had an invisible best friend. Actually an invisible *only* friend was the way Fitch had put it.

"I'm okay," Finn said. "I'm up and around, that's the main thing."

"It's a large part of it," she agreed. She was studying him frankly, and Finn wondered at this unusual attention. Miss Minton had never had much time for either him or Fitch—he was a little surprised to find she even remembered him.

Noticing that Paul, tired of waiting in the car, was coming toward them down the boardwalk, he said hastily, "Nice to see you again! I've got to get off this leg."

Miss Minton followed the direction of his gaze. "*What* is that?" she asked disapprovingly, watching Paul cast his scarf over his shoulder and toss his head.

Finn muttered, "Excuse me."

He hobbled to head off Paul, who greeted him as though he'd been given up for lost, and they made their way to the station wagon parked beside Miss Minton's battered old pickup. Hiram joined them a couple of minutes later.

"Was that the local witch or *what*?" Paul inquired as the car left the marina.

Finn couldn't help the edge that crept into his voice. "No."

"Quaint. Very quaint. It explains a lot, I think."

"What does?"

"This place. You. You and Fitch both. You especially, though. You're sort of…well…a throwback."

To *what*? Finn clipped, "Gee, thanks!"

"It's not an insult. It's not a compliment, I admit, but it's not an insult. So are you working on anything?"

"No."

Paul sighed disapprovingly. "I thought that was the excuse for coming back to Salem's Lot?"

Finn glanced at Hiram, who could have been a cigar store Indian for the interest he showed in their conversation. "I never said that."

"You did. You said you thought it would be good for your painting."

He probably *had* said that, although he hadn't meant it in the way Paul imagined.

Paul thrust his head forward from the backseat. "My, my. You're interestingly pale all at once. Not feeling well?" he suggested.

Finn snapped, "I'm fine. Tired, that's all."

"Your head's hurting again, isn't it? Why don't you take some of those painkillers you've been taunting me with?"

Finn glanced at Hiram, who was chewing the inside of his cheek and seemingly still not paying any mind to either of them. He said, "I don't want to get in the habit."

Paul shook his head. "Now *there's* where you're making a mistake. We are *all* creatures of habit." He rattled cheerfully on, and Finn's headache, which had only been the faintest suggestion, bloomed into full-blown pain.

"...was reading an article about migraines in *Scientific American*. You have to catch them before they really get their claws into you. What you want to do is disrupt the *pattern*—it's like an electrical disturbance in the circuitry of your brain..."

Finn listened without hearing and nodded and told himself that he was really glad that Paul was there to keep babbling so that he couldn't sit and brood in peace, because thinking about the past was getting him nowhere fast. It wasn't healthy.

They reached the house, and Paul enthused about the view and the fresh air and the sea breeze and the architecture, and then they were inside and Martha was bustling up to meet them, wiping her wet hands on her apron.

"Lunch is all ready," she said briskly. "Your uncle is working in his study."

She seemed to be trying to telegraph some warning to Finn. He said, "We won't disturb him, then."

Martha nodded, but he had misread her. She said, "And Con Carlyle is waiting for you in the parlor."

CHAPTER FOUR

"**W**hy do I know that name?" Paul asked into the silence that followed Martha's words.

Instead of replying, Finn asked curtly, "Why is Con here?"

Martha looked uncomfortable. "I...snum he wants to talk to you."

"*Snum,*" murmured Paul delightedly.

Finn was less delighted. He opened his mouth, but what was he going to do? Ask Martha or Hiram to throw Con out? Even if it were possible, it wasn't practical. The island was too small and all their lives too intertwined to allow him to really avoid Con.

Anyway, there was always the possibility that Con really did have something of importance to say to him—like oh-by-the-way-I-forgot-to-mention-Fitch-is-now-living-in-Australia. So he nodded at Martha, told Paul he'd join him in a couple of minutes, and squared his shoulders, heading for the parlor.

Con was standing at the bookshelves by the bay windows that looked out over the ocean. He was looking through *Treasure Island*—the edition featuring Holloway Barret's illustrations. He looked up at the tap of Finn's cane.

"Martha said you wanted to see me," Finn said with determined aggressiveness.

Con closed the book with a snap, slid it back into place on the bookshelf. "I think I owe you an apology. When I thought it over later, I realized how…"

He didn't *quite* realize it since he couldn't seem to think of the word.

"Unwelcome?" Finn suggested, and Con's face tightened. "Inappropriate?" Finn offered. "Overbearing?"

"Look," Con said shortly. "Whether you want to hear it or not, the fact is I owe you an apology. Not for yesterday, for what happened three years ago."

The light flooding through the window behind Con was very bright. Finn had to narrow his eyes against it; in fact, it was easier to turn away. Con said, "I treated you badly. Maybe I need to say it more than you need to hear it. Either way, it needs to be said."

"All right, you've said it," Finn said.

"No, I haven't." Con was walking toward him, calm, measured steps, and Finn felt ridiculously at bay—mostly because he couldn't easily walk away. "I hurt you…badly. I know that. There's no excuse for it. I've regretted it every single day since. I'm very sorry. Sorry for what it's cost me, but mostly sorry for hurting you. That was the last thing I ever wanted to do."

Finn made an impatient sound. Con had hurt him all kinds of ways that summer. Betraying him with Fitch was merely the *coup de grâce*. He kept his face turned, but he couldn't shut off his awareness of the other man. He was very much afraid he was going to start shaking—from tiredness and not feeling well, but Con was liable to read that all wrong.

He came right up to Finn, and his breath was warm against Finn's cheek and hair. He ran a light finger down Finn's forearm as though he didn't dare touch him but couldn't quite stop himself either.

Softly, he said, "I realize after yesterday that you don't feel the same anymore—I guess I didn't really expect that although I'd hoped, obviously, that we might have another chance. That probably wasn't realistic on my part. Both of us have changed."

Finn risked a look, but it was a mistake because Con was right there, gazing into his eyes, watching him far too closely. He should say something, of course, agree with Con or at least have the grace to accept his apology since there was no reason not to on these terms.

"Maybe...I don't know. Maybe we can one day be friends," Con said. "I'll leave that decision up to you."

Finn managed a grudging nod. Con seemed to be waiting for something more. When nothing was forthcoming, he turned away, moving toward the door.

Finn struggled with himself, cleared his throat, and said, "Con... thanks."

Con paused. He said, "If it had been anyone but Fitch, would there have been a chance of you forgiving me?"

Finn said, "If it had been anyone but Fitch, it would never have happened."

"So that's the famous Con-man," Paul said when Finn sat down at the dining room table. Paul was staring out the window, watching Con, tall, lean, and long-legged, striding down the gravel drive toward the woods.

"That's him," Finn said unemotionally, reaching for his water glass.

"What does he say happened to Fitch?"

Finn knocked back a couple of pain pills. Swallowed. "He hasn't said anything."

"That's a little suspicious, don't you think?"

Finn stared. Paul was joking, but not entirely. For reasons more unfathomable than any murder mystery, he was a big fan of the Margaret Rutherford Miss Marple movies. When they had roomed together, he had coaxed and cajoled Finn into watching all four films several times.

Finn admitted, "Well, in fairness, I haven't asked him."

"You haven't *asked* him? Kind of an oversight, don't you think? I mean, he's probably the last person to see Fitch alive."

"What are you implying?"

"Isn't that what you were getting at, at ye olde tavern?"

Finn opened his mouth to deny it, but the fact was, once the idea of foul play had infiltrated its way into the back of his brain, he couldn't quite shake it.

"It's your theory," Paul pointed out graciously. "You're the one saying Fitch vanished off the face of the planet, that no one's mentioned seeing him in three years."

"Well, yeah. But that doesn't mean..."

"What *does* it mean?"

Good question. If no one had seen Fitch since he left Seal Island...

Finn sat very still, taking it in. Fitch...*dead*? He realized he was shaking his head, denying it. "I'd...know," he said. "I'd feel it."

"Uh..." Paul's pale brows were meeting his hairline. "You'd *feel* it? When did you develop the psychic powers?"

"We're tw...twins." He actually swallowed on the word, a caught breath as the implications sank home. He'd been so angry for so long, it hadn't ever occurred to him how he'd feel if there was no chance of ever making it up, no chance of ever seeing or talking to Fitch again.

Paul must have seen something in his face because he said hastily, "True. True enough. I've read plenty of articles on the twin thing. Maybe you *would* know. And maybe he did split for Australia."

That pretty much killed the lunch table conversation.

* * * * *

The light station at Seal Island had been established in 1870, but it hadn't been operational since the 1920s. The eighty-one-foot tower was built of rubble stone and originally painted pristine white. There were two levels to the cast-iron lantern at the top of the tower: a watch room and the actual lantern room above, where once upon a time the whale oil lamp had hung. The small attached keeper's dwelling was built of creamy white brick. Tattered berry bushes grew along the side of it, and the casement windows had been boarded up. The door wasn't quite fastened, though, and he'd pushed it open wide...

It had taken Finn's eyes a few seconds to adjust to the darkness, to make out the two figures tangled in desperate humping need on the tarp on the floor. Recognizing too late what he was looking at, he stood frozen, and they had looked up, shocked at that blaze of sunlight, both their faces briefly lit as though by a flashbulb.

Not one of them had said a word.

Finn had turned and walked out, letting the door swing back on its rusted hinges, letting that broken shriek speak for him. He had not looked back, not faltered or flinched even when Con called out to him. Con had shouted twice...and then...nothing.

That vast nothingness filled only by the waves and the shrill cries of the sandpipers.

He had walked until he had run out of beach, and then he had climbed up to the highest point on the island—Ballard's Rock—and he had sat there motionless and numb while the sun climbed up the sky and then slipped down again. What he most remembered of that time was his amazement that anything could hurt that much and not kill him.

It never occurred to him that Con might have mistaken Fitch for him—and for that he was grateful. Grateful that he didn't try to tell himself any comfortable lies because that's all it would have been. Con knew them apart, always had. He knew them in bright sunshine and he knew them in the darkness. Funny that it had never occurred to Finn just why that was.

As for Fitch...Finn didn't waste his energy trying to understand. He knew he would never in a million years understand. If he thought about Fitch at all, it was to acknowledge that this really shouldn't come as a surprise. Fitch firmly believed in the old saw about asking forgiveness being easier than asking permission.

Con had found him as he was making his way down the trail that night. Finn had been moving very carefully down the hillside. Moonlight was not enough to guide him, and he was damned if he was going to break his neck and have everyone think it was over Fitch and Con.

He was halfway down the rocky slope when Con materialized out of the shadows ahead of him.

"Where the hell have you been? I've been looking for you everywhere!" He sounded both angry and weary—and there was another note in his voice that Finn couldn't quite place. Worry? Fear?

Finn didn't know and didn't care. He had stepped around Con, and Con had tried to put his arm around him. Finn had shoved him off.

Con had stopped walking. "We have to talk."

"There's nothing to say." It was the first and only thing he said to Con that night.

He kept walking, and when Con realized he wasn't going to stay and chat, he came striding after him.

"I know you're hurt. I'm sorry. I'm truly sorry. I wouldn't hurt you for the world. You know that."

Finn had stared straight ahead, calculating how far to the beach, and then how far from there to the road that cut through Bell Woods.

"It was a mistake. I don't even know why… It was…stupid. I'm very sorry. Sorry you saw it, sorry it ever happened. I haven't been with him since you and I— It's only the one time, and it will never happen again. I swear to you."

And Finn had thought about how weird it was that the stars never changed. Even when something like this happened—you would think it would be raining stars—but the world never missed a beat. Ink blue waves washed gently, rhythmically, against the pale sand, and the stars were still and bright and cold.

"You're being childish, Finn. It didn't mean a damn thing. You know it didn't. You know I... Can't you stop for one minute and listen to me? This is crazy." He reached a hand out, but Finn moved his arm away without ever breaking stride, so that it was a ghost touch.

"Finn. *Finneas.*"

Any second now Con was going to call him Huckleberry, and Finn was going to turn around and punch him in the mouth.

But Con didn't. He continued to stride beside Finn, watching him, talking to him all the way down the beach, climbing up to the main road, through the woods, and all the long walk back to The Birches. It got a little stream-of-consciousness by the end with Con telling him how he'd looked for Finn all day, how afraid he had been that Finn might do something rash, how every minute he'd regretted what he'd done, what he'd risked—and for what? For nothing. Fitch meant nothing. Finn was all that mattered.

On and on. Words Finn would have given anything to hear twenty-four hours before, but that now meant nothing. Nothing. Because something had died inside him that morning when he had opened that door.

When they reached the drive leading to The Birches, Con's voice was husky with talking so much—he wasn't used to it. Finn was the one who always did all the talking, although Finn was not by any stretch a chatterbox.

Con's footsteps dragged a little as they got closer and closer to the house—reluctant to face Fitch perhaps? Or Thomas. He said huskily, "It's no use talking to you now, I can see that. I'll talk to you tomorrow. I'm not going to let this destroy what we have together."

But he followed Finn right onto the porch. Finn reached the door-step with a feeling of relief. Sanctuary. He grabbed the handle and slipped inside.

Behind him, Con had said quietly, steadily, "I love you, Finn."

Finn had closed the door.

Finn watched the shadows of the sea's reflection moving on the ceiling of his room and let himself remember the things he had refused to consider for three years. He was mildly interested to find that he had been healing during that time because he could remember without pain.

Or maybe it had something to do with Con's apology. Maybe he had needed to hear it as much as Con needed to say it. He believed Con now. He had not believed him at the time; not that Con lied—far from it—just that he thought Con didn't know what he felt—or was confusing regret at hurting Finn for something more. He knew Con was fond of him, liked him, liked fucking together, but Con had warned him early on to lighten up, to not make too much of it, to not try and turn it into some big romance.

Really, when he looked at it like that, his own shock and hurt seemed childish—exactly what Con had feared at the start.

No, the only real surprise should have been that Fitch hadn't come after him.

Oh, not immediately. Fitch knew better than that. Fitch knew to give his twin time to cool down. But to not come at all? That was the one surprise of the day. Fitch couldn't bear it when they quarreled, couldn't bear to be cut off from Finn—even more than Finn couldn't bear to be cut off from him. Even that day. Even that day, part of what Finn grieved for was the knowledge that Fitch too was lost to him. Lost forever.

Because he wasn't going to be able to forgive him.

Maybe Fitch sensed that. Maybe that was why he never came.

Safe to say, he wasn't fleeing out of remorse or guilt because Fitch had never experienced such emotions. Embarrassment at getting caught, maybe. At least that was what Finn had thought before, when he had allowed himself to think about it all. Now he had to wonder.

Suppose something had happened to Fitch when he reached the mainland? Suppose he had been mugged or hit by a bus? But if either of those things had happened, Uncle Tom would have been notified by the authorities. It was barely possible that Fitch had been ashamed of what he'd done and split for parts unknown, but even if Finn could convince himself of such a scenario, he couldn't believe that Fitch would stay away for three years. It wasn't in his nature.

And it was perfectly obvious Fitch had not returned to their old stomping grounds. Even if he'd taken new lodgings, made new friends, hung out at new places...at some point their paths would have crossed.

So what were the remaining possibilities? Foul play? That was Paul's theory—an appropriately melodramatic one. And yet...what else was there? Amnesia? Kidnapping? Murder?

Murder.

But if someone was going to murder Fitch...wouldn't it be the people he had spent the summer with? His nearest and dearest? It was too hard to believe he'd caught the eye of a roving homicidal maniac. And if someone on Seal Island had wanted Fitch dead, would they have waited to strike until he left the island?

Yes. If they wanted to make it look like an accident. But in order to make it look like an accident, Fitch needed to turn up looking accidentally dead—not vanish into thin air.

Finn studied the row of model ships on his bookcase—collected one by one with loving care through his childhood. It had been rather a long childhood, now that he thought about it. But he wasn't a child anymore, and it was time to face things.

Suppose...Fitch hadn't left the island?

CHAPTER FIVE

"**S**crew Frank and Joe," Paul growled. "I want to be Nancy!"

Finn gave him a long look, and Paul giggled delightedly.

"No pun intended."

"Would you tone it down?"

Paul raised his eyebrows. "Maybe it's something in the water. You seem to be turning straight."

"I'm not turning straight. I... This is a small town. It's not even a town. It's a...a conservative little backwater."

They were sitting in the station wagon in the marina eyeing the harbormaster's office.

"That's their problem," Paul pointed out. "What does it have to do with us?"

"Get real, Paul. We're trying to get information out of people. We need their cooperation. We don't want to put anyone's back up." Paul opened his mouth, and Finn said, "You know what I mean."

"Unfortunately, I think I do." Paul shook his head, his blond hair swinging against his cheek. "Look, Frank, I can't be anyone but who I am. Deal with it." He got out of the car, and Finn slowly followed.

Was he in the wrong here? He wasn't sure.

Despite everything, he had slept well again the night before, and he was starting to feel a little more like his old self. His leg wasn't giving him constant hell, and even his headache had been a no-show nearly twelve hours now.

They went into the harbormaster's office, empty on a Wednesday morning, and asked the girl working behind the old walnut desk if there was a way to verify what boats had left for the mainland on the afternoon of August 18, three years previous. They'd got the date from Martha, who had managed to piece together history based on her reminiscences of family disasters—her own and the Barrets'.

The girl went into a back room. Finn moved to the window and stared out at the wharf and thought about what it would take to capture that dazzle of sunlight on water. If he used a glaze of Ultramarine Blue over both the shore and sea, it would reduce the values... He could paint the ripples into the water using a mix of blues, greens, and Titanium White...then mix the Titanium White with Flake White and a bit of Cadmium Yellow, work it with a bit of Liquin into an impasto paint to catch the glitter of the sun on water. It calmed him to focus on something besides whatever information that girl was going to dig up in her dusty files.

Paul poked around, making uncomplimentary comments on the décor. Finn glanced around. Paul had a point. Gray walls, nautical charts, and a girly calendar from the year before.

The girl returned from the back room. *"The Sea Auk,"* she verified. Her expression was commiserating.

"Is that a problem?"

"The Sea Auk sank last year. I don't think you're going to have much luck tracking down her captain—he's in Florida now—let alone her passengers."

Paul and Finn exchanged long looks and returned to the station wagon.

"That's *awfully* convenient!" Paul said when they had closed the doors against the stiff, salty wind.

Finn laughed. "What, you think someone sank *The Sea Auk* to cover up the fact that Fitch wasn't onboard three years ago?"

"If the flipper fits…"

"I don't think it does. Not that flipper, anyway. Not sabotage."

"Fine. The boat conveniently sank, so we don't know for sure if Fitch took it or not. That doesn't mean this is a dead end. It's merely…a *cul-de-sac*. What I think you should do is start with the person with the strongest motive for getting rid of Fitch and then work backward."

"That would be me," Finn said.

"Ah. Then…second strongest motive. And that would be Con-man."

Irritably, Finn said, "Don't call him that."

Paul chuckled. "Int-ter-esssting."

"No," Finn said.

"No? What do you mean? Are you telling me you don't have any feelings for him at all? *Hmm?*"

"I'm saying I don't want to talk about it with you. I don't ask you about what happened between you and Fitch."

"That's because you already had Fitch's version."

"That's one side of the story."

"It was probably true. I never knew Fitch to lie. Even when it would have been the smart or kind thing to do."

That was true. Fitch was not a liar. Brutal frankness was his specialty. According to Fitch, he had grown bored with Paul's jealousy and tantrums. But then Fitch always found something to grow bored with.

Paul said, "Well, personally I rule you out. At least for now. Which still leaves Con Carne or whatever his name is. You need to go and ask him the obvious question, which is: what happened after you ran off?"

"I didn't *run* off. I walked off in a slow and dignified manner."

"Whatever. What we want to know is, what did Con and Fitch chat about after you stalked off? Can you imagine being a fly on *that* wall?"

No. He couldn't. Or maybe he didn't want to, because he was sure whatever had been said would have hurt him even more badly. He said, "I still don't see why Con would have a motive for getting rid of Fitch."

"Oh my God. Keep your day job, lambkin! Fitch deliberately seduced him and broke up his relationship with you. Of course he would want to strangle him."

Finn sighed, staring unseeingly at the mountain of lobster traps to the side of the car. "It wasn't like that, though. First of all, Con had told me that he wasn't interested in anything long-term, and that he wasn't going to make promises to be monogamous. Secondly, although I was too stupid to see it at the time, Con had had some kind of relationship with Fitch before I ever came into the picture."

"You're kidding!"

Finn shook his head again.

"And they both kept that from you?"

"Fitch wasn't staying on the island when Con and I started up. He came home later that summer—Con was already getting restless. I knew that. I could see the signs. He kept doing stuff to push me away." Finn's mouth curved bitterly. "I saw it, but I was in love with him."

Paul considered this grimly. "That doesn't mean he didn't resent being manipulated by Fitch."

"What makes you think Fitch manipulated *him*?"

"You forget. I was on the receiving end of Fitch—and I mean that in every possible sense—for nine months. I know exactly how he operated. And it wasn't pretty."

Finn considered Paul. Fitch could be—and frequently was—a bastard, but Paul was the only one of Fitch's ex-lovers—that Finn knew of—who carried a grudge against him. And Paul definitely carried a grudge. He'd taken Fitch to small claims court for three months of back rent and the monetary equivalent of several gifts.

"What kind of temper does Con have?"

"I never thought of him as having a bad temper."

"Maybe he's the type that represses it, and when it blows...*kaboom!*"

Finn said doubtfully, "I just...don't really see that."

"You're not being very helpful." Paul tapped his tooth with a buffed fingernail. "Fine, who else would have had it in for Fitch? Who inherits his share of the family fortune?"

"I don't know... I guess it would be split between me and Uncle Tom. But if money was the motive, why conceal the fact that Fitch is dead?"

"Good point." Paul started the engine. "It's Con. It's got to be. You need to go talk to him."

Finn gave a disbelieving laugh, staring as Paul guided the car across the uneven road. "You think he's a killer and you want me to go talk to him? Thanks!"

"Are you afraid of him?"

"Of course not." He felt a little indignant at the idea, for reasons probably best not to analyze.

"So what's the problem? It was probably an accident."

If it had been an accident, then Fitch's body would have turned up. You didn't accidentally dispose of a body.

Paul said thoughtfully, "*Could* it have been an accident? I mean, could he have fallen into the ocean?"

Finn considered it. "I don't think so. He'd have washed up sooner or later. If not here, then on one of the other islands or the mainland." He shivered, stared unseeingly out the window at the choppy green-blue water.

* * * * *

Martha was beginning to "take against" Paul. Finn knew the signs. It was not so much what she said as what she didn't say, uncharacteristically cryptic as she fed them a late lunch of smoky potato soup with bacon croutons after their return from a hard morning of snooping.

Her dark gaze rested on the back of Paul's head with a certain grimness, and when she caught Finn watching, Martha gave a little disapproving sniff. Paul represented Finn's new life, which was probably reason enough right there for Martha to dislike him.

It was a shame because Martha was generally a gold mine of information, but her suspicion of Paul made her closemouthed. Granted, she had not been on the island the day Fitch left. She had not been there that entire week. She had been tending to her sick sister on the mainland. By the time Martha returned to the island, it had all been over and both Finn and Fitch were gone—Fitch perhaps forever.

After lunch, pressured by Paul, who had decided sleuthing was the only credible means of entertainment on Seal Island, Finn went up to Uncle Thomas's study to ask if he remembered anything about the day Fitch had disappeared.

Uncle Thomas, up to his elbows in art books, looked up distractedly and frowned. "Disappeared? You mean the day he left? I wasn't here."

"But you came back that evening."

Uncle Thomas frowned. "I don't recall seeing you or Fitch."

"Fitch was already gone by then. We just didn't know it."

"Perhaps he left the following morning."

"No, because *I* left the following morning. Hiram had to walk down to the village to get the car."

"I'm sorry," Uncle Thomas said, a fraction impatiently. "What was the question again?"

That really was the crux of it. What was it that Finn was hoping to learn? And why was he asking the people most unlikely to have reason to want Fitch dead? Was he stalling because he was afraid to face the person to whom he should most obviously be talking?

"If Fitch is dead," he asked finally, "who inherits?"

Uncle Thomas looked taken aback. He answered without having to consider it, "You do. You and Fitch equally inherited your mother's share of this estate. If one of you predeceases the other, the survivor takes all."

Since Finn seemed to have nothing to say to that, Uncle Thomas went back to his research, and Finn went downstairs to find Paul. Hearing him out, Paul seemed unreasonably amused.

"We're building quite a case against *you*," he said.

"I'm laughing so hard."

"It's ironic, don't you think?"

"Mostly irritating."

Paul smirked. "Well, my suggestion is we—meaning *you*—go talk to the only real suspect we have."

Finn rubbed his face in his hands without answering.

"You said you weren't afraid of him."

"I'm not," he replied, his voice muffled behind his hands.

"You can take my cell phone, and if I don't hear from you in…say, one hour, I'll start yelling my head off."

"I'm *not* afraid of Con."

Which wasn't exactly true—although he wasn't afraid of Con for the reasons Paul probably imagined.

In the end, he decided to walk down to the cottage. He needed the exercise, and he wanted time to think before he arrived on Con's doorstep. But no sooner did he close the door on The Birches than he seemed to be facing Con's front door, and he could not claim that the walk had done anything to clear his thoughts.

He knocked before he had time to change his mind and beat a retreat.

Con came to the door. He wore jeans and a heather-and-blue tweed sweater. Reading glasses were pushed back on his forehead, and he held a green-and-white paperback titled *The Princes in the Tower*, keeping his place with a finger between the pages. He stared at Finn as though he were the last person in the world he expected to see—which was probably about right.

"Are you busy?" Finn asked awkwardly since it was obvious Con was.

"Not too busy for you." He said it simply and moved aside so that Finn could step inside the cottage.

The last time he had been here, he had been too tired and pained to really look around, but his impression of time unchanged seemed accurate now. It was all as it had been: the same comfortable furniture and rugs, the same pictures on the wall—including Finn's painting of the cave at Otter Cove, the first place they had made love. Well, Finn had made love. For Con it had been fucking, but that was all right. Either way, Finn had good memories of that day.

The computer was a new one, and there were a couple of framed snapshots on the fireplace mantle. Finn noticed because Con had never been one for family photos.

"Did you walk down here?" Con was frowning.

"Yeah." As Con's frown deepened, he said, "I'm supposed to walk. Really. It's good for me."

"It's two miles from The Birches. I doubt if your doctor had that kind of hike in mind."

Finn didn't really register that because he had realized that while one of the photos on the mantle was of Con and his family at some anniversary celebration, the other one was of Fitch. It gave him a very strange feeling, and he missed the next two things Con said.

Picking up the frame, he studied it. They were standing outside some kind of antique store, and Fitch was smiling. He looked relaxed and happy—and so did Con. He had draped a casual arm around Fitch, who was holding a large handcrafted model of an "Ironsides" yacht.

When the hell had Fitch and Con gone off together...? Finn had the peculiar sensation of missing a step in the dark because...it *wasn't* Fitch in the photo, it was him. He had completely forgotten that trip to Union—

less than a week before he'd walked in on Fitch and Con in the lighthouse keeper's cottage.

Ironically, he had started to believe that weekend that Con was falling in love with him.

"Finn, what's the matter?" Con asked for the third time, and by now he sounded alarmed. He put a hesitant hand on Finn's shoulder. "Why don't you sit down?"

That seemed like a good idea, and Finn dropped into the nearest chair, still holding the framed photograph.

"You can't keep doing this," Con said, and if it had been anyone besides Con, Finn would have considered him to be fussing. "You can't keep doing these marathons until you're stronger. You could fall, you could faint—"

Finn looked up into his hard, anxious face. "What happened between you and Fitch that day?"

His question cut Con off midsentence. "What do you mean?" He sounded wary.

"After I left the lighthouse cottage. What happened between you?"

"Nothing."

Finn was abruptly irritated. He put the framed photo on the table next to him with a clatter. "*Nothing?* Something must have happened. You must have had *something* to say to each other. Like…*gosh, this is awkward!*"

"I don't recall what I said to him." Con's expression was bleak. "I think—"

"What?"

After a hesitation, Con said, "I think I hit him."

"You…hit him?"

"He was laughing. I don't even remember what he said, but I…I seem to recall punching him."

Finn closed his eyes for an instant. "Did you kill him?"

"What?"

Finn opened his eyes, and Con was staring at him, aghast. "No, I didn't *kill* him. What the hell are you talking about?"

"No one has seen Fitch since that day."

"What? What are you saying?"

Finn didn't bother to repeat it. Con's black gaze seemed fixed on his.

"That's not possible. He left the island. Someone had to have seen him go."

"I haven't found anyone so far."

"Wait a minute," Con said, and it was his normal, brisk tone. He sat down in the chair across from Finn's, leaning forward, his expression intent—he could have been applying his mind to any academic puzzle. "Let me get this straight. You're saying no one has seen Fitch in three years?"

"Right."

"That's not possible."

"It's not possible if he's still alive."

"You think he's dead?"

Finn said carefully, "As far as I can make out, you were the last person to see him alive."

Con drew back. His expression was startled, but not...particularly guilty. He seemed astonished more than anything.

"I didn't kill him, Finn." Con said it plain and simple, and Finn found that unexpectedly reassuring. "I was angry, but...it was mostly at myself. What I'd done. What I'd...destroyed."

"What happened after you hit him?"

"I didn't wait to see. I went after you. I spent the entire fucking day searching the island for you. I thought you would go to the cove. I waited there. Then I thought you might come here. Then I thought you might go into the village. Then I tried the cove again. Then I tried The Birches. Finally I thought of Ballard's Rock, and that's where I was headed when I found you that night." He swallowed hard. "By then I was...terrified..."

Finn's smile was caustic. "You thought I'd done something dramatic like pitch myself from the cliff?"

Con said quietly, "All I knew was that you loved me and I took that love and shoved it right back in your face. You weren't the most worldly kid."

"I wasn't a kid."

"You were twenty-three, but you'd spent most of your life on this rock in the company of folks who were a lot older than you. People who thought queer only happened to other people. People in big bad cities—like Sodom and Gomorrah."

Finn said defensively, "I had Fitch."

Con said nothing.

"You don't know a damn thing about it," Finn argued hotly. "No, I wasn't *worldly*, but I did get that I was only a passing thing for you. And I wasn't about to kill myself over it."

"I know," Con said. "I realize that now. At the time I was…scared."

Unappeased, Finn said shortly, "So you punched Fitch and left him there, and in all this running around the island, you never ran into him again?"

Con shook his head.

"What about when you went to The Birches?"

"I didn't see him—" Con paused, and his expression changed.

"What? What did you remember?"

"When I was waiting for you outside the cave in Otter Cove, I vaguely remember seeing someone up in the lighthouse tower. My first thought was it was you, but then I remembered your tracks had led away down the beach."

"So who was it?"

"I couldn't tell at that distance, but at the time I think I assumed it was Fitch. If he'd wanted to see where either of us went, the tower would have given him a bird's-eye view of half the island."

"What time was that?"

"Less than half an hour after all hell broke loose." Con studied Finn's face. "Are you serious about this? You honestly believe Fitch is dead?"

"I...don't know."

Con was frowning, watching him. "Then why does everyone believe he left the island that afternoon?"

"Because his things were gone. His suitcases and clothes were gone, and Hiram's station wagon was left at the wharf as though Fitch had driven down there and caught the boat for the mainland. And it made sense given everything that happened."

"Does it? But didn't Martha see him come back and pack? Didn't Hiram drive him? Didn't he say good-bye to Tom?"

"Martha was in Harpswell that entire week. Her sister was sick. Hiram was clearing out poison ivy at the back of the property all that afternoon. Uncle Tom was in Portland stuck at the airport. Everyone assumed Fitch came in, packed, and drove the station wagon down to the village himself."

"He didn't leave a note or anything?"

Finn shook his head. "But that wasn't so unusual. He always came and went as he liked. Anytime he left a note, it was for me. He wouldn't have done that this time..."

"I'm not so sure. I always thought that scene was more about Fitch's jealousy over you, than Fitch's jealousy over me."

"I don't know what that's supposed to mean."

"It means," Con said dryly, "that you were the most important person in Fitch's life, and he didn't like sharing you. Especially with me." Finn opened his mouth to object, but Con was already following another thought. "Someone at the wharf or in the village must have seen him leave that day. There would be a record of a ticket sale, a ship's log—something that would prove either way?"

"Paul and I did some checking earlier. The only ship that Fitch could have sailed on was *The Sea Auk*, which sank last year in that freak storm.

No records. As for anyone remembering seeing Fitch…it was the summer. There were all kinds of visitors on the island. If this had happened last week…but three years ago? Nobody remembers anything. Even Martha and Hiram aren't that clear on the details, and they're part of the household."

"But you realize what you're saying?" Con asked quietly. "If Fitch didn't leave the island, you're hypothesizing that someone went into the house, packed up his things, and borrowed the station wagon to make it look like he did. You're saying someone deliberately concealed the fact that Fitch was dead."

Reluctantly, Finn nodded.

Con's voice was very low. "You're suggesting that someone murdered him."

"It could have been an accident."

Con was shaking his head. "If it was an accident, why wouldn't that person come forward? Why go to elaborate lengths to hide the truth?"

"I don't know."

"If what you're suggesting is true, I don't believe it could have been an accident."

Finn's gaze met Con's dark one. "But I don't see why anyone would deliberately… I can't believe that anyone would want Fitch dead."

Con reached out and squeezed his uninjured knee; he withdrew his hand immediately. He said neutrally, "There was a side to Fitch you didn't see—or didn't see it until that day."

"What are you saying?"

"Only that…for one instant in that cottage, when you walked away and Fitch was standing there laughing, I wanted him dead. I'm not the only person who ever felt that way."

Finn straightened, unconsciously bracing himself as Con continued, "Fitch had a cruel streak. I don't know why or what made him the way he was, but he enjoyed being rude, he enjoyed seeing people squirm, he enjoyed hurting people."

Finn got up fast—and awkwardly, belatedly steadying himself on the chair, ignoring the pain in his injured leg. "That's not true!"

Con rose too. "It is true. Are you telling me you never heard the way he talked to Thomas? Or Hiram? Or plenty of other people?"

"He was joking."

"He wasn't funny. He was cruel. *You* never talked to anyone that way."

"I…"

"Don't make excuses for him. The reason you never noticed any of that was because you were such a nice, sweet-tempered guy."

"Oh, great!" Finn's face twisted in comical disgust. "*Nice.* There's the kiss of death right there."

"I know." Con's smile was crooked. "Awful, isn't it? But you were the nicest guy I've ever known. And I wish to hell I had appreciated it at the time. I mean that as a compliment. Fitch was different with you, and you… didn't see the way he was with others."

"So you're saying he made fun of someone and they killed him?"

"I don't know what happened. I know that Fitch could have said the wrong thing to the wrong person at the wrong time—sometimes that's the way it happens."

That was the historian talking. "But if someone did all those things… packed his clothes, took the car…then it was premeditated."

"Not necessarily."

"If someone hid his body…"

"That's the question, isn't it?" Con said. "It's not that big an island. So where would someone hide Fitch's body?"

Finn sat down again. "I can't believe we're casually talking about this, talking about Fitch being dead. Murdered." He rested his face in his hands. "I can't believe it."

Con came over to him, squatted down next to him, putting an arm around his shoulders. It took all Finn's willpower not to lean into him.

"You might be wrong. I hope you're wrong…but you've made a pretty convincing case. Now I'm wondering. More than wondering. Frankly, I think Fitch probably *is* dead."

Neither said anything for a time. Finally Finn raised his head. He said wearily, "I don't know what to do. Should we call the state police? I haven't even talked to Uncle Tom about the possibility yet. What if I *am* wrong?"

Con's gaze seemed to linger on his mouth, and for an uncomfortable moment Finn thought Con might lean forward and brush his lips against Finn's. Instead, he drew back, rising.

"Let's wait a bit," he said. "Why don't we try this: why don't we go out to the last place we know Fitch was alive?"

Finn stared at him. "The lighthouse?"

Con nodded. "The lighthouse."

CHAPTER SIX

"Who is Paul?" Con asked as they took the long, meandering road that wound up to the abandoned lighthouse. "You said you and Paul went down to the marina to check when Fitch might have left the island."

Finn, distracted by any number of unpleasant reflections, dragged his gaze away from the rise and fall of the road ahead. "Paul Ryder. He's a friend."

"Close friend?"

"Close enough." Finn added, "We're not lovers, if that's what you mean. He came because...I needed some company. At least, I thought I did. I wasn't sure what to expect here. Paul's an art dealer—a pretty successful one—so his schedule is, well, he makes his own schedule."

There was nothing to read in Con's voice or profile. He might simply have been making polite conversation. "He must be a pretty good friend to drop everything to keep you company."

"He's a pretty good friend," Finn agreed. "But I think part of the attraction was he wanted to see where Fitch grew up. They had a thing a few years back, and I don't know if Paul ever really got over it. I mean, he's still pretty caustic, and sometimes that means there are still feelings there."

"Yes," Con said. "Indifference is the worst."

Finn stared out the window at the trees, the flash of brisk blue water behind the golden wall of autumn leaves. The sun was very bright. He'd forgotten sunglasses, and he put his hand up to shield his eyes.

"All right?"

He hadn't realized that Con was watching him so closely. "I'm okay."

"There's an extra pair of sunglasses in the glove compartment."

Finn shook his head. "I hate them. I won't wear them until I don't have a choice."

Con's brows drew together.

After another mile of silence, Con's voice jerked him out of his thoughts again. "The guy who was killed in the car accident that injured you...?"

"Tristan. Another friend," Finn said unemotionally. "He might have been something more. We never got the chance to find out."

After a hesitation, Con said, "I'm sorry."

"Yeah."

They did not talk the rest of the way. It was not a long drive, but the road was a roundabout one snaking through the hills and woods. As the road wound its way, Finn glimpsed the lighthouse through tree branches. He studied Con's profile and thought that Con's expression was peculiar. Remote and yet resolute. As though feeling his gaze, Con glanced at him and then—perhaps misreading Finn—slowed the Land Rover.

Finn *was* increasingly tense as the miles passed, but it was not the fear of another accident. In fact, he couldn't understand his own mounting stress.

It wasn't until the final stretch of road at last uncoiled at the top of a green hillock overlooking the ocean, and Con rolled to a stop in the sandy square beside the keeper's dwelling, that Finn recognized what was disquieting him. He glanced at Con's grim profile, stared at the small white brick building with the boarded windows, and all the while his heart was pounding in hard, hollow slams as though someone were kicking an empty oil drum. Suddenly he was very sure he did not want to take this any further. Very sure that he would be happier not knowing what he was about to find out.

Con opened his door, and Finn said desperately, "Con—"

Leaning back inside, Con said, "What is it?"

"I'm not feeling— Can we do this another time?"

"What's wrong?"

Finn shook his head, but Con was already coming around the front of the Land Rover, opening the door on Finn's side. "What is it? What's wrong?" He slipped his arm around Finn and helped him out of the vehicle, his hands very gentle, his face concerned. "It's your eyes again?"

"Yes. No. I'm okay," Finn said. "Maybe a little—"

"Carsick?" Con asked. "Light-headed?"

Try afraid of you, Finn thought. Because as he stared into Con's buccaneer eyes, he couldn't help remembering that everything Con had told him that day indicated that Con was the person most likely to have murdered Fitch—if Fitch *were* truly dead and not playing some cruel game.

"Jesus," Con said, sounding alarmed as he eased Finn back against the side of the Rover. "You're as white as the fucking stones. Do you want to— What do you want, sugar? You want to sit down, or do you want to walk a little?"

Sugar. Finn could have cried at the old pet name. Why did Con have to do that? Why didn't he call him something stupid, like "Huckleberry"? Why did he have to be so tender and…loving *now*? Why did he have to do any of this?

But it was Finn who had started it, not Con. It was Finn who had made the mistake of coming back here, coming back to Seal Island. He should have let well enough alone. He should have left this place and all its memories to slide into the past and sink to the bottom of his consciousness.

"Rest for a minute. You're pushing yourself too hard." Con was worrying aloud. "These headaches… I keep forgetting you're only a couple of days out of the hospital. This could have waited."

"I just need a…little air," Finn said desperately because he couldn't think while Con's hands were moving in conscious or unconscious caress on his shoulders, and Con's face was mere inches from his own.

"You want to walk?" Con was watching him intently. "I'll help you. Lean on me."

He tried to slip his arm around Finn's waist, but Finn freed himself clumsily. "In a minute. Why don't you…why don't you go up into the lighthouse and see…if there's anything to see?"

"You don't want to look for yourself?" Con's dark eyes never left his own.

Finn shook his head.

"Are you all right if I leave you for a minute or two?"

Finn nodded tightly.

Con scrutinized him for another few seconds, clearly divided; then he said, "All right. I'll run up and take a quick look around. The place may be locked up for all I know."

Finn licked his dry lips, nodded again.

Con turned away and strode toward the boarded-up dwelling. Finn watched him try the door. It opened with a soprano screech of frozen hinges, and Con disappeared inside.

Finn reached into the Land Rover and grabbed his cane. He hadn't been kidding about needing air. He felt woozy with a combination of dread and confusion. At least part of it was that irrational fear of going into that claustrophobic dark of the keeper's dwelling, but the rest was genuine foreboding that he had started something that couldn't be stopped.

If he forced himself to look at the situation with cold logic, Con had opportunity, means, and motive—by his own admission. And as Paul would no doubt have pointed out, Rutherford's hatchet-faced Miss Marple was always boisterously enthusiastic about such a criminous trifecta. Con had not wanted to call the police. Con had wanted Finn to come out here alone with him. Why? So he could kill Finn too?

But…this was *Con.*

He was the most civilized man Finn knew; he still used the library for God's sake. Con who drank Earl Grey tea and read fantasy and listened to Barber and wrote histories about long-ago injustices in an effort to set the score straight. Con, who had held Ripley in his arms to the very end when the old dog had to be put down. Con, who, despite his determination not to get enmeshed in a relationship, had been the gentlest and most painstaking lover Finn had known. That weekend they had gone to Union, staying at a quaint bed-and-breakfast, going to the Farnsworth Art Museum, Damariscotta Lake, the Antique Toy and Art Museum…that had been the single best weekend of Finn's life.

It wasn't…possible.

But what else made sense? Fitch had his faults, God knew, but the idea that someone had killed him because…because he was rude to them? Because he had been insensitive?

He got Paul's cell phone out and began to dial the house.

"Finn, you're closer to the edge than you realize." A hard hand came down on Finn's shoulder, and he nearly jumped from the rocky cliff all on his own. Lost in his own thoughts, he hadn't heard Con's approach, and there was no hiding his alarm as he turned, dropping the cell phone and knocking the other man's hand away, ready to fight.

"What's the matter with you?" Con's expression was startled.

Finn clutched his cane with both hands, braced for whatever was coming. But it seemed that nothing was coming.

The surprise on Con's face hardened slowly into disbelief, then anger.

"You think *I* killed Fitch?" He didn't wait for an answer. "And then what? Brought you up here to murder you too?"

"What's in the lighthouse?" Finn croaked.

"I don't *know* what's in the fucking lighthouse because it's too dark to see and I forgot to replace the batteries in my flashlight. What do you think is in the lighthouse? Proof that I killed your brother?"

"Did you?" Finn got out between stiff lips.

"How can you even ask me that?" Con cried, and the anguish in his voice seemed too raw to be faked. "I already told you I didn't. I told you exactly what happened that day."

"And you told me that you punched him and that for a minute you wanted him dead. Maybe when you hit him, he fell and hit his head—"

"If I had accidentally killed Fitch, I'd have gone to the authorities. I wouldn't have tried to hide it." There was contempt in Con's voice. "I wouldn't have spent the afternoon searching for you—which, by the way, I can prove. In part at least."

"All right. Prove it."

"Barnaby Purdon was fishing in Otter Cove most of the time I was waiting there after I left Fitch—alive—here."

"That doesn't prove anything! I only have your word that Fitch was alive when you left him. Besides, you said yourself it was too far away to know for sure who was in the lighthouse tower."

"Well, who else could it have been?"

Finn shook his head stubbornly. "I-I don't know. But it's not proof, Con."

He raked an impatient hand through his pale hair. "All right. Try this on. Estelle Minton was working in her garden when I walked up to The Birches. I think she'll be willing to testify I wasn't carrying a body."

"Don't make fun of it. For God's sake!"

"No. You're right," Con said tightly. "There's nothing funny about this. And there's no point discussing it with you. If you think I killed your fucking brother, then go call the state police. Go do whatever the hell it is you think you need to do, Finn. But stay away from me."

He turned and walked away to the Land Rover. He got in, started the engine, and drove away without looking back.

Finn painfully lowered himself to the ground, picked up the dropped cell phone, and dialed The Birches. He got Martha, who instructed him to invite Con to supper. He told her Con was otherwise engaged and asked for Paul.

Paul's fluting tones answered a couple of seconds later.

"I'm at the lighthouse," Finn told him. "Can you bring the station wagon? And can you borrow a couple of flashlights from Martha. Tell her…I don't know. Something. Tell her I want to paint the tower or the cliffs from above and I need to get into the old building to look around."

"Are you going to paint the tower?" asked the ever-hopeful art dealer.

"No."

"Oh. What did you find out?" Paul demanded. "Did he admit it?"

"No, he didn't admit anything. I don't believe he did kill Fitch." Finn added shortly, "I think Fitch might be playing some cruel game on all of us."

There was a sharp silence. "Are you serious?"

"Yes. Oh, I don't know! It's…very hard to believe that anyone would kill Fitch. And I sure as hell don't believe Con did."

"What did he say that so convinced you?"

"Among other things, he told me to call the cops."

"Oh."

"Can you bring the car?" Finn asked wearily when the empty buzz on the line persisted.

"On my way," Paul said and hung up.

It was about twenty minutes before the station wagon tires crunched onto the sandy shale and parked in front of the lighthouse. By then Finn was chilled through and completely depressed.

He picked himself off the ground as Paul unfolded from the station wagon and waved cheerfully.

Paul loped up, inquiring, "Is Martha a blood relation?"

"Technically she's not any relation at all."

"That's good. So she can't actually send you to bed without supper? Because those were the dire threats she was muttering when I left."

Finn snorted.

Paul studied his face. "What's up? Why so glum?"

Finn shook his head. "Did you bring flashlights?"

Paul held up a cautioning finger and ducked back into the car. He brought out two high-powered flashlights. "I don't know how you're going to get up those stairs with that leg, though. You probably should leave it to me."

"I'll be fine."

Paul shrugged. "Suit yourself."

They opened the front door of the keeper's cottage, flashlight beams stabbing through the darkness. Faded daylight pried through the boards nailed unevenly across the windows, throwing odd bars of light here and there on the stone walls.

Plenty of light…really. Anyway, he couldn't spend the rest of his life afraid of the dark.

"Gadzooks. It's like a cave in here!"

Finn swallowed hard, said conversationally, "I'm amazed the place hasn't been totally trashed."

Paul retorted, "I think you must mean *trashed* in a relative sense."

He had a point. The wooden floor and wall paneling had been pulled up and removed, and there was silver graffiti painted over one wall—a pentagram and some odd symbols—but otherwise the structure was mostly unharmed. It smelled strongly of damp and animal.

Finn's heart was ricocheting around his rib cage in panic. It made him angry. He was not giving in to this, not giving in to irrational, superstitious fear. He forced his voice to stay steady, unhurried. "It's so far from the village, there's nothing really to tempt anyone out here but hikers and photographers." He shone his flashlight to the black oblong at the end of the room that had once served as a kitchen. "There's the entrance to the tower."

"It looks like the doorway to a tomb." It did too.

"Nice," Finn growled.

"Well, you know. One tries," Paul said breezily, but his voice sounded as nervous as Finn felt. It helped a little knowing he wasn't the only one struggling. Paul added in that strained tone, "This place isn't haunted or anything, is it?"

"It didn't use to be."

"Nice one yourself!"

They moved slowly to the door of the tower and looked upward. Light from a window midway up the turret cast a perfect square on the opposite wall. In the blue light filtered from the windows in the lamp room, the narrow spiral of iron staircase looked like the interior of some exotic conical seashell.

"Do you think it's safe?" Paul inquired, shining his flashlight at the cobwebbed lowest step.

"I think *safe* is another one of those relative terms." Finn directed his own beam around the circular room. "We used to play in here when we were kids. It felt different then. Not so…empty."

"How tall is it?"

"The entire tower is about eighty feet, but that includes the lamp."

Paul shone his light in Finn's direction. "Not that I wouldn't like to see the prices of your work appreciate, but I'd hate them to skyrocket because of a fatal accident. I think you should stay down here while I go up."

No way was he staying down here with only this watery blue light to hold the darkness at bay. "You can go first," Finn said. "I'll take my time."

"I'm not sure what we're looking for at this point."

Finn wasn't sure what to make of this about face. Paul had pushed him to question Con, but now he seemed to be leery of the idea of investigating further. Was he maybe a little freaked inside the creepy old structure? Finn couldn't blame him for that.

"I don't know. That's why we're looking."

Paul started up the staircase. The metal steps rang hollowly beneath his feet. He stopped.

"I'm not sure what the point of this is," he said, a little testily. "It's not like his body is going to be up there." In the silence that followed his words, he said, "I didn't mean it like that. You know what I mean."

"It's all right if you don't want to go up," Finn said. He was moving very slowly, very cautiously up the staircase, holding tight to the metal banister with his free hand and his cane with the other.

"You're going to break your neck, and your housekeeper is going to send *me* to bed without supper."

Finn stopped. "Paul, you don't have to go up, but I do. I don't know why, but I feel like I do. This was the last place anyone saw Fitch alive."

But had it *been* Fitch in the light tower that morning? Con was not sure. Finn shrugged that thought away.

"Oh, fuck!" Paul said and turned, marching up the staircase. It clanged noisily in the wake of his steps.

"Wow!" Finn heard him say after a time.

His own progress was tedious and painful. Soaked in sweat by the time he made it to the top, it wasn't until he was tottering on the last step that he began to consider how difficult the trip down was going to be in the fast-encroaching dusk.

"That doesn't look too promising," Paul said as Finn stepped out onto the circular landing. He nodded out to sea, where the sky was turning an ominous black and green. Witch lights seemed to flash and flicker in the roiling clouds.

"There's a storm moving in," Finn said.

"Duh. I recognize it from the movie. The one with *gorgeous* George Clooney and Marky Mark."

Finn snickered, wiped his perspiring face on his sleeve. It had been a long time since he'd experienced an island gale. He wasn't thrilled at the idea. It usually meant power outages and being completely cut off from the mainland for hours, if not days. "It may pass us by," he said without much hope.

"I have to admit," Paul said after a pause. "It's quite a view."

In accord, they stared down at the gray-green surf churning over the rocks far below them.

Paul said finally, "If...someone fell, he'd have gone straight into the drink."

"It depends on the time of day and year," Finn said. "In the morning, at that time of year, the tide was probably out. He'd hit the rocks."

"Lovely." Paul heaved a heavy sigh. "Well, I don't know what you're thinking, but there's no way Fitch jumped. And there are much easier ways of killing someone than dragging them up seventy-three stairs and pushing them off a balcony.

"He climbed up to look for something that morning—there was something he wanted to see on the island. I'm wondering what it was." Finn slowly traversed the metal platform staring out over water, rocks, hills, treetops, hills, and more rocks and water.

"See anything?" Paul asked when he rejoined him.

Finn shook his head. They stood in silence, watching the storm rolling toward them over the choppy water.

"I think we should go down before that hits," Paul said. "This tower must act like a lightning rod in a storm."

Finn nodded.

Paul pushed away from the side, crossed the platform, and started down the stairs, his feet clanging on the metal rungs. Finn started to turn away, stopped. The railing around the platform was painted a dull brick color. It was weathered and chipped in places. Where Paul had been standing, there were several long, narrow marks where the paint had scraped away. The marks curved over the top of the railing and continued down the other side—dropping away to nothing.

Finn counted the scratches in the paint. There were ten of them.

Chapter Seven

Wednesday evenings for as long as Finn could remember, Barnaby Purdon came to The Birches for dinner and checkers with Uncle Thomas.

Barnaby had been a teacher on the mainland, and before his retirement he made the trip back and forth from the island every weekday. Finn and Fitch had been homeschooled, but Barnaby had overseen their education as much as anyone could be said to have overseen it, and Finn had always liked the pale, twitchy but enthusiastic young man Barnaby had been. Barnaby had a way of pointing out the gossipy, interesting bits of academia, so Finn and Fitch hadn't only studied geometry, they had learned about Harappan mathematics, and the *I Ching*, and Plato.

No longer young, and no longer twitchy, Barnaby was still enthusiastic, and he greeted Finn warmly that evening. "How's that brother of yours?" he inquired as Uncle Thomas handed whiskey sours—another part of the Wednesday evening tradition—all around.

Barnaby was smiling quizzically. Gazing into his pale face, Finn abruptly remembered that here was another person Fitch had not cared for. He had called Barnaby the White Rabbit and mocked him in secret—and sometimes openly. Finn had always tried to ignore it, tune it out, but Con's words of the afternoon resonated even though Finn had tried to deny them.

"I haven't seen him in three years," Finn answered and took a cocktail glass from the tray.

Barnaby raised his white eyebrows. His blond hair had turned silver now, and that reminded Finn of Miss Minton. That was something he *really* didn't want to remember: the way Fitch had mocked Barnaby about Miss Minton being in love with him.

As little as Finn wanted to admit it, Con had been right. Fitch's sense of humor could be cruel sometimes. He had been cruel about Miss Minton and Barnaby, and if there had been the tentative beginnings of something between them, it had shriveled by being exposed to merciless light too early on.

"Out of the country, is he?" Barnaby asked. "He always did have itchy feet."

"They have powder for that," Paul chimed in. "In Fitch's case, I'd have recommended rat poison."

Barnaby looked surprised, and Uncle Thomas coughed. Paul met Finn's glare innocently.

Finn said, "To tell you the truth, I've been trying to find out what happened to him. No one seems to have seen him since he supposedly left the island three years ago."

"Supposedly?" Barnaby repeated.

"Finn," Uncle Thomas said uncomfortably and then stopped.

As though speaking to the at-home viewers, Paul said airily, "He's very stubborn. Once he gets something into his head, it's impossible to shake him loose. He's convinced that Fitch is dead. That he was murdered."

Into the shocked silence that followed Paul's words came the sound of smashing glass from the dining room. They all turned as Martha appeared white-faced in the doorway.

"What are you saying?" she asked. Her eyes were enormous in her stricken face.

"Why did you have to put it like that?" Finn asked Paul, moving to Martha.

"What in God's name is going on?" Uncle Thomas demanded, looking from face to face.

"It's not true," Martha said to Finn, but she sounded like she was begging for reassurance, not really denying it.

"I don't know," Finn said. "I mean, I'm not sure. There's no proof that Fitch ever left the island. And no one ever saw him again after that day."

"What day?" Barnaby asked, sounding bewildered.

"The day Finn found Conway Twitty and Fitch fucking in the lighthouse," Paul said.

"That's about enough of that," Uncle Thomas said in a tone Finn had rarely heard. "I won't have that kind of talk in this house."

Paul laughed. "You do know your nephew is gay, right?"

"That's Finn's business. I'm not going to—"

"This is totally off the track," Finn interrupted. "The point is that Fitch disappeared three years ago and hasn't been seen since. I think something happened to him that day."

"You think he's dead," Paul corrected.

Three horrified faces turned his way. Finn said, "I do. Yes."

Martha faltered, "But if…if there had been some accident…"

"I don't think it was an accident. Someone packed his things to make it look like he left on his own. That couldn't happen accidentally."

"But that's…that's crazy," Uncle Thomas said. Barnaby glanced at him but said nothing.

"I knew it," Martha moaned. "I always felt something was wrong, him leaving like that and Finn the next day. I knew when Finn said he hadn't seen him…"

"No." Uncle Thomas spoke firmly. "*No.* It's impossible. Ridiculous. No one would do such a thing. And if it were true…where are his things? Where is the…the body?"

Martha moaned again. Rain shushed softly against the windows.

"No one's looked for them," Paul said. "No one's looked for *him.* If someone started looking…"

"Have you called the police yet?" Barnaby asked calmly into the stunned silence.

Finn shook his head, gazing at his uncle. "I wanted to talk to you first."

"C-Call the police?" Uncle Thomas was practically stuttering. "That's the craziest thing I've heard yet. Call the police based on…on what? This is Fitch we're talking about, is it not? He's just as likely to be deliberately playing some hoax on us."

"For three years?" Martha cried. "He wouldn't. Not for three years."

"Martha's right," Finn said. "I think three years negates the possibility of this being a hoax."

"Although I don't put anything beyond him," Paul said casually, moving to take a layered cream cheese biscuit off the tray on the credenza.

Uncle Thomas put his glass down. "Finn, I don't believe you've thought this all the way through. Do you have any idea how truly unpleasant a police investigation would be? It would be in the papers, you understand? They would ask questions of all of us, and they wouldn't stop until they had all the details of that day—the whole story of what happened between you and Con and Fitch."

Not for the first time, it occurred to Finn to wonder how, if Fitch had never returned to The Birches, everyone at the house seemed to know what had taken place that morning at the lighthouse? He blurted, "How do you know about that?"

Uncle Thomas looked at Martha, and Martha, oddly enough, was the one who answered. "Mr. Carlyle came to the house to find you the next afternoon. It wasn't hard to put together what must have happened. Fitch was… Well, he had his funny ways. No mistake."

"Fitch was jealous of you," Paul said. "He was jealous of you, and he was jealous *of* you, if you get what I mean."

"Huh?"

"He competed with you, competed with you for attention from people like Con. From everyone, I imagine. But he also wanted you all to himself. He was jealous of time and attention you gave others, right?"

Finn stared at them bewilderedly. This was very much what Con had said, but Finn had never seen any of this in his relationship with his twin. He wanted to tell them that they were all wrong, but he was too much of a realist to believe that everyone else could see it the same way and still be mistaken.

Martha said uncomfortably, "Mr. Carlyle was... Well..."

"Con was distraught," Uncle Tom said crisply. "I don't see what's to be gained by digging all this up now."

"I think Tom's right," Barnaby said quietly. "Best to let sleeping dogs lie."

"I don't understand."

Paul said, "They want you to shut up about it. They want you to forget about Fitch."

Finn stared at the ring of faces watching him with varying degrees of wariness. He said to Martha, "You don't believe that, do you? You don't believe we can—we should—just forget this? Forget that Fitch has been murdered?"

"We don't know that for sure," she faltered. "He might have left the island. Just because we can't prove it doesn't mean he didn't leave of his own free will. And if the police start digging...and the papers...it's going to be...bad. Bad for all of us."

"Murder is bad for all of us," Finn said.

"It's not merely you and your reputation at stake," Uncle Thomas said flatly. "There's my own name and reputation—this family's name and reputation. There's Con's name and reputation. A thing like this could ruin us all."

Finn opened his mouth to make an impatient reply, but Barnaby said, "Have you thought about the fact that you'll be under suspicion as well?"

"Me?"

"If I understand correctly, there was some falling out between you, Fitch, and Conlan Carlyle. That means that you and Carlyle will be the prime suspects."

"Do you have an alibi for that day?" Paul inquired sweetly.

Finn stared at him.

"You're talking about disrupting a lot of lives...and we don't even know for sure that Fitch isn't perfectly well and merrily raising hell in some other corner of the world." Uncle Thomas picked up his drink and sipped it. With an air of having said the final word, he said, "Martha, is dinner about ready?"

Martha made a visible effort to pull herself together. With a guilty look at Finn, she nodded to her employer and left the room.

"I don't believe this," Finn said at last.

Barnaby smiled uncomfortably at him—offering that same sort of silent half apology Martha had—before handing his glass to Thomas for a refill.

Finn opened his mouth. He closed it. Clearly, if he was going to proceed, it was going to be against the will of everyone at The Birches—with the exception of Paul, who moved to his side and said under his breath, "Don't worry. We'll find proof."

Dinner was a strange affair. The food, as always, was excellent. Roast beef and Martha's shrimp-stuffed triple-baked potatoes. Barnaby and Uncle Thomas chatted pleasantly about politics and general island business, directing comments to Finn and Paul, but not pausing long enough for either of the younger men to really join in the conversation—let alone redirect it. On the surface, everything seemed normal. The conversation in the parlor might never have occurred, but as casual as Uncle Thomas and Barnaby seemed, Finn was conscious of being carefully and deliberately corralled.

The discussion regarding Fitch was clearly over.

It was unbelievable, and yet…it was a perfect example of how life on Seal Island had always been…isolated and self-contained. It was as though they none of them realized how unrealistic—otherworldly—their attitude was. In fact, scooping the creamy, steaming-hot filling out of the potato shell, Finn couldn't help wondering if maybe *he* was the one missing the point. Maybe he *should* leave well enough alone.

Not only did he dread the idea of being the focus of a police investigation—what the hell kind of an alibi did *he* have for that day? He'd spent it sitting on top of a mountain, staring at the ocean and trying not to think. He was horrified at the idea of dragging Con into the limelight. Nothing could have convinced him of Con's innocence as effectively as his hurt fury at the lighthouse that afternoon.

He remembered only too clearly how fiercely protective of his privacy Con had always been.

In fact, every time he thought of Con, his stomach knotted with anxiety. It had been much easier when he was confident in his unyielding anger and rancor. But Con's remorse, his continued displays of affection and caring, were wearing Finn down. Equally wearing were the times when Con seemed to indicate that he was moving on or losing interest in pursuing anything with Finn. When it came to Con, Finn was a mess of contradictory feelings—the bottom line being that whether he could sort them out yet or not, he did still have feelings for Con. Con was making it hard to ignore those feelings. And now Finn had weakened his own position of utter inviolate righteousness by doing something fairly unforgivable…like accusing Con of murder.

'Cause nothing put a damper on romance like suspicions of homicide.

But Fitch…as angry and hurt and unforgiving as Finn had believed himself…he couldn't bear not knowing what had happened to Fitch. Nor could he bear the idea that someone had killed Fitch and was going to be allowed to get away with it. Perhaps that was ironic, given how certain he had been that he could never forgive his twin—but knowing that now there truly would be no chance for reconciliation had changed everything.

At the same time, he couldn't help being afraid of waking this particular old hound dog. It was a small island, and he was painfully aware that he could rule out the possibility that Fitch had been killed by a passing madman. The odds were, whoever had killed Fitch was someone Finn knew quite well. Maybe loved.

Granted, Fitch had had his secrets—certainly Finn hadn't known about Con and Fitch until the day that he'd discovered them in the lighthouse. Maybe there was someone else on the island who had known another side of Fitch.

Or maybe someone had followed Fitch to the island. Finn glanced across the table, and Paul met his eyes.

No.

No, right? Because if Paul had been going to kill Fitch, it probably would have been when they were still together. Who waited years? And Paul had moved on. Well, he didn't have a steady lover—but neither did Finn. No. But it wouldn't hurt to ask whether Paul had an alibi for that weekend.

When at last the meal was finished, Uncle Tom and Barnaby took their brandies and went off to the study to play checkers.

"Where can we go to talk?" Paul asked in a stage whisper.

Finn shook his head, rising. He led the way upstairs to Fitch's bedroom. A little frisson rippled down his spine as he pushed the door open and turned on the light.

Looking around himself, Paul said, "This was his room?"

Finn nodded. There was an obstruction in his throat that made it difficult to speak.

The room was the twin of his own—same window seat flanked by dormer windows, same funny-sloping ceiling and long bookshelves. The heavy, mismatched furniture was similar—both rooms had been furnished from other rooms within the house. As with his own room, nothing had been moved or changed, although the room was neatly dusted, the bed made.

How weird to stand here in this room again. Finn closed his eyes, trying to remember, trying to…perhaps reach out to Fitch. But all he sensed was a room that hadn't been used for a long time. He opened his eyes. There were photos stuck on the mirror over the dresser: a snapshot of himself crossing his eyes for Fitch's camera, a much older picture of them together swimming, and several shots of people unknown to him. There was a small bowl on the dresser with loose change, a couple of fishing lures, and a pair of dice.

Paul opened the closet door. "His clothes are still here."

Finn joined him, looking inside. There were some odds and ends pushed to the side. A fishing vest, a couple of flannel shirts, a heavy parka. "Those are mostly his older things. Stuff he'd outgrown or only wore here on the island. He took—well, someone took—most of what he'd brought with him that summer. His suitcases are gone."

Paul backed out of the closet and looked around the room. "There's not a lot here."

"He didn't like collecting junk."

Fitch had never been one for acquiring possessions. He had a few books, not nearly the number Finn had—nothing from his childhood. There were no games, no equivalent of Finn's collection of old sailboat models. There was a fishing pole behind the door and a tennis racket in the closet.

"Did he keep a journal?" Paul asked.

Finn shook his head.

Paul went over to the dresser and took the photos down from the mirror, one by one. "I know some of these people."

Finn joined him, glancing at the familiar and unfamiliar faces. "Anyone with a grudge against him?"

Paul snorted. "I have no idea why, but most people thought Fitch was perfectly charming—even when he was screwing them over."

Finn moved to the desk and examined the desktop calendar. It was open to August 18. There was nothing noted for the day. No "betray my brother before breakfast" reminder. He flipped through the back pages, but they were all blank. He said slowly, his thoughts on Uncle Thomas and Barnaby, "I can't decide if they honestly don't believe Fitch is dead, or if they're afraid he really is."

"I think they know he's dead. I think your uncle has suspected it long enough that it's not even a shock."

Finn sighed. "They're right, though. I can't go to the police without something more than this."

"You could file a missing persons report and let it follow its natural course. Let the police decide if there are grounds for a murder investigation."

"Yes, but what they said is true. If I open this can of worms, there's no way of controlling it."

"So?"

"So? So if the police determine that a murder investigation is warranted, Con and I will both be prime suspects."

Paul studied Finn, head tilted to one side. "*Did* you kill him?"

"Ha-ha."

"I wouldn't blame you if you had."

"I didn't kill my brother," Finn said shortly. "If I had, I wouldn't be pointing out to everyone that I thought he'd been murdered."

"You might," Paul said seriously. "If you thought it had been long enough that people were going to start wondering and asking questions."

Finn said wearily, "If I had been going to kill anyone that day, it would have been myself. And I wasn't about to kill myself."

"You still had too many wonderful paintings left to give the world," Paul trilled, waving his arm in a broad gesture toward the room's only painting—one of Finn's early studies of the lighthouse.

"Yeah, actually. You can laugh about it, but as miserable as I was, I still had a strong sense of the work I wanted to do. I knew it wasn't always going to be as bad as it was right then."

"I suppose that makes sense." Paul eyed him speculatively. "And so you fled to me."

"You were the only person I knew in Manhattan."

"Now don't spoil it because I've always been immensely flattered that you came to me."

Finn spluttered, "I told you that day when I apologized for barging in on you."

"Shhhhh, don't speak...no no no...don't speak," Paul said, seemingly channeling Dianne Wiest in *Bullets Over Broadway*. "Now that I think of it, I wonder why we never got together. We had an obvious natural bond."

Was rage at Fitch an *obvious natural bond*? Finn answered, "Because I was still in love with Con and you were still in love with Fitch."

For a long moment, Paul stared at him. He smiled—he had a surprisingly sweet smile. "I guess that's true." He put a hand on his hip, surveying the room thoughtfully. "All right. So if you were a body, where would *you* hide?"

CHAPTER EIGHT

It was a small island, but there were many places one could hide a body. It could be buried in Bell Woods or in the soft sand of the cave at Otter Cove. It could lie undiscovered beneath the wildflowers in one of the meadows or on a hillside beneath a cairn of stones.

The first challenge would be in transporting a corpse in broad daylight.

If Fitch had died at the lighthouse—and Finn and Paul could not agree on this point, as Paul did not concur that the scratches in the light tower looked like marks left by clawing fingernails. But for the sake of argument, if Fitch *had* died at the lighthouse…the simplest thing would have been to bury him there. The lighthouse was off the beaten track, and there was less chance of discovery by a stray hiker's dog. It also eliminated the need to move the body any distance.

"It wouldn't be hard to lift you," Paul commented, examining Finn, who was sitting on Fitch's bed. "Even when you're your normal weight, you're pretty skinny. Maybe one forty, one forty-five? Fitch was more muscular—not a lot a heavier, though."

"A deadweight is different."

"Even so. I could do it. You could do it if you didn't have to carry someone too far."

Finn considered. "We should talk to Miss Minton. I don't know if her memory is as sharp as it used to be, but in the old days, no one traveled the road to The Birches without her seeing them. Con said she saw him that day. She might have seen someone else."

"Is there another way to get to this house besides the main road?"

"There isn't another drive. There's a trail that leads to the back of the property." He remembered that Hiram had been clearing poison ivy out that day along the path.

There was a tap on the door frame, and both Finn and Paul jumped guiltily.

"You boys have been up here awhile," Martha said, bringing a tray into the bedroom and setting it on the desk where Paul sat. "I brought you some hot chocolate and lobster butter cookies."

Paul spluttered and put a hand over his mouth, his gaze finding Finn's.

Martha straightened and eyed Finn sternly. "Mr. Carlyle called a little while ago. He wanted to make sure you got home safely."

Paul laughed outright. Finn ignored him. He said to Martha, "Con and I argued. It's not anything new."

"I don't understand these things," she said. "It seems to me that Mr. Carlyle still has powerful feelings for you. And despite what you say, I think you still have feelings for him. Is that such a bad thing? It's not like there's so much love in the world that people can afford to go turning it away."

Finn tried to imagine what Con must have said to Martha to inspire that little speech.

He opened his mouth, but Paul forestalled him, saying, "Martha, between us, who do you think might have killed Fitch?"

She turned slowly and stared at him. "I loved Fitch," she said. "But I'll tell you right now, sonny, you're meddling in things best left alone. And you're dragging Finn into dangerous waters with you."

"No one's dragging me into anything," Finn said quietly. "If someone killed Fitch, I can't ignore that."

"There are all kinds of things we have to ignore every day," Martha said. "Sometimes it's better for everyone to let certain things go."

"You're talking about turning a blind eye to murder, not spitting on the sidewalk," Paul said shrilly.

"I know exactly what I'm talking about," Martha said grimly. She looked at Finn. "Don't you stay up too late, Finn."

Paul closed the door after her with a suggestion of a bang. Catching Finn's expression, he burst out laughing.

* * * * *

It was still raining on Thursday morning, a steady wash of silver rain that was almost invisible in the gray daylight. Fog shrouded the sea, pierced here and there by a dripping tree. It did not look like a particularly auspicious day for sleuthing.

"You don't think it's going to snow, do you?" Paul asked, meeting Finn on his way down to breakfast.

"It's not cold enough."

"Are you kidding me? I thought the next ice age had come last night."

Finn threw Paul a guilty glance. He'd been perfectly warm; Martha had brought him extra blankets before he'd fallen asleep. Well, perhaps there was a blanket shortage at The Birches these days. Or perhaps not.

Probably not—as Martha still seemed a little stern when they found her in the kitchen. She ordered them to the table and began piling their plates.

It brought back comfortable memories. The kitchen was very warm and smelled deliciously of bacon and coffee and cinnamon rolls. Martha had the radio on low as she listened to the weather report.

"Paul and I are going to borrow the station wagon this morning," Finn told her as she refilled his coffee cup. "Unless you or Hiram need it for something?"

Martha directed a disapproving look at Paul, who was busily eating his haystack eggs—baked eggs on fried potato sticks with cheese and bacon topping.

"Dangerous driving conditions today," she pronounced like a hash-slinging oracle.

"We'll be careful."

Martha hmphed. "I don't need the car today." She didn't say more, though it was clear she wished to. Paul grimaced at his plate without looking up.

Breakfast finished, Finn and Paul climbed into the station wagon—Paul driving—and headed slowly and cautiously down the muddy road to Estelle Minton's.

"So your uncle and the ex-schoolteacher... Are they...?" Paul peered over the steering wheel at the lazy whorl of fog before them.

"Are they— Huh?" Finn stared at him and did a double take. "Uncle Thomas and Barnaby? God no. They've been friends forever."

"So?"

"You better get your gaydar recalibrated. Neither of them is a member of the sisterhood. I think Barnaby used to have a thing for Miss Minton, and Uncle Thomas was once engaged to a lady from the mainland."

"What happened to the lady from the mainland?"

"The story is she declined to live on an island, and Uncle Tom couldn't picture living anywhere else."

"Uncle Tom is a little set in his ways, isn't he?"

"Here it is," Finn interrupted. "You can pull to the side of the road, but don't get stuck in the mud."

Most days Miss Minton could be found working out in her yard, but today there was no sign of her, although the battered pickup in the drive indicated she was home. White trails of fog wreathed the rosebushes and trees as though dragged there by the rain. A wheelbarrow sat tipped over next to stacked bags of fertilizer and soil amendment.

Finn swore as his cane sank into the mud, and Paul laughed.

"Need a hand?"

"How about a new leg?"

Crossing the deserted road, they entered through the gate. They knocked on the front door, and after a few seconds it opened. Miss Minton, dressed in comfortably baggy flannels and jeans, stared at them in surprise.

"Finn Barret. Something wrong at The Birches?"

"Nothing like that," Finn said apologetically. "I was hoping to maybe have a word with you?"

"Well, well." She directed a skeptical look at Paul. "I expect you'd better come in."

They followed her into a large room with a picture window that looked out on the road. The room was comfortably furnished in crisp blue and white. A fire burned cheerfully in the grate. A black cat leisurely groomed itself on the pillow-piled sofa.

"Well, you'd better have a seat," their hostess said. "This isn't weather for fooling around on the roads. It must be something pretty important to bring you down here?"

Finn glanced at Paul, who was watching him, clearly wanting Finn to take charge here. Which was all very well, but it seemed sort of tactless to hint to Miss Minton he thought her longtime friends and neighbors might be murderers.

"This is going to seem like an odd request," he said. "I wanted to put that famous memory of yours to the test."

Miss Minton raised her eyebrows but said nothing.

"August, three years ago…Fitch and I both left the island." He paused, but Miss Minton had nothing to say to that. "I left on the nineteenth. It was a Tuesday, about eleven o'clock in the morning. We always thought Fitch left on the previous Monday afternoon."

"But?"

"But no one ever saw him again," Finn said. "At least, if they did, they're not admitting it."

Miss Minton's brows knitted. "I'm not sure what you're getting at. Are you saying… What *are* you saying?"

"We think Fitch is dead," Paul said as Finn groped for a less shocking way to break the news. "We think someone on this island might have killed him."

Finn turned on him, and meeting that exasperated stare, Paul said, "What? That's what we think!"

To Miss Minton, Finn said, "It does seem like Fitch never left the island, and what we were wondering was whether you remembered anything that might have stood out from the ordinary."

"When?"

"That Monday. The eighteenth of August. I thought you might remember because it was during the time you were still taking art lessons from Uncle Tom."

Miss Minton looked taken aback. "You expect me to remember something that happened three years ago? Such as what?"

"Like who traveled to and from The Birches that day."

She was watching him with a peculiar alertness. "Ah," she said finally. She seemed to look inward. At last she said, "My lessons were Mondays and Wednesdays, but I don't remember taking a lesson that week."

"Uncle Tom was supposed to fly to Boston or somewhere for an art show or a lecture. His flight was canceled on Monday, but he spent most of the day in Portland at the airport."

"That's right…" Miss Minton said slowly. "I do remember. Con walked past here about lunchtime right before I came in from the garden to change clothes. I don't remember seeing him walk back, but he wasn't at The Birches when I arrived about half an hour later. No one was there at all, and I came back home."

"Did you see anyone else pass here on their way to The Birches that day?"

"It was a long time ago, Finn. I seem to remember your uncle driving past early in the evening. And you and Con walked by about an hour and a half after that." Her smile was wry. "Con's voice carried. I remember that."

Finn colored.

"I'm surprised I remember that much after all this time," Miss Minton commented, reaching for the cat and cuddling it in her arms.

"Why do you suppose that is?" Paul asked.

Miss Minton gave him a considering stare. "I don't know. I guess the reason it stayed in my mind is because it *was* the summer—the very week, in fact—the Barret Boys left Seal Island."

* * * * *

"She's like something straight out of Stephen King," Paul commented as they got back into the car. "Or possibly, *What Not to Wear.*"

"I don't see that," Finn replied irritably. Sometimes Paul's casual unkindness reminded him of Fitch. "She's had a hard life."

"So had Dolores Claiborne. So had Cujo."

Finn sat unmoving, not really listening. The fog blanketed the car in white, giving them the illusion of complete and utter privacy. "She used to be different when she was younger."

Paul groaned. "*Why* do people always say that? *Everyone* is different when they're younger. Nobody is born a crotchety old fart." Studying Finn's profile, he asked reluctantly, "Different how?"

"Happier. Softer. Pretty."

"I'll take your word for it."

"I didn't know her well, but she and Uncle Tom have been friends for years. She used to babysit Con—I didn't know her *then*, naturally, but she was always crazy about him. They're third or fourth cousins, I think."

"Toto, I have a feeling we're not in Arkansas anymore."

"I don't mean that way. She never married, never had kids of her own. Actually, I always thought those art lessons were more about the way she liked Uncle Tom than her really wanting to become a painter."

"Sacrilege. I thought it was old Barnaby she had a thing for?"

"She did. Well, I mean...I have no idea. What do kids know? She might have been sweet on Barnaby or he might have been sweet on her."

"As fascinating as Miss Minton's love life is, where to now?"

Finn said slowly, "The lighthouse."

"I think so, yeah."

There were a few alarming seconds while the car's tires spun in the mud, but then they gained traction and were on the road once more, proceeding with great caution through the white nothingness.

"For the record, I hate driving in this," Paul said.

Finn nodded absently.

"The fact that she didn't see anyone but Con that day doesn't mean that no one else went up to The Birches," Paul said when Finn's silence persisted. "They could have gone in the back way. We didn't talk to Ezra or whatever his name is."

"Hiram."

"Right. Maybe he saw someone. Or maybe she missed them. Him."

"Maybe."

The car bounced along the uneven track, Paul accelerating as the mist thinned out in patches. "If you think about it," he said, "it's kind of hard to believe that someone would simply walk up and shove Fitch off the tower, and then what? Scrape him off the rocks and hide him under a bush?"

Finn rubbed his forehead, smoothing away the little ache in his temple.

"True. To really hide a body you'd either have to weight it down and dump it in the ocean or dig a grave deep enough that no one would accidentally uncover it."

"If he was dumped in the ocean three years ago, we're wasting our time."

"I know."

"Obviously, if he was killed at the lighthouse, whoever did it couldn't take a chance on moving a body around in broad daylight. That's what we think, right? That he was killed in broad daylight?"

"Yes. No one seems to have seen him after he and Con parted ways."

"Which leads me to wonder—and you won't like this—how could anyone know he'd be up there?"

Finn sighed. "Either it was Con, and he killed Fitch when he hit him—which I don't believe—or it was someone who was maybe following Fitch?" He said slowly, working it out, "*Or* maybe it was someone Fitch had originally planned to meet? Because I remember that night Con was saying to me that it hadn't been planned, that it hadn't been arranged, it had just happened. That he'd actually come up to the lighthouse to find me because I was supposed to be sketching there that day."

Paul's eyes were trained on the road ahead. He grunted. "Not bad."

"Here, you've missed the turn."

Paul braked sharply, reversed, and turned off the road leading up to the lighthouse.

"So…you think Fitch arranged to meet this person, but Con showed up first, and Fitch grabbed the opportunity as it presented itself? Yeah, I can see that. He'd enjoy rubbing someone's nose in it."

Finn shot him a sideways look and said nothing.

"It could have been someone who was there for another reason, though." Paul spoke meditatively, "Someone who hiked up there for the view or to sketch…"

Finn's stomach did an unpleasant flip-flop.

Paul rambled cheerfully on. "Maybe this person had an innocent reason for being there but went a little crazy when he saw what was happening. Maybe he pretended to walk away and hid, and when Con left, he came back and killed Fitch. Because it seems to me that whoever killed Fitch must have been someone Fitch wasn't afraid of."

"Fitch wasn't afraid of anyone."

"No. He wasn't."

Finn added, "And I didn't come back and kill him. It happened exactly like I said it did."

Paul chuckled. "I never doubted you. Here we are." The lighthouse swung suddenly into the windshield's view, seeming to loom up out of the mist.

They took their flashlights and jackets, got out of the car, and stood staring up at the white tower. A gull appeared out of the mist, crying eerily and disappearing once more.

Paul said, "Let's put our emotions aside for a sec and look at this logically. If Fitch was killed here, then there's a good chance he's buried here. Somewhere. I can't see anyone taking the risk of moving a body very far."

"I can't either."

"Could he be buried inside? Maybe put into a wall or stuck under the flooring?"

It took Finn a moment to control his voice. "I guess that's what we're going to find out."

Without further discussion, they went into the light keeper's dwelling. In silence that seemed to grow heavier with each passing minute, they moved around the small residence, checking the empty built-in closets and cupboards, pounding against the walls, which all seemed perfectly solid. The wind picked up, whistling mournfully through the boards across the window, moaning down the chimney. Far, far beneath their feet was the slow, distant pound of the surf hitting the cliffs in phantom heartbeat.

"We should have brought shovels," Paul said.

"That would have gone over well. There's no sense upsetting people if we don't need to." Finn moved the flashlight over the broken flooring.

"You mean if we don't find anything?"

Finn studied the moldering earth beneath the broken patches of boards. Yes, Paul was right, they should have brought shovels.

Paul said shortly, "That *is* what you mean, right? If we don't find anything, you're not going to let them cover this up? You're not going to let them get away with murder?"

Finn stared across the room at Paul's weirdly shadowed face. "Them?"

"Yes, *them*. All of them. Are you going to call the police or not? Or do I need to do it?"

"What's the matter with you?"

"If you killed him…then I understand. I can forgive it. But if it wasn't you—"

"I told you I didn't kill Fitch."

Paul lifted a negligent shoulder.

"I'm not lying." Finn's flare of temper caught even him off guard. "And I'm not going to let anyone get away with anything, but you're not making the call on this. And I'm not doing anything until I've thought it through. Until I know what I'm dealing with. And one of the things I don't understand is why the hell you're so hot to see Fitch get justice. You hated him."

"I *loved* him!"

"You loved him? You *sued* him."

The beam of Finn's flashlight caught tears glittering on Paul's cheeks. "So what? I was angry and bitter—and jealous, I admit that. But I never stopped loving him. Even when I hated him."

Finn opened and then closed his mouth. Finally he managed, "Really? Well, you've hid it pretty well all this time."

"What do you know about it? You've been moping over Conway Twitty for three years. Which ought to tell you something right there since I'm pretty sure you thought you hated *him*."

That struck a little too close to home. Finn said, "In that case, and since you're so quick to scream for justice, where the hell were you on the eighteenth of August three years ago?"

Paul gasped as though mortally struck. Tears gave way to astonishment and then outrage. "What are you saying to me?"

"I'm saying...you're so quick to want to call the cops, fine. Only they're going to ask you where you were three years ago—especially since, according to you, you were still in love with Fitch. It was one thing when you were an interested bystander, but now you're a potential suspect."

"You...*bitch!*"

"Hey"—Finn shrugged—"I'm just pointing out the obvious. You're a suspect here too. So before we go flying off to drag the state police into this, I suggest we figure out exactly what we're dealing with. Because we're both going to be very unpopular if it turns out Fitch isn't dead. And if he is dead, we're going to be even *more* unpopular—not to mention one of us might end up getting arrested for a crime he didn't commit."

Paul stood very still. "You're turning this around on me to protect Carlyle. He's the only one who could have done this, and you know it."

"Do you have an alibi or not?"

"I don't know! I don't remember where I was three years ago. I might have an alibi. When I get home, I'll check!"

"Great. In the meantime, let's keep our mouths shut till we know something for sure. Because right now we don't know *anything*. We don't even have a body."

"Well, why don't I go get a couple of shovels?" Paul offered with acid sweetness. He stared challengingly at Finn.

Finn stared back. "All right," he said finally. "Why don't you?"

"Do you mean that?"

"Of course I mean it. I already told you I—" He shook his head wearily. "Just...try not to let anyone see you. They're going to be very upset if they think—"

"Give me credit for some discretion," Paul said. He propped his flashlight on one of the window shelves and picked his way across the broken flooring.

Finn forced himself to stay where he stood as he heard the car engine fade away. Blackness was *not* the absence of color. If you mixed every color together, what did you get? You got black. Close enough. So there was nothing to fear in the darkness. No reason to stand here with his heart in overdrive and sweat breaking out over his body, because nothing in the darkness could hurt him. And even if there was something buried in the soft, wet square of ground next to his foot, it could not be Fitch. It was not big enough for Fitch.

He forced himself to stand there for another wrenching second or two, and then he crossed the broken floor and stepped outside. The fog had mostly dissipated; the rain was coming down in a fine misting. But overhead, the sky was heavy and dark with the promise of worse weather, and the sea looked black.

He took a couple of deep lungfuls of oxygen, and then he forced himself back into the cottage. The cottage door swung restlessly back and forth on its creaking hinges, and he propped it open with a large flat rock.

Fresh air, daylight. What more could he ask? Grimly, he took his cane and began to poke it into the soft dirt near the far corner of the house where he thought he had seen an unnatural indentation in the bare earth. The ground was very soft. The tip of the cane slid in deep and struck something—which then gave.

He straightened up, stood motionless, looked to the doorway. It stood open and empty. The door tugged in the wind, bouncing against the rock anchoring it.

Finn looked down at the square of damp earth.

An old rug?

It hadn't sounded like that. He lowered himself carefully, kneeling awkwardly, scraping at the thing buried in the soft, damp earth.

After a time he stopped, looked around for something else to use as a shovel. He spotted a broken piece of flooring and grabbed that, carving and scraping, digging away as ferociously as a terrier despite the uneasy feeling crawling down his spine. It had to be the cold of the cottage working its way into his bones; he gritted his jaw against the incipient chatter of teeth.

"It's a suitcase," he got out, and the sound of his own voice startled him.

He dug more quickly, the wood making a rough whisper against the cloth of the suitcase, and then the suitcase was free and he used all his strength to drag it out of the hole in the floor. He braced a hand against the wall and pulled himself up again.

Hauling the suitcase out into the soft, rainy mist, he laid it on the patchy grass and brushed away rust and mud, struggling to yank the zipper open. The smell of rotted material and mildew wafted up. Inside were a jumble of clothes and odds and ends. Finn recognized the moldy remains of a black checked shirt, a moss green sweater, red briefs, the cotton discolored, the elastic deteriorated.

He touched the shirt—his own. Fitch had borrowed it one day, and Finn had never thought of it since.

At last he closed the suitcase lid and sat there, shaking a little with cold and exhaustion and nerves. He had not really, entirely believed it until now, but there could be no doubt.

Fitch was dead. Murdered.

He was not sure how much time had passed by the time it occurred to him that Fitch had had two suitcases. That meant the other must still lie in the cottage in another corner of wet, cushioning earth.

He forced himself back on his feet and back into the pitchy interior of the cottage. Was it darker than before, or was that his overactive imagination?

Not so overactive as it turned out.

Finding his discarded cane, he began to poke again in the spongy sections of bare earth.

From outside came the rumble of thunder. He ignored it, jabbing the metal tip of the walking stick into the moldering earth. It took a while, but on the opposite side of the room, near the doorway leading to the light tower, again he struck something in the soil.

And as he did, a blast of wind, harder than the previous gusts, slammed shut the door to the cottage.

His heart seemed to stop. And then, after a moment of utter, abject, paralyzed fear, it jump-started, speeding back into life.

Finn began to feel his way across the uneven boards, reminding himself all the while that he had a flashlight—two flashlights, for Paul's still shone from the window shelf—and that his fear was an irrational, foolish thing.

Except that wasn't right. Maybe there wasn't anything in the darkness to fear, but Fitch had been murdered—and that murderer could only be one of a handful of people, and they were all still on this island.

He was still absorbing the full shock of that when the cottage door was dragged open again. Instinctively, Finn turned off his flashlight as a black outline filled the doorway.

"Finn?" Con called out.

CHAPTER NINE

Silently, instinctively, Finn moved back, slipping through the doorway that led to the tower. Watery light from the windows high, high above moved in the base of the tower like ghosts.

"Who's in here?" Con called.

Finn didn't move a muscle. Didn't breathe. He could hear Con stepping carefully; hear the crunch of his shoes on broken concrete and splintered wood. Con was coming his way. Soundlessly, he crept behind the stairwell, hiding in the shadows. He knew the impulse telling him to climb was a false one. If he went up the stairs, he would be trapped, and yet everything in him was clamoring for light and air and distance from the threat coming steadily toward him.

If he could stay perfectly silent, perfectly still...Con might leave. Might see the tire tracks in the yard and assume that whoever had been at the lamp had come and gone.

But no. The suitcase was still in the yard. He would see it, surely? Would he believe that they had left it behind? Doubtful.

Con was not leaving. Finn could see the golden circle of Paul's flashlight beam coming toward the tower door ahead of Con's footsteps.

Finn's nerve broke and he went for the staircase, trying for silence but needing to move.

"Finn, you're scaring the hell out of me," Con said, and Finn was so startled he misstepped and came down hard on the staircase, which clanged noisily—no concealing that. In any case, for a red wash of an instant he was in too much pain to worry about it. His cane slithered and fell through the railing, hitting the wall of the tower as it dropped to the ground.

Out of the corner of his eye, he saw a shadow move into the tower—caught briefly in the blue light from above.

"Finn?"

"Here," he got out. Dimly, it occurred to him that he had resolved his fear of Con. It had been that disarming *Finn, you're scaring the hell out of me.*

"*Jesus.* What happened?" And Con was at the stairs and bending over him. "How far did you fall?"

"I didn't. Exactly. Just came down wrong."

Con was running hands over him, checking for broken bones. His fingers were cold, his breath warm. He smelled like rain and aftershave.

"I'm okay," Finn said.

"Are you sure? You could have killed yourself."

He opened his mouth to reiterate that he hadn't been far up the staircase, but stopped. He didn't want Con to know he had tried to run from him. He felt stupid for his earlier fear. He had known in his heart Con couldn't be a killer, and yet a part of him had persisted in doubting. Partly it had been the horror of finding Fitch's suitcase, having his worst fears confirmed. Partly, though, he had feared Con.

Grabbing on to the railing, he drew himself up. Con's hand brushed his back, offering support or maybe reassuring himself that Finn was still in one piece. "You're sure?"

Even in that eerie light he could feel Con's gaze. He met it and couldn't look away. "I'm sure." It was mostly embarrassing now. Had he fallen down the stairs it would have been different—fatally different, probably.

"What in the name of Christ were you doing?"

"I needed the light," he said.

"Finn, sugar..." Con said, and there was a wealth of emotion in his voice that Finn couldn't understand. Con's head bent, his mouth covered Finn's, and he kissed him. It was a strange kiss, though. Strangely tender. Strangely restrained. But maybe that wasn't so strange given everything else.

Finn kissed back, tentatively. How long had he waited for this? No, that was wrong. He hadn't waited. Hadn't anticipated or hoped. Hadn't let himself think about it all—because he had believed there was no chance of it ever again. But he had not forgotten. Not forgotten Con's taste or scent or feel. He'd forgotten nothing—and nothing had changed. Finn was no longer tentative—and neither was Con. Suddenly it was hot and sweet and all the colors of the rainbow.

Finn's fingers clenched in Con's wet jacket, and Con was stroking his hair, kissing his face, kissing his hair. "I'm so sorry," he said, and he found Finn's mouth again, his own hungry and insistent. Finn opened to that delving kiss, that firm, deep, hungry kiss that seemed to call forth everything that had been wounded and sleeping deep inside him. He was waking up all right, the reds and yellows of the color spectrum were alive and well, dancing beneath his eyelids, and his cock was getting hard for the first time in what felt like a very long time.

It was Con who broke the kiss. Finn swayed a little as contact ended, hanging on for support, and Con yielded, softly mouthed the edge of his jaw, his cheekbone, before pulling back again. His voice sounded uneven as he said, "I saw the suitcase."

And it all came crashing back—Fitch was dead, murdered—and Finn was standing here making out. It was...a jolt. He turned, looking blindly for his cane.

Seeing his fumble, Con moved, finding the stick where it had fallen behind the staircase. He grabbed it, then pressed it into Finn's hand, wrapping Finn's fingers around it.

"What are you doing here?"

"I came to check the tower out. After yesterday…" Con didn't finish it, instead taking Finn's arm and guiding him through the darkness of the cottage. There was something unusually protective in the way Con was hanging on to him. Sort of sweet, but sort of quaint too. Not that Finn minded. It was nice to have Con's arm around him, nice to have a little help getting across the obstacle course of the broken floor. But Con had never been overly watchful.

"The other suitcase is in that corner." He nodded to where he had been digging.

Con stopped. "So it's true." His tone was flat but unsurprised. "You should never have come here on your own, Finn. This is… You know what it means."

"I know what it means. I wasn't on my own. Paul came with me. He went back to The Birches to get shovels."

"What the hell was he doing leaving you on your own?"

Con sounded really angry, and Finn looked at him in surprise. "I sent him to get the shovels."

"I don't care. He had no business leaving you on your own." Con was moving forward, still holding Finn's arm as though Finn couldn't be trusted out of his sight. Which was getting a little odd.

Finn freed himself as they reached the door and stepped out into the murky daylight. Con loosed him reluctantly. "I wish you could trust me."

"I do." He realized it was true. He did trust Con. He knew he hadn't killed Fitch, although maybe that was instinct more than logic. He knew that Con regretted the way things had ended between them.

"Do you?" Con's expression was weary. Almost sad. "I know it's my fault. I wasn't there for you the last time, but I will be there for you this time. If you'll let me."

"If I'll let you what?"

Con was giving him the strangest look. "I was hoping you would tell me, but it's not hard to put the pieces together."

"It's…not?"

"I was afraid when no one at The Birches would talk about it—about your accident. I know how hard this is, but you've got to learn to rely on others a little with…this hanging over you."

Finn stopped, staring. His heart was pounding hard as Con's words sunk in. "What do you mean?"

He was afraid he knew only too well what Con meant, so it was a shock when Con said calmly, "I know you're…losing your sight."

Finn blinked. "I'm…"

Con said, "Do you think it makes a difference to me? It doesn't. I still love you. Still want to be with you. Nothing could change that."

Finn felt a crazy desire to burst out laughing—at the same time tears stung his eyes, closed his throat. "*Con.* Jesus. I thought you were going to accuse me of murder—like I did you."

"I know you didn't murder Fitch." Con dismissed the idea as not worth considering. "I didn't kill Fitch. I give you my word. I know you don't have any reason to accept it—"

"Yes, I do. You never lied to me," Finn said. "You weren't always kind, but you never lied."

"I lied to myself," Con said grimly. "I told myself all the time we were seeing each other that it was just sex, a fling. Nothing more. I told myself I didn't want to get involved. That you were too young for me. I couldn't picture myself in a long-term relationship—an open relationship. But the only person I was fooling was me. There isn't any getting over the way I feel about you, Finn. The way I've always felt about you. I've had three years of trying, and when I saw you again, I knew that, for me, nothing had changed." He put a hand up and lightly traced the scar on Finn's temple. "The car accident—"

"I'm not going blind," Finn said.

Con held very still. "You're…not?"

Finn shook his head. Wiped at the tears welling at the corner of his eyes. "No." He gave a watery chuckle. "I can't believe that's what you thought. Were you really prepared to take care of me?"

"Hell yes." Con was staring at him. "I had a speech all ready about how you needed—" He stopped. "Why the hell was everyone so mysterious about your accident?"

"Were they?"

"Yes. No one would tell me anything." Con began to sound incensed. "I could see you were having trouble with your eyes—and all those headaches—"

"Well, yeah, but that was—"

"And what about that comment in the car yesterday about not wearing dark glasses until you had to?"

Finn tried to remember what comment Con meant. He really didn't remember saying anything that should have created such a dramatic impression.

Con said bluntly, "You're terrified of the dark."

Finn's smile faded. "Yes. After the accident...yeah. I couldn't see, and they did think for a time...there was a chance I'd lost my sight." He couldn't meet Con's gaze. There was too much there. He said gruffly, "It... shook me. Not least because of my painting. It's my livelihood, and it's... my passion. My life. I think that was the worst part. Realizing that *all* I had was my painting. And if that was gone—"

"But it's not?"

Finn shook his head. "I'm going to be fine. Even the headaches have gotten better since I've been home. I'm not sure I believed it at first. I think I was afraid to. But...I'm going to be okay." He grimaced. "Now I just have to get the nerve to pick up a paintbrush again."

"Thank God," Con said and pulled him into his arms.

At which point, with cosmic bad timing, the skies opened up. It wasn't quite the effect of being doused with a bucket of cold water, but it wasn't far from it. Con grabbed Finn's arm, and they haltingly ran for the Rover, then slammed inside. Rain ticked noisily down on the metal roof.

Laughing unsteadily with a combination of stress and nerves, they were back in each other's arms and kissing again with a near-frantic hunger, as though they had drawn back in time from some terrifying precipice. Con's mouth was hard and soft, sweet and harsh all at the same time.

The windows began to steam.

"Ow. *Ouch.* This isn't going to work." It wasn't easy, but Finn pulled away, trying to ease his cramping leg despite protests from other frustrated parts of his anatomy.

Con let him go, but his hands lingered. "Let's go to my cottage."

"Paul is going to be here any minute." His body was already aching with thwarted desire. Well, it never rained, but it poured—literally, it seemed.

"Call him and tell him to meet us at the cottage." Con's smile was mostly grimace. "Better yet. Tell him to forget about it." His breath was warm as he leaned forward to nip the side of Finn's throat.

"Con."

"I don't mean that." Con sighed. "It's too late even if I wanted that. But this storm is going to get worse before it gets better."

He was right. The storm was moving in, black clouds sliding across the sky, flashes of lightning flickering over the water.

"Anyway, your part in this is done. We both know what that suitcase means. It's time to call the state police."

"Yes."

It was the lightning that decided Finn. That, and the fact that if he didn't get some kind of sexual release soon, his guts would be in knots.

He pulled Paul's cell phone out and called The Birches.

Martha answered with the news that she had not seen Paul. Finn thanked her and told her to have Paul call his cell if he did turn up. Clicking off, he said to Con, "I told him to make sure no one saw him, so I guess that's not surprising. He's probably on his way back now."

They were silent while the rain beat down on the roof, and the interior of the Rover filled with the peculiarly erotic scent of damp wool and frustrated desire.

"We can't leave the suitcase out there anyway," Con said suddenly. "I'll grab it and leave a note for Paul inside the cottage."

He was out of the vehicle before Finn could object—not that he had a real objection. He was eager to get away from the lighthouse, to get away from the memories—and from what the future must bring.

* * * * *

Con was smiling, tracing Finn's collarbone, fingers brushing sensitized skin. He kissed the hollow at the base of Finn's throat.

Finn shivered.

"Cold?"

He shook his head. They were lying on the cushions and rugs before the roaring fireplace in the cottage. The firelight cast heated shadows over their naked bodies as they moved together, exploring with hands and lips.

Con nuzzled his way up Finn's throat, and Finn opened his mouth, panting a little beneath that delicate, shuddery pleasure of grazing lips and tongue. When Con's mouth covered his, he moaned softly. Their tongues touched tentatively, withdrew.

Con raised his head, and they smiled at each other.

"Am I rushing you?"

Finn chuckled. "I don't think anyone could accuse you of rushing me."

"You don't know." Con shook his head—apparently at himself. "I've been desperate from the minute I saw you come walking down the path the other day."

"You hid it pretty well."

"No. You didn't want to see it, that's all. I've been wondering if I could keep sane if I had to watch you walk away again."

Finn smiled uncertainly. Con had to be joking, exaggerating, because he had never seemed anything but in control of his feelings.

"I'd given up on you ever coming back." Con's return smile was twisted. "You don't know how much I wanted to go after you, to find you."

Finn shook his head. "It wouldn't have worked then."

"I know. That's what Thomas said."

"You talked to Uncle Tom about…us?" That must have been some conversation.

Con nodded. "He said… Hell, it doesn't matter now. He was right, though, and I'd pretty much accepted that I wasn't going to get a second chance. Then Martha told me that you'd been in an accident…that it was bad."

"Bad enough."

"When I heard you were coming home to recover, I canceled my book tour."

Finn examined the proud, patrician features—the dark, hungry eyes that held his own gaze.

"I love you, Finn."

"Con—"

"Let me say this," Con said, suddenly harsh. "Let me…get it off my chest. I didn't intend for it to happen. The thing with Fitch and me had been over long before you and I met. I mean met as—"

"I know what you mean."

Con's shadowy gaze never wavered from his own. "I came to find you that morning. I was going to…break it off." Finn closed his eyes. But he could hear the undernote of emotion more clearly. "I was going to tell you I was going to Europe for a few months. It had gotten…so intense between us. And I couldn't handle it. I was afraid to feel that much for you, afraid it was getting out of control. So when I came upon Fitch at the lighthouse, and he made his move…I went with it. I swear to Christ I didn't mean for you to see it. I didn't ever intend to hurt you like that. But I was glad to… take that opportunity to distance myself from you. Do you understand?"

"No." He did, of course, but it hurt like hell. Even now.

"But when you walked in on us, when I realized what I'd done and that there wouldn't be any turning back from it, I knew I'd made a mistake."

Finn opened his eyes. Con was still watching him.

"I don't know why it took that to make me see how I really felt. But it's the truth. I'd been so busy feeling…trapped and pressured that I hadn't stopped to consider how much I cared for you. I'd have done anything to erase those goddamned stupid fifteen minutes with Fitch."

Finn opened his mouth, and Con kissed him—a baby's breath of a kiss, a dragonfly wing of a kiss. "Forgive me," he whispered.

The kiss went from soft to seductive to searing. They seemed to kiss forever, seeming to find new ways every few seconds, the press of mouths, the taste of tongues, the slide of skin on skin, rolling and pushing against each other as they grew more fierce for union.

Finn's healing nerves and muscles protested, but he ignored the various twinges and pains because Con's touch was sending chills of pleasured sensation down his spine and into his groin.

Con's kisses were harder now, demanding and yet coaxing—making his case for him where words might have failed. His cock was like a steel pole, and Finn shuddered in a kind of sensory overload as Con's hand went to that junction of thigh, stroking Finn's slower reactions to stiffness.

Con was breathing hard, like he'd had to fight his way to get to this moment, and in a way he had. "What do you want? Whatever you want—"

Being asked to choose, to think, was more than Finn was prepared to do. He was running with the tide, riding that wave of feeling all the way out. He gasped while Con did those wicked, wanton things with his hands, eyes closed, listening to the crackle of fire, the rush of rain—

Con shifted abruptly, lifting up. Finn's eyes flew open, and then he arched, bit back a cry at the warm, wet shock of envelopment. So good, so intensely good it was frightening. Physical response pulsing through his body, flashing up and down his bloodstream like a drug, the rush of release like no other.

Con made it last and last, skilled, yes…but more than that. Loving. Loving in a way it had never been before. Or maybe he was just more experienced now. Maybe he knew enough now to recognize what neither of them had recognized three years ago—until it was too late.

Con worked him with expert hands and mouth, and orgasm ripped through Finn, a kind of convulsion of delight that left him sobbing and breathless while his cock shot spumes of white like sea foam that Con swallowed down as though it carried some magical properties.

"What about you?" Finn finally managed when the tilting world settled back into its frame. Con was holding him, nuzzling his cheek. One hard warm arm lay across Finn's belly, hand cupping Finn's genitals.

Con chuckled, bumped his hips against Finn's backside, and Finn realized from the sticky softness there that Con had come too.

They dozed for a time. It was the crack of thunder that brought Finn back to awareness. He opened his eyes, and he could see the rain sluicing down the windows across the room.

"Why hasn't Paul called?" he asked.

Con lifted his head. "Because he's tactful?"

"He's not tactful. It's been well over an hour now. It's been two hours."

Con considered this. "He must not have talked to Martha."

He sounded unconcerned, and he was probably right, but Finn couldn't help the spark of uneasiness he felt. "He should have seen your note when he got back to the lighthouse, in that case."

"Maybe it took longer than either of you expected."

"How long could it take to grab a couple of shovels?"

There was a pause while Con digested the implications of that. "You think Fitch is buried here? At the lighthouse?"

"I don't know."

Con raised his head, studying Finn's profile. "He couldn't be inside the keeper's house, Finn. Most of the flooring is still intact. A suitcase, maybe two, yes. A man? No. And he couldn't be buried on the grounds—someone would have noticed a mound that size and shape."

Finn shivered. "He could be in the woods."

Con kissed Finn's naked shoulder. "That would be taking one hell of a risk—burying him in the woods there."

"But someone did take a hell of a risk."

Neither spoke for a time; then Finn said, "Paul wouldn't give a damn about disturbing us. We argued earlier, and he was set on going to the state police with or without proof."

Con expelled a long breath. "You think he's up there digging on his own?" Finn's gaze found his. "You want to take a run up to the lighthouse and see what's keeping Paul?"

Finn nodded slowly.

"Okay. Let's get it over with." Con got to his feet in a quick move. He grabbed Finn's discarded sweater and jeans, then tossed them to him.

CHAPTER TEN

Paul was not at the lighthouse.

Con's note was still pinned beneath Paul's flashlight inside the doorway to the keeper's cottage.

"He didn't come back." Finn stared at Con.

"Maybe common sense prevailed. Nobody's getting across from the mainland this afternoon. He probably decided to stay warm and dry up at The Birches."

"That isn't the way Paul thinks."

Con considered this. "Of course not. Well, what do you want to do?"

Finn was already dialing The Birches as they made their way back to the Land Rover.

He got Martha again, and after reassuring her that he was perfectly all right—and with Con—he asked about Paul and was told he'd never arrived back at the house.

"Something's wrong," he told Con as he clicked off.

"He probably got stuck in the mud," Con reassured, turning the key in the ignition. "The roads are hell right now."

That was reasonable. Paul wasn't used to driving rural roads, and the wind and rain made for terrible visibility. All the same, Finn was rigid with anxiety as they bumped and slid down the road from the lighthouse.

"He'll be okay, Finn," Con said without taking his eyes from the road.

"I should never have started this."

"Do you mean that?"

Did he? Despite his bitterness and anger at Fitch's behavior, despite everything—

Finn shook his head. "No."

"No." Con's voice was quiet. "Murder will out."

The wind shook the Rover and plastered soggy leaves against the windshield as they made their way beneath the storm-tossed trees. There was no sign of the station wagon along the road.

Finn rubbed his head, which was starting to pound with tension. "Who could plan something like that? If you and Fitch really didn't intend to meet that morning—"

Con did look briefly from the road at that. "You said once I didn't lie to you. I'm not lying about this. I didn't go up there to meet Fitch."

If he and Con were going to try and make a go of this—and if he was honest, he wanted to try at least—Finn was going to have to stop throwing the past in Con's face. He was going to have to let it go. So he said neutrally, "Do you think Fitch was at the lighthouse to meet someone that morning?"

"No. Fitch followed you that morning. He wanted you to go over to the mainland with him. There was some art show he wanted you to see."

Finn closed his eyes and then opened them. "So whoever killed him… it couldn't have been premeditated."

"I guess it could have been an accident." Con sounded unconvinced. "But why didn't this person come forward?"

"I don't know. I guess there could have been a reason."

Con didn't say anything else. He didn't have to.

They were passing Miss Minton's when Finn said, "Wait a minute. Stop. Paul might have come here."

Con was already pulling to the side of the road, searching for a safe place to park in the wet road. "Why would he?"

"I told him to try and get shovels without anyone at The Birches noticing; he might have thought to ask to borrow Miss Minton's. She's got every tool known to man."

Con killed the engine. Finn opened the door, climbing down cautiously before Con could get around to help him. He slammed shut the door against the wind, shrugging into his jacket and glancing down the woody embankment, and froze.

"Con."

Con came around quickly and followed the direction Finn was pointing down the gully. The brown station wagon was at the bottom of the embankment, hood buried in the overhang of trees.

Con swore. Turned to Finn. "I'll go down and check."

"He must have gone off the road."

"Stay right here. I'll be right back."

Con went slipping and sliding down the muddy slope. Gripping his cane, Finn watched tensely as he reached the station wagon and dragged open the driver's side door. He turned and waved all clear.

"He's not here," he called up.

"Where is he?" Finn demanded, which was about as dumb a question as he'd ever asked.

Con spread his hands and started back up the hillside. Finn looked over the muddy tracks along the side of the road. He found the spot where the station wagon had been parked. Had Paul tried to back out and gone over the side? But the car was nose-first down the gully, so he'd have had to deliberately pull forward over the edge.

It didn't make sense.

Con reached the top of the embankment. "There's no blood inside the car," he reassured. "He can't have been badly hurt. It's not that far down the hillside."

The idea occurred to them at the same time, and they gazed across the road at Miss Minton's wall of rosebushes and the house beyond.

"He must have gone across to Mitty's," Con said.

"But if he had an accident, why wouldn't he call The Birches?"

"Could he have decided to walk back for some reason?" Con had a supportive hand beneath Finn's elbow as they started across the muddy road.

"I think the normal thing would be to—" Finn broke off as Miss Minton's battered pickup came barreling through the gate toward them.

There wasn't time to think, and there was no way he could have moved fast enough with his injured leg. Con grabbed him and shoved him hard to the side. Finn went sprawling as the pickup swerved, just missing Con and taking out a section of white picket fence before tearing up the muddy road, water flying up behind its tires.

Finn barely had time to register what had happened before Con was kneeling beside him.

"*Finn.* Jesus. Are you all right? You're not hurt?" Con's face was white, his hands shaking as he dragged at Finn. "Finn?"

"I'm okay," Finn managed, clutching his injured leg and rocking a little with the pain.

Con was swearing in between ordering Finn to let him see the damage.

"We've got to go after her," Finn said, pushing him off.

"To hell with her."

"Con. Listen to me. She's not on her way to the fucking hairdresser. She's heading for the lighthouse. We have to go after her." Finn groped for his cane, and Con got up, reaching down and pulling Finn to his feet.

With Con's help, Finn made it across the road, slamming shut the Rover door as Con ran around to the driver side, then slid behind the wheel and started the engine.

"Call The Birches," he ordered. "Tell Martha to call the state police."

Finn spent the remainder of the short, rough drive on the phone with Martha trying to explain what was happening—which wasn't easy given that he wasn't exactly clear himself what was happening.

He clicked off the phone and asked Con, "Could Paul have stolen Miss Minton's truck?"

"Paul wasn't driving."

There went that theory—that Paul had arranged to meet his ex-lover and ended up killing him. It hadn't been much of a theory to start with, but the other possibility seemed even crazier.

"You saw her? Miss Minton was driving?"

"I saw her. She deliberately swerved in order to miss me."

They were tearing back up the slippery road to the lighthouse. As they topped the crest, Finn could see lightning flashing out over the ocean. Miss Minton's pickup was parked near the cliff's edge. The tailgate was down, and she was dragging something across the grass to the verge.

Con sped forward across the green, braking sharply. He was out of the Rover and running toward Miss Minton. Miss Minton, who was dragging an unconscious Paul by his legs across the short space to the ledge, dropped him and turned.

Finn, moving more slowly than Con, dropped down beside Paul, who was unconscious and gray-faced, his blond hair soaked in blood. But Finn was only dimly aware of this, his focus on Con as he struggled with Miss Minton. For one truly horrific moment he thought Con and Miss Minton were both going over the side, but Con dragged her back.

Miss Minton was shrieking. It was difficult to make out the words through the wind and rain, but Finn thought he heard her scream, "They should have drowned him at birth!"

* * * * *

"I've been thinking…I'd like to paint you."

Con's mouth twitched, but he didn't open his eyes. He murmured, "Oh yes? I think I'd look good in a nice robin's egg blue."

"Funny." Head propped on hand, Finn studied him. Sunlight gilded Con's hair and turned his skin honey-brown against the peach-colored sheets. It was late Monday morning, and they were still in bed—they had barely been out of bed since arriving Saturday night at the little bed-and-breakfast they had stayed at in Union three years earlier.

Con reached over, lacing their fingers and bringing Finn's hand to his mouth. He kissed it lightly and opened his eyes.

He smiled, but there was a certain melancholy in those black-cherry eyes that Finn understood only too well.

It had been four days since Miss Minton had confessed to the attempted murder of Paul Ryder and the murder of Fitch Barret three years earlier. With true New England reticence, she had declined to discuss her reasons for either crime with the state police, but she had talked to Con on the drive back to The Birches. In fact, she and Con might have been alone in the Rover for the attention she paid to Finn anxiously cradling an unconscious Paul in the backseat.

"He was bad. He was a bad seed, that one. Selfish and cruel from the day he was born. Everything he put his hand to, he spoiled."

Finn couldn't see Miss Minton's face; her hair and clothes were soaked and her voice was a hoarse croak he had to struggle to hear over Paul's stentorian breathing.

"I saw him that day. I saw him laughing as he spoiled your life the way he spoiled mine. Spoiled every chance I had for love and happiness. First with Barnaby Purdon and then with Thomas Barret. He did it deliberately. Nothing made him happier than when he was hurting people, seeing them cry."

Her eyes rose, unexpectedly catching Finn's gaze in the rearview mirror. She said harshly, "You don't know. He was laughing that day. You ran off, and Con knocked him down, and he was still laughing. And then he went up in the tower to see where you'd got to. And I followed him up and pushed him off. It was the easiest thing in the world."

Finn had put his head down at that point and stopped listening.

When they had reached The Birches, everything had grown surreal. Martha had fixed tea and provided dry clothes for everyone, and they had waited together in the kitchen while Con phoned the mainland, requesting emergency services and the state police. Miss Minton had stopped talking by then. She was silent and eerily docile.

A LifeFlight helicopter made it to the island to transport Paul to the mainland, where he was currently in critical but stable condition. Miss Minton had declined to say why she'd attacked Paul, but from what she'd said during the drive from the lighthouse, Con believed that she had mistakenly thought Paul had shown up at her cottage to accuse her or blackmail her—that her own guilty conscience had fooled her into thinking Paul had somehow figured out the truth.

That evening, after the state police had taken Miss Minton away, Barnaby Purdon came to the house, and there was more muted, shocked discussion. The house had the feel of death after long illness…and after all, that was close to the truth of it.

Barnaby Purdon was the one who remembered that Miss Minton had been gathering gravel at the lighthouse all that long-ago week, transporting it by pickup truck to her cottage, traveling sedately back and forth along the road.

She was a strong, vigorous woman used to hauling rocks and bags of fertilizer and mulch, used to taking care of her own property. It wasn't so hard to picture her dumping Fitch into her wheelbarrow, shoving him into her pickup, and driving him away…to bury him beneath the bloodred roses in her garden—the roses she'd been planting that August afternoon when Con had traveled the road to The Birches.

As their nearest neighbor, Miss Minton had a key to The Birches, and she'd been in the habit of going up to the house for art lessons. She knew her way around, knew that the house was deserted that day, and she had packed Fitch's things in his suitcases, dumped them at the lighthouse, driven the station wagon down to the wharf, and then walked home.

Once he knew the why of it, Finn had stopped listening. He didn't care about the details of how and where and when. He was grieving for Fitch. Maybe Fitch was all that Miss Minton said and believed, but he had been more than that to Finn, the best loved companion of his childhood—his other half. He had grieved for him three years ago, and he continued to grieve for him now. It was a strange comfort to think that Fitch had climbed up the light tower. He wanted to believe that Fitch had regretted what he'd done, that he'd wanted to find Finn and had gone to look for him. Con had listened to him and kissed him and said nothing, letting him talk late into the night.

The police had questioned them all; then the reporters had descended on the island, and Con had taken Finn away to Union. For two days Finn and Con had been getting to know each other again.

Now Finn admitted, "I've been afraid to try anything since the accident."

"But you've only been out of the hospital a week or so."

"I know but… From the time I left college—not a day went by that I didn't work. Even if it was just to sketch something. Until the day I woke up in the hospital and couldn't see."

Con didn't say anything at first, his brows drawing together as he surveyed Finn's face. "But you're okay, Finn. There's no reason you can't start working again."

Finn nodded.

Con said, "You can paint me." His eyes were bright beneath the soft fall of blond hair. "You can do whatever you like to me."

Finn looked interested. "Is that right? Because I've been thinking I might like to experiment with different mediums…"

Con bit his fingers lightly. "This sounds promising. Tell me more."

Finn lowered himself to Con's arms. "I think I'd prefer to show you."

Ghost of a Chance

Personally, I'm pretty much a scaredy-cat. I love ghosts—or at least the idea of ghosts—but no way in hell would I willingly spend the night in a haunted house. I think that's probably one reason why I like my spooky to be heavily diluted with laughs and humor.

CHAPTER ONE

Like the philosophers say, the line between genius and stupidity is a fine one.

Actually, it wasn't the philosophers, it was Nigel in *Spinal Tap*, but the point is still a valid one. Which is why what seemed like a perfectly good idea at the time—namely, prying off the screen and crawling through the open window of Oliver de la Motte's front parlor—turned out to be a really bad decision.

It's not like I hadn't *tried* to use the key Oliver sent. I'd tried for about two minutes, turning the damn thing every possible way—not easy in the dark of three a.m., and not pleasant either with that clammy sea breeze on the back of my neck—and rustling the overgrown shrubs. Not that I'm the nervous type, or I wouldn't hunt ghosts for a living—well, for a hobby. No one hunts ghosts for a living.

When I couldn't get the key to work I jumped off the porch and walked around the side of the house till I found an open window. Pulling out my pocket knife, I pried loose the screen, hoisted myself up and climbed through…

And that's when all hell broke loose.

Something rushed out of the darkness and tackled me around the waist, hurling me to the hardwood floor. The very hard wood floor. My tailbone, elbows, and skull all connected painfully. My glasses went flying.

"Christ!" I yelped, trying to get away.

"Guess again," growled a deep voice.

Human.

Definitely human. And male. Definitely male. I was wrestling six feet or so of hard, lean male. *Naked* hard, lean male. Definitely not Oliver who is sixty-something and built like the Stay Puft Marshmallow Man. And no one else was supposed to be here. Was my assailant a burglar? A naked burglar? The guy had muscles like rocks—speaking of which: I brought my knee up hard.

His breath went out in an infuriated whoosh. His weight rolled off me. I rolled over and tried to crawl away, but the rug beneath me bunched up and slid my way. A small table crashed down just missing my head, and I heard glass smash on the floor.

"You little son of a bitch," said the burglar who was probably not a burglar, looming over me.

I tried to scoot away, but a knee jammed into my spine pinning me flat. He grabbed my right arm and yanked it back so hard I thought he'd dislocated it. The pain was unreal. I stopped fighting.

For a minute there was nothing but the ragged sound of our breathing in the darkness. Then he reached past me and turned on the table lamp.

I had a blurred view of a forest of scratched claw-foot furniture, miles of parquet floors, and a herd of dust bunnies. I could make out my glasses a few feet away beneath a wide ottoman.

"I don't understand what's happening here," I got out.

"What part do you not understand?" he inquired grimly.

"Who *are* you?"

It must not have been the question he expected. "Who the hell are *you?*" He didn't ease up on my spine, but there was something in his tone…a hint of doubt beneath the hostility.

"Rhys Davies. I'm a-a friend of Oliver's."

He made a disgusted sound. "Yeah, you and every other cheap hustler in the greater metropolitan area—"

"Cheap hustler!" I'm sorry to say that came out sounding way too much like a squeak. The squeak factor was partly due to the fact that with every shallow breath I inhaled his hot-off-the-sheets scent. He'd had a shower before bed, and that sleepy, soapy skin smell was even more alarming than the fear he was going to crack my vertebrae.

"Oh, sorry," he said, not sounding sorry at all. "Cheap is the wrong word. These things are never cheap."

"Things?" I repeated. "I'm not...you've got this all wrong."

"Is that right?" He seemed unimpressed.

I requested with an effort, "Could you ease up on my arm?"

He let go of my arm. It flopped weakly down. I flexed my fingers, surprised that they still seemed to work.

"What are you doing here?" he asked. "Oliver's out of town for the next month."

"I could ask you the same question."

"Yeah, but I asked first." He patted me down with brisk, impersonal efficiency. "If you're not one of Oliver's boy toys, what are you? Reporter? You're not a burglar, that's for sure."

And neither, obviously, was he. So who the hell was he?

"I told you who I am," I bit out. "I'm a friend of Oliver's. He invited me to stay."

His weight shifted off my back, and he ran his hands along the outside of my legs—then the inside. He seemed to know what he was doing, but it was invasive, to say the least. "Ever hear of knocking?"

"I didn't know there was anyone to hear me knock. I tried my key— the key Oliver sent. It didn't work."

"*Your* key?" He felt over my crotch with what felt like unnecessary familiarity. And in a tone I didn't like, he said, "I see."

"Hey! Then what's with the Braille!" I recoiled as much as you can with two hundred plus pounds of beef pinning you to the floor.

He hesitated, but only an instant, before pulling my wallet out of my back pocket. He thumbed through it, taking his time.

"Rice Davies," he said.

"It's pronounced Reece," I retorted, muffledly. "Like in Reese's Pieces."

Now why had I said that?

Amusement threaded his voice as he continued, "Ten forty-five Oakmont Street in West Hollywood. You're a long way from home, *Reece*."

Yes, apparently I had turned left after the Outer Limits. "Can I get up?"

"Slowly."

He stepped out of range as I sat up, wincing. I looked up—a long way up. He was a big blur; I had an impression of dark hair, big shoulders narrowing to more darkness, and miles of long brown legs.

"Can I get my glasses?"

The blur stepped away, bent, retrieved my glasses, and handed them to me.

I moved onto the settee and put them on. My hands were a little unsteady. I haven't been in many fights. Not that academia isn't a jungle, but generally we don't end up brawling on the floor.

The man now sitting on the giant ottoman across from me came into sharp focus. He was not entirely naked after all. He wore cotton boxers with little red and blue boating flags, thin cotton very white against the deep brown of his tanned skin.

He stared back at me with equal curiosity.

His black hair was unruly—which could have been the result of an impromptu wrestling match. His eyes were very green in his tanned face. His features were too harsh to be good-looking. He looked…mean. But he wasn't quite as burly as he'd seemed in the dark. About six feet of strong bones and hard muscle.

"You're Oliver's nephew," I guessed, rubbing my wrenched shoulder. "The cop."

Something changed in his expression, shuttered.

"Bright boy. That's right. Sam Devlin."

I didn't know what to say. This was an unwelcome development, to say the least.

"I didn't know you were staying here."

He cocked a dark brow. "I didn't know I needed your permission."

"It's just…I'm here to work."

"What did you have in mind?" he asked dryly.

I remembered the leisurely way he'd groped me earlier and felt an uncharacteristic heat in my face.

"I teach a course in paranormal studies at UCLA," I said. "I'm working on a book about ghost hunting along the California coast. Oliver invited me to stay here for a few days while I researched Berkeley House."

I'm guessing most people never saw that particular expression on Sam Devlin's face. After a moment he closed his jaw sharply. He studied me with narrowed green eyes.

"Well, well," he said mildly. "A ghost buster."

I hate that term. I hate that movie. Well, okay, there are funny bits: Rick Moranis as Louis Tully is a scream—but really. Not good for the image.

"Parapsychology is a science," I said firmly.

"Yeah, weird science." He considered me without pleasure. "This oughta be cozy," he said finally. Planting his hands on his muscular thighs, he pushed up to his feet. "Okay, Mr. Pieces. I can't see anyone making up a story that dumb. Help yourself to one of the bedrooms. I'm upstairs on the left. There are clean sheets and towels in the cupboard at the end of the hall."

I stopped massaging my shoulder, gazing up at him doubtfully. "That's it? You're going to bed?"

"Did you have other plans, Professor?"

That was going to get old fast. I said a little sarcastically, "I thought you'd demand to see my teaching credential at the least."

He said through a yawn, "Is that what they call it these days? I think it can wait 'til morning." Heading for the hallway, he tossed over his shoulder, "Impressive though it may be."

I was treated to a final glimpse of his long brown legs vanishing up the staircase.

CHAPTER TWO

A cheap hustler?

Now *that* was a first. Pretty funny too. Sort of. C.K.—my ex—would have thought it was a riot.

After a moment or two, I pulled myself together and went outside to get my bags from my car.

The distant moon hung soft and fuzzy above the sharp tips of stiff and silent pine trees. I cut across the lawn, unlocked my car, and hauled my laptop and suitcase out of the back of the Volvo, setting them on the gravel drive. I was relocking the trunk when I caught a flicker of light out of the corner of my eye. I turned.

Beyond the tall wall of pine trees stood the cliffs overlooking the ocean. And on the cliffs perched Berkeley House. It looked like the illustration on the cover of a Hardy Boys novel—or a smaller version of Cliff House near Ocean Beach, which was where C.K. and I had been dining when I first got the idea to write the book.

As I stared, light drifted across one of the upstairs windows.

I removed my glasses, wiped them, and looked again.

The house sat in total darkness. But as I watched, that eerie glow appeared once more in the corner room window on the second floor.

Interesting.

In ten years of researching the paranormal I'd never yet come across something that couldn't be explained by natural causes or human intervention. I had to admit, though, this looked pretty authentic. Not Marfa Lights; this illumination really did seem to be inside the house, hovering from window to window. Probably too powerful to be a flashlight beam— the house was about half a mile away. Maybe a reflection off the sea below, or some trick of moonlight? I was pretty damned tired, maybe I was dreaming...

Fascinated, I started walking toward Berkeley House, watching for that mysterious light. It seemed to float from window to window, then disappear—only to reappear on the other end of the house.

I rounded a bend in the road, and the house vanished from view. I kept walking. The night smelled of the pines and the sea. It was quiet except for the sound of my footsteps on the dirt road; I was a city kid and not used to that kind of quiet. It should have been nice. People always talk about the peace and quiet of the country, but it made me a little uneasy.

I looked back, and Oliver's house was now lost to sight. The woods crowded in on me.

I shook off my disquiet, focused on my destination.

It couldn't be a coincidence—a physical manifestation practically the moment I arrived? But who, besides Oliver, knew I was coming to investigate Berkeley House? Not even the nephew, apparently.

Just supposing the ghost lights *were* for real? As unlikely as that was, I decided I couldn't wait for morning. I needed to check this out now.

I hurried along the dirt road as quickly as I could safely go without risking a sprain or a fall.

When at last I emerged from the copse, I found myself on the edge of what must have once been a formal sunken garden. The hedges were overgrown with brambles and berries, an oblong pool filmed over with scum. A couple of wind-bent eucalyptus dotted the grounds as though placed there by Salvador Dali. Broken statuary littered the weeds like bone fragments.

I stared across the ruins of the garden to the house. The upstairs windows were unlit. Nothing moved. It could have been a painting—maybe one of those gloomy efforts by Atkinson Grimshaw.

I continued to wait for…something.

But nothing happened. The woolly moon sank further down the sky.

Something swooped overhead, and I ducked. A bird? A bat? Or—the way my night was going—a flying squirrel?

I peered at the luminous dial of my watch. Four fifteen. The sun would be up soon. I rubbed the grit from my eyes and decided to call it a night.

Starting back for Oliver's place, the woods were even darker and creepier, pine needles whispering underfoot, the sea breeze sighing through the tree branches. My night vision was never great, and it was especially bad when my eyes were tired. The shadows seemed to shift and slide. I kept my attention on the mostly overgrown road, having zero desire to spend the night in the woods with a sprained ankle.

Rounding the bend that took Berkeley House from view, I realized that someone stood in the road ahead of me.

I stopped dead thinking—hoping—the shadowy figure was just a trick of my tired eyes. The hair rose on the nape of my neck. It—he—was so still. I blinked a couple of times and willed him to disappear. No luck. There he stood: tall, dark, and alarming.

Could it be a manifestation? I preferred to think it was a manifestation and not a transient. I waited for him to move or speak.

"Hi," I offered.

Bushes rustled to my left. I turned instinctively. When I looked back, the figure was gone.

Granted, I might not be the best judge, but I didn't think that was normal behavior.

Was he lying in wait for me? I stared at the empty road.

Abruptly, I decided to take the shortest distance back to Oliver's house even though it meant cutting through the woods. I slipped into the bushes to my right, hoping like hell this wasn't the right time of year for poison oak or lively rattlesnakes.

I was caught between feeling foolish and genuine unease; all the same I stayed low, sticking to the shadows. I moved as quietly as I could, pushing through the branches. Every few feet, I stopped and listened. There was no sound to indicate anyone was following me. I could imagine what C.K. would say if he could only see me now. I was probably going to end up with a tick down my collar and broken glasses.

Except...when I remembered that still, silent figure blocking my way, I wasn't so sure I was overreacting. There had been something weird about the way he stood there. Something...menacing.

It took about fifteen minutes before I stepped out of the woods, brushing myself down, feeling my clothes sticky with pine sap and God knows what. By then I was too tired to care if Barnabas Collins himself was after me. I wanted a bath and bed. Actually, I just mostly wanted bed.

Oliver's house looked peaceful in the moonlight. I started across the lawn, belatedly remembered the whole reason I'd come outside, reversed, and headed for my car and the bags still sitting where I'd left them on the gravel drive.

Some sixth sense caused me to glance over my shoulder.

I froze.

The blunt outline of a man stood unmoving near the woodline. What the hell? Was this guy *following* me?

He sure as hell was watching me.

Okay. Enough was enough. I diverted my flight pattern from the car and redirected to the front porch. The peacock blue door, which I'd left propped open with an umbrella stand from inside the hallway, was now closed. The umbrella stand rolled gently in the night breeze.

I crossed the porch and tried the door.

Locked.

Again.

I could have howled my rage and disbelief to the now-nonexistent moon.

Once more I tried the handle. Still locked. I shoved my shoulder against the unyielding wood. The only thing likely to give was my shoulder.

I pulled my keys out. This was where I'd come in.

I looked behind me. Did a double take. The figure was now halfway across the lawn. A slash of black silence. For some reason the fact that he didn't move or speak was more alarming than if he'd made some obvious threat that I could respond to.

I turned back to the door. Leaned into the bell.

No response from inside the house.

I glanced over my shoulder.

He was closer still—only three or four yards from me. Even so I couldn't make out his features, nothing but a smudge of darkness where his face should be. But that was the light. The lack of light. But the way he stood there...motionless, staring...

I turned back and pounded the door. "Christ," I muttered. "Open *up!*"

The porch light blazed on above me. The door suddenly swung open, and I half fell into Sam Devlin's arms. For a split second a brawny pair of arms closed around me and my face pressed into a warm, hairy chest.

We disengaged hastily. I threw a nervous look behind me. The lawn was an empty stretch of...nothing. I blinked. There was no sign of the man who had followed me.

Nothing. Not a trace.

"What is this, some kind of sleep deprivation experiment?" Devlin inquired in less than patient tones. I straightened my glasses and looked back at him. His hair was a lot more ruffled, and the addition of gruesome pillow creases down his face didn't add to his looks.

"Someone was following me."

"From your car?"

"From Berkeley House. I walked over to see it. There was a light in one of the upstairs windows—" I broke off at his expression. "Someone was out there. He was standing there not two minutes ago."

"Are you on some kind of medication?" he asked. "Never mind. Dumb question. Have you maybe skipped your medication?"

I didn't totally blame him. If I didn't know me as well as I knew me, I might wonder about me too. And we hadn't started off on the best footing. All the same, Sam Devlin was getting under my skin like no one I'd ever met. But then I've never been impressed by big macho alpha males.

"You don't believe me? Fine," I said. "Can you just wait here while I bring my bags from the car?"

He groaned and rubbed his eyes. "Make. It. *Fast.*"

"Two minutes," I told him. I sprinted to the car, grabbed my laptop and suitcase, and ran back.

Several times I glanced toward the woods and the road, but there was no sign of anyone.

Sam Devlin's long form threw a sinister shadow on the grass as I lugged my bags across the lawn, hiked up the stairs, and squeezed past him. He only stepped aside at the last moment.

"Thanks," I huffed.

"Are you sure you're in the right line of work?" he inquired. "Fear of the dark seems like it might be a handicap in your profession."

"Funny."

"Not really. Are you done for the night?"

"Mission accomplished," I said, heading straight for the main staircase. "Sorry to have disturbed your beauty rest."

Amazingly enough no sarcastic comment followed. I heard him slam the front door and lock it after me. The downstairs lights went off as I reached the upper level.

Keeping in mind that Devlin was in the first room off the left, I staggered down the hallway past the master bedroom and two additional rooms—putting a safe distance between me and Joe Friday.

Finally I opened a door into a room with an empty bed. I guess there was other furniture beneath the sloping roof, but all I cared about was the bed. I dropped my bags, climbed onto the mattress, and pulled the quilt up. Sleep settled over me.

* * * * *

The smell of coffee woke me.

For a few moments I lay there, trying to remember where I was. Not at home. Not at C.K.'s... I waited for the inevitable stab of pain. It would never be C.K.'s again. And then I remembered.

I opened my eyes. The shadow of the wisteria growing outside my window moved against the white ceiling.

I blinked, checked my wristwatch. Nine thirty. Late for me; I never needed much sleep, and lately my sleep patterns were worse than ever. My nose twitched at the promise of caffeine.

Throwing off the quilt, I padded into the adjoining bath. A quick shower and a shave later, I dug a clean pair of Levi's out of my suitcase and pulled on a T-shirt.

The bedroom window looked down on a sparkling pool and a brick courtyard. Flowering vines twisted through the top of a redwood pergola. Tidy green lawn stretched in all directions and vanished into the woods. I could just glimpse the blue of the ocean behind trees. It was a beautiful place. A little isolated, but that untouched quality was all part of the scenic charm. I thought I understood what had inspired the elegant, passionless landscapes of Oliver's early career.

I went downstairs and was making my way across the carpeted hall when Devlin's voice reached me from the kitchen.

"Flakier than pie crust. And a little old for Oliver. Normally he prefers them straight out of the shell."

Silence. He was either talking to himself or he was on the phone.

"Early thirties, at a guess." He added sardonically, "A natural blond. In every sense."

Me. He meant me.

It's not like I hadn't heard all the stupid, closed-minded comments before, but my gut tightened anyway. The fact that Devlin thought I might turn tricks for a living sort of appealed to my warped sense of humor, but that he thought I was dumb? I didn't find that so funny.

Maybe the polite thing would have been to pretend I didn't hear him. I guess I'm not that polite.

I strolled right into the kitchen. He stood by the gleaming stainless-steel counter, coffee machine bubbling over beside him, and I had the satisfaction of seeing him jump. He recovered instantly, turning away and speaking quietly into the mouthpiece. "I'll give you a call if I hear anything, Thad."

Hanging up, he nodded to me without warmth. "Morning."

"Morning." I nodded at the volcanic spill. "Is it okay if I pour myself a cup of coffee?"

"What's Oliver's is yours. At least for the next ten minutes."

"What happens in ten minutes?"

He handed me a clean mug from the cupboard, his eyes greener than the untidy stretch of woodland behind the house. "Oliver doesn't have a long attention span."

"Can we get this settled here and now," I said, pouring coffee. "I think Oliver's a charming old guy, but I'm here to investigate Berkeley House. Period."

"If you say so."

I gritted my jaw against a lot of stuff that would make future encounters with this asshole awkward, and looked up to meet his gaze. "Look, your uncle invited me to stay for a couple of days, and if there were any strings attached, I'm not aware of them. Since he's not even here, they'd have to be pretty long strings, wouldn't they?"

"Puppet-length."

I took a sip of coffee and nearly choked. "This is *terrible*."

He nodded gloomily. "Yeah."

"It's probably the worst cup of coffee I ever had."

"I know."

I couldn't quite read him. "Do you… prefer it this way?"

He took a mouthful from his own cup and shuddered. "No. It just always turns out like this."

He was permitted to carry a gun but couldn't figure out how to use a coffee machine?

"Would it be okay if I made another pot?"

For a moment I thought he was actually going to smile. "Knock yourself out."

I poured the seething black contents of the current pot down the drain and set about measuring coffee into the machine. Devlin watched me thoughtfully. He wore a black T-shirt and faded Levi's that emphasized his narrow hips and long legs. He had a perfect body, no doubt about it. It made an interesting contrast to his homely face.

"Where'd you say you met Oliver?"

"An art exhibit in San Francisco. C.K. Killian introduced us."

"The art dealer?"

I was surprised he knew that. He looked like his idea of art would be calendars with sport cars.

"Yep."

"And what were you doing at an art exhibit?"

I wondered if it were possible for him to ask a question so that it didn't sound like he was interrogating a hostile witness.

"C.K. is—was—is a friend."

He raised those black eyebrows again. "Is he a friend or not?"

"He's a friend," I said shortly. I wasn't about to go into my relationship with C.K. My former relationship.

"And somehow you and Oliver got talking about this book you're writing, and he invited you to scope out Berkeley House?"

"Pretty much. Yes." When I raised my eyes he was watching me narrowly.

Sure, there was a little more to the story—like the fact that I was drunk off my ass and had actually—humiliatingly—cried on Oliver's surprisingly comfortable shoulder about getting dumped by C.K.—but no way was I ever going to share that information with him. Or anyone. I sort of hoped Oliver had forgotten it.

Devlin said reluctantly, "For the record, you were right about seeing someone in the woods last night."

"Are you keeping a record?" I gazed at the coffee machine, willing it to hurry along that precious life-saving elixir.

When he didn't answer, I glanced his way. "So who was roaming in the woods last night besides me?"

"Thaddeus Sterne. Our nearest neighbor—our only neighbor—unless you count your ectoplasmic buddies at Berkeley House."

I ignored that crack. "Thaddeus Sterne? The painter?"

"That's right."

"Wow." I meant it. Thaddeus Sterne was a legend in the art world. Even more of a legend than Oliver de la Motte. Probably because Sterne sightings were rarer than albino whales. He was like the Garbo of the oil paint set. According to C.K., the last time Sterne had made a public appearance was the 1980s.

Then I remembered the stillness, the silence of the man who had followed me through the woods, and some of my pleasure died. Sterne might be a genius, but last night I'd felt threatened.

He said curtly, "Yeah, well, see that you don't disturb him while you're poking around out there. The property lines are clearly marked."

"Correct me if I'm wrong, but he was on your property last night."

"*He* can go where he wants. If you see him, get out of his way." He studied me, his eyes flinty in his blunt-featured face.

I swallowed my irritation—which tasted only slightly better than the bitter coffee had.

"Understood. Anything else I need to know before I head over to Berkeley House?"

Talk about a foolish question. Sam Devlin contemplated me for a long unsmiling moment. "I think we better discuss that, as well," he said. "Are you aware that the property is condemned?"

"The house? Yes."

"Great. Well, if you want to wander around the grounds at your own risk, that's one thing, but it's not safe to go inside the house."

"I already signed a waiver—"

He interrupted, "I don't care what you signed. You saw the place last night. One good push and the building will be in the sea. You don't go inside."

"I've already arranged this with Oliver—the guy who owns the property."

"I don't care what you arranged. You don't put one foot inside that house. Understand?"

What, was the entire *universe* supposed to be his jurisdiction? I stared at him. It was a stare I had perfected through years of dealing with insolent adolescents and asshole adults. He stared right back. I finally managed a terse, "Yeah, I understand."

He nodded curtly. "Good. I've got a call in to Oliver, but just so you know, I believe this story of yours about writing a book." He managed to make it sound like he figured I was capable of any lunacy.

"Gee, thanks," I practically stuttered. He was actually going to dou-ble-check my story? Who the hell would make up a story like this?

He shrugged. "No offense, but Oliver is a sucker for a pretty face and a sob story."

Unfortunate choice of words under the circumstances.

I smiled. It probably looked more like a baring of teeth, because he blinked. What an arrogant asshole he was. Poor Oliver. I could just imagine the lectures he had to listen to from Mr. Law and Order.

"I'll keep it in mind," I said.

"Do that."

Apparently he also needed to have the last word. I struggled to control myself. I couldn't remember the last time somebody had this kind of effect on me.

"Is there more, or am I dismissed?"

To my surprise he gave a twist of a smile. "Not easily," he said.

CHAPTER THREE

"**H**ey, be careful there!"

I turned away from my survey of Berkeley House's pallid and dissolute face—hollow-eyed windows and gaping broken door mouth. A man in jeans and a plaid shirt hurried across the threadbare lawn toward me.

As he reached me, he said earnestly, "You weren't thinking of going inside? It's a death trap."

He was about my age. Attractive. Medium height and comfortably built; hazel eyes, soft brown hair, and a carefully groomed beard.

"Hi," I said. I gestured with my camera. "I was just taking a few photos."

He studied me, and something changed in his face. In mine too, probably. The old gaydar picking up those high frequency waves. "It's private property, you know." He said it almost apologetically, his smile rueful.

"I know," I said. "I'm staying at Oliver de la Motte's." Remembering Oliver's reputation, I added hastily, "I'm writing a book about haunted houses along the California coast."

"Seriously?" The genuine interest was refreshing after Sam Devlin. He offered a hand. "Mason Corwin. I'm president of the local historical preservation society." His handshake was firm. "So you know the history of the house?"

"Just the bare bones."

"Interesting choice of words. There are plenty of skeletons in the Berkeley House closet."

"I'll bet. David Berkeley was a magician, right?"

"A 20th Century illusionist. By profession and philosophy. He really did subscribe to the notion that the material world was just an illusion."

"Yeah? How does that tie in with his committing suicide?"

Mason smiled wryly. "Beats me. I personally subscribe to the here and now theory."

I smiled back, then glanced at the house, feeling its tug once more.

"Come by the museum," Mason invited. "You can look through our collection. We've got all kinds of photos, newspaper clippings, and memorabilia on Berkeley."

"I'll do that."

He smiled at me again. "How long are you staying for?"

"Just through the weekend."

"Too bad."

"Why?" I caught the meaning of his smile. "*Oh.* Thanks."

His gaze wavered, edged past me. I glanced around. He said, "Old Thad Sterne. He's another reason to be careful around here. He's kind of on the weird side. Take a piece of advice?"

"Sure."

"Ghost hunter or not, don't hang around here after dark. It's not safe."

"Thanks for the warning."

He nodded. Glanced at his watch. "I've got to get back. The museum opens at noon on Fridays." He hesitated. "But I'll be seeing you, right?"

I smiled. "Right."

I waited until Mason vanished into the woods; then I ducked around the back of the house. I could do with less of an audience.

Immediately I saw what Devlin and Mason meant. Originally the mansion must have sat several hundred yards from the cliff, but time and tide had done their work. The back porch stairs were now literally inches from the edge.

One of these days—and not too far in the future—the entire structure was going to tip over the side.

I stared down at the hypnotic green swirl. White foam washed across the bronze rocks below. The wind seemed to sing eerily off the cliff beneath me. That might explain any mysterious noises coming from the house, but I couldn't see anything that would create the mirage of ghostly lights in the upper story windows.

I dipped under the rickety railing, climbed cautiously onto the wrap-around porch.

Exposed to the unrelenting elements, the porch was in bad shape, the remaining wooden planks silvery and fragile. I picked my way across and then pushed open the sagging French doors, which gave with a screech of rusted hinges.

The glass doors opened onto an empty sunny room. Despite the obvious disrepair and smell of damp and mold, the bones of the house— the black wood floor, the arching windows, and graceful architecture— were still beautiful. A giant chandelier, missing crystal teeth and beads, hung from the ceiling, winking and glinting in the light streaming through the windows.

Once this must have been a lovely room in a gracious home. Now...

I stayed quiet, trying to pick up a feel for the house. Listened to the wind moaning down the chimney, keening at the window casements.

The reflection of the water flickered against the bare ceiling and walls.

It was sort of soothing, but I didn't feel soothed. I felt nervous and keyed up. I told myself it was from having to sneak into the house—the mistrustful awareness that Sam Devlin was probably the type to come and check up on me.

Moving to the window, I considered the choppy water, the wind rippling through the grass. Not hard to imagine that unceasing whisper preying on the nerves of a guy who wasn't maybe totally right in the head to start with.

The light was very good in here. I pulled my camera out and took a couple of photos of the cobwebbed chandelier.

I proceeded to the next room, which turned out to be a wide and elegant hallway. Chunks of plaster molding littered the floor. A graceful curving staircase led to the second story. I studied it, wondering what kind of shape it was in. It didn't look obviously unsafe, but that didn't mean a lot given the condition of the rest of the structure.

I started cautiously up. Seven careful steps and there was a loud crack. I hesitated. Took another tentative step—my tennis shoe shoved right through a rotten board.

"Damn."

Grabbing the carved railing for balance, I pulled my foot out and started back down. Another snapping sound and the edge of the next step broke off right under the heel of my foot. Only my grip on the rail kept me from pitching forward.

Shit. It really was unsafe, Super Cop hadn't been exaggerating.

I leaned over the railing and looked down at the dusty blackwood floor. An easy drop. I tested the railing; it groaned but held. I swung a leg over and jumped, landing in a crouch. The crash of my touchdown sounded like I was going to slam through to the cellar, but to my relief the flooring held.

I'd have liked to get some shots of the second story, but it wasn't crucial.

It did make the lights in the upper story windows a little more problematic. I wasn't a particularly big guy, and it would have to be someone a lot lighter than me to make it up this staircase. So...natural phenomenon?

Or was there another way upstairs?

Since Berkeley was supposed to have topped himself in his downstairs library, I didn't see why spooklights would be manifesting themselves upstairs, but it's not like the supernatural had to abide by the rules of human logic. Especially since half the humans I knew didn't abide by them.

I spent the next couple of hours wandering through the downstairs rooms, using my flashlight to guide the way through the dark interior, brushing aside cobwebs as long as tattered draperies. I took some pictures and made some general notes.

On the inland side of the house I came to a long room overlooking the woods. Daylight spilled through the cracked windows, revealing built-in bookshelves and the cracked and fissured façade of what must have once been an elegant fireplace. Silvery sheets of velvety wallpaper peeled off the scarred walls.

Presumably the library. The room where David Berkeley decided to end it all.

And what a way he'd chosen: using the specially made guillotine from his stage show. Gruesome but effective.

To me, it felt like an empty room in a dead shell of a house. But then I've never been particularly sensitive—at least, not in the psychic sense. According to C.K., I was ridiculously oversensitive in every other way.

On impulse, I sat down in the center of the room, closed my eyes, and just…listened.

Wind worked its way through the holes and loose boards: an eerie chorus in a multitude of different tones and pitches.

Was it just the wind?

I closed my eyes, listening…feeling…

"What the fuck are you doing inside here?"

If Sam Devlin wanted to pay me back for catching him off guard that morning, he got his money's worth. It's hard to retain your dignity when you're scraping yourself off the ceiling, but I tried. At least I didn't actually scream—although I'm guessing my shocked expression was just as bad.

Not that he spent time gloating. He leaned in through the open window frame, his face hostile but unsurprised—apparently not much of anything surprised him—and said evenly, "I told you the house was off-limits."

"I told you I've got Oliver's permission."

"I don't give a goddamn. I told you to stay out of the house."

Apparently he read my silence correctly because he said levelly, "Last warning. Get out before I come in and get you."

I wasn't sure if he would try it or not. If he did decide to throw me out, it wouldn't be much of a contest; he was a lot bigger than me, and I didn't doubt he was a lot tougher. In any case, there was no point continuing now with him draped over the windowsill. Talk about blocking reception.

Feeling a little silly to have been caught trying to…well, what had I been trying to do? Commune with the dead? I crossed over to the window, and he backed out, looking as grim as though he'd caught me trying to wriggle out of my straight jacket. I started through the open window, and his big hand closed on my shoulder, dragging me out.

"Come on, pretty boy."

"D'you *mind*?" My shirt—and skin—caught on a nail. "Christ, watch it!"

"All right, all right." He unhooked me. "Hope you've had your tetanus shots."

"Yeah, since you missed your rabies vaccine."

He gave a little snort that might have been a laugh.

I got through the window without any further help. Mouth compressed, Devlin watched me as I checked the tear in my shirt.

"Come on!" he said impatiently after a second or two.

"Go. I don't need a police escort."

"You've got one anyway."

I raised my head and glared. "What, you're escorting me off the premises?"

He made a sharp gesture with his chin and turned, obviously expecting me to trail after. So, in answer to my question, yes, I was apparently being escorted from the premises.

Devlin strode off across the patchy lawn, and I followed at a normal pace. No way was I trotting after him. I watched him stomping along ahead of me through the shambles of the old sunken garden, his dark head gleaming in the late afternoon sunlight.

I fantasized about picking up a piece of broken statuary and lobbing it at his thick skull. But enough damage had been done to the property without me adding to it.

At the end of the garden he paused, waiting for me.

"I think we'll wait to hear from Oliver before you do any more exploring," he said when I finally joined him.

"Oh, for—! I've only *got* the weekend!"

He shrugged. Clearly not his problem. "I'm sure he'll call this after-noon," he said indifferently.

I shook my head, not trusting myself to speak, and he turned and stalked off again. I guess I should have been grateful he didn't insist that I march in front of him with my hands on the back of my head.

When we reached Oliver's, I went straight upstairs to shower off the cobwebs and filth of Berkeley House.

Devlin called up to me as I was changing into a clean pair of jeans and flannel shirt.

"Hey, Professor. Phone call for you. It's Oliver."

I came downstairs and took the phone from him in the hallway. "See," he said laconically. "Told you he'd call."

"Thanks." I took the phone without meeting his gaze. Waited for him to depart—which after a minute he did.

"Hi, Oliver. It's Rhys. Sorry to bother you."

"Well, my dear. How are you getting along?" I pictured him instantly: tall and elegant with iron-gray hair and amazing green-gold eyes. I figured the connection to the Neanderthal now slamming kitchen cupboard doors had to be by marriage. Probably a forced marriage.

"Well…"

He laughed that plumy laugh. "You mustn't mind Sammy. He has a very suspicious mind. It comes of being a cop. But it's all right. I've vouched for you."

I doubted that meant as much as he imagined it did.

I glanced at the door of the kitchen, through which Prince Charming had vanished. "The thing is, Oliver, he's making it all but impossible for me to step foot inside Berkeley House."

"Mmm. I heard," Oliver said vaguely. "But you can surely work around that, yes? You're a resourceful boy."

I blinked this over. "Uh, yes. I guess."

Oliver sighed. "I was so hoping that you and Sammy would hit it off."

"Hit if off?" I added ungrammatically, "Me and *him*?"

"Yes! Oh, I know how brusque and hard Sammy seems, but he's not like that really. Just a big softie, once you get to know him."

"Sure," I said, not believing it for a moment.

"You'd be lovely together, you know. You're just what he needs. And he's what you need, my dear. Someone you can really count on. Someone steadfast and loyal."

"You make him sound like a St. Bernard." I was joking, but I was sort of appalled. Was that why the old reprobate had given me permission to investigate the house? So he could pimp me out to his socially retarded nephew?

"His bark *is* much worse than his bite. I've known Sammy his entire life..." He ran blithely on with a full listing of the Boy Scout virtues, but I'd stopped listening as Sammy appeared in the kitchen doorway.

He gave me a level look. Maybe I'd already used up my one phone call privilege. I said, cutting Oliver off, "Okay, thanks. Did you need to speak to him again?"

"No, no. Just give Sammy my love," Oliver said archly.

I returned something noncommittal and hung up.

"He sounds like he's having a good time," I said into Devlin's formidable silence.

"Oliver knows how to have a good time."

I wondered if he knew Oliver's hopes that we would hit it off. If so, I couldn't blame him for feeling a little hostile. There's nothing like matchmaking relatives. I'd had my own share of that.

"Satisfied that my intentions are honorable?"

His smile was sour. "You've certainly got Oliver convinced."

But obviously not Sam Devlin.

"So is it settled? Can I get back to work?"

"If by that you mean going back into the house, no."

"Christ! What is your problem?"

"Look, it's not safe. You had to have seen that much for yourself today."

I gazed out the window at the failing light. I wasn't looking forward to walking through those woods in the dark.

"I don't get it. I've signed a waiver. I'll be careful. Oliver is okay with it."

He sighed. "Oliver hasn't been inside that place for decades. He has no idea of the shape it's in."

"Fine," I said shortly. "I'll stick to the grounds."

He eyed me skeptically. It began to get under my skin.

"I said I'd stick to the grounds. What do you want?"

"Your word is fine."

He said it mildly, and I ignored the little stab of guilt that went through me. We stood there for another minute, and he said slowly, "So, Professor. By any chance do you know how to cook?"

CHAPTER FOUR

I assumed it was some kind of crack, but as I stared at him I realized he was perfectly serious. Strange but serious.

"That depends. What is there to cook?"

"Follow me."

I followed him through the large and modernized kitchen, then downstairs to the basement and a tomb-sized industrial freezer.

"Perfect for storing a body," I murmured.

"Yes. Don't annoy me too much."

I looked at him, and he laughed.

"Funny," I said. I stared at the frosty packs of food. "This is all frozen solid. What do you expect me to do with it?"

"I thought we could defrost something in the microwave." He actually looked...conciliatory. Not an expression that fit naturally on his dour face.

"I guess we could. It's not ideal, but yeah, we could defrost something. What did you have in mind?"

He reached right into the ice cavern and pulled out a neatly wrapped packet in white butcher's paper. "Pork chops?" he said hopefully.

I thought it over. It couldn't hurt to try and make friends with him. Well, *friends* was unlikely. What I pictured was more in the spirit of throwing a bone—or a pork chop—to a big ugly guard dog.

"If I cook, you clean up, right?"

"Deal," he said so quickly I thought it must be some kind of trick.

But apparently he was just desperate for a hot meal. He sat at the kitchen table, watching every move I made as though he feared I might take off with his precious pork chops.

I checked out the refrigerator, opened a few cupboards, pretended he wasn't there, but after a few minutes his silence sort of got to me. I leaned against the counter, waiting for the microwave to melt the block of pork chops, "So are you on vacation or something?"

Nothing.

He was an alien life form, and I was wasting my time trying to communicate.

The microwave bell rang, and I popped open the door.

"Or something." Devlin spoke curtly from behind me. To my surprise, after another long pause he said, "How did you get involved in the ghost-hunting racket?"

I searched the spice rack, selected cumin seeds, black peppercorns, coriander, and sea salt. "It's more of a hobby than a business," I said. "I mostly teach history."

"How'd you get interested in paranormal studies?"

I realized two things about him: he was a better listener than he appeared to be, and he was not easily sidetracked. I guess that was useful in his line of work.

Combining spices in one of those anchor-sized frying pans, I tried to decide if I was going to be candid or not. On the whole I thought candor with someone like him was a bad idea, so I was startled to hear my voice begin, "My brother was killed…"

I stopped, appalled. Where had that come from?

"Sorry," he said brusquely.

Silence. I pushed the spices around the pan.

"What happened?" Unexpected as it was, Devlin's voice jarred me out of my reflections.

I said, "It was a long time ago. I don't know why I brought it up." And I really didn't know.

He said, "How did it happen?" A cop's curiosity, I guessed.

Easier just to get it over with. I said, "Dylan, my twin—" And was even more startled when I swallowed mid-sentence. I spoke quickly to get past that little stumble. "Was killed when I was eleven. We were riding bikes, and a car hit him. It was…fast. One minute he was right there… laughing…and the next minute he was gone."

I stopped the film running in my head. Stopped myself from saying anything else. I had already said too much. I threw Devlin a quick look. Waited for him to say something—bracing for sarcasm or traffic death statistics or, worst of all, sympathy—not that he looked like the sympathetic type. To my relief he didn't say anything. His face was expressionless, his eyes alert and curious.

I stirred the spices, and the room grew fragrant with the toasted scents. I said, "It just seemed to me…has always seemed to me…that the line between life and death is so…*fine*…"

"It is fine."

"But it seemed like because it was just a matter of seconds…" I stopped, realizing I was never going to be able to explain it to someone like him. He thought by "fine," I meant fragile—that was natural since he was a cop—and while I agreed that life was fragile, that wasn't what I was talking about. I meant that the dividing line was so flimsy, so insubstantial that it seemed possible—even probable—that you could just reach right across… If you knew how. If you had the courage.

I flashed him a quick, meaningless smile. "So that's my traumatic childhood. Sorry you asked?"

His brows drew together as I pulled the blender away from the wall, dumped the spices in and turned it on. The whir of the blender made speech impossible, and I was glad of that. I couldn't imagine why the hell I'd told him about Dylan. Low blood sugar, probably.

While the pan grew hotter, I scooped out the blended spices and began to dry rub the meat with them. The smell of the heating pan and the spices, the warmth of the kitchen, and the scent of Sam Devlin's aftershave and freshly laundered flannel shirt had a weird effect on me. I became conscious of my bare fingers deeply massaging the warm raw meat—and that Devlin was watching me with close attention.

I said at random, "So what kind of a cop are you? Oliver never said."

Another tense pause—I wasn't sure why the question should make him tense. He wasn't undercover, right? So what was the big deal?

"I'm a sergeant at the Park police station. Burglary division."

"That must be interesting."

He gave me an ironic look.

I tried anyway. "Do you...like it? Being a cop?"

"Yes." He couldn't have made it any terser. His eyes went back to my meat massage.

I gave up. Nodded at the wine rack on the far side of the room. "You want to open a bottle of wine?" By then I needed a drink.

He rose, opened the wine with quick efficiency, and poured me a glass. Our fingers brushed as I took the glass—and why the hell I would even notice beat me. I took a sip. A very nice pinot noir. I took another sip, set the glass down, and placed the chops in the heated pan.

The room began to feel very warm—the effect of wine and the stove.

"What do you want with the chops?" I asked, squatting down to look for a sauce pan.

He cleared his throat. "Whatever you..."

I glanced around. His gaze appeared to be pinned on my ass. He took a gulp of wine and said, "I think there's some canned corn in the cupboard."

"Okay. Toss me a can."

He got up, opened the cupboard, and tossed me the can of corn— across the table. I almost suspected he didn't want to get too close to me.

Studying the can of creamed corn, I considered the peculiar likeness of the Jolly Green Giant to present company.

I studied Devlin under my lashes. He was a big man, no question. It was probably handy in his line of work. He looked intimidating, and he had the voice and manner to back it up. I wondered what kind of social life he had, being a cop and looking the way he did. It couldn't be much of one since he was spending his vacation all by himself at his uncle's isolated retreat. Maybe he'd be in a better temper once he was fed and watered. Granted it would take a lot of feeding and watering…

"I could make stuffing," I offered.

His face changed. He looked at me with something close to respect. "Could you?"

I nodded. Maybe when he was in a better mood I could work on him again about Berkeley House. Considering the house's state of disrepair, it would be safer to have someone aware of where I was all the time; I didn't want to have to lie and sneak around, but no way was Sam Devlin getting in the way of this book.

Searching the refrigerator I came up with limp celery, a loaf of stale nut bread, and half an onion. I set about making stuffing. Sam Devlin watched me all the time, and unwillingly I watched him back, uncomfortably aware of long legs, wide shoulders, powerful arms.

"So why did you become a cop?" I asked into what began to feel like a very long silence.

"I wanted to make a difference," he said sardonically.

I sighed. It really was pointless trying to talk to him, but I like talking to people. Generally the wrong people, according to C.K. "And have you?" I asked.

He was silent. Gee, what a change. I glanced at him, and once again he was observing me in that assessing way.

"Maybe."

It took him so long to answer that I'd forgotten I'd even asked a question. I didn't pursue it.

Dinner was ready in just under an hour, and by then I was feeling the effects of two glasses of wine on an empty stomach. When Devlin came over to the stove to inspect the results of my efforts, I felt awareness of him in every pore.

"You really can cook," he said, as though he hadn't believed it until all the evidence was presented.

"My dad's a chef. Or was. He's retired now." I was proud of my impromptu efforts: home-style pork chops and stuffing. It smelled great if I did say so myself.

Devlin made an uninterested noise. "I'm going to build a fire and eat in the study," he said, serving himself out of the pan.

For the life of me I couldn't understand why I felt hurt. He had asked me to cook dinner, not dine with him. And I didn't want to dine with him anyway, right? Because what could be more uncomfortable than trying to choke down food in his silent and disapproving presence. Too much wine, I decided. I was just feeling a little blue, missing C.K.

"Sure," I said. I set my plate on the table and pulled out the chair.

He eyed me for a moment. "It's warmer in the study, but suit yourself." He turned on heel and vanished from the doorway.

I stared after him.

Oh. Okay.

I picked up my plate and trailed down the hall to Oliver's study.

It was easy to picture Oliver in this room—urbane and easy in a silk smoking jacket, pouring cognac from a decanter, and chatting amusingly about art or whatever caught his fancy. If Oliver had ever been a starving hard-scrabble artist, I didn't know about it; this room provided the perfect setting for him. The walls were a deep green, the trim and molding white, the furniture leather and masculine. Paintings covered the walls, mostly oils, but a few watercolors—one or two of them looked like Thaddeus

Sterne's work. Not that I was an expert, but you pick up a few things dating an art dealer.

Devlin sat on the floor in front of the fireplace, staring into the flames. His powerful body was relaxed and graceful, one arm resting on an upraised knee, the other leg stretched out before him. In the muted light he looked almost attractive, I thought, and then had to bite back a laugh.

"Something funny?" he asked, catching me by surprise.

"Uh, no." I sat down across from him. Avoiding his eyes, I stared up at the paintings—a small fortune in artwork. I couldn't believe there wasn't a state-of-the-art security system to protect it. Maybe Devlin *was* the state-of-the-art security system.

"He's amazing, isn't he?" I said, meaning Oliver. I thought of his kind-ness that day at the art gallery and felt an unexpected lump in my throat. Oliver had most certainly been on the prowl that afternoon, but the minute he'd figured out what was up with me, he'd been absurdly kind.

"Every day in every way," Sam returned. An unemotional tone but I realized that there was a sense of humor in there—a sarcastic sense, which appealed to me since I was a little on the sarcastic side myself according to C.K.

I really didn't want to think about C.K. tonight.

We chewed for a while, and he said, "This isn't bad."

"Thanks."

"In fact," he said grudgingly, "it's pretty good."

I nodded, biting back another laugh.

Silence but for the scrape of forks on plates, the crackle of the fire-place, and the howl of the wind.

"It doesn't stop, does it?" I said, lifting my head to listen.

"What's that?"

"The wind."

"No. It doesn't stop." His head lifted, and there was a gleam in his eyes.

I felt my mouth tugging into a smile. I said, "No, I am not spooked by it. I'm not afraid of the dark, either. Or ghosts."

He actually grinned. He had one hell of a smile—when he let himself smile for real instead of that usual sardonic twist.

"Or lions or tigers or bears," I added.

"Oh my," he murmured right on cue.

And we both laughed. For real. A shared moment and a genuine laugh.

After that it was a little easier—another bottle of wine helped. Sam asked about the other ghost houses I was writing about, and I told him about some of the things that had happened during my research of other houses. He listened politely—unimpressed, I think, but polite—which was an improvement in diplomatic relations.

I was telling him about the elderly owner of a Monterey B&B who had invested quite a bit of money in her resident "ghost," when he startled me by bursting out laughing.

"I'm serious," I said. "She had to be in her seventies, and she was climbing along the outside railing of this giant staircase with a long pole and a makeshift rubber foot attached—all covered in phosphorous paint."

"What size foot?"

That struck me as hysterically funny. He watched me, smiling, but his eyes were dark and serious. I eventually got control of myself and said, "I forgot to ask. Anyway, she may have been a fraud, but she made the best oatmeal raisin cookies I ever ate in my life, no lie. The *best*."

His smile widened. He said, "So the fact is, you're actually trying to disprove these ghosts, aren't you?"

That sobered me fast. "Not at all."

"No? Seven haunted houses and every one of them a fake?"

I shook my head. "It's not my fault they're all a bunch of frauds. I'm trying to find proof that these ghosts really exist."

He looked unconvinced, and for some reason it seemed important that he be convinced.

I said, "I want to believe. I really do."

"Then maybe you shouldn't ask too many questions."

I frowned. "That seems like an odd philosophy for a cop."

"You're not a cop. I didn't say it was my philosophy."

Maybe he didn't mean to sound as brusque as he did. Maybe he was just too used to talking to bad guys. I changed the subject. "If you spent summers here as a kid, did you ever go inside Berkeley House?"

"Yeah, and it wasn't safe back then," he said.

"Okay, okay. I get it," I said. "Did you ever see anything…?"

He shook his head like I was confirming his suspicions.

"What's the big secret? Did you see something?"

His mouth did the sardonic thing. "Not really."

"So there *was* something?"

Amused, he said, "How do you work that out?"

"Well, if there was nothing, you'd have said *nothing*, but you said, *not really*, so there is something."

He studied my face for a moment. I'd had a lot to drink, and I wondered if it showed. I wasn't slurring or anything, but I felt very…relaxed.

He said slowly, "Yeah, there *is* something…" And he leaned across and kissed me on my open and astonished mouth.

Since Devlin seemed a little on the socially inept side I was taken aback by the skill of that kiss. He didn't look like an expert in seduction, but that mouth—pressing coolly and firmly against mine—had had a lot of practice. I found myself wondering hazily who would have dared kiss him…and what I was doing kissing him when I wasn't sure I even liked him.

"Uh…"

He reached over and carefully removed my glasses. I blinked at him uncertainly. The muted firelight turned him into a fuzzy shadow. I had the impression of gleaming eyes and five o'clock shadow, and then he found my mouth again, parting my lips with gentle insistence. It was the gentle-ness that undid me.

That, and way too much wine, and not enough sleep, and missing C.K., and…

A lot of excuses for giving in to what simply felt…great.

I found myself tipping back, big hands cradling me as I landed on the rug, His kiss deepened, heated. Still gentle, but now exploring…

I lay in his arms responding without hesitation, my hunger surprising even me. I pushed up his T-shirt, ran my hands down his sides. His body was warm and brown and lean; muscles rippled beneath my fingers as he shifted position. It felt good to hold on to someone, to feel bare skin. I wanted more. Needed more. His fingers worked the button of my shirt, his mouth still on mine, his knee insinuating itself between my legs.

He finished unbuttoning my shirt, and I half raised to shrug out of it; he pulled his T-shirt up over his head and tossed it away. His hands went to the button fly of my jeans and I thrust up at him, already so hard the stiff denim was torture. My hands fastened on his belt, and I worked it like I had seconds to disarm a bomb—which is what it was starting to feel like. Sweat broke out on my forehead, my breath came fast. I felt wild, out of control with wanting him. Wanting him *now*.

He had me free of the constriction of briefs and jeans, yanking them down where they hung up on my tennis shoes, and I didn't give a damn because by then I had got him free as well, and his dick, hard and thick, was giving the high five to my own.

"Oh, *God*," I groaned.

He didn't say a word, his breath fast and rough and scented not unpleasantly of the spices and wine. Usually I'm a little more vocal, but his silent intensity shut me up.

I bit my lip as we humped and ground against each other, fast and frantic like this had been on our minds from the first meeting—which was crazy. The slide and slap of feverish bodies. It didn't take long at all before

I was coming. I yelled and bumped my head into his shoulder, pressing my mouth to the hollow there, somewhere between nipping and nuzzling.

Sam came a couple of heartbeats later in hard, economical thrusts, and I felt that blood-hot spill between us.

A shudder rippled through him and then another exquisite little after-shock of pleasure, but he still didn't say anything. Just expelled a long heated sigh against my ear, stirring my hair.

CHAPTER FIVE

We lay there for a few moments, recovering our breath. Sam's powerful arms felt good about me, comfortable. Right. I like to be held; C.K. hated it, wanted—needed—his space immediately after sex.

And about the last person I wanted to think about right now was C.K.

Not that thinking about Sam Devlin was an improvement because I felt a little stunned at what I'd—we'd—done.

On Oliver's Aubusson carpet no less.

"Wow," I said finally.

He gave a short laugh and let me go. I was sorry about that. Sorry as he lifted off me and moved away. Dazedly, I felt around for my glasses.

"I begin to see the attraction," he said.

"What's that?"

He said clearly and calmly, "Now I understand why Oliver's developed a sudden interest in psychic phenomena."

It took a moment for the meaning of his words to sink in.

I stared at the dark blur with the even voice. That's what comes of having sex with people you don't like—and who don't like you. And how stupid was I that I felt like he'd slapped me?

I slipped my glasses on and got up in one quick movement. I thought he tensed—it was hard to tell in the dim light, but maybe he'd had a lot of experience with people wanting to hit him after sex. He stared up at me, apparently waiting for some reaction.

"Yeah, well, there's no accounting for taste," I said. "Mine in particular." It wasn't a bad exit line, and I took advantage of it, heading for the door.

He didn't say a word, and I left him there in the shadows.

* * * * *

I opened my eyes and groaned.

It was morning. I'd slept through the entire fucking—no pun intended—*night*. Instead of getting my ass over to Berkeley House and doing what I'd come here for, I'd gone upstairs and, feeling stupidly, illogically sorry for myself, given in to the urge to lie down for a couple of minutes' rest. Only my quick nap had turned into the entire night and now it was…I checked my wristwatch…ten o'clock.

I'd lost an entire night. Totally wasted it conked out in Oliver's guest room. The entire night and a good portion of the morning as well.

In a very bad temper I rose, showered, and went downstairs. No homely scent of witch's brew coffee this morning, which gave me hope that Prince Charming had taken himself off somewhere—like the cliff behind Berkeley House—but no such luck. There he sat reading the local paper.

He looked up and nodded briefly as I entered the kitchen.

I nodded even more briefly back, felt him watching me as I opened the fridge and scanned the contents. I ignored him.

"I thought you might prefer to make the coffee this morning," he informed me, like this was a concession on his part.

I snorted. "Thanks. I'll just get something in town." I removed a carton of orange juice, poured myself a glass, and drank it standing at the sink, staring out across the woods at the rooftop of Berkeley House.

He shrugged and went back to his paper. I glanced to see what was so fascinating, but the local headlines seemed to consist of a couple of burglaries, the results of the annual garden show, and a successful library fundraiser.

I finished my OJ, rinsed the glass out, and left the kitchen.

Ventisca was one of those quaint little seaside villages, though not so quaint that it didn't have a Starbucks, of course, and I headed there post-haste to up my caffeine intake to appropriate levels. I ate a pumpkin cream cheese muffin while I got directions to the Historical Society.

I found the Historical Society nestled in between two calculatedly adorable bed and breakfasts. It was the only building on the street that didn't have flower boxes in the windows or a brightly painted entrance. Mason Corwin was unlocking the black front door when I pulled up. I got out of the car, waved, and he waved back, his expression lightening.

"Well, hi there! I was hoping you'd turn up today." He looked relaxed and approachable in a blue striped polo shirt and jeans, and his obvious pleasure was balm to my ego after Sam Devlin.

"If this is a busy time, I can look around on my own."

He chuckled, gesturing me inside. "We're not exactly on the Must See list for most tourists."

I looked around while Mason went about the ritual of opening the museum. There were the usual displays of Indian life and Spanish influence. I skipped over the collection of arrowheads and beads, ignored the sepia photographs of the town's early history, and bypassed the local arts and crafts section. There were a couple of very nice watercolors by local artists—nothing by Oliver or Thaddeus Sterne—and a lot of battered antique furniture.

And then I saw the guillotine.

It was roughly twelve feet tall and painted in some kind of shiny black lacquer. Golden sphinxes formed the feet of either side of the two tall guides; tiny jeweled eyes winked at me from the birdlike faces. Egyptian gods and goddesses ambled their way down the sides of the "bed," and the circular collar that held the victim's head in place was covered in crimson velvet. The morning sunshine glinted cheerfully off the sharp-angled blade hanging above my head.

"Christ, is that real?" I asked Mason. "Is that the guillotine he used to kill himself?"

He joined me, smiling faintly. "No. This was a second guillotine Berkeley designed to use in his show. See, his assistant's head would fit down here." He leaned across and pressed a small lever. "A dummy head would fall into the basket. The assistant would never be in any actual danger, although it looks pretty realistic from where the audience was sitting."

"It looks pretty realistic from where I'm standing." I added slowly, "It's huge. I don't know why that never occurred to me."

"That's show biz." Mason pointed to the far wall where a large oil portrait hung. "And that's David Berkeley."

I'd seen photographs of this portrait, but the real thing was startlingly vivid. Somber eyes stared out of a long, pale, intense face. Flat black hair and a dapper mustache and beard. The background was green like the sea beneath the cliffs at Berkeley House. I couldn't think how I'd missed it earlier because once I'd noticed the painting, it was hard to ignore it. I could feel the gaze of those black eyes as though a real person were watching me.

"Creepy," I commented.

Mason laughed. "Yeah. It's painted so that the eyes seemed to follow you wherever you are in the room. I'm used to him now, though."

"Who painted it?"

"No one."

At my glance, he clarified. "No one famous, I mean. It was done by a local artist. Aaron Perry."

"The same Aaron Perry who ran off with Berkeley's fiancée?"

"The same. Very good. You've done your homework. According to the stories, the three of them were inseparable growing up. The girl—"

"Charity Keith," I supplied, and Mason laughed.

"Now you're showing off."

"Yeah. It's an interesting story. Sad. Romantic. Like most ghost stories."

"Pure soap opera, if you ask me. Charity agreed first to marry Berkeley, but then changed her mind and ran off with Perry. Berkeley committed suicide at the peak of his fame and fortune—such as it was. The guy was not exactly Houdini."

He guided me through the rest of the display. There were fragile posters of Berkeley's performances and yellowed newspaper clippings of his modest triumphs. He'd definitely been junior varsity. No appearing before the crowned heads of Europe and his performance at the Pan-American Exposition had been marred by the assassination of President McKinley.

I glanced over the notice of Berkeley's engagement to marry Charity Keith and studied the formal still posed portrait of the happy couple. Apparently not that happy since Charity had eloped with Berkeley's good friend Aaron Perry.

Even in his engagement portrait Berkeley looked...harrowed. Charity, on the other hand, had that grim expressionless countenance most brides wore back then. Possibly something to do with women not having the right to vote until 1920.

"Are there any photos or pictures of Perry?"

"Not that I know of."

"Too bad." It would have been nice for the book, a picture of the love triangle. I mused, "An elopement must have been socially awkward in a town this size."

Mason laughed briefly. "I bet."

I moved down the row of black-and-white photographs, pausing at a picture of Berkeley in Paris. I felt a prickle down my spine as I picked out his tall figure standing next to the unsettlingly realistic guillotine. Something about that tall dark figure in top hat and cape caught my attention; seemed somehow familiar.

"This was the guillotine he used to kill himself?"

Mason peered over my shoulder. He smelled appealingly of pipe tobacco and citrus. He was sucking on a lemon drop, and he shifted it with his tongue before saying, "I don't know. There were two of them, and they were identical, I guess, until Berkeley doctored one for his own personal use. That one was destroyed after the inquest."

The shudder that rippled down my spine caught me off guard. Mason laughed. "Berkeley's story really got to you, didn't it?"

I laughed, trying to brush my unease off. "Maybe. It's all these gruesome props. Usually I have to use my imagination more. A lot more."

"I can imagine. Have you ever seen a real ghost?"

"Me? No." I glanced over my shoulder, feeling those strange painted eyes again.

"Well, if it's any comfort, it was all about the illusion for Berkeley. He didn't really chop the heads off volunteers."

Mason was teasing, and I forced a smile in response; I had no idea why David Berkeley's story affected me like no other I'd investigated so far. It wasn't a rational response, that was for sure.

He left me to examine the rest of the photos and memorabilia at my leisure, and I spent the morning glancing over the colorful ephemera of placards and postcards, puzzling over birdcages and boxes and other vintage odds and ends. I took photos of the clippings and the portrait of David Berkeley. I had more than enough information on him for the book, but the more I learned about him, the more fascinated I became.

I was the museum's only visitor that morning, and I wondered what Mason did to while away the long hours.

"We get a lot more visitors in the summer," he assured me, when I asked. "Berkeley might never have been a household name, but he's still pretty well known in magic circles." He watched me screw the lens cap on my camera and asked a little diffidently, "What do you think about lunch?"

"I'm all in favor of it."

I really liked his smile—and the fact that smiling wasn't a struggle for him. "There's a little place down the road that makes terrific meatball sandwiches."

"Sounds good," I said, and was treated to the easy smile again.

I followed Mason to a little Italian restaurant with a great view of the ocean. The tables were covered in red and white checked table cloths, and there were candles in Chianti bottles and faded photos of 1960 Rome for ambiance.

Mason ordered the meatball sandwiches, and I went for pepperoni and black olive pizza, having no idea when or if I'd have dinner.

"How long are you staying for?" he asked as we sipped beer from chilled mugs.

"Just 'til Sunday night."

"I guess, living in L.A., you don't get up this way a lot?"

I thought of all the plane trips, all the Friday night drives up the coast to see C.K. How come it had never occurred to me that I was the one doing all the driving and flying and jumping through hoops? Never again.

"No," I said.

He nodded, stared at the table top.

Someone had left a newspaper folded on the table next to us, and my wandering gaze lit on the story about the recent rash of burglaries—which reminded me of Sam. Now that I had a little distance from the night before, I could see that a certain amount of cynicism was probably part of the cop job description. And it's not like I was so inexperienced I put undue importance on sex. I was irritated with my earlier reaction to his misanthropic view; what did I care what he thought about me? I put it down to Oliver planting ideas in my head about him.

"What's the crime rate like here?" I asked, to distract myself from the direction my thoughts were going.

"Almost nonexistent." Mason followed my gaze to the newspaper headline and shook his head. "Oh, that. That's something new for us.

Started a couple of weeks ago with summer houses getting broken into and robbed. Luckily no one's been hurt."

I nodded absently.

We chatted about the usual things. Mason was full of praise for small town living. He had moved to Ventisca from San Jose following the death of his longtime partner three years earlier.

"I'm sorry," I said.

He smiled sadly. "Yeah. People sort of forget that AIDS is still killing us."

I wondered if he had tested positive for the virus or not. I liked him and found him attractive, but I wasn't at the point where it mattered to me personally one way or the other. His uncomplicated admiration and openness was refreshing after Sam Devlin. Not to mention C.K.

But I was still unsettled about my stupidity in having sex with a stranger the night before—unprotected sex at that—and it put me on my guard. I returned the conversation to neutral ground. "So what's the local word on the ghost?"

"Ask around and you'll hear plenty of accounts of flickering lights and strange noises. You know: the ghostly slide of a guillotine blade echoing through the woods."

He grinned, and I grinned back, but I remembered the eerie sensation of those silent woods closing in on me.

"Have you ever seen anything?"

He hesitated. "I hate to tell you this, but I'm not a big believer in the supernatural."

"Sure. Which means anything you've seen will be more interesting. Or at least more reliable."

He took a swallow of beer and wiped the foam from his mustache. "I've seen the lights. I go out to Seal Point sometimes with my telescope. The lights are supposed to be Berkeley traveling from room to room searching for his lost bride."

"But she wasn't his bride, right? She ran off before they married, so why would he be looking for her in the house?"

Mason shrugged. "Never thought about it. Maybe ghosts aren't logical. Maybe his ghost forgot what happened. He did chop his head off, after all."

I laughed. "Good point."

I liked the way his eyes crinkled at the corners when he smiled. I said, at random, "Berkeley killed himself eight months after Charity ran off?"

"So the story goes. Yep. That much is documented."

"It seems like a weird way to commit suicide, using the guillotine. You think he'd just throw himself off the cliff or blow his brains out."

"He was a showman up to the end, I guess."

"I guess. So did you ever hear—"

He chuckled. "I know what you're going to ask. Did I ever hear the ghostly scrape of the guillotine ax?"

"Did you?"

His face was rueful. "Nope. I've made a point of never getting that close to the house at night."

"Seriously?" Mason didn't look like the nervous type.

"Seriously," he said, and his eyes were without their habitual twinkle. "And, if you'll take my advice, you'll steer clear of those woods after dark."

CHAPTER SIX

Mason and I talked a little longer, and then I reluctantly declined dessert and coffee and headed back to Oliver's. This time I took the back road, skirting Oliver's home and parking in the woods not far from the cliffs.

I could smell the sea salt and eucalyptus and hear the cries of the gulls circling high above the rocks as I unloaded my gear and lugged it across to Berkeley House. Once I had everything out of the car I lifted it through the broken front windows of the library and began setting up my equipment.

The afternoon was warm and unusually sunny, the wind down to a murmur. I could hear birds singing in the trees. The unease I'd felt the previous day seemed silly now.

I mounted the video cam on its tripod in the corner of Berkeley's library where it wouldn't be easily spotted by anyone peering through the window. Setting the timer, I hurried back to the car.

As I pulled away, I was caught between guilt and triumph. Yes, I'd given Sam Devlin my word not to go back into the house, but I'd been coerced into it, so it didn't count.

Not really.

Besides, Devlin was a jerk.

It took about ten minutes to drive to Oliver's. I parked in the shady front drive and went inside the house, using the key Devlin had given me before I'd left that morning.

There was no sign of him, and that was a relief.

Sitting down at my laptop, I entered my notes from the museum. I worked for about an hour when the sound of splashing filtered through my consciousness. I rose, went to the window, and looked down at the brick patio and swimming pool beyond.

Sam was in the pool. I watched him for a while. He swam with a single-minded ferocity. Gleaming brown arms cut glistening arcs in the air, strong legs kicking as he shot through the water. Each time he reached the end of the pool, he did one of those quick underwater summersaults off the wall and started back across the water.

I was struck again by the beauty and power of his body; I didn't want to remember how it had felt to be held by him, how his mouth had tasted on mine, the roughness of his cheek, and the softness of his hair. I wanted to forget the night before had ever happened, so it was annoying as hell to find it difficult to tear myself away from the window.

But I did. I went back to work, finished entering my notes, and then read them over. I thought Berkeley House was by far the most interesting of my chapters, and I wondered if it would be feasible to use David Berkeley's portrait on the book cover.

"Hey," Sam yelled upstairs some time later. "You want some dinner?"

I opened my mouth to yell my refusal, but my stomach growled, practically loud enough to answer for me. And the answer seemed to be yes.

I closed my laptop and went to the top of the stairs. "Is that your way of asking if I'll cook?"

He stared back, but then his mouth quirked like he just might smile. "It's for your own protection," he said.

"That's what I thought," I said.

His expression altered. "If you want me to cook, I'll cook."

I must have looked unconvinced because he said, "I defrosted a couple of steaks. I can do steak."

I was too hungry to ignore this olive branch—in fact, I was hungry enough to eat an olive branch, so I shrugged ungraciously and joined him downstairs in the kitchen.

"There's beer in the fridge," Sam said, peppering two enormous steaks. "I went to the market earlier."

I opened the refrigerator and saw that he had indeed stocked up. There was plenty of imported beer as well as perishables like milk and bread and lettuce. Apparently he was planning on staying for a good while. It didn't matter to me now; I wouldn't be staying beyond Sunday, and I'd already figured out how I'd work around him.

"How was your day?" he asked, his eyes very green in his tanned face.

"Fine."

"How'd the ghost hunting go?"

I stared at him. Was he *making conversation* with me? Why?

"It was okay," I answered warily.

"Learn anything useful at the museum?"

My hand slipped opening a bottle of Beck's, and I almost spilled some of the precious elixir. "How'd you know I went to the Historical Society museum?"

He raised thick brows at the suspicion in my voice. "I saw you with Mason Corwin coming out of Mama Louisa's. I put two and two together."

"Oh?"

His mouth twitched a little at my tone. "Is that a touch of paranoia? I was going into the market. I have the produce to prove it."

Well of course he wasn't following me; I hadn't thought he was, but it still gave me a funny feeling, especially since he was being so uncharacteristically cordial.

"Speaking of which, do you want me to make a salad or something?" I offered, mostly to change the subject.

Sam smiled, his expression informing me that he knew exactly what I was doing. "Sure, that'd be great."

It occurred to me that the offer of beer had simply been a ploy to get me to open the fridge and see the vegetables awaiting my expert hand. "Are you sure you're gay?" I inquired. "You seem pretty helpless in the kitchen."

"I'm sure." He gave me an unexpectedly direct look. "My skills lie in another direction."

Anybody else, I would have thought he was flirting. As it was, blood rose in my face remembering exactly how skilled he was—and my own uncharacteristic response.

I busied myself tearing up and washing greens, and Sam took the steaks out to the back patio. Apparently his idea of cooking was BBQ.

I gave myself time, drank some beer, then followed him outside. He was sitting in one of the wooden Adirondack chairs, idly swiping at flies with the extra-length spatula while the coals heated. I straddled one of the weathered benches, taking a turn at observing him for a change.

"How do you want your steak?" he inquired into the silence.

"Medium—hold the flies."

He turned a gleaming look my way. "Extra protein," he observed.

"Ha."

He resumed gazing at the sun-glittering pool.

I swallowed a mouthful of beer, listened to the sound of the pool filter and the scrape of dead leaves on the bricks. Bees hummed around the bougainvillea winding up the wooden posts of the pergola, brilliant scarlet and yellow flowers.

"So what happened between you and the boyfriend?" Sam asked suddenly.

"Huh?" I stared at him, astonished.

"The art dealer boyfriend," he clarified, as though I had so many I might have lost track.

I continued to stare at him, and his face reddened as though it belatedly occurred to him that maybe this was just slightly intrusive. I figured that

Oliver must have filled him in on me—preparatory to handing me over as human sacrifice du jour.

"He didn't do monogamous," I said. "Or long term." I stood up, swung my leg over the bench, aware that he was still watching me with that bright alert gaze. "Are we eating inside or out?"

"What did you want?"

Somehow everything spoken in the last couple of minutes seemed laden with undertones and secret meaning. It took me a second to gather my thoughts. I said, "Outside, I guess. It's nice tonight."

"It is nice," Sam agreed. He rose and applied himself to the grill.

* * * * *

The steak at least was perfect.

After his odd question about C.K., Sam seemed to have little to say. We ate mostly in silence, while the little lights strung across the open patio and threaded through the vines blinked into life like fireflies or tiny stars. Pool lights illuminated crystal water. The evening was perfumed with charcoal and chlorine and freshly mown grass.

Every so often I'd glance up from my plate and Sam would be staring at me with an expression I couldn't quite pin down. Each time I'd catch his gaze, he'd look away.

"You want another beer?" he asked on his way into the house.

"No thanks."

We were both sticking to beer—and not too much of it.

"How did your family acquire Berkeley House?" I asked when he returned with his beer. "Berkeley wasn't a relative, was he?"

"No."

"The house was abandoned after Berkeley's death?"

"Near enough. The house went to elderly relatives of Berkeley's back east. They had no interest in moving out west, and the house had a bad reputation locally. Finally it was sold off with the surrounding acreage to

Cornelius Wagnalls, who built this house. Wagnalls lost everything when the stock market crashed in 1929, and Oliver's grandfather bought the estate in auction."

"And the house was left closed up all that time?"

"Mostly. There are stories about Wagnalls offering the house to his daughter as a wedding present, and her walking inside and walking straight out again." He raised his black eyebrows suggestively. "Atmosphere," he said.

"Or thirty years of dust." I smiled absently, reminded suddenly of the previous evening, the way it had felt being together. It was still hard for me to believe that I'd done that. Or that he had.

It seemed risky to even question it. It had been a one off. It had felt good at the time, but now I needed to forget about it. So how the hell come I kept thinking about it?

I said briskly, talking myself away from my wayward thoughts, "Are you ever going to tell me what you saw at Berkeley House way back when?"

Sam tilted his beer bottle up, his eyes studying me wryly over the top.

"Is this going in the book?"

"Not if you don't want it to." That was a rash promise; I wasn't sure if it would go in the book or not, but I wanted to hear what he had to say.

"Okay, well, it's not like I have an actual incident to report. I used to go over to the house. This is about twenty years ago."

How old was he? Late thirties? Early forties? I tried to picture him as a little kid. I kept getting tall, grim-faced with five o'clock shadow.

"What did you see?"

"Nothing."

At my expression he said, "I never *saw* anything, but…it was an… uneasy place. It had a vibe, I'll give you that."

"Did you ever go upstairs?"

"A few times." He shrugged. "By then there wasn't much left to see, but when Oliver was a kid there was still some furniture and bits and pieces of Berkeley's magic apparatus."

"For real?"

"Yeah. No one seriously ever tried to secure the premises, so piece by piece, it all vanished or was destroyed by vandals. Oliver's grandfather donated the best of what was left to the Historical Preservation Society."

"What kind of stuff was there?"

His eyes rested on my face; it was probably my imagination, but for a moment his expression seemed to soften. "Books mostly. A guillotine. A portrait of David Berkeley."

"I saw that guillotine today. Pretty impressive. The portrait too."

He smiled reluctantly. "You love this stuff, don't you? Everything from the magic tricks to the spooky old house."

"Well...it'll make a great chapter for the book and...yeah. I do." I waited for him to say something rude or belittling, but he just grimaced and reached for his beer.

"What was it like upstairs?"

"Like the downstairs."

I opened my mouth to object, and he said patiently, "There was a lot of junk and a lot of cobwebs and dust. A few skeletons of seagulls that flew in through broken windows and couldn't get out again."

"Did you go through all the rooms?"

"Yes," he said. "I did. And I crawled around in the attic."

Here was a valuable resource if he'd be willing to cooperate.

Correctly reading my expression, he said, "That wasn't the creepy part."

"What was?"

"The cellar."

His eyes flicked to mine, and I wasn't sure if he was about to pull my leg or not. "Cold as ice. A cold like nothing I've ever felt. I only ever went down there once. That was enough."

"The cellar? Not the library?"

"The cellar."

"But Berkeley killed himself in the library."

"So the story goes."

I fastened on this. "Is there any reason to think he didn't kill himself there?"

"Not that I know of."

There was nothing about the cellar in any of the stories about Berkeley house, so I couldn't figure why there would be a cold spot in the cellar. Lights in the upper story and an unnatural chill in the cellar: two supernatural manifestations that didn't make any sense.

Whether they made sense or not, I wanted to check the house out, experience its secrets for myself.

Afraid that Sam might read my thoughts—he seemed pretty good at that—I changed the subject again. "How long have you been a cop?"

His face tightened. "Ten years."

Yes, there was something there. Something to do with his job.

"So you must like it."

"Yeah. I like it."

"Are you on vacation now?"

He gave me a long level look, planning, if I read his look correctly, to tell me it was none of my fucking business. But instead, he said neutrally, "I'm on...leave."

"Oh." Medical leave? He looked healthy as a horse. What other kinds of leave were there?

I was still thinking it over as he changed the subject, turning the tables once more.

"Oliver says you teach at UCLA?"

I nodded, reached for my beer.

"You've got a pretty good football team heading into spring practice."

"Twenty returning starters and an experienced core group of players."

"And you teach history?" He really had been listening the night before.

"Mostly. One course on parapsychology."

"How long?"

"Six years."

He nodded thoughtfully.

It was the slightly awkward conversation you make on a first date. I almost asked him how he felt about Oliver trying to set us up, but remembering how quiet and intense he had been when we'd fucked, I held my tongue. It seemed to me that he was not a guy to tease.

I must have been looking at him oddly, though, because he raised his brows. "What?"

I shook my head. "Thanks for dinner. My turn tomorrow night."

"Are you staying for dinner? I figured you'd be taking off early. Beat the traffic."

Meaning he'd *hoped* I would be taking off early? Probably.

"I…was thinking I might stay over Sunday." *I was?*

Sam raised his brows.

"Unless you have a problem with that?"

He shrugged. "It's not a problem for me. You're Oliver's guest."

"Right. Well…good." For some damn reason I couldn't come up with anything else to say. I'd thought—well, I hadn't really thought anything. I'd *hoped*—no. No, I definitely wasn't hoping for anything. In fact, I had no idea what the hell I was thinking or why I had suggested staying another night.

Sam said slowly, "Did you know Berkeley was found just moments after he used the guillotine? The local story is that when they picked up his severed head he opened his eyes and spoke."

I stared at him. I knew it was just a story, but for some reason my face felt stiff as I formed the question, "What did he say?"

"Dum spiro, spero."

A chill rippled down my spine. "Which means what?"

"It's Latin."

"For what?" I asked a little impatiently.

Gravely he said, "While I breathe, I hope."

He laughed at my expression, and I was glad it was too dark for him to see that I was red as well.

"Funny," I managed.

He was still laughing.

"So is there actually any story about Berkeley being found after he used the guillotine?"

He sobered. His eyes, black in the uneven light, met mine. After a moment, he said, "No. Of course not."

I realized he was lying.

"You know, there are scientists who believe that when a head is suddenly severed it takes the brain a while to realize what's happened. There are recorded instances of severed heads responding to someone speaking their name or touching their cheek."

He said flatly, "Berkeley was found days later. There's no story about his severed head."

"How do you know when he was found? I've never read anything about it."

"Anecdotal evidence. There are still a few old-timers with stories about Berkeley." He rose and picked up his plate and mine. "Don't let your imagination run away with you, Professor," he threw over his shoulder.

After a moment I stood, gathering the rest of the dishes, following Sam into the house. He had the dishwasher open and was loading it.

"I'll wash up," I told him, and he nodded and left me to it.

It didn't take me long. I finished loading the machine, turned it on, and went upstairs to bed.

Setting my wristwatch for eleven thirty, I lay down to nap, but it took a long time to relax. I could hear the TV downstairs, little twitches of the house settling down for the night, the wind...

I woke at the creak of floorboards down the hall and the sound of Sam's bedroom door shutting. Raising my head, I checked my wristwatch. Ten thirty. Early yet. I closed my eyes and drifted back to sleep.

My wristwatch was going off softly next to my ear. I rolled over, peered at the luminous dial in the gloom. Eleven forty-five. Time to get moving.

I sat up, pulled on my jeans and shirt. Found my shoes and socks, holding them in one hand as I eased open the bedroom door. I paused.

Moonlight dappled the floor like silver lily pads on the shiny dark wood.

Not a sound from down the hall.

I tiptoed down the lily pads past Sam's closed door, hesitating at the squeak of a floorboard.

I waited. Behind the door on my right, I could hear Sam snoring, and I bit back a grin.

I continued down the hall, down the stairs, and out through the front door, which I locked quietly behind me. I sat down on the porch steps and slipped my tennis shoes on, pulled my sweatshirt over my head.

Rising, I glanced back at the black window of Sam's bedroom.

I hoped to God the neighborhood burglars didn't pick tonight to hit Oliver's.

* * * * *

Berkeley House was, unsurprisingly, quiet as the grave on a crisp and chilly Saturday night.

I crawled in through the library window and hesitated for a moment in the darkness. It was very dark with only my flashlight to guide my way across the uneven floor.

The video camera whirred softly away in the indistinct gloom of the library. I checked the meter. It had only started running two hours ago, so there was still plenty of time and tape.

For laughs, I tried tapping on a few walls. Berkeley was an illusionist. I thought it was likely he might have a hidden room or a secret passageway built into the house. But the place was huge and some of the rooms were no longer even accessible due to broken flooring and tumbled walls. I wondered if it would be possible to lay hands on a set of blueprints for the house. Mason might know.

Remembering Sam's comments about the cellar, I started hunting for the kitchen. There were two doors at the end of the long former dining room. One door turned out to be false, apparently existing only to add symmetry to the room's architecture. The second door led down a short passage to the enormous old kitchen. The flashlight picked out where the ovens had stood, the wreck of cupboards, and another door leading into what must have been the pantry.

Staring up, I saw the gallery where the lady of the house would have stood to drop her instructions for the day's menu down to the kitchen staff. Of course there had been no lady of the house in Berkeley's day, so maybe he had stood up there himself.

For some reason the image of that tall, thin figure standing up in the gallery gave me goose bumps. I turned away, making my way to the far end of the kitchen where an empty door frame led out onto a porch.

That couldn't be it.

I started back across the wasteland of dirt and debris.

The flashlight beam picked out another door I had missed when I'd entered the kitchen. It was positioned near the kitchen entrance, set off to the side of the hallway. I studied the peeling surface for a moment and reached for the tarnished knob. It seemed stuck. I tugged harder, and the handle came off in my hand.

The door swung gently open.

The dank breath of the cellar gusted out. I could feel clammy stink against my face. A chill wave of sick horror came over me.

Okay. Maybe not.

I shoved the door closed and stood there for a moment panting in the wake of that cold miasma.

What the hell *was* that?

I backed up trying to make sense of it. I'd experienced a few cold spots in my investigations—though nothing that couldn't be explained by underground springs or faulty architecture—and occasionally I'd felt something that prickled the hair on the back of my neck, but this was the first time I'd ever felt anything quite that...extreme.

Mouth dry as sand, heart banging away in my chest in that flight or fight instinct, I began to reason with myself. It was just bad air. Stale air.

It was dust. Mold. Mildew. The damp.

That scene from the movie *The Haunting* flashed into my mind. Gloomy old housekeeper, Mrs. Dudley, warning poor doomed Eleanor, *There won't be anyone around if you need help. We couldn't even hear you, in the night. In the dark...*

Right. In the night. In the dark. In the damp.

That seeping damp...pervasive and oppressive...like a gust of swamp gas or the tainted air from a crypt. It brushed against my face like a veil.

Even if there was some kind of presence—no, *not* presence. Presence was the wrong word. Even if there was some kind of supernatural manifestation, that didn't mean there was any danger. Outside of the movies, no one has ever been killed by a ghost.

I was still telling myself this as I stumbled back toward the door opening onto the dining room. I grabbed the handle, relieved when it turned. Why wouldn't it turn? Why was I overreacting over a little bit of moist and mildew?

I made my way through the broken planks and plaster, almost falling over a loose floorboard in my haste.

Christ. I was acting like the very nitwit Sam believed I was.

Blundering back into the hallway, I paused to get my bearings.

Something moved in the surrounding pitch blackness, and my heart stopped. I swung my flashlight in the direction of that soft sound. A mouse froze in the glare of my flashlight and then whisked itself away behind a baseboard. I sucked in a sharp breath, told myself to get my shit together.

Okay. There were good reasons not to explore the cellar. It was a foul place, and it wasn't even mentioned in any of the stories about Berkeley House. So no need to prove anything to myself. Logically, there was no reason to go down there.

If I did decide to explore the cellar, it would be better to do that during the day. But actually it would be better to just forget about the cellar because Sam was right. It was dangerous down there. The house really was unsafe. I could break a leg easily. Or my neck.

I reached the library with a feeling of relief.

The relief was short-lived.

As I stood there listening to the breeze through the broken window scuttle leaves or old newspaper around the floor, I got that sensation of being watched.

A feeling of increasing anxiety crept over me. I turned my flashlight into the cobwebbed corners of the room.

Nothing.

I shone it at the black mouth of the doorway.

A prickly shivering darkness seemed to lie in wait beyond the doorway.

Yeah. Right.

Really, what the fuck was my problem?

I resolutely turned from the doorway and scouted out a reasonably clean place of floor space near to the wall. Wrapping myself in my blanket, I sat down with pad and pen.

The spring moon moved slowly across the floor, the shadows lengthened, deepened...

The repetitive rasp of sliding metal, a cold hollow thunk, and the jangling pull of a chain filtered into my dreams.

I started awake.

To a crisp and eerie silence.

I listened tensely.

To nothing.

I rubbed my eyes, checked my watch. Three thirty. The camera was still running. I took a look at the electromagnetic detector. The needle was trembling, indicating strong, erratic, fluctuating EMFs.

I watched it in the circle of my flashlight beam. The needle stilled.

I waited for something else to happen.

Nothing did. I jotted down the time and event in my log , then made myself sit down again to wait.

Outside the window I could hear crickets chirping.

Bed sounded better and better. Especially since I couldn't seem to keep my eyes open.

Electromagnetic fields could result from a number of things, but that sound had been so...real. I could still hear the echo of the slow distinct draw of chain, the swift steely bite, and the crunch of blade on...on flesh and bone?

Too much red meat, that's what this was about. A heavy dinner and not enough sleep.

Unfolding painfully, I set the mostly unused pad aside—I wasn't about to write down my dreams—folded up the blanket, and crawled out through the window.

I hurried through the shambles of the garden, pausing on the edge to look back at the house. The scent of eucalyptus hung heavy in the night air. I told myself that if I saw lights in the second-story windows, I would go back, so it was a relief to see only black and broken panes reflecting the night sky. I started back up the road toward Oliver's house.

It seemed a long way that night—as though the overgrown road were elastic, stretching further and further despite the energetic pace I set.

I began to think about the figure in the road the previous evening.

Except...not a mysterious figure, after all, but rather a famous and well-respected artist. With a penchant for sauntering through the woods at night.

Well, everyone needs a hobby.

But the way Thaddeus Sterne had followed me through the woods—that wasn't normal behavior. That was...disquieting. The way he'd stood there watching me, moving closer and closer across the lawn. He'd practically emanated malevolence.

Or had my tiredness and imagination got the better of me?

Given the direction my thoughts were going, I guess it wasn't surprising that when someone stepped out of the bushes right to the side of me, I shot off the ground like I'd had springs installed in my feet.

A blast of fear and adrenaline surged through me; I turned and bolted—slamming right into a thick tree trunk.

CHAPTER SEVEN

I was seeing stars.

"Are you all right?" The voice floating above me was soft and alarmed. A black bulk bent over me.

I jackknifed up—and just missed banging heads with the owner of the voice. "I-I think so…" Actually, I felt a little sick in the wake of that rush of fear and adrenaline—not to mention the shock of hitting my head.

I had a blurred impression of massive shoulders and silver fur. It didn't do much to settle my nerves.

Feeling around in the grass, I found my glasses and examined the wire frames doubtfully. The lenses were fine, but the frames fit crookedly when I slipped them on. I viewed my companion.

He was big—even bigger than Sam. Tall and broad with a dark hawkish face and long silver hair and beard. Silver eyebrows too.

"Here, let me help you up." Forceful hands fastened on my upper arms and lifted me onto my feet. "I didn't mean to frighten you."

"You didn't." I put a hand to my forehead, brought it away. No blood as far as I could tell. That was good, though I could feel a knot rising beneath my cautious fingers. It pulsed, tender to the touch.

"You're Oliver's little friend." His eyes were very dark, like black holes in his face.

I irritably shook off my fancifulness. An elderly man and the safety of Oliver's house within sprinting distance: there was nothing here I couldn't handle. I bent to brush myself off.

"I don't know if friend is quite the right word." I glanced up. "I don't know if *little* is quite the right word. You make me sound like a pet rabbit."

He chuckled. "Sure you're all right?"

"Mostly. You're Thaddeus Sterne, aren't you?"

"Yes." He did that chuckling thing again.

I said as though we were standing in C.K.'s gallery, "I'm a great admirer of your work."

"Are you?" He sounded amused. "Would you like to come back to my house and see some of it?"

It seemed an odd time for a visit, even if he was one of the living legends of the art world. "I should probably be getting back," I said regretfully.

"I think you should come with me," he said gently. "David Berkeley's waiting for you."

"I...what?" I jerked upright, interested at how calm I sounded. Calm and a little faint. Which was pretty much how I felt.

"Look." He pointed down the road. I stared. There in the bend where the trees dipped low and the shadows were deep I could see—

No. I didn't see anything but shadows. And Thaddeus Sterne was almost certainly off his rocker.

But my eyes wouldn't seem to look away, and as I focused I seemed to be able to pick out the tall, faceless figure. A tall man standing silent in the center of the path.

This was what I had seen the night I arrived. Not Thaddeus Sterne at all. The shade of David Berkeley.

Ridiculous. I was just reacting to the suggestion...

"Why would he wait for me?" I asked carefully, unable to tear my gaze away from the umbra in the path.

"I don't know." I could feel Thaddeus's gaze on my profile. "You keep returning to the house. Maybe he thinks you're looking for him."

I was too tired to work this out. And then it occurred to me that I was having a very strange dream. It had to be a dream. I could imagine myself telling Sam about it over dreadful coffee in the morning: *I was standing in the woods talking to Thad Sterne about David Berkeley—and David Berkeley was right there listening to us.*

I said to Thaddeus, "I thought it was you following me the other night."

He said, "You'd better come back with me and let me take a look at that bump on your head."

Yeah, I had to be dreaming. I was tucked up in bed right now. So it was okay to go along with this—it wasn't for real, and I was curious about how it was all going to work itself out.

I nodded, keeping one eye on the dark shadows where I thought I'd seen…Berkeley's specter.

We didn't take the path, though; Thaddeus pushed right through the bushes, and I followed him so there was no need to pass that point in the road where Berkeley waited.

"It's not far," he assured me. He moved in long powerful strides once we cleared the shrubbery. I trailed after him.

We walked until we came to a house that looked like an Arts and Crafts masterpiece: a rambling shingle-style in dark wood with a multitude of brightly lit windows. Thaddeus trudged up the interlocking stone front path and pushed open the unlocked front door.

"You're not afraid of burglars?" I asked.

He tittered, holding the door so that I could precede him inside. "No danger of that. What do I have that anyone would want?"

I stared around at an informal wall-to-wall gallery of paintings, a fortune in Thaddeus Sterne art work. It seemed to me pretty obvious what someone might want, but I let it go. There's no point debating with people in your dreams.

Thaddeus led the way to a large room that was also lined with paintings. Obviously the rumors were wrong; he hadn't quit painting. He had just quit exhibiting.

I sank down on the nearest surface: a velvet-covered sofa straight out of a Victorian novel. My head hurt, but mostly I just felt tired and a little woozy. Sterne left me for a few moments and returned with an old-fashioned ice pack. I applied it cautiously to my forehead.

Disappearing again, he reappeared with a decanter. He poured two cognacs, one of which he handed to me. I said apologetically, "I probably shouldn't after a knock on the head."

He shrugged, set the glass on the flimsy table next to the sofa, and then dropped down in a giant brocade chair. He leaned forward, frowning beneath the shaggy silver eyebrows.

"Tell me about Oliver?"

I shifted the ice pack. "Tell you…what?"

"How did he look?"

"Good. Healthy. Happy."

He nodded. Stared at his drink. Had that been the wrong answer?

"Did he say when he was coming home?"

"Not to me." I added uncomfortably, "I think he's in Paris now."

"Yes. He loves Paris." He tossed back the cognac in his glass. "You must have made quite an impression on him."

I said honestly, "I think he felt sorry for me. I'd broken up with my boyfriend and…I wasn't taking it well."

He stared at me.

"He can be very kind," he said at last.

"He was to me."

There was a very strange silence. I realized that more than anything I wanted to lie down on this velveteen couch and go to sleep.

"We grew up together, me and Oliver. We've always been together."

I guess it was all how you defined "together."

I searched around for something to say. He obviously was only interested in one topic. "What was he like back then?"

He said dryly, "Like he is now, only faster on his feet."

"Did you know Sam when he was a boy?" I heard myself ask—proof that I'd been knocked harder on the noggin than I supposed.

Sterne smiled, his face unexpectedly relaxed. "Oh yes. He spent all his summers here when he was growing up. Sammy's a sweetheart."

I made a noncommittal noise. I hadn't seen that side of him yet, but he certainly had the Silver Panther vote.

Sterne chuckled again. I wished he wouldn't. It raised the hairs on the back of my neck. Then he leaned forward and whispered, "You shouldn't go in the house. It isn't safe. Especially for you, I think."

I stiffened. "Why especially for me?"

"Not every door you open is possible to close."

"That's certainly cryptic."

He just eyed me in that calm way.

"Did you ever see…?" I realized it was a foolish question. He had seen whatever I had tonight. The question was what had we seen? How much of it was imagination—or suggestion—and how much of it was bad lighting?

"Sam said he used to play—" I paused, wondering if "play" was the right word to describe anything Sam might have done.

"Boys will be boys," Sterne remarked. He reached for my untouched cognac. "Oliver and I used to prowl through the house when we were lads, too."

"You know the story about Berkeley killing himself in the library?"

"Using the guillotine from his act? Oh yes. The guillotine was long gone by then, of course, but you could still see the bloodstains on the floor."

The ice pack was leaking cold water down the back of my neck. I shuddered, studying Sterne, not sure whether to believe him or not. He smiled maliciously.

"Or maybe we just hoped that's what those stains were." He eyed me speculatively.

I said, "Is there some legend about Berkeley's severed head speaking when he was found?"

He laughed heartily. "Where did you hear that old horror story?"

"So there is such a story?"

"*Amor et melle et felle est fecundissmismus.*"

"Which means what exactly?" Did everyone in this damn place speak Latin?

"Love is rich with both honey and venom."

I stared at him. "That can't be true." Why had Sam lied?

"Of course not." His eyes were puzzled. "It's just a story some fool made up. You know the legend of course? Berkeley killed himself when his childhood sweetheart ran off with his best friend."

"A local painter by the name of Aaron Perry."

"That's right!" He looked pleased. "Have you seen the portrait?"

I nodded.

"It's not bad, is it? Aaron Perry had something. It's a shame none of the rest of his work survived. Berkeley was at the height of his fame when that portrait was painted. Fame being relative. He traveled all over the world: England, Spain, Paris—" his voice was bitter on the word "Paris." "He performed in music halls and carnivals and circuses. Anywhere he could. He didn't come home for years on end, but I suppose he thought the girl would wait forever. She didn't."

The silence was definitely awkward.

"I should probably be getting back," I said.

"Do you know the way?"

"Yes. I think so."

"Take the road. Don't cut through the woods."

I didn't answer that. I wasn't sure that he wasn't deliberately trying to spook me—no pun intended.

Sterne followed me to the front door. "Thank you for visiting," he said politely. "I don't get much company. Everyone thinks I'm crazy." He chuckled and closed the door in my face.

* * * * *

"Shit!"

Sunday morning I studied myself with dismay in the steamy bathroom mirror. A colorful bruise marked my brow bone where the tree branch had whacked me the night before. Now how was I supposed to explain that?

I raked my hair over my forehead. If I didn't mind it in my eyes, it was long enough to cover the special effects. I just had to remember not to move my head around too much. I sighed and reached for my shaving cream brush. Not so pretty a boy this morning.

Lathering my face, I considered last night's adventures. If I didn't have the bruises to prove it, I'd have wondered if I'd dreamed the entire evening. As it was, the events had an *Alice in Wonderland* quality to them. Or maybe I was thinking of the Jabberwocky. I'd definitely experienced a sinister moment or two in that house. Probably my own overactive imagination, but I couldn't wait to get hold of the video camera and see what might have been captured on tape.

"What the hell happened to you?" Sam asked, looking up out of the paper when I wandered into the kitchen a short time later.

So much for my hair disguising the damage. I walked over to the coffee maker. This morning Sam appeared to be boiling tar in it. Perhaps he planned on working on the roof.

"I—er—went for a walk last night and banged into a tree," I replied, wondering if Thaddeus would confirm my story or whether he'd come up with his own version, which was liable to include details about me climbing out of Berkeley House at three o'clock in the morning.

"A walk in the woods?"

"It's true, believe it or not."

To my alarm he tossed the paper aside and got up, coming over to examine me. I flinched as he raised his hand—and he halted mid-reach. Just for an instant hurt flared in his eyes. "Rhys—"

I had a sudden understanding of how often people reacted to his size and rough-hewn looks, without giving him an opportunity to be anything else. That wasn't my problem, but how could he know that?

"Really, Sam, it's okay," I said awkwardly.

He brushed the hair off my forehead. I went stiffer than a plank of wood, feeling that gentle touch in every cell of my body. I swallowed nervously, my throat making a little squeaky sound.

"That shade of purple just about matches your eyes," he said with wry humor.

I smiled weakly. It felt funny having to look up into his eyes—funnier still was the expression in them. I couldn't make it out, but just for a second I thought he was about to...

Actually, I don't know what I thought.

"There's coffee," he said laconically, lowering his hand and moving back to the table.

"Is that what that is?" No wonder he was such a grim guy if he started every morning out with a dose of molten lava.

"I ground the beans myself."

"They have a machine for that, you know."

He grinned a wolfish grin. "I waited for you as long as I could."

Oddly, I remembered Thaddeus saying that Berkeley had assumed his sweetheart would wait forever. Which reminded me.

"I ran into Thaddeus Sterne last night."

His face changed, the friendliness draining out of it. I said defensively, "I wasn't looking for him. Why would I? He stepped out of the trees and startled me. That's how I got this." I pointed at my forehead.

After a moment he relaxed and nodded. I felt a flicker of guilt. And unease. Maybe I should have shut up about Sterne; now it was sure to come up between them as a topic of conversation.

"How was he?" he inquired.

"I think he misses Oliver. A lot."

"Yeah." He sighed. He didn't seem like the type to waste time sighing over what couldn't be changed, but that was the impression I had. Then he jerked his thumb back at the stove. "I fried up some Spam and eggs, if you're hungry."

"No you didn't," I said.

He looked puzzled. "Yeah, I did."

"Spam? Nobody eats Spam."

"I got news for you. Spam is delicious and nutritious."

"I'll give you delicious. No, actually, I can't in good conscience give you either of those."

"Suit yourself," Sam said. "There's probably a stale box of oatmeal somewhere."

I raised the lid on the frying pan, and the warm, salty smell of fried eggs and ham hit my salivary glands. I hadn't realized quite how hungry I was.

"Well, I guess I have to eat something," I conceded, reaching for a clean plate.

"You do eat a lot for such a little guy."

"'Little guy?' Excuse me, King Kong, but I'm nearly six feet." His eyes flickered at the King Kong crack, but then he laughed.

"Better keep your strength up then, Cheetah. Especially if you're going to be taking many moonlight strolls." It was suddenly hard to avoid his gaze. "What brought on that sudden desire for fresh air, by the way?"

I could come clean right now. I could tell Sam everything that had happened—or at least everything I had dreamed. But if I told him, I knew without a doubt he'd have my equipment out of Berkeley House and me packed and on my way back to Los Angeles before my Spam and eggs were cold. That's what I told myself, anyway, but what I really shied away from was risking this jokey almost companionable truce between us.

"I wanted to see if I could catch another glimpse of those lights over at Berkeley House."

He was silent. I kept my eyes pinned on my plate while I shoveled in eggs, waiting for him to press it. I tried to decide if lying by omission was as bad as lying straight to his face—and whether I had it in me to lie straight to his face in any case. I wasn't sure I could anymore.

So it was a relief—and a surprise—when he all he said was, "Did you see the lights?"

"No."

He nodded, and then went back to his newspaper.

After my delicious and nutritious breakfast, I went out to the pool to have a heart attack and read over my notes in peace.

Not that Sam was disturbing me, except that somehow his presence was harder and harder to put out of my mind. In fact, I was astonished to realize that I hadn't given C.K. a single thought in almost twenty-four hours.

It was warm and sunny by the pool; summer wasn't far off now, and the events of the night before felt more and more distant and unreal. I turned my laptop on, working while the pool water lapped soothingly against the filter and the sun moved lazily across the bricks.

As I tapped and clicked, I began to wonder about Aaron Perry and Charity Keith. Their story seemed to stop with the event of their running off together; no source ever mentioned them after the elopement. Of course, I had never thought to ask anyone about them before...

I plugged "Charity Keith" into Google but came up with nothing. "Aaron Perry" brought up musicians, actors, and basketball players—none of whom fit the profile. There was quite a bit of information on David

Berkeley—a lot of it totally inaccurate—and there were several mentions of the runaway lovers, but nothing about what had become of them.

Nothing about the talking head either, for what that was worth. I was pretty sure Sam had brought that up to freak me out, and then for some reason changed his mind and turned it into that silly joke.

Had the eloping couple never returned to their hometown? A little drastic, surely? Or was public opinion so strongly in favor of Berkeley that they had decided they needed a fresh start?

Or had they feared some reprisal from Berkeley?

I thought about this for a moment, eyes narrowed against the sunlight dancing on the water. I wasn't sure why that idea had come to me; perhaps it was the unsettled feeling I had about Berkeley's—alleged—specter. If it *hadn't* been Thaddeus Sterne in the woods that first night…if it really had been the shade of David Berkeley…then there was no denying the sense of threat I'd had.

But maybe the Perrys had returned. Maybe no one mentioned them because David Berkeley was the star of that show, and what interest was there in a couple of ordinary newlyweds settling down to run-of-the-mill domestic bliss?

Why had none of Aaron Perry's other paintings survived if he had continued to live and work in Ventisca?

Maybe they weren't any good? Maybe they had survived but no one recognized them as Perry's since he wasn't a famous artist? Maybe he had stopped painting and got a day job. The absence of other paintings didn't prove the Perrys hadn't returned to Ventisca; it was just interesting, that was all.

I could check out the local graveyard. Maybe check church records?

A shadow fell across the lounge chair. I glanced up.

"Feel like taking a break?" Sam asked.

"What's up?"

He said very casually, "I was thinking of going into town for lunch. Want to come?"

I did—how much was unsettling—but as I opened my mouth to say yes, I realized I would lose a much-needed opportunity to slip over to Berkeley House and change the video tapes, resetting them for the night. I might not get another chance. Besides, I needed to hear whether the ghostly guillotine sounds had been in my imagination or had actually been recorded.

"I'm not at a place where I can stop," I said reluctantly, nodding to the laptop.

He glanced at his watch and said tentatively, "Well, how about in another hour or so?"

"I—uh—I really need to keep working," I excused. It was hugely disappointing, but I didn't see a way around it. "Rain check?" I said hopefully.

Even as I said it I realized how stupid that was. When would there be time for a rain check? I'd be leaving tomorrow.

"Sure," Sam said indifferently, his face closing up again into its usual hard lines. "See you later."

He went back into the house, and I stared unseeing at the computer screen.

The minute I heard his car pull away, I shut down my laptop and ran inside the house.

I pulled on Levi's, stepped into tennis shoes, and hot-footed it over to Berkeley House. There was no sign of anyone in the woods—for a change—and my fears of the night before seemed the result of not enough sleep.

Slipping through the broken library window, I quickly changed the tapes, stuck the recorded video in the smaller video cam, and started out again.

Leg over the sill, I hesitated.

Why not take a look at the cellar in the daylight?

Last night I had been overtired and, I had to confess, I'd let the atmosphere of the old place get to me. But today the house was just a slightly depressing wreck, and there was no reason not to check out the cellar. In fact, there was every reason to take a look since it was my job to investigate paranormal occurrences, right?

I ducked back under the sill and made my way down the hall and through the ruined dining room. The chill hit me as I slipped through the dining room side door, but it was cold inside the center of the house, removed from the light and warmth of the day.

Rounding the corner, I stopped, letting my flashlight play over the scratched and battered door to the cellar.

The door was closed again. The knob had been replaced on its spindle. I stared at it for a long time, trying to remember when I'd replaced it.

I reached for the knob and then let my hand drop back to my side.

My skin crawled at the thought of opening the door to that...to that *what?* What was my problem?

I yanked open the door.

Cold. Bitter cold seeping through my clothes, my skin, right to my bones...

I slammed the door shut.

Fuck. I couldn't do it. I couldn't make myself step through that door, let alone go down the steps to the cellar.

And that fact alone seemed to indicate that there was something here, something at least worth mentioning in the book.

I'd never felt anything like it.

Everything else...the shadowy figure in the woods, the lights, the noise of the guillotine, everything else could be put down to fatigue or imagination or suggestion.

But whatever was on the other side of this door...

Suddenly I wanted out of that house about as intensely as I'd ever wanted anything in my life.

As I crossed the hall to the dining room my foot stuck to the floor. I shone my flashlight on the sole of my shoe.

A dime-sized piece of plastic.

Not plastic.

Hard candy.

I could see a candy wrapper blowing inside the house, but there was no way a half-sucked lozenge of candy had wafted here on its own. And there was no way David Berkeley's ghost—with or without a head—was eating hard candies.

Someone—a human someone—had been inside the house besides me.

CHAPTER EIGHT

Kids, I thought. Not that I had seen any kids around, but candy and trespassing in haunted house seemed to indicate an adolescent hand.

Or perhaps...Thaddeus? He didn't seem particularly fearful of the house, but he also didn't seem like the candy-popping type. Or maybe he did. How would I know?

There was a reasonable chance I had the answer on the video tape—assuming the candy-sucking intruder had shown up during the hours I'd been recording.

I remembered the floating lights in the attic and the sounds of sliding metal and clanking chains—had someone faked guillotine sounds and a ghostly presence? Why?

The house was already abandoned, and no one seemed to show much of an interest in it aside from me—and my interest was temporary. It's not like I planned to move in there. The house itself didn't seem long for this world.

I stick-stuck my way across the floor, the dirt on the wood gradually working the candy loose and off my shoe sole.

Climbing out the library window, I was startled to see that the day had grown overcast, the sun retreating behind heavy cloud cover. A cold salty wind blew off the sea. I crept my way through the overgrown garden and then slipped into the woods, making my way back to Oliver's.

Sam was still not back, but as I glanced at the grandfather clock in the hallway, I saw that it was nearly four thirty. He might be on his way back now. He'd been gone all afternoon.

I hunted around until I found a television hidden inside a lavish antique armoire. It took a few moments to figure out the inputs, but at last I had the camera hooked up to the TV.

I pressed play and stood back to watch.

Gray snow and the ear-blast of static.

I turned down the sound and tried different channels. No good. I hit fast forward.

The tape was blank.

"Damn."

Camera malfunction? Pilot error? I couldn't make sense of it. I'd used this camera dozens of times without problem.

Could someone have tampered with it? A candy-sucking saboteur? But why wouldn't such a person simply have turned the camera off—or smashed it?

Hearing the sound of a car in the drive, I snapped off the TV. I wiggled the cord free, grabbed the camera, and ran for the stairs.

Foot on the bottom step, I heard Sam's key in the front door lock. I froze, spied the hall closet door, and jerked it open, setting the camera inside.

I turned as the door swung open. Sam was balancing white bags of takeout while trying to pull his key from the door.

I felt a weird mix of pleasure and guilt at the sight of him, and although I had been planning to make my escape upstairs with the evidence as quickly as possible, I found myself walking toward him.

"Hi."

"Hi." He smiled a little self-consciously. "How'd the work go?"

"Good."

This was ridiculous. I actually felt...*shy.*

"I thought tonight we'd both get a night off." He held up one of the bags. "You like Chinese?"

"I love Chinese."

He gave another one of those lopsided smiles like he was still practicing getting the expression right.

"Grab some plates and a bottle of wine. We'll eat in the study." He added as an afterthought, "If that's okay with you."

"Yeah, it's okay."

His eyes met mine.

I waited 'til he vanished into the study; then I opened the closet door, grabbed the camera, and took the stairs two at a time. I dropped the camera inside the doorway of my room and raced downstairs.

No sign of Sam, but I could smell woodsmoke.

I uncorked a bottle of wine, found glasses, and carried the plates into the study. Sam had dragged a short table over to the fireplace and was setting out little white cartons.

"Cashew chicken, barbecue spare ribs, sesame beef..."

I poured the wine into the glasses and settled on the floor beside him, facing the fire.

Something was different. Something had changed. I could feel it, even though I couldn't identify what it was. I knew the change was partly in myself—and I knew the change was partly in Sam. Every time I met his eyes—which was frequently—something in his gaze warmed me, lifted my heart.

Suddenly there was a lot to say, each of us rushing into speech, pausing, smiling, to let the other talk. I let Sam refill my glass a couple of times, and I looked forward to the night ahead.

When we finished eating, Sam slipped his arm around my shoulders, and I turned my head to find his mouth. I closed my eyes, liking the feel of his mouth on mine, firm and warm, liking his gentleness and liking his assurance. My heart started to pound hard in my chest as his tongue brushed my upper lip.

"I've never known anyone like you," he said against my mouth. It almost sounded like an apology.

I smiled and his tongue slipped into my mouth, a dark and sweet kiss. Our tongues pushed delicately against each other, whorled, withdrew.

I laughed, snatched a quick unsteady breath. It had been a long time since kissing had been a big part of my sexual repertoire. With C.K. time had always been of the essence, both of us busy with our careers and outside demands. I hadn't realized quite how many outside demands C.K. had until one of them insisted he break up with me.

Sam rested his hand on my jaw, turned my face to his, and kissed me deeper still, taking my breath away as his tongue touched, tested, tasted. Weren't there something like eight thousand taste buds on an adult tongue? Every one of mine seemed to be experiencing its very first burst of flavor: a smoky blend of alcohol and cashew chicken and something uniquely masculine—uniquely Sam.

The phone rang above our heads.

Sam stiffened. I moaned. He tore his mouth away.

"Who the hell is *that*?" I complained.

He kissed the corner of my mouth and sat up. "Thad probably. No one else ever calls here."

The phone continued to shrill away. Sam rolled to his feet and picked it up.

I listened to the one-sided conversation. Since that was Sam's part of the conversation, there was basically nothing to hear.

"Yeah…Okay…Sure…No. No problem, Oliver. I'll handle it."

He hung up the phone and studied me ruefully. "Feel like a walk in the woods?"

"Seriously?"

"Oliver says he got a strange phone call from Thaddeus a while ago. He wants me to go over there and check that he's okay."

I sat up. "Okay."

We grabbed jackets from the hall closet and locked the front door behind us.

The moon was lost behind the heavy clouds as we cut through the woods, but our two flashlights provided enough light as we pounded down the dirt path.

"What are you smiling at?" Sam asked during the silence that had fallen between us. If he could tell I was smiling in the dark, he had to be paying pretty close attention.

"I was just thinking I'd put money on you over David Berkeley's ghost any day of the week."

"I thought you weren't afraid of ghosts?" He sounded amused.

"I'm just sayin'." Actually, I was saying too much, but I wasn't used to having to deceive anyone in the course of my work. And I liked less and less having to lie or conceal things from Sam. I tried to think of a way to tell him I'd been sneaking into Berkeley House before Thaddeus brought it up, but I hated the thought of losing this newfound harmony.

And maybe Thaddeus wouldn't say anything. Maybe whatever had us hot-footing it over to his house in the middle of the night would require all his attention. And if he did bring it up, maybe having a third party present would keep Sam from getting too angry, and give me a little time to explain my side of it.

Only one light was on at Thaddeus's house. Remembering the blaze of lamps the night before, it struck me as ominous. Sam banged on the door, but after a pause that seemed long enough to confirm my fears, Thaddeus swung open the door. He was wearing a purple paisley silk dressing gown, and his hair looked like he had stuck his finger in a wall socket. He reeked of booze.

"Oliver sent you," he said immediately.

"He's worried," Sam said. "Can we come in?"

Thaddeus's eyes moved from Sam to me. He said, "He's not so worried that he'll come home."

For a minute I thought he was talking about me. He continued to stare at me.

"Can we come in, Thad?" Sam repeated. And after a moment Thaddeus moved aside and led the way into the house.

We trailed him into the room where he'd played host to me the night before. Sam sat down as though it was an ordinary visit, and after a moment, I sat too, choosing a chair off to the side. I was sort of hoping Thad might forget all about me.

We watched as he poured himself another cognac. His hands shook.

"You think that's going to help?" Sam asked.

"It can't hurt," Thaddeus retorted. He poured another glass and handed it to Sam. Looking blearily around, he spotted me. "There you are." He poured a third unsteady glass, and I half rose to take it from him.

Sam savored, swallowed, and said, "What's going on, Thad?"

"I'm old and I'm tired and I'm lonely," Thad said pretty crisply for a guy who'd apparently downed a half bottle of cognac. "I've come to the end of my rope."

Sam didn't have an answer for that, and I recognized it would be best if I kept my mouth shut. I swirled the tulip-shaped glass and then sniffed the volatile aroma.

"I want Oliver to come home," Thaddeus said. "If he loves me, he'll come."

"You know it's got nothing to do with that," Sam said.

Thaddeus turned his dark, bitter gaze my way. "I know what it has to do with. It has to do with using pretty little boys like that one to keep the dark at bay."

I lowered my glass. Granted, I was outside my weight division with those two, but I wasn't a midget, and I was over thirty. I opened my mouth but caught the warning look Sam shot my way. By now I had an idea of Oliver's track record, so I bit back what was on the tip of my tongue.

"It's still got nothing to do with you," Sam said.

"No?" Thaddeus laughed—nothing like his usual nutty chuckle—and tossed back the rest of his drink.

Sam said quietly, "Thad."

Thad refilled his glass from the decanter at his elbow. "Don't be a boor, Sammy. Allow me my little farewell party." He raised the glass and toasted something out there in the night.

"Oh, that's just great," Sam said disgustedly. "What? You're planning to off yourself because Oliver's a spoiled, overgrown adolescent?"

Thaddeus glared. "This is farewell to *a dream*," he said with great dignity. "I wouldn't give him the satisfaction of killing myself."

"For what it's worth, I don't think Oliver would find your death very satisfying."

"It doesn't matter what he would or wouldn't find," Thad returned. "It's over. I've finally given up. I've been a fool. I see that now. Flesh and blood can't compete with…" Once more he turned that dark hostile gaze my way. "Well, it's finished. Over. Oh, don't worry. I won't do anything drastic. That's why you're here, I suppose. You can call Oliver right back and assure him I'm not going to cut my throat. I'd have to care to cut my throat, and I don't care anymore. I don't feel anything anymore."

And he drained his glass once more.

"Why don't I help you to bed, Thad?" Sam suggested. "You'll see things differently in the morning."

"Oh, go home, Sam," Thad said wearily. "And take *him* with you."

Sam's eyes met mine apologetically. I shrugged. I accepted that Thad's dislike wasn't personal; I just happened to represent everything he blamed for his unhappiness.

We didn't stay much longer. Sam made a couple more attempts to help Thad to bed, but they seemed to piss the old man off more than anything, and in the end even Sam had to concede defeat. Thad seemed to be settling into a boozy doze when Sam nodded silently to me. I rose, setting my empty glass aside.

We let ourselves out, standing for a moment on the porch. The wind had picked up again, rustling the tree leaves around us.

"Will he be all right?"

Sam shrugged. "I guess so. He's not a child. And he's not self-destructive—unless you count wasting your life loving someone like Oliver."

"Oliver must care a little. He called you to come check on Thad."

"Oh, he cares. In his own way." He added quietly, "The best thing for Thad would be if he *could* stop loving Oliver. But how do you break the habit of a lifetime?"

That was a depressing thought. I felt tired and dispirited as we headed back to Oliver's. No wonder Sam was cynical about relationships with a role model like Oliver. And, if I remembered correctly, his parents were divorced as well.

"They grew up together?" I asked.

"Oh, yeah. They were boys together, went to art school together, achieved fame and fortune together."

"They were lovers."

"They *are* lovers. That's the weird thing. No one means more to Oliver than Thad."

"I guess I understand Thad's confusion." My own sour memories must have echoed in my voice because Sam glanced my way and then put an arm around my shoulders.

He said, "I don't understand Oliver. I don't understand why being with the person he loves the most isn't enough for him. But it's not. He needs the fame, and he needs the adulation—he likes being a celebrity, and he likes being a legend in his own lifetime. And if that's all it was, it would be difficult enough for Thaddeus, who doesn't care about any of that."

"But Oliver also likes pretty little boys."

"Yes." He sighed. "Thad isn't in the best of health, although he won't tell Oliver that—won't let me tell Oliver that. So Oliver's going to wait too long, and that will be that."

"And you don't think maybe you should speak up before it's too late?"

I felt him glance at my profile. "No, I don't."

I thought it over, comfortable in the circle of his arm.

"Did you ever hear the story of David Berkeley?" I inquired. "He was a Twentieth Century magician who was so busy building a career based on creating illusions that he fooled himself and lost the woman he loved to another man."

He said wryly, "Okay, okay. I know about Berkeley, and Oliver knows about Berkeley. Oliver knows life is short—that's a big part of Oliver's problem."

"Non-interference. It doesn't seem like a cop attitude."

"I'm not a cop with the people I love." His voice was different, although I couldn't define how. "And if it was me, I'd try to spend every minute with the person I loved, instead of focusing on the pain of losing him one day."

"Is that what it is?"

"I don't know. Partly, I think."

I thought it was funny how easily he spoke of love and caring and commitment. He didn't look like a guy who would waste five minutes on mushy stuff, let alone be able to articulate his feelings. Of course, he didn't look like a world-class kisser, either, but he was that all right. My mouth still tingled pleasantly from our after dinner encounter.

I started to speak but caught sight of Berkeley House through the trees. I stopped stock still. "Look!"

Sam followed the direction I pointed. In the distance we could see hazy lights moving eerily from window to window on the upstairs floor.

He was silent.

"You see that?"

"Yeah." He let go of me, automatically reaching up with his free hand, and I knew he would ordinarily have been wearing a shoulder holster. "I need to check that out."

The last thing I wanted was him investigating the house and finding my equipment. I said, "Unless someone's using a trampoline, I don't understand how that can be of human origin. The staircase has rotted through, and the dumbwaiters are wrecked."

He snorted. "What, you think that's David Berkeley looking for a lost sock or something?"

"Maybe he's looking for his head."

He glanced at me. "Now that's a gruesome thought, Professor."

I shrugged.

"It might be some kind of refracted light. Ships off the ocean?"

I didn't even bother to answer that one.

"Okay, what do you think it is?"

"You can't even *consider* the idea that it might be a paranormal phenomenon?"

He opened his mouth and then apparently rethought the first words that came to him. "I didn't say that." His spoke painstakingly, and I realized that he was making a conscious attempt not to offend me. "But I need something more than—"

He fell silent as the light vanished. We waited for a few moments, but the windows stayed dark.

"The moon reflecting off something maybe," he said doubtfully.

"Whatever it is, it's over for the night," I said. "Let's go back to Oliver's."

He thought it over. "Come on," he said, and to my relief—and pleasure—he put his arm around my shoulders again.

As we continued on I was thinking about my assertion that supernatural forces had to be at work, but what about the lozenge of candy I'd found?

I knew I should tell Sam.

If local kids were fooling around in that house, it had to stop. The place was a death-trap.

But maybe I could wait 'til tomorrow; 'til after whatever was going to happen tonight had developed. We'd have a better chance of weathering Sam's discovery of my deception if things went well tonight. And if I could get my stuff out of the house tomorrow without him finding out, maybe I could find another way to let him know about the house's other trespassers.

"What are you thinking about so seriously?" he asked.

"About the way things work out. I'm glad Oliver invited me to stay."

His hand rested lightly against the small of my back, warm, possessive. "Me too."

When we got back to the house, Sam poured us each a brandy and then called Oliver. It was a brief call, and Sam was unusually curt with his uncle. At least, that's how it seemed to me, listening in.

He said finally, "Maybe you should tell Thad, then."

He listened to Oliver and then said with great finality, "Then I guess it comes down to trust."

Trust. A little frisson of alarm unfurled down my spine, and I was glad I'd kept my mouth shut about sneaking back inside the house. In fact, I was definitely going to get my stuff out of that house without Sam finding out. I could probably pretend to leave tomorrow and then swing back around and park in the woods again.

Sam concluded his call with Oliver. For a moment he gazed down at the phone; his head raised, he met my gaze. "Feel like a moonlight swim?"

"A…swim?"

He smiled—and I found myself smiling too.

* * * * *

We swam naked in the warm buoyant water of the pool behind the house, our voices quiet in the cool empty night air. A tear in the canopy of thick cloud cover revealed the dusting of stars glittering high overhead. Sam had turned on the living room stereo, and the music drifted out from the window, a lazy seductive saxophone flirting with a sexy-shy piano.

After a couple of lazy laps, I floated on my back and stared up at the sky. The fleecy black clouds looked low enough to touch. Steam rose from the water. Sam swam up beside me; he moved like an eel in the water, smooth and fast, the water barely rippling around him.

"What time are you leaving tomorrow?"

"I should probably be on the road by lunch time. I have an evening lecture."

He sank down, swimming under me, slick body brushing my own, surfacing so that I was lying across him. His genitals bobbed against my backside; he was half-hard—and now so was I. The languid graze of hands and legs, the bump of bodies, the glide of water on sensitive skin: it was playful and erotic at the some time.

"Do you—?" I wanted to ask if he ever got down to L.A., but he interrupted quietly, "Yeah, I do." And his hands slid under me, turning me without effort so that I was lying on top of him.

He kissed me, his lips cool and tasting of chlorine and Sam. I kissed him back.

His legs wrapped around me, his arms slipped under my own, holding me tight. His mouth fastened on mine again and we slowly submerged, the water closing softly over our heads.

I realized I was out of my depth in more than one way.

CHAPTER NINE

I breathed out a gentle stream of bubbles through my nose while Sam's breath filled my mouth and lungs. I opened my eyes as we sank past the pool lights, the underwater world washed out aqua and bright as daylight. It was like being in our own sphere, warm as the womb; I let go, let Sam control it, relaxed in his arms as we drifted down. His mouth exhaled softly into mine. Our feet touched against the floor of the pool, and he pushed off. We shot back up again in a silver spill of bubbles.

Our heads broke the surface, the night air cold against our wet faces.

It was black as pitch. It took me a moment to realize the house lights were off and the music had stopped.

"Hey," I said to Sam, wiping my face. "That was some kiss. The fuses just blew."

The pool water swelled like ink around us as the wind rose again. Sam's feet and legs brushed mine as we tread water.

"It's an electrical storm," he said, staring up at the clouds.

Sure enough, as we watched, lightning forked against the night. The air around us seemed to crackle with a charge—followed by the boom of thunder.

"Oh hell," Sam said. "Swim, Rhys."

I didn't need to be told twice. We raced for the steps, reaching them as the night flashed white—followed by another ear-splitting crack of thunder.

Sam was up and out, reaching back for me. With one hand he practically lifted me out of the water and onto the cement—and I realized exactly how strong he really was.

"It's close." I gasped as another flare lit our way across the bricks to the back door of the house.

"Too close," he agreed. He kept a hand fastened on my upper arm, guiding me through the blur of wooden patio furniture and potted plants.

The wet slap of our feet left footprints that vanished on the paving behind us like ghost steps. Sam felt for the doorknob and pushed into the kitchen. The curtains billowed in the wind from the open windows, shadowy and indistinct in the darkness.

"Stay there and I'll find candles," he ordered.

I didn't bother to answer, stepping back outside, finding my way to the table where I'd left my glasses. I slipped them on and stood there for a moment beneath the vine-covered pergola, watching the lightning flash above the ocean. The air snapped with electricity. The hair on my arms prickled with it.

"Rhys?" Sam called from inside the house.

"Right here," I called back.

Sam appeared in the kitchen doorway, holding a thick candle. The flickering shadow cast sinister angles across his face.

I said, "This would seem to limit the evening's entertainment options."

A slow and wicked grin crossed his face. "I wouldn't say that," he said.

* * * * *

"You're beautiful," Sam said huskily. His big warm hand stroked my belly like he'd stroke a cat. It felt extraordinarily nice, and if I'd known how to purr, I would have. My own laugh was unsteady as my cock filled, twitching like a witching wand.

"So are you."

"You're right. That is funny."

I shook my head, but it was hard to concentrate. I just wanted his hand around me. I dug my heels in the mattress of his bed and thrust up a little. Instead his hand slid upward, stroking my chest, scratching my nipples with his thumbnail. I groaned.

He murmured, "Beautiful and funny and smart—and a liar."

My eyes flew to his face. "I'm not lying," I said—and because my conscience was guilty, I sounded abrupt and defensive.

"I'm teasing you," he said. "I know you're not lying. You're trying to be nice. You don't have to bother. This mug of mine is useful in my line of work."

I stared up at his face; there was strength and character in his harsh ugliness. In fact, he no longer seemed ugly. I liked the fact that he didn't look like everybody else. He seemed familiar and increasingly important to me. Too important to lie to.

"Sam," I began hesitantly.

His mouth touched mine, stopping my words as though he knew what I was going to say, as though he didn't want to hear it, as though he didn't want the moment spoiled. And because I didn't want the moment spoiled either—because I *needed* this moment—I let his lips press me into silence, opening to him in another way.

Sam's kisses made me feel like I'd never been properly kissed before, like it was the first time—like the best of all the firsts: the first giddy swoop of alcohol in your bloodstream or the first sweet bite of dark chocolate on your tongue or the first time you saw a shooting star or felt a man's mouth close on your dick.

His hands gathered me close, hard and competent but cherishing too. I could feel every beat of our hearts echoing in my veins and nerves, beat and answering beat. I felt safe and complete in Sam's arms.

His mouth lifted from mine. "What would you like?" His soft words gusted moist and warm against my ear.

I said with simple certainty, "I want to be inside you."

And he nodded, surprising me with an astonishingly sweet smile. "Sure. How?"

We angled around, knees and elbows bumping, but it was relaxed and easy, as though we were already used to each other, comfortable with each other. Sam stretched out before me, long, strong, and bronzed in the candlelight. Everything in beautiful proportion, the ripple of muscles beneath supple skin, the black dusting of hair over limbs and genitals. His hands and feet were carefully groomed, the nails trimmed and buffed. His hair was neatly cut. He took care of the details, so he did care to some extent about appearances. I felt unexpected tenderness for him, a desire to make up for things.

Bending, I kissed the back of his strong neck, and he shivered.

There was a tube of sunscreen next to the bed, and I squeezed a dollop of creamy white smelling of sea and sand on my fingers, separating the globes of Sam's tight buttocks with one hand and probing that tight little hole with the other.

I pushed a delicate finger in, and Sam uttered a long, low groan, his body clenching.

I smiled. "All right?" I leaned forward, pressed a damp kiss between his shoulder blades. The ring of muscle pulled at my finger as I slid in and out.

"Believe it," he grated.

I took my time, although I could tell he didn't really need it, and then I pressed a second finger in, stretching him, seeking that nub of nerves and gland. Sam pushed back at my hand, drawing me in deeper.

"You're so gentle..." He raised his head, smiling. "Knew when I saw those long, sensitive fingers of yours...*fuuuck*..." His back arched as I found his P-spot.

I moved forward, trying to find his mouth at that awkward angle, massaging the spongy bump with careful fingers. My own cock was rock hard, my balls aching. Sam shuddered and moaned as I lowered myself on top of him. I loved the hard heat of his body down the length of mine.

"This feels so good," I said into his muscular shoulder. "I think I've wanted this practically since that first night."

"You're killing me here, Professor," Sam muttered. His buttocks humped back against my groin, and I pulled my fingers out, replacing them in that moist heat with my dick. So...*good.* I whimpered as his sphincter muscle contracted around me. Began to push and slide in that hot darkness. I couldn't have stopped to save my life.

Sam let out a deep sound, something between a groan and a growl, and began to rock back hard against me. I thrust back at him, closing my eyes, just concentrating on that welcome velvet grab, trying to push deeper, needing to feel joined, united. Heat on burning heat. His fierce silence in contrast to my own wounded sounds as I pumped into him, reaching further and further for that desperate release—

And finally...after delicious and due diligence...at last...there it was. Rolling up out of the yearning struggle of hungry cock and willing ass, slow sweet climax that pulsed through me, warming me with every heartbeat.

"Sam...Sam..." I couldn't help it. Couldn't help the helpless noises as I began to come, pouring out stupid emotional things while my muscles turned to rubber and my cock spurted sticky relief into the clench of his channel.

I collapsed on top of him, gasping for breath, quivering head to foot. I'm ashamed to admit I didn't even know if he'd come. Although the linens felt soggy enough for several orgasms.

A long, long time later, Sam stirred, tipping me off him and pulling the covers over us. I wrapped my arms around him, still wanting the closeness, quietly delighted when his arms wrapped around me again, cradling me against his warmth. He kissed my brow bone and my nose, and I smiled, opened sleepy eyes.

Over his shoulder I could see the candle on the bedstand, hissing and guttering hot wax. "Does that candle look funny to you?" I mumbled. "Kind of green and glowing…?"

He half rolled away, blew the candle out, and pulled me back against his body.

* * * * *

The storm had passed.

I slipped out from under Sam's arm. Slid out of the warm bed, found my glasses, stuck them on my nose. The clock next to Sam read half-past midnight. For a moment I stood there watching Sam sleep in the moonlight, the hard planes of his face relaxed, his hair tumbled, his mouth soft. He was snoring, a tolerable buzz. I found my jeans and tiptoed out of the room while Sam slept deeply on.

Making my way along the hall, I headed downstairs, retrieving my shoes in the hallway.

I was moving swiftly, refusing to acknowledge any unease. I needed to make this fast, needed to get back in case Sam woke and wondered what happened to me. I didn't know how heavy a sleeper he was, and I didn't want to find out the hard way.

So if David Berkeley was lurking in the trees, I didn't see him as I ran through the woods. I came out on the edge of the sunken garden, paused, hands braced on thighs, to catch my breath. The moon, reflected in the black windows of the house, gilded the eucalyptus trees and the broken statues. Cautiously, I made my way down the moss-slick stone stairs, finding a path through the weeds and brambles.

Skulking along the side of the house, sticking to the shadows, I drew near the library window—and froze. Were those voices I heard? I inched closer, trying to see through the shadows and darkness.

I reached the library window and listened.

Silence.

No—there it was. Echoing down the hallway. It sounded like something heavy being dragged along the floor.

Hands on the window ledge, I hesitated. Leaned in.

I heard it again. A voice. Masculine. I couldn't make out the words. I swung myself up, ducking under the shattered window, and the roof crashed down on me...

* * * * *

Cold.

Bitter cold. I shivered—had been shivering if the ache in muscles was anything to go by.

My head ached too, the sick pounding of my temples seeming to rebound through my entire body, pulse hammering, heart thudding too hard. Shell bursts flared behind my eyelids.

What was wrong with me? Was I ill?

I pried my eyes open. Pitch...black...nothing.

Panic washed through me. Was I blind? What had happened to me?

I made an effort to sit up. Sweat broke out on my body, nausea roiled through my belly. I twisted to the side and threw up. I groaned. Threw up again.

When the worst of it seemed over, I scooted back painfully, dropping back shaking onto the cold stone. Why was I lying on the floor? *What* floor?

What...the...fuck...had happened to me?

For a few moments I lay there shuddering, fighting the sickness bubbling in my guts. My head throbbed in time to my heavy heartbeat. The cold of the stone floor seeped...

Cold stone?

Where the hell was I?

I forced my lids open again. Passed my hand in front of my eyes. I could just make out a pale glimmer.

It wasn't my vision. At least…it wasn't only my vision. I was somewhere very dark, somewhere with a stone floor…

It didn't make sense. I tried to remember… I recalled swimming with Sam. Warmth washed through my body. I remembered making love to Sam.

That was the last thing I could recollect. It wasn't a bad place for memories to end, but…

I pushed myself up, having to wait on my hands and knees for the next wave of nausea to subside. I dragged myself the rest of the way to my feet, and hands outstretched, tried to get an idea of the size of the room that held me.

Three steps forward and my hands touched wood. Old wood. Rough and splintered. A door.

Dizzily, I closed my eyes and leaned against the wooden surface.

No way.

No. This had to be a nightmare. I was lying next to Sam right now. Dreaming. And hopefully he would wake me up any minute.

I waited in the unstable blackness. My balance was off, and I needed the support of the door to stay upright. I needed to lie down again. But not here. I needed out of wherever here was…

Vague flashes of running through the woods, the moonlight gilding the ruined garden, and then…nothing.

My heart accelerated, zero to ninety in nothing flat.

I was in the cellar at Berkeley House.

I knew it as sure as I knew anything…which was maybe debatable considering the dumbass way I'd managed things so far.

One thing for sure, no ghost knocked me over the head and threw me into the cellar. I told myself this a couple of times in an attempt to distract my awareness of the sickening chill pressing in on me.

Numbly, I moved my hands over the door, trying to find a knob. A handle.

No reason for panic. Even if there was…something…wrong with the house…and there wasn't. Of course there wasn't. Even if there was…it had nothing to do with me. It had nothing to do with my being in the cellar.

I jerked my head around at a whisper of sound behind me.

Was there motion? A breach in the wall of darkness? I turned back to the door, urgently feeling over its surface.

There it was again, the stealthy slide of something metallic. A tinkling like broken glass—links of a chain?

My groping fingers closed on metal. A handle. I twisted it. Tried the other way. The door stayed firmly closed. I yanked hard. The door didn't budge.

Another insinuation of sound. I threw a frantic look over my shoulder and froze.

Something seemed to stir that utter darkness. Yes. There was movement. Definite movement.

I turned, planted my back against the wood, facing…the wisp of smoke that seemed to unfurl in the void a few feet from me.

My eyes strained to see.

From overhead came the slow draw of a chain. I looked up, flinched as something glinted overhead.

"This isn't real," I said desperately. "I don't believe in this."

I caught motion out of the corner of my eye, jerked my gaze forward. A filmy, cadaverous mist was gathering a few feet away.

No.

I shook my head to clear it. Mistake. The room slanted sickeningly. I could feel something warm trickling down my face. Blood? Tears? My head swam. I blinked hard.

Above me I heard again the metallic rasp of links through a pulley, but I couldn't look away.

The mist was taking shape before me…a tall figure in old-fashioned garments…shoes with spats…trousers…vest beneath overcoat…a top hat…

but all of it indistinct, vaporous, seeming to waver and wane as though moving in a breeze.

The drag of chain was louder, harsher...deafening. It was destroying my ears.

The mist seemed to reshape, a familiar face taking form: long, narrow, diaphanous, with hollow burning eyes and a cruel thin mouth.

Overhead the pulley stopped.

"You're not real," I told the baleful haze. "I don't believe in you."

The eyes seemed to find me in the darkness. *It sees me*, I thought bewilderedly. The cruel mouth turned upward.

I heard the screeching release of chain, felt something heavy hurtle my way. I cried out in shock as something massive and glacial and terrifying slammed into me.

From a distance I heard David Berkeley laughing.

* * * * *

"Thatta boy."

The words trickled through the warm blankness. Someone was stroking my face. My hair. A warm callused hand smoothing from temple to jaw, a long, slow, comforting sweep over and over.

"That's it. That's better."

Sam.

I unstuck my eyelashes.

An indistinct form leaned over me—and beyond his shoulders, the red ball of the morning sun. I was lying on the ground. I could feel the fragrant tickle of weeds and grass, feel the damp warmth of the earth beneath me. Tears of relief flooded my eyes.

I unglued my lips. "Sam?" I croaked.

"Welcome back," he said. He brushed the back of his knuckles against my cheek, wiping the wet away.

"I can't—" It was an effort to get my lips to form sentences. I felt battered, exhausted. "Are my glasses—?"

"Your glasses are broken. I found them outside the house." He added grimly, "That's how I knew to look for you inside." He repositioned, slipped an arm beneath my shoulders. "You think you can sit up?"

I nodded. Sat up with his help. "Sorry," I said to the blur of his face. "Are you pretty pissed off?"

"Yeah, I am. You want to try standing up?"

I nodded. Rested my head in the warm curve of his neck and shoulder. Closed my eyes.

* * * * *

When I next opened my eyes I was in my bed at Oliver's, and it was late afternoon. I squinted at the clock on the bedside table. Sometime after three? My spare pair of glasses sat next to the clock. I slid them on.

3:12 on Monday afternoon.

Shit.

I needed to call the university. I shoved aside the pile of blankets and sat up cautiously. My head ached but nothing like that morning. I reached up, touched a square of gauze and tape. Sam to the rescue, apparently.

I was slowly trying to process everything that had happened since that very long ago night we had spent together, when the open door to the bedroom pushed wide, and Sam, wearing black jeans, black T-shirt, and a black expression, looked in.

We gazed at each other for a silent moment. He had the advantage. There's nothing like being knocked over the head and caught out in a lie to take the wind out of your sails—sitting there in nothing but my underwear didn't help, either.

"Hi," I said, subdued.

"Hi. How do you feel?"

"Okay." That was overstating it. I felt like shit.

"Good. Because I want to know what happened. You up to getting dressed and coming downstairs?"

I guess I could understand why he had no wish to sit with a nearly naked me in my bedroom. "Yeah."

"I'll see you downstairs."

"Sam—"

But he was already gone.

I got up slowly, dressed still more slowly, and went downstairs. Sam was in the kitchen, sitting at the table. There was a mug of tea in front of him.

I took a seat at the table, moving with careful deliberation, trying to jar my head as little as possible.

He watched me without particular sympathy. "You want some tea?"

"Please."

"Milk and sugar?"

I nodded and wished I hadn't.

"You've got a mild concussion," he said, observing me. "I had Oliver's doctor take a look at you while you were out."

"Thanks." My spirits sank lower still at his flat tone.

He placed a mug in front of me. I picked it up, hand shaking. I sipped the hot liquid and felt a little better. I wondered if this doctor had left any tablets for my head.

"So fill me in on what happened after you snuck out of the house." He didn't sound angry, exactly, just...empty.

I told him everything I could remember—which wasn't a lot—and I apologized a couple of times for...not listening to him.

"You mean lying?" he asked, the second time I said it.

I cleared my throat. "Yes."

He was silent for a moment. "Have you ever blacked out like that before?"

"I didn't black out. Someone hit me over the head."

"When I pulled you out of that cellar you were...you appeared to be catatonic."

I stared at him.

"Has that ever happened to you before?"

"No." I took another mouthful of tea, concentrated on keeping my hand steady. "I didn't dream it. There's something in the cellar," I said.

His green eyes rested on my face. This was the face that people across the interrogation table from him saw. I'd blown it with him; I knew that. He wasn't somebody to take a light view of being lied to.

"You mean like a ghost?" he asked at last.

"I mean like..." I stopped. "Yes. Like a ghost," I admitted.

He looked sorry for me. "Rhys."

So I told him everything. I told him about seeing the shade of David Berkeley in the woods the night I had arrived, how I thought it had been Thad, but now I knew for sure it hadn't. I told him about hearing the sound of a guillotine when I'd fallen asleep in the library. I reminded him of the horrifying cold emanating from the cellar.

"You said yourself you'd never felt anything like it," I said.

"It's an unpleasant place. That doesn't mean there's a—an *entity* setting up house down there."

"Thad saw David Berkeley too."

"*Thad?* Thad is not what I'd call a reliable witness."

Neither was I apparently. It didn't look like he was going to bother humoring me at this point.

I said, "What happened to my equipment?"

"Loaded in your car."

I nodded, looked down at my mug. My fingernails were torn and bloodied; I must have clawed the door of the cellar trying to get out; I was just as glad I didn't remember that part.

"There's something down there," I said.

He stared at me with those hard green eyes.

"I think David Berkeley is insane—was insane."

"I think he's dead," Sam said with finality.

I began, "If there is such a thing as life beyond the grave—" His wearied expression stopped me. I said, "Is it unreasonable to think that if someone was driven mad in life, their spirit might be...troubled as well?"

"Yeah, it is. Dead is dead. Over. Done with."

I had the sick feeling he wasn't just talking about mortal coil stuff.

I said, still trying although even I wasn't sure why, "There's something in that house. Something that can't rest. Something that won't let David Berkeley rest." I rubbed my head. Speaking of rest, I wanted nothing more than to lie down again.

Distantly I was aware that Sam had risen from his chair. He dropped a hand on my shoulder, squeezing, then letting go. "You should get some sleep," he said. "You've got a long drive tomorrow."

CHAPTER TEN

I was packing when Mason showed up that evening.

The door bell rang, and then Sam bellowed for me from downstairs. When I came down only Mason sat in the front parlor.

"How are you feeling?" he asked, rising as I entered the room. "You look okay." He stepped toward me and then stopped.

"I'm fine. Just a slight headache." I gave him a wan smile.

Had I been interested in Mason? It seemed as vague as everything else that had happened to me since crawling out of Sam's bed Sunday night.

Mason sat back down and so did I.

"The whole town's buzzing with the news you got yourself clobbered by the local burglars."

"I did?"

"Yeah." He looked puzzled. "Didn't you know?"

"I don't remember much about it."

"Apparently the gang was using the house to store the stuff they stole."

I stared at him, dumfounded. "I didn't see any sign of that."

He smiled his nice, uncomplicated smile. "They were using a hidden room."

"A hidden room?"

He chuckled at my tone. "'Fraid so. Not so hidden as it turned out. Sam Devlin knew all about it."

"He knew about it?" I didn't seem to be able to do more than echo Mason's words.

"Apparently he spent a lot of time in the house when he was a kid."

I felt irrationally hurt that Sam had not shared this knowledge with me. Had he thought it would tempt me too much to return to the house? Little did he know.

"So they caught the burglars?" I asked.

"No. They recovered some antiques, a couple of stereos, and some TVs equipment. They won't catch anyone. I'm sure they wore gloves. Everyone knows that much."

"Yeah," I said slowly. "How would these burglars have known about the hidden room?"

Mason got a funny look on his face. "Now that's an interesting question." He lowered his voice. "It would have to be someone familiar with the house." His eyes shifted to the doorway which led to the room where, from the sound of things, Sam was watching TV—loudly. "Did you know he's on suspension? Something about missing property in a police investigation."

My head was really starting to throb again. I stared at Mason. "You think *Sam*—"

"I just think it's very convenient that he happens to be the guy who discovered the hidden room was full of stolen property right before the sheriffs descended on the place."

I absorbed this slowly, shook my head—unwisely—which made me curt. "That makes no sense at all. He couldn't have been the one who hit me. When I left he was sleeping."

Silently we both absorbed the implications of my certainty on this point.

Mason said, "He wouldn't have been the only person involved, you know."

"He wouldn't have pulled me out of the cellar if—" I stopped because I already knew the answer to that.

Mason said earnestly, "He wouldn't have wanted to kill you. No one would have wanted that."

I nodded. I knew what he was suggesting didn't make any sense—I knew Sam was not part of any local burglary ring—but I was too weary and muddled to reason out how I knew.

Mason rose. "Anyway, glad you're okay. I guess…"

He stopped. I stood up.

"Thanks for coming by," I said. "And thanks for your help…and everything."

"Yeah. You won't be headed this way again?"

"My work here is done." I was trying to put the right note of levity in, but it just sounded dull.

"Sure. Take care," Mason said.

After he left I spent a few moments sitting in the parlor feeling sorry for myself. I listened to the television blasting from the next room.

Finally I rose and followed the sounds to their source.

Sam was sitting in the dark, watching some nature program. Snarling tigers and velvet-eyed antelope—the antelope were getting the worst of it, as usual.

"Can I talk to you?" I asked from the doorway.

A noticeable pause, and then he said, "Sure." He pointed the remote control at the TV.

I sat down across from him and said, "I think you should dig up the cellar."

I couldn't read his face in the flickering light of the television set, but he said without inflection, "Is that so?"

"That cold, that…miasma—it's classic outward manifestation of a haunting."

"Look, you weren't hit *that* hard on the head."

"Just listen to me for a moment. A ghost or a spirit is the sentient presence of someone which stays in the material world after the individual dies. Conventional wisdom is that the ghost is the spirit of a murdered person who wants justice."

"Or someone who died violently and is confused about passing over." Sam turned his head my way. "I read plenty of ghost stories when I was a kid. I know the drill."

"I've investigated a lot of so-called haunted houses, but I've never seen or heard anything like Berkeley House. I guess the sounds and lights can be explained by the burglary gang wanting to scare people off—and maybe someone was dressing up like David Berkeley in the woods—but nothing explains that cellar."

"I think a case of concussion explains that cellar."

I was afraid he had a point. "Okay, maybe, but you felt the cold yourself. You said you'd never felt anything like it."

"The house is built on a cliff over the Pacific ocean. Of course it's cold. Of course it's damp."

I said stubbornly, "I can't believe that what I experienced down there was all due to concussion. You said yourself I was in shock when you pulled me out."

He said, "I know you're not the most honest guy in the world. For all I know, you're not the most stable guy, either."

Well, I sort of had that coming. I said, "I'm sorry I lied to you, Sam. I let my enthusiasm for the book get in the way of my judgment."

He was shaking his head, and I knew he wasn't interested in hearing it.

"But don't let your personal feelings for me get in the way of hearing what I'm saying. I've never had anything like that happen, never experienced anything that didn't have a rational explanation."

He moved as though he were going to get up and walk away, but he stayed seated. "Rhys, Jesus. It's a creepy room. All right? I don't think

David Berkeley was murdered, and he had plenty of time to figure out what he was doing when he set the guillotine up."

"I think Berkeley is trying to hide or protect something in the cellar."

There was a long moment of silence.

"So what's in the cellar?" Sam asked evenly at last.

"The remains of Charity Keith and Aaron Perry."

"Really." It was not a question. Sam's tone was uninterested.

"I might be wrong—"

"You might."

"But I think the reason no one ever heard of Perry or Keith again, why they never turn up in any of the historical accounts, is that Berkeley killed them. And I think that's why he killed himself eight months after they supposedly ran off. Either he couldn't live with what he'd done or…"

"I'm going to hate myself for asking. Or…?"

"Their spirits were haunting him."

"Okay," he said calmly. "Appreciate the theory. What time did you want to hit the road tomorrow?"

* * * * *

My office phone was ringing Thursday afternoon when I got back from giving a seminar on historical research and interpretation. I shrugged out of my tweed jacket, reaching for the phone with my free hand.

"Davies," I said.

"Hello," Sam said. "How are you?"

I sat down hard; I hadn't expected to hear from him again. He sure as hell hadn't indicated he'd be giving me a call when he said his curt good-bye Tuesday morning.

"As good as new," I said. "It's nice to hear from you."

"Yeah. Well. Oliver's on his way home. He liked your idea of digging up the cellar, so he's inviting you back for the weekend."

"Ah," I said. Oliver was inviting me, not Sam; that was clear. And Oliver had initiated the call; it wasn't Sam's choice. My happiness drained away; I was embarrassed to have felt it. Of course it was over. It hadn't even begun, really. We'd fucked a couple of times, and it had been nice, and that was that. Leave it to me to start building it into something more.

As tactful as ever, Sam questioned, "Is that a yes, no, or whatever?"

"Whatever," I said.

Silence. Nothing new there.

"Is that what you want me to tell Oliver?"

It took a little effort, but I got a grip on myself. "No, of course I want to see whatever there is to see. What time should I be there?"

"They're breaking ground Saturday morning." He added, like he was reading a script, "You're welcome to come up Friday evening."

"Okay. I'll see y— Tell Oliver I'll see him Saturday morning."

Silence. "Okay," said Sam.

Another silence. It was torture.

I opened my mouth, but he said, "Drive safe," and hung up.

* * * * *

The sun was shining when I pulled up at Berkeley House on Saturday morning. I could smell the brine and eucalyptus on the breeze. There were a couple of trucks parked in the clearing. Voices and the unmistakable gravelly pound of distant jackhammers echoed from inside the house.

I slammed my car door and started walking but stopped at the sound of someone calling my name.

Oliver waved to me from the sunken garden. Thaddeus was with him—and the contentment on his face was almost painful to see.

"Hello, dear boy," Oliver greeted as I came down the mossy steps to meet them. "Have you seen Sam?"

That answered one question; I'd been wondering if Sam would be around for the festivities. I replied, "I just got here."

"He's probably inside, overseeing the slaves. You'd better go talk to him. He has some bad news for you."

"In that case I can't wait to see him."

Oliver chuckled, exchanging a knowing glance with Thaddeus, who chuckled right back. I never realized how much alike they sounded.

I hiked up to the house, ignoring the anxiety spiraling through my guts. I wasn't sure if I was more uneasy at the thought of facing Sam or the cellar again, but either way, the best thing was to get it over with.

The boards blocking the front door had been removed, and thick brick-colored hoses ran through the doorway and disappeared inside the structure. I stepped over the hoses, following them to the dining room.

It was amazing how the light and noise and bustle diffused the atmosphere. Sam stepped through a side door and spotted me. It seemed to me that he hesitated for an instant. Then he pointed the way I'd come and yelled over the sound of the drills and shattering stone and mortar, "Let's go outside."

I nodded, turned, and preceded him back out. The sunlight and fresh air were a relief. I hadn't realized how much I didn't want to go back inside.

And yet…it suddenly dawned on me that I hadn't felt that sick taint flowing from the cellar.

Sam took my upper arm, surprising me, drawing me to a halt. "I wanted to tell you before you found out some other way. Mason Corwin's been arrested for burglary."

"You're kidding me."

He let go of my arm. "No. He turned up on that video tape you recorded Sunday night. Him and another local man."

"Mason knocked me out and threw me in the cellar?"

"Mike Klinger, the other guy, knocked you out. But Mason let Klinger put you in the cellar, which was pretty stupid since I'd never have started poking around the house if they'd just dumped you in the garden."

I thought this over. I'd wondered what happened to the second video tape. Confiscated as evidence, apparently.

I said, "He must have found out about the hidden room by reading through Berkeley's private papers."

"That's right." His green eyes were approving—and I was sorry to note how much that mattered to me. "He pretty much admitted everything when the sheriffs questioned him. Anyway."

I shrugged. I was sorry about Mason, but... A little maliciously, I said, "He'd suggested that maybe you were involved."

Sam snorted. "Did he?"

"He said you were on suspension because of some missing evidence in a case."

Sam's face hardened. "Small towns. Yeah, that's true. But it's ancient history now. I was cleared, and I've been reinstated. I start back at work next Monday."

"Congratulations."

"Yeah." He gave me a funny look from under his heavy brows. Reluctantly, he asked, "Are you...pretty upset about Corwin?"

"Me?"

"Yeah."

"No."

"Because I thought maybe—"

"While I was sleeping with you?" I interrupted, offended.

To my surprise, he grinned. "Not so much sleeping."

"Not so much." I turned my profile to him, stared at the house. The sounds of the drills seemed to have stopped.

He said quietly, "I don't like being lied to. I don't like the idea of being manipulated."

"Manipulated?" My voice rose. His hand closed around my arm again, but the funny thing, I was relieved by that hard grip. Relieved that he seemed to have trouble keeping his hands off me.

"Shhh." He nodded toward the garden where Oliver and Thaddeus seemed to be in deep conversation by an overgrown hedge. "I may look like a dumb ox, but I'm not." He was smiling, but it didn't reach his eyes.

"If you think I was manipulating you, you're dumber than I thought you were," I said.

"That could be," Sam said evenly.

Oliver was laughing. His voice drifted up from the garden. I watched Thaddeus watching Oliver, and even from this distance I could see the hunger and longing on his face. It made me sad.

And I thought I had an inkling where this particular insecurity of Sam's sprang from. He'd had a lifetime of seeing Oliver operate. And Oliver was quite an operator.

"Is that back on again?" I asked.

"Apparently."

"How long is Oliver home for?" I asked.

"He says for good." Sam watched the two older men. "Thad scared him this last time. We'll see how long that lasts."

I nodded. I could feel Sam watching me. I said finally, "I'm sorry I lied to you. It didn't seem like a big deal at first, and then when it was, I didn't know how to get out of it. There was no manipulation. I…liked you. A lot. I mean, after I got used to the fact that you can be a real jerk."

He didn't smile as he drew me forward. His mouth brushed mine lightly, and something tight and angry in me relaxed. I kissed him back, and for a moment there was nothing and no one else.

"I realize I'm not exactly your type," he said abruptly. "Guys like me generally don't have a chance with guys like you."

"Is this your unique lead in to asking me out?"

"Yes."

One of the workmen stuck his head through the window. "Hey, you better get in here," he said to Sam. "There's something under this floor all right. It looks like a skeleton. Or maybe two."

Sam's eyes met mine. "Congratulations, Professor."

"Kind of gives you a dim view of romance, doesn't it?" I remarked.

He said quite seriously, "I'm willing to take a chance. If you are."

"Okay," I said. "Just this once."

A VINTAGE AFFAIR

A tongue-in-cheek salute to the Southern Gothic literary tradition. I think the story holds up just fine even if you had no idea there was such a thing as a Southern Gothic literary tradition, but I can't deny I really had fun writing this one. That said, I hope A Vintage Affair also has some genuinely poignant moments.

Chapter One

The house was one of those old antebellum mansions—though more reminiscent of *Hush...Hush, Sweet Charlotte* than *Gone with the Wind*. Four fluted, peeling columns and short white railings lined the once-elegant façade. Faded green shutters framed the windows. There was a large moss-covered fountain in the front courtyard and an iron gazebo that looked like an inhospitable birdcage. The house was named Ballineen. They named houses here in the South. Then again, they also married their first cousins, so that was hardly a recommendation.

Austin caught his expression in the rearview mirror of his BMW 507.

"It can't be that bad," he muttered and slid out of the roadster, slamming the door briskly behind him.

It needed to not be that bad. He couldn't afford any problems with this cellar appraisal. Not with Whitney Martyn already hunting for a reason to get rid of him and replace him with Whitney's fiancée, Master Sommelier Theresa Bloch. Losing his position as auction director for one of the oldest wine shops in North America was a thought too painful to contemplate. Austin had worked too hard to get where he was. His family thought his career was frivolous; being an unemployed master of wine would make him a bigger joke than he already was.

He turned at the rattling scrape of metal on stone. A young black man was raking dead leaves and twigs from a narrow walkway. He wore black jeans, a red leather jacket, and a purple do-rag. As he raked, he sang tunelessly along with an iPod.

Austin slung his laptop case over his shoulder and headed for the house. As he strolled past the fountain, it spat up a trickle of gray water. The whole place had an odd earthy scent—like an herb garden gone to rot. The petals of cherry blossoms littered the courtyard and steps to the front veranda like dirty pink confetti after the parade has passed. Spring in Georgia was supposed to be very pretty, but this was March, the wettest month. The skies were slate, and an eerie light seemed to bounce off the dark stone urns with their dead vines.

As Austin reached the covered front porch, the door swung open, and a young woman dressed like the last of the Southern belles in a yellow satin ball gown leaned seductively against the frame and smiled at him.

"Why, hello," she drawled. She was probably in her early twenties, a bit younger than Austin, petite and very pretty with dark curls and dark eyes. "Y'all must be Mr. Gillespie."

"That's right." Austin automatically shook the unexpectedly square, blunt-fingered hand she offered.

"I'm Carson Cashel, the daughter of the house. Did you have any trouble finding us?"

"Uh, no." With five stepmothers and four stepsisters, Austin liked to think there wasn't much a woman could do to surprise him, but he couldn't help staring. Carson Cashel was wearing a hoop skirt, for crying out loud. "No, no trouble."

Just make a hard right after the end of the civilized world.

She smirked at him. "What do you think of my dress, Mr. Gillespie?"

Blushing, Austin tore his gaze from her bodice. Not that he was scoping her out—hardly—but her creamy, pert breasts were all but popping from that nest of lace and ribbon like a pair of doves about to take flight.

"It's very pretty."

"It is, isn't it? I thought you'd look different. Older. Like one of those wine snobs."

Austin smiled lamely because what was he supposed to say to that? He was, probably by definition, a wine snob. Snobbery was part of the master of wine job description. He was paid to be a snob. An articulate, witty snob with a trained palate and a sensitive nose.

Carson burst into a peal of laughter. "I guess y'all are wondering why I'm dressed like it's Halloween."

"Well, I…"

"I'm modeling my costume. For the annual Madison Masquerade Ball on Saturday." She turned away, throwing him a sassy look over her bare shoulder. "Well, come on! You'll want to see the cellar straightaway, I guess."

He wiped his feet on a grungy-looking mat and stepped over the threshold. "Thanks. I think I'm supposed to meet with Mr. Roark Cashel."

"Oh, Daddy is…*indisposed* just now. He'll see y'all later." The bottom of Carson's gown swept along the parquet floor as she bustled along leading the way. Austin had a glimpse of her bare feet as the hoop skirt billowed lightly from side to side.

The house had clearly seen better days. The carpet was a patched and faded blue laurel-wreath pattern; the wallpaper was coming loose in places and had discolored through time and trouble to an uneasy butterscotch hue. There was a lot of furniture, some of it good, a lot of it rubbish. The rooms smelled of rain and disinfectant and…burned bacon. It was at times like these that having a highly trained nose was a liability.

As they passed open double doors leading into a room that appeared to be some kind of back parlor, a woman's thin voice called out, "Carson, honey, is that him?"

"Yes, ma'am!" Carson called back. She paused a few feet down the hall and whirled to face Austin. The full skirt of her gown nearly knocked over a small table. A red vase that looked a lot like Ming rocked wildly. Not that Austin was really an expert, but Rebecca, Stepmother #3, collected Ming ceramics.

"That's Auntie Eudie," Carson whispered. "You don't want to talk to her right now."

"Okay," Austin said. It was true enough.

"Not unless you want to spend all afternoon confabulating your family tree."

"My family tree?" Proof of Austin's own prejudices, he thought she must be implying something social or even racial. He had inherited his mother's wide, rather exotic hazel eyes and her honey-colored complexion—courtesy of Eurasian ancestry—but in most respects he was as WASPish as a man could get and still make his living buying, writing, and consulting on wine. He was certainly as WASPish as one would expect of any of Harrison Gillespie's offspring.

"Genealogy. Six degrees of reparation, Cormac calls it."

"Cormac?" He was starting to lose track. How many people lived in this mausoleum?

"My little brother." Carson whirled away again and narrowly avoided crashing into the man who had appeared soundlessly behind her.

"Why, Jeff, you startled me!" Carson's Georgia drawl suddenly seemed to go still slower and stickier. Austin could practically see the peach juice dripping from every vowel. "I thought you were still in bed."

Jeff certainly looked like he had just crawled out of bed. He was wearing a snug pair of faded jeans low on his tanned hips and nothing else. His blond hair was appealingly tousled. His light eyes met Austin's over Carson's curly head. He winked.

"Why, honey chile, what would be the point without you?"

"You!" She smacked his muscular brown arm. Austin expected to hear a *fiddledeedee!* at the least, but no. She settled for the love tap. "Mr. Gillespie, this is Jeff Brady. He's a...friend."

In a perfectly normal—well, for a Southerner—tone Jeff said, "Hi, Mr. Gillespie. Nice to meet you."

"Hi," Austin replied.

"You're here to catalog the wine cellar?"

"That's right." Austin smiled politely in answer to Jeff's white smile. Jeff Brady was just too good-looking. Austin didn't trust anyone that handsome. Jeff looked like he should be selling toothpaste or seducing a congressional page.

"You've got a job ahead of you."

"He does, doesn't he? That cellar's one thousand square feet if it's an inch." Carson smiled at Austin too. "Well, come on. Time's a wasting." She turned, her gown swirling like churned butter around her.

"Nice dress," Jeff said as she passed him. He smiled at Austin again, and Austin smelled the scent of his shampoo: green apples.

As they started down a long staircase, Carson inquired, "Are you married, Mr. Gillespie?"

"No."

"Goody!" Carson threw him another of those friendly, flirtatious glances. It was probably second nature to her, but it made Austin self-conscious.

They turned down another hallway. The decor seemed to consist of dark wainscoting and a couple of chandeliers that looked ready to fall out of the ceiling.

Carson chattered blithely as they made their way down the murky corridor. "It was such a shock Granddaddy going like that. I don't mean in the arms of Miz Landy, because we *all* knew about *that* peccadillo. I mean his heart giving out. We all thought the doctors had removed it with his appendix years ago. I guess it's a blessing, really."

"A blessing? Really?" Austin offered since she clearly expected some comment from him. He was concentrating on not walking under the sagging light fixtures in case they tore loose and crashed down.

"Oh yeah. What do they call that medical condition when people start stockpiling lots of useless junk?"

"Collecting baseball cards?"

Carson laughed. "You! Naw, *hoarding*. That was Granddaddy. He was always buying and hoarding wine. Whatever money was left, it's all gone now. Or at least it's down in the cellar."

She prattled cheerfully all the way down the narrow stairs that led to a scratched, dark wood door. A key stuck out of the tarnished faceplate.

"It's not locked?" Austin asked, shocked. This wasn't merely tantamount to leaving a liquor store standing open; given the fortune in wine reputedly stored in the cellar, it was equivalent to leaving a bank unlocked.

Carson opened the door. "It's never been locked."

On the other side of the door was an even more rickety staircase. They went down it, Austin taking pains not to step on the hem of Carson's dress and send them both plummeting to their deaths.

A bare bulb threw muddy light against the dingy walls. The cellar smelled of damp and mold and even less pleasant things. At the bottom of the staircase, an elderly black man in a dark suit was spraying a can of Raid as though it were air freshener. He turned at the pound of their feet on the wooden steps.

"Faulkner, Mr. Gillespie is here to catalog Granddaddy's wine," Carson announced. To Austin, she said, "Faulkner is what I guess you'd call our faithful family retainer."

"Uh…" Austin had grown up with full-time domestic staff, but he couldn't imagine referring to anyone as a faithful family retainer.

"Suh," Faulkner said. The exaggerated, deferential tone was at odds with the shrewd dark gaze that met Austin's. Faulkner was probably in his late sixties, his lined skin still supple-looking, though his gray hair and mustache were grizzled.

Carson hitched up her dress and frowned at a black-soled foot. "When we used to be rich, Faulkner was our butler. He was a better butler than he is housekeeper."

"You shouldn't be running barefoot in this cellar, Miz Carson."

Miz Carson ignored that. "Oh, good. Everything is already set up for you." She gazed at the card table and folding chair beneath the gently swinging lightbulb. "If you need anything else, just ask Faulkner. He'll be pleased to give you any help you need."

"Thanks, I should be all right." Austin held up his laptop case. "I've got your grandfather's—"

She interrupted blithely, "Oh, I wouldn't put too much stock in Granddaddy's record keeping, Mr. Gillespie. He was never one for figures, especially at the end. Well, not the arithmetical kind!" She threw the former butler a sly look. Faulkner remained as impassive as one of the battered statues lining the front drive.

Gazing about himself, Austin feared Carson was probably right. But if even half the bottles Dermot Cashel had claimed were in his cellar existed, this cobwebbed dungeon would prove a treasure trove.

"I've set up a table and chair for you over here, sir," Faulkner said, as though Austin could possibly have missed the effort at creating a work space—positioned as it was beneath a giant spiderweb. "I'm afraid there's no electrical extension."

There was barely electricity, if the pallid light from overhead was anything to go by.

Austin thanked him and moved to the table, setting down his laptop case.

"I guess I'll leave you to it," Carson said after a moment as he removed his laptop. "Will you join us for lunch?"

Austin, his attention caught by the nearest rack, bottles blanketed in velvety dust, barely registered that. "Yes, thank you," he said automatically.

"We'll see you at one o'clock," Carson called, grabbing her full skirt in two fists and trotting up the staircase. The stairs shook beneath the energetic pound of her feet. Faulkner unhurriedly followed. The door slammed shut behind them with the finality of the last nail in a coffin lid.

Austin turned his attention to the wine racks. He lifted a bottle from the nearest shelf and gingerly wiped the dust away to study the label. His heart jumped.

A 1970 Château La Gaffelière. The La Gaffelière was a Bordeaux that generally aged well. The 1970 should still be powerful with a good tannin structure. This was a very promising start. Austin returned the bottle to its cradle and looked around for something to wipe the dust off his hands. He should have worn jeans and a sweatshirt, that was obvious, but he preferred to introduce himself to the client looking as professional as possible. He wasn't afraid to get his hands dirty, but that came later.

Gingerly wiping his hands on an oil-stained rag, he moved along the tall racks, looking but not touching.

Cheval Blanc, Gruaud-Larose, DRC, Lafitte, Mouton... Oh yes. This was most definitely worth the trip from DC. Austin could admit now he'd had his doubts when he'd learned Martyn, North, & Compeau had been hired to catalog and evaluate the late Dermot Cashel's extensive wine cellar. He'd even suspected Whitney might be trying to get him out of town in order to further his own plans for bringing his girlfriend on board.

But this was the real thing. Even without the Holy Grail of the legendary Lee bottles, this was an appraisal Austin wouldn't have trusted to anyone else.

And if the Lee bottles really *did* exist?

If they did exist, it was going to be fun trying to find them. As far as Austin could tell, there was no rhyme or reason to the way the shelves had been organized. Bottles of whites and reds were mixed—as were years and vineyards.

He reined in his impatience to delve and returned to the card table, where he switched on his laptop and watched the screen for a wireless connection. No signal. Not even the promise of a signal. Austin sighed. Annoying not to be able to access his e-mail, but he could do that at the hotel this evening. He clicked on the document file he'd saved to his hard drive, and glanced over his notes.

The spreadsheet before him was his own rough effort at estimating the contents of the Ballineen cellar based on the crinkled, purple, ruled sheets of notepaper he'd received from Whitney. He'd deliberately underestimated. The purple stationery and nearly illegible writing did not induce confidence. But even underestimating—and not counting in the Lee bottles—the Ballineen cellar added up to a treasury.

If by some miracle the Lee bottles were here, the chances of their being the real thing were slim. Who could forget the drama of the Jefferson bottles in the 1980s? The greatest wine hoax ever? The very thought of another Jefferson's bottles scandal was enough to raise the hair on the back of his neck. Not many careers could have withstood that hit. His would have crashed on the reef for sure. Fortunately, in 1985 Austin had been four years old and rarely drunk anything stronger than Yoo-hoo.

But had the Jefferson bottles been the real thing? That was the seduction, wasn't it? The allure. Because wine wasn't merely a beverage. Wine was history and art and romance and civility and culture...and maybe a bit of magic.

Austin moved his cursor down the spreadsheet, noting quantities, and then glanced at the towering shelves around him. It was probably going to be easier to take it shelf by shelf, listing the contents and location and then matching it against the inventory sheets.

Especially since the cellar wasn't kept locked. For all he knew the family had been enjoying the Lee bottles with their fried-chicken dinners over the four weeks since Dermot Cashel's death. It was a sickening thought, but it had to be faced. Austin was pretty sure from what he'd seen of the self-titled "daughter of the house," she wouldn't know a bottle of Montrachet from a bottle of Asti Spumante. There was no reason to hope the rest of the clan was any more savvy.

Not that there was anything wrong with drinking what you liked to drink—or not drinking at all, for that matter. Austin really wasn't *that* much of a wine snob, and growing up in Harrison Gillespie's house had been all about learning restraint. Moderation in all things was one of his father's guiding principles—except when it came to marriage.

As a matter of fact, good old Robert E. Lee himself hadn't been much of a drinker. Lee had put his thoughts about the use of liquor in writing: *"My experience through life has convinced me that, while moderation and temperance in all things are commendable and beneficial, abstinence from spirituous liquors is the best safeguard of morals and health."*

Austin pulled a legal pad and pen out of his laptop case. He mapped the cellar floor plan and layout, sketched the shelving units, and labeled each one: *A, B, C*, and so on. He numbered the individual shelves.

At least the thick stone walls of the cellar ensured that the temperature remained cool and stable.

Shrugging out of his jacket, he hung it over the back of the folding chair, rolled his sleeves up, and loosened his tie. He picked up the pad and pen and moved to the first shelf.

Forty minutes later his hair, shirt, and shoes were covered in dust, and the palms of his hands were black. He had never worked on quite so cruddy a site. It was bad enough that he considered going back to his hotel and changing then and there, but it was a thirty-minute drive back to the town of Madison.

The smell of insecticide was fading, only to be replaced by something worse. Far worse.

It smelled like something had died down here.

Austin continued to work—he was on the bottom row of the first shelf—but he began to feel queasy. The smell was truly awful. Did they keep the garbage bins down here? Or were the canned goods going bad?

He put down the pad and pen and wandered back through the maze of tall shelves and racks. The light dimmed the farther he moved into the recesses of the cellar. He was going to need a flashlight when he worked back here. The back portion was nearly in darkness. The shelves and broken furniture threw bizarre geometric shadows against the dingy walls.

Austin's sense of unease, of disquiet, mounted. At the end of the farthest aisle, he stopped and peered more closely at the floor. It was hard to tell in the poor light, but it looked like…

What *was* that?

He took a hesitant step forward.

Something white and waxen rested in the aisle. It sort of looked like a hand stretching out from behind the very last shelf.

Austin stopped.

Yes, it looked like a hand: palm up, fingers outstretched…

He moved warily, reluctantly, forward another step.

It *was* a hand. A man's hand. Not just a hand, because it was attached to a wrist, and what the wrist might be attached to…was concealed by the tall shelving.

"Hello?"

His voice sounded nervous in the cavernous chill of the cellar.

He took another unhappy step forward. He could now make out gray fingernails and dark hair on the backs of curled fingers. He could see every detail, it seemed, every freckle, every hangnail—not that there were any hangnails, for this man's hand was manicured. He could see the glint of a gold watch too. It was as though Austin had suddenly developed bionic vision. Time seemed to slow as he took another dragging step forward.

"Are you all right?" he asked.

He already knew the answer to that. No one who was all right had gray fingernails and skin the color of wax. No one who was all right was that motionless.

The toe of his shoe stopped a couple of centimeters from the lax fingers. Austin closed his eyes, opened them, and made himself look around the corner of the shelf.

The man lay on his back. He was middle-aged. Maybe older. His clothes—expensive clothes—were rumpled and dirty. He needed a shave. His mouth was slack and open, his lips blue-gray. His black hair was mussed and had fallen in his dull, sunken eyes. He stared sightlessly up at Austin.

Chapter Two

Austin drew hastily back. He leaned against the shelf and closed his eyes, sucking in a couple of deep, quavery breaths.

"Crap."

He needed to do something. What? It was so unbelievable. He peered around the shelf again.

Yes. Believable or not, it was still there. *He* was still there. The dead man.

The only dead person Austin had ever seen before was his mother. He had been nine, and even in death she had been very beautiful. Beautiful but not alive. Despite the things one read about the dead, she had not looked like she was sleeping. This guy did not look like he was sleeping, and he was not beautiful.

Who was he? What was he doing back here? How had he died?

Austin couldn't tell at a glance, and he didn't want to look more closely than that.

He turned and walked very calmly, very quietly back to the front of the cellar, then up the stairs, through the scratched and paint-blistered door, and up the next flight. It seemed strange to be moving with such calm deliberation when people in movies either fainted or screamed and ran, but that was probably shock. Or maybe *this* was shock. This blank lack of feeling.

A man was coming down the first flight of stairs. He wore black jeans and a black sweater. He was too much like Carson to be anyone but a brother. Same slim build, dark eyes, dark curls. He checked at the sight of Austin.

"You're Gillespie?" He too had that soft Southern inflection.

"Yes. I just found—"

"I don't think y'all should be down there on your own."

Truer words were never spoken. Austin started to speak again, but the man, his own age or younger, said, "I tell you what. I'll stay down there with you. I'm Cormac Cashel." Cormac was scowling, but the look he directed at Austin was definitely a considering one.

In another time and place, Austin might even have welcomed that *au courant* appraisal. He and Richard had split up three months ago, and he just hadn't had the time, energy, or inclination to get out and meet people. As rattled as he was, he couldn't help noticing that Cormac was very attractive, though his interest seemed a bit surreal at the moment.

"I found something in the cellar," Austin blurted.

Cormac went rigid. "Then it's true? You've found them? You found the Lee bottles?"

"No. No, I mean there's some*one* down there."

"Oh." The eager attention faded. "That's Faulkner. Don't let him scare you."

"No, it's not Faulkner. It's...someone else." It occurred to Austin that the corpse in the cellar probably belonged to a family member and that he was about to deliver terrible news. "He's not...well."

"That'll be Daddy," Cormac said sardonically. "He's often not well. Y'all want me to throw him out of there so you can work?"

"Uh...I don't know how to say this..."

Footsteps pounded lightly down the stairs, and another figure appeared behind Cormac. Austin recognized the too-handsome Jeff Brady. He'd put on a white tailored shirt but still exuded a sexy, just-rolled-out-of-bed-and-not-because-he-was-sleeping air. He halted, spotting Cormac and Austin, and Austin guessed that Brady had been planning to pay him a visit too.

Maybe there was no TiVo this far from town?

"Something wrong?" Brady asked, looking from one man to the other.

"Naw," Cormac said, throwing him a look of dislike.

"Yes," Austin said. He wasn't sure why he was now talking to Jeff, except that he had the impression that Jeff was not part of this family. Plus Jeff appeared able to handle pretty much anything that came his way. A sort of cool, smiling authority; Beauty Stuart confounding the Union commanders.

"What is it?" Jeff inquired. "Or would you rather show me?"

"I think I'd better show you." To Cormac, Austin said, "I'm sorry, but I have bad news. I think your father may be... There's a body in your cellar."

"What?"

Cormac recoiled, and Brady pushed past him on the narrow staircase. "Show me."

Austin did an about-face and led the way quickly downstairs. Jeff was right behind him. Austin wasn't sure if Cormac followed or not. He sort of hoped not, but mostly he was thinking that the scent of green apples made a welcome change from Raid and death.

"How did you happen to find him?" Jeff asked, brisk and businesslike.

"I was trying to work out why it smelled so bad down here. I couldn't concentrate."

"Yeah, I guess you must have a pretty sensitive nose in your line of work."

"I don't think anyone could have missed this." Despite the old-house smells, the damp and the decay, Austin was still baffled no one had picked up on that putrid odor earlier. As he and Jeff reached the bottom, the smell of rotting garbage made his stomach churn. He'd have liked to wave Jeff on to the back of the cellar without him, but pride insisted that he lead the way.

All the same, he stood on the other side of the shelving, hand protectively shielding his mouth and nose while Jeff went around the corner.

There was a long moment of silence, and then Jeff reappeared, his handsome face grim.

"What makes you think that's the old man?"

Austin lowered his hand. "Isn't it?"

"Naw."

"Who is it?"

Brady opened his mouth, then closed it. "I think we'd better call the police."

Austin nodded, grateful to escape the cellar and its grisly contents.

They started upstairs only to be met by a delegation of concerned citizens. A tall, thin, beaky-looking man with curly silver hair and a beard that looked like pheasants could live long and prosper in its strands was leading the charge. Cormac and Carson followed—the resemblance between them was even more striking now that Carson had changed out of her ball gown and into jeans—seeming torn between an adolescent mix of nervous amusement and awkwardness. Behind them was a washed-out woman with alarmingly red hair and a very nice triple strand of pearls. Sasha, Stepmother #4, collected pearls in all shapes and sizes, and Austin knew a nice set when he saw them.

Pearls, that is.

Trailing them all was Faulkner, looking as impassive as ever.

"What the hell is going on here?" demanded the bearded gentleman, who Austin guessed was Roark Cashel, the patriarch.

"There's a corpse in the cellar," Jeff announced. "Everyone needs to go back upstairs."

"That isn't possible," quavered the lady in pearls. The genealogical Auntie Eudie, Austin presumed.

Carson and Cormac gripped each other's arms.

"Nonsense," Roark said. He tried to propel his way forward, and Austin nearly overbalanced on the narrow stairway. Jeff steadied him with one hand—and planted the other in Roark's chest.

"I'm sorry, sir, but you've got a crime scene downstairs."

"This is my house!"

"Sure, but you don't want your fresh fingerprints found down there, Mr. Cashel. It'll just confuse things when the police get here."

"Police!" repeated all four of the Cashels.

"That man didn't crawl in here to die a natural death," Jeff said. "Of course we have to call the police."

Roark smelled of whiskey and sleep sweat and something else. Fear. Reaction suddenly hit Austin. His stomach lurched, and he wondered if he was going to vomit on the old man's striped socks. And how unsanitary was that? Running around in socks in these ruins? Now that he thought about it, Roark's feet didn't smell any too sweet either.

"Can someone let me through?" he requested.

His desperation must have made itself felt because they all began to back up and shuffle around, the staircase squeaking and groaning ominously beneath their feet. The Cashels were talking at once, but Austin didn't listen. His sole concern now was getting out of there without disgracing himself.

He jumped when Jeff placed a light hand on the small of his back. Kindly meant or not, that was not a normal gesture from a straight guy. Austin had pegged Jeff for aggressively heterosexual the minute he'd seen him, but nonetheless that casual touch seemed to reach right through him and cup his balls in a friendly fashion.

The clumsy procession reached the top level at last, and Austin managed to work his way to the front of the line while yet restraining himself from actually shoving anyone down the stairs. Carson discreetly indicated the powder room off the front hall, and he strode quickly down the corridor to a tiny room with red velvet wallpaper and dark paneling. After locking himself behind the flimsy door, he turned the taps on the sink and proceeded to be quickly and comprehensively sick.

After he'd flushed the toilet, he splashed a gallon of cold water on his face, rinsed his mouth, and gazed in disgust at himself in the diamond-shaped mirror. He tried to imagine his father in this same situation. Harrison Gillespie losing his breakfast just because he'd seen a dead body!

"Man up, for crap's sake," Austin muttered to his wan reflection.

He splashed more cold water on his bloodless face and finally abandoned the refuge of the powder room.

He could already hear what Whitney was going to say when he heard about this. Austin watched enough TV to know that the cellar was going to be labeled a crime scene and he was probably not going to be allowed back in there for days. Maybe weeks. Whitney was going to be seriously pissed. In fact, he was liable to see this as Austin's personal failure.

Speaking of personal failures, now that Austin had a chance to think, he needed to get his laptop out of the cellar immediately. He couldn't take an even remote chance that it might be confiscated. It wasn't like he could do any more damage to the crime scene than he'd already unwittingly done, after all.

He started down the hall. Not tiptoeing, exactly, but trying to walk quietly. He could hear voices—agitated voices—drifting from one of the side rooms. By the sound of things, the Cashels were not taking the news of the body in the cellar well. But then he couldn't blame them. He wasn't taking it well either.

He had just reached the hall entranceway when his cell phone sounded with the countdown-to-spaceship-launch ringtone that meant Ernest was calling.

Austin reached for his phone. Jeff Brady stuck his head out of the parlor doorway.

"There you are. I was starting to wonder whether y'all decided to sneak out the back."

Since there was nothing Austin would have liked more, he gave Jeff a withering look and answered his cell.

"Hey, Ernesto."

Ernest said in his gruff voice, which made him sound more like ninety than nine, "They're sending me to boarding school in the fall."

Uh-oh. He'd known this was coming—just not so soon. He should be in Maryland, not way down yonder in the land of cotton.

"It's for sure?"

"Harrison broke it to me half an hour ago."

For some reason Ernest had called their father by his first name from the time he had been old enough to speak. And more astonishing, Harrison had allowed it. But then Ernest was a remarkable kid. The family joke was he'd been speaking in complete sentences at nine months and offering his opposing political viewpoint at eighteen. The real joke was that it wasn't a joke.

"McDonough is a good school," Austin said. "They've got riding stables and a great science program."

"I don't want to go." Uncompromising.

Austin licked his lips, tried to find the right words. "It's not like you imagine. A lot of it is really fun."

"I've done my research. I don't want to go."

Sometimes it was easy to forget that despite the 159 IQ and his unequivocal way of expressing himself, Ernest was just a little kid.

"Listen, Ernie, I got through it. Harrison—Dad—got through it. It's... just part of growing up."

"I'm not going."

"We'll talk about it when I get home, okay?"

"When are you coming back?"

Austin looked at Jeff Brady, who was listening in on his phone conversation with unabashed interest. "Well, it might be sooner than I was thinking. But I'll call you from my hotel tonight. We can talk more then."

"We can talk, but I'm not changing my decision."

"Try to keep an open mind."

"I don't see any point. I already know it will interfere with my work." Ernest's voice wobbled infinitesimally as he added, "And I'll be homesick."

Austin's already sensitive stomach knotted unhappily. "I'll call you tonight. It's hard to talk right now."

"What time?"

"I'm not sure. But I will call." For an instant it went through Austin's mind to tell Ernest the setup. He probably knew more about a homicide investigation than Austin.

"Bye." Ernest disconnected.

Austin turned off his iPhone, and Jeff asked curiously, "Your son?"

"My brother." Half brother, actually, but it wasn't a distinction Austin made.

"Are you, er, married?"

"Er, no."

Jeff scratched his jaw thoughtfully and gave Austin a funny look from beneath his long, dark lashes. "Domestic partnership?"

"I'm not involved with anyone," Austin said shortly. It wasn't anyone's fault that things hadn't worked out with Richard, but it was another failure, wasn't it?

Jeff smiled. On a scale of one to ten, with one a wallflower and ten charismatic world leader, the smile was a devastating nine. Austin narrowed his eyes in the full force of it.

"I...see," Jeff said, forcing those lazy, no-account Southern vowels to put in a full day's work.

Austin stared. He began to think he had got Jeff Brady all wrong. "I need my laptop," he said. It was the first thing that popped into his mind.

Jeff seemed to follow the non sequitur without trouble. He looked regretful. "Sorry. The cops said to keep the cellar sealed off till they get here."

"You don't understand. If they hold on to my laptop for any length of time, I'm ruined."

Jeff's blond brows rose. "You got naughty pictures on there or something?"

"Of course not." Did he? It was Austin's personal computer. There were a lot of things on there he wouldn't choose to share with the public. Nothing illegal. Opinions of wines, vineyards, vintners, and others that didn't need to be public. Not without softening them considerably. "I've got my notes for my next column, the rough draft of this week's blog—and I have to be able to check my e-mail. My entire work world is on that laptop."

"They're not likely to hold your laptop," Jeff reassured. "They might glance through it just to verify that you are who you say you are. I'm sure it wouldn't be more than a few hours. Maybe overnight."

Austin blanched. He *lived* on his laptop. It was like being told he wouldn't have access to his body for a day or so.

"Jeff…" He stopped. What could he say? Why should Jeff Brady care about Austin's problems?

And yet…Jeff tipped his head, seeming to consider all that Austin was not saying.

His eyes were green, Austin noticed absently. The rich, mysterious green of an old Bordeaux bottle.

Seeing Jeff's indecision, Austin urged, "Please. I can't do any more harm than I've already done. My fingerprints and footprints are all over the place."

"True." Jeff glanced back at the parlor where the Cashels were, from the sound of things, having some kind of family debate. "Okay. I'll do this for you." It seemed sort of a solemn way to put it, but Austin was too relieved to analyze, and Jeff added, "But we better make it quick."

Austin flashed him a grateful look and sprinted down the dark hall. Jeff was right on his heels, running lightly, swiftly. They pounded down the staircase.

The cellar looked undisturbed, but breathing in that horrifying stink now, Austin couldn't understand how he hadn't smelled it the minute he'd walked in. The insecticide had masked it very effectively.

He turned off his laptop, waiting impatiently for it to power down while Jeff prowled restlessly back and forth. Every now and then he threw Austin a look that seemed both curious and expectant. Austin didn't know what to make of it.

Watching Jeff, then glancing back at the shadowy recess where the body lay, Austin said, "You know him, don't you?"

"Who?"

"The dead man."

Jeff stopped walking. "What makes you say that?"

Austin thought back to those moments when Jeff had first seen the body. "You weren't surprised when you saw him. You were…taken aback, but not really surprised."

"You lost me."

"You were surprised he was dead, but you weren't surprised that, if someone *was* dead, it was him."

Jeff stared. He laughed. "That's not bad."

Absurdly, Austin felt a flicker of pleasure that Jeff seemed even fleetingly impressed. "When I asked you who he was, you almost answered. Then you thought better of it." Austin's laptop screen went dark. The keyboard lights went out. He grabbed the laptop and thrust it into its case, zipping it up.

Jeff was still gazing at him with that funny smile—almost like they knew each other. What was that about? Austin felt like he was missing something. Like there was an undercurrent running that he was unaware of.

"How did he die?" He slung the bag over his shoulder.

Jeff was already moving back to the stairs, clearly uneasy about the possibility of their being discovered down there. "Couldn't you tell?"

Austin shook his head, swallowing queasiness as he remembered the dead man's face.

"Someone slammed him on the side of the head with that good old favorite: the blunt instrument." Jeff added thoughtfully, "But I don't think this cellar was where he died."

"Then where did he—"

But Jeff was already running up the stairs. Austin had a very nice view of Jeff's trim, tight ass and the flex and bunch of muscles beneath his jeans as he moved—and he moved well. A natural athlete.

They reached the first-landing door. Jeff glanced back. "I'd appreciate it if you'd keep those thoughts to yourself for now."

"You mean if the police ask—"

"Not the police, naw. I'm not worried about the police. I mean, don't say anything in front of the family."

What was the big deal? It wasn't like they had tampered with evidence. Jeff definitely seemed on the paranoid side. Not that it mattered. He owed Jeff, and it was a harmless enough request. Jeff wasn't asking him to lie to the police, after all. Austin nodded. "Sure."

"Thanks...Austin."

It was a casual comment, but something in the deliberate way Jeff said his name, said *Austin* as though he was testing it, trying the sound of it on, affected Austin in an almost visceral way. For an instant they stared into each other's eyes.

Jeff treated him to another of those winning smiles and held the door for him.

"Where've you been?" Cormac demanded as Austin and Jeff walked into the parlor.

Austin started to respond, but Cormac interrupted. "I mean him." He glared at Jeff with loathing.

Jeff gazed coolly back. "I went to check on Mr. Gillespie."

"You poor child," the fragile, titian-haired Auntie Eudie murmured to Austin. "You come and sit right down here." She patted the green velvet upholstery, and a gust of dust moved through the air. She sneezed.

It had been a long time since anyone had called Austin a child. Not that twenty-nine was so old. In oenophile terms, he was still a young wine: light, fresh, and...um...fruity. He obeyed her summons and sat gingerly beside her on the sagging sofa.

She peered at him nearsightedly. "Are you feeling better?"

"Yes, thank you," Austin answered hastily. He was embarrassed about earlier. That had been more about his sensitive nose than his sensitive nature.

Roark stood at the liquor cabinet, putting away what appeared to be fine Kentucky bourbon and living up to the reputation of the gin blossoms on his nose and cheeks. He asked of no one in particular, "Who *is* the infernal fellow? That's what I want to know. What the hell was he doing in our cellar?"

Auntie Eudie said, "Mr. Gillespie is here to appraise Papa's wine cellar, Roark."

"Not *him*. Not the damned Yankee." Roark was impatient. "The dead man!"

The Cashels all gazed expectantly at Austin. Did they think he'd brought the dead man along in his laptop case?

"I never saw him before in my life," Austin asserted.

"'Course not," Carson said. She gave a shiver and went to Jeff, who put his arm around her wide shoulders.

"Now, now, honey," Jeff murmured with all the sincerity of an AT&T recording.

"Just who *are* you?" Cormac demanded, watching Jeff cuddling his sister.

Carson flushed. "Hush, Corrie. Mr. Brady is a friend of mine."

"Since when?"

"Since last night at the Blind Pig Tavern."

Cormac's face grew even tighter and more sullen, and Austin began to wonder if all those alarming Southern plays he'd had to study in school hadn't maybe got it right.

Roark said, "I find it most suspicious that this man appears at the same time a body turns up in the cellar."

"What are you suggesting?" Jeff was grinning.

"I just find it most suspicious that these two events should coincide."

Carson giggled. "Exactly which two events are you referring to, Daddy?" She was an engaging minx. Austin had to give her that.

Roark's already red face went the color of the Confederate flag.

"Mr. Gillespie, are you by any chance related to the Macon Gillespies?" Auntie Eudie inquired, ignoring the unpleasantness brewing around her.

"I don't think so."

"I thought you were going out with Blythe Landreth," Cormac said to Jeff as Roark launched into a diatribe about respecting one's elders.

Jeff replied, "Blythe and I see each other now and then. And I see other people now and then." He smiled at Carson.

Auntie Eudie looked disappointed. "The Gillespies are lovely people. An old and respectable family. I believe they own a pine-tree plantation down Middle Georgia way."

Austin murmured politely, his ear attuned to Cormac and Jeff's cool exchange. Not that it was any of his business.

Faulkner appeared in the doorway. He waited till the Cashels had stopped bickering and fallen silent. When he had their attention, he spoke to Roark using that exaggerated accent. "The *pohleece* are *heah, suh.*"

Roark knocked back the rest of his drink. "Show them in, Faulkner."

Chapter Three

The Morgan County sheriffs turned out to be a paunchy, gray-haired investigator and an eager, young black officer, both in spick-and-span powder blue uniforms. Austin was expecting shades of *In the Heat of the Night*, but the two sheriffs were professional and courteous. Captain Thompson, the senior partner, greeted Jeff by name and invited him to accompany them downstairs, asking the rest of the family to wait in the parlor.

"Well!" Auntie Eudie remarked after Jeff and the sheriffs disappeared down the hallway.

"I told you there's something not right about him," Cormac said triumphantly.

"Where did you say you know that young man from, Carson?" Roark demanded.

"We went to the same high school, Daddy. Jeff was starting quarterback the two years the Bulldogs won the league championships."

"I thought he moved to Savannah," Cormac said. Clearly, he felt Jeff should have stayed in Savannah.

"He did, silly. To go to college. He came back." Carson was smiling at her brother; a smile both teasing and understanding. It seemed to appease Cormac in some indefinable way. The resemblance between them was really striking. Not *just* brother and sister, Austin thought. Fraternal twins.

Confirming his thoughts, Carson ruffled her brother's hair. She said to Austin, "Corrie is the baby of the family."

"By ten minutes!" protested Cormac, flushing.

"Jefferson Brady!" Auntie Eudie exclaimed. "I thought I recognized him. He has the Brady eyes. A very distinct color. Myrtle green," she informed Austin. He nodded politely. "Yes, there have been Bradys in Morgan County as long as there have been Cashels. Maybe longer. I expect Jefferson came home after his daddy died. *Such* a tragedy."

"What was?" Austin asked. He couldn't pretend that he wasn't curious about Jeff Brady.

"Richmond Brady killing himself like that. He shot himself right beneath the portrait of old Gideon Brady." Austin must have been looking blank because she added helpfully, "The general."

"Eudora, nobody gives a rat's ass about Jefferson Brady's family," Roark informed her.

Eudora's cheeks went pink. "Mr. Gillespie does."

"It's none of Mr. Gillespie's business," Roark returned. "You shouldn't be discussing our friends and neighbors with a Yankee wine merchant."

It was so outrageous that Austin nearly laughed. With the exception of Jeff and the sheriffs, they were all like something out of a play. Though more along the lines of *While the Lights Were Out* than *A Streetcar Named Desire*.

"Now, Daddy." Carson came to join Austin, perching gracefully on the arm of the old sofa.

Roark ignored her. "Did you find those bottles?" he demanded of Austin.

"The Lee bottles? Not yet."

"They're not there," Roark said with bitter satisfaction.

"You've looked for them?"

"Of course not. They were never there."

Something about the way Roark said that didn't quite ring true. Was that because he feared the bottles had never been a reality or because he knew what had happened to them? "You know that for a fact?" Austin inquired.

"Daddy," warned Carson.

"Don't *Daddy* me. You know as well as I do your granddaddy's warped sense of humor. He's laughing in hell right this minute at the notion of us thinking our fortunes are saved because of those damned wine bottles."

"If those bottles are real, they're worth a fortune," Austin told him.

"Those bottles are a myth. Robert E. Lee was not a drinking man. Anyone who knows anything about him knows that much. Lee understood the Southern gentleman's duty to present an example at all times." Roark drained his glass and set it on the cabinet. He dropped into a spindle-legged chair upholstered in faded silver grape leaves and directed a challenging look Austin's way.

"Lee was a man of temperate habits. That's true," Austin said. "I've done a lot of research on him in the past weeks. He kept a fully stocked wine cellar, as befitted his rank and position. We know that for a fact because we have the letters his wife wrote him regarding moving the contents of the cellar before the Federal occupation of Arlington House in the spring of 1861."

"Take that, Daddy." Carson's fingers lightly played with the hair at the back of Austin's collar. He started at that playful graze of fingertips. She winked. "Your collar was turned inside out."

Cormac said suddenly, "I've been reading your 'Message in a Bottle' column."

"Oh?" Everything Cormac said was in that same intense, semibrooding manner, so Austin had no clue whether that was a compliment or a prelude to vivisection.

"I want to be a writer too."

"You should read Cormac's stories. They're wonderful," Carson said. Austin's collar was still not right. He tried not to jump this time, but it was weird, right? This tickling the back of his neck in a room full of people?

"Cormac is such a clever boy." Auntie Eudie sighed. "Although I do wish everyone didn't die or go mad in his stories."

"I want to write novels," Cormac said, scowling as though he expected someone to object.

"That's great," Austin said. "I only write nonfiction."

"Yes," Cormac said grimly, obliquely.

Who knows where that might have gone, because Jeff and the sheriffs tromped back in.

"Folks, the crime-scene people have arrived, and we're going to let them get down to business," Captain Thompson stated. "Meanwhile, we're going to interview each of you privately." His gaze fell on Austin.

Pick me, pick me. He wanted out of this nuthouse posthaste. It was obvious he wasn't going to be doing a cellar appraisal anytime soon, so the faster he got back to Maryland and his endangered job, the better. He didn't trust whatever machinations Whitney might be up to in his absence.

But after that considering appraisal, Captain Thompson said, "Why don't we start with the ladies. Ma'am?" That was addressed to Auntie Eudie, who rose all aflutter, tugging nervously at her woolly pink cardigan and touching her hair as she led the sheriffs to a room where they could "set up camp."

Jeff took her place on the sofa beside Austin.

"How're you holding up?" He offered a glimpse of that spectacular smile, although his eyes were serious.

"Fine. Good." Austin realized he was nervously tugging at loose threads on the sofa arm and stilled his hand before the last of the upholstery unraveled.

Jeff started to speak, but Faulkner appeared in the doorway.

"Shall I serve sandwiches and coffee here in the parlor, Miz Carson?"

"Oh!" Carson looked perplexed. Austin saw the dilemma. They needed to eat, but sitting down to luncheon with a murder investigation going on around them was a tad socially awkward. Sandwiches on a tray was probably the ideal solution, although the idea of food sent his own stomach somersaulting.

A loud snoring interrupted Carson's response. They all glanced to the corner where Roark slumped in his chair, sleeping. His mouth was slightly ajar, his face twitching as though he was still arguing in his dreams.

"That would be lovely, Faulkner," Carson said with the perfect self-possession developed by generations of Southern beauties in the face of flood, famine, and Civil War. "I guess you better serve those sheriffs something to eat too. We don't want them to get in a bad mood and arrest somebody."

Faulkner nodded graciously and withdrew.

"Where are you staying tonight?" Jeff quietly inquired of Austin.

"The Stonewall Jackson Inn in Madison." Why were they practically whispering? Austin wasn't sure, but he was increasingly confused by Jeff Brady's signals. Assuming they *were* signals and not just Southern discourse.

"Very nice," Jeff commented.

Austin nodded. The hotel was nice. Nineteen individually themed, luxury guest rooms' worth of nice. Distractedly, he checked his watch. One thirty. He couldn't believe how late it was. He mustn't forget to phone Ernest.

"I guess you'll be driving back tomorrow morning?" Jeff persisted.

"I suppose so. Assuming they don't arrest me."

Jeff chuckled.

Auntie Eudie returned with sparkling eyes and flushed cheeks. She looked like she'd been having a wonderful time.

"They want to see you next, honey," she said to Carson.

Carson left the room. Jeff rose so that Auntie Eudie could take his place on the sagging sofa. He sauntered across the room and leaned against the wall beneath a gold-framed portrait of a dashing-looking Confederate officer. There was, Austin thought wryly, a marked resemblance, although presumably Jeff wasn't aware of it. Arms folded, he was studying the others while not seeming to pay them much attention.

"It was very exciting," Auntie Eudie informed Austin. "They showed me a snapshot of the dead man and asked me if I recognized him."

"Did you?"

"No. He does have the Williams eyebrows. I wonder if he might be a relation."

Jeff asked, "Did you ever see him around here?"

Roark spluttered in his sleep.

"No." Auntie Eudie was definite. "I've never seen him before."

Cormac said suddenly, roughly, "I was wondering if you'd like to take a look at my work."

Austin realized he was being addressed. "Now?"

Cormac nodded, scowling.

"I don't think we're supposed to wander around till we've been interviewed, do you?" Austin was asking Jeff. Possibly because Jeff seemed like the only normal person in the house. Although that was stretching a point.

"Naw. Nobody gets to leave till everyone has been questioned."

Cormac said accusingly, "You were wandering around!"

Jeff shrugged.

"*He* was wandering around," Cormac informed Austin. Was Austin supposed to take sides?

Faulkner reeled into the room, bearing an enormous silver tray, and just managed to lug it to the table in the corner without overbalancing.

"Thank you, Faulkner," Auntie Eudie said vaguely. "I suppose we ought to feed those police persons too."

Faulkner gave her a speaking look and departed.

"Why are you so tight with the police, anyway?" Cormac asked Jeff. "Are you a cop?"

"Naw." Jeff pushed lazily away from the wall and went to the table where Auntie Eudie was examining the insides of sandwiches and making pleased noises.

"Ham or turkey?" Jeff asked Austin.

Austin consulted his stomach and decided turkey was the lesser of two evils.

He rose as Auntie Eudie asked, "How do you take your coffee, Mr. Gillespie?"

"In a Starbucks cup, I bet," Cormac said.

"I don't drink Starbucks." Austin nearly added *or wine from a box*, but that really was snobbery. Besides, he'd had some decent boxed wines. He took a cup from Auntie Eudie. "Turkey, please," he told Jeff.

Jeff started to hand him a plate with a sandwich.

"Now that's woman's work!" Auntie Eudie exclaimed, and Jeff reddened and dropped the plate as though it were on fire.

"Corrie, they want you now," Carson said, returning to the room.

Cormac swore.

"It's not so bad, honey." Carson came straight to the table where the others stood exchanging plates and cups. "Well, what do you think?" she said to Jeff.

Jeff seemed to be studiously avoiding Austin's gaze. "What's that, honey?"

"The dead man is Dominic Williams."

"I knew I recognized those eyebrows," Auntie Eudie mumbled through a mouthful of ham sandwich. "But I don't recall a Williams boy named Dominic. Who is he?"

"Among other things, he's the master sommelier at Old Plantation House." Carson was looking directly at Austin. "Now what do y'all think of that?"

"The *master sommelier*?" Austin repeated uneasily.

"What is a sommelier?" Auntie Eudie inquired.

"A wine steward with a fancy title," Jeff replied. He was studying Austin too, his expression unrevealing.

"That can't be a coincidence," Austin said slowly.

"Nope. I'd say not."

"Did you know Dominic?" Auntie Eudie asked Austin.

"Me? No." At least...he didn't think so. It was always possible he'd run across Williams professionally at a wine tasting or a workshop or some other industry event. It was hard to judge by the one glimpse he'd had of him.

"The sheriffs sure don't think it was any coincidence," Carson said. She selected a ham sandwich. "I must say it was a terrible shock seeing Dom like that."

"How exactly did you know this gentleman? You never brought him here." Auntie Eudie turned to Austin. "You're not eating anything, Mr. Gillespie?"

Austin picked up a sandwich and tried to look like he was between bites.

"Dom and I used to run into each other now and then." Carson was blushing.

Jeff gave a wicked chuckle, and Carson laughed, but she still looked uneasy. "I just don't see why Dom would be in our cellar."

"Maybe he missed you?" Jeff teased. "Maybe he was hoping for a midnight assignation."

Carson seemed to give this serious thought, chewing contemplatively.

"Or maybe he was searching for those wine bottles." Jeff was looking at Austin as though he thought Austin might have a theory.

"If the plan is to auction off the cellar, maybe he was trying to get a firsthand look at the inventory," Austin offered. It seemed unlikely the sommelier of a fine restaurant would have to resort to sneaking through his neighbors' cellar, but then everything that had happened since he'd arrived in this house seemed unlikely.

"Maybe."

Carson said, "If he wasn't in *our* cellar, I'd say Henry knocked him off."

"Henry?" Austin looked from Carson to Jeff, who had started to speak but instead took a bite of sandwich.

"Henrietta. The current Mrs. Williams. I never met a more jealous hag than Henrietta Williams. We were at school together."

Cormac returned, looking grouchier than ever. "Daddy!" He shook his father awake. "Daddy, the sheriffs want to talk to you."

Roark came awake blinking and mumbling, "The light was green when I entered the intersection."

"You'll never guess who the man in our cellar is," Cormac informed them. "It's that good-for-nothing lowlife Dominic Williams. The one who was sniffing around Carson all this winter."

Roark took his hand from his face and snarled, "Why, I told that bastard if I saw him around here one more time, I'd fill him full of lead."

Jeff suddenly laughed. Austin looked at him. "Your expression," Jeff said. "You look like you think you wandered into a Flannery O'Connor story."

"All that's missing are the peacocks."

"We used to have peacocks," Auntie Eudie said. "Faulkner's nephew shot them all with his BB gun when he was thirteen, bless his heart."

"They're saying they think Williams might have fallen and hit his head outside. He could have crawled into the cellar and died," Cormac said. "The storm doors are unlocked."

In the peculiar silence that followed, Roark rose unsteadily and left the room.

Though no one had argued, Cormac insisted, "It could have happened like that."

"Hit his head on what?" Jeff was frowning.

"On…anything. On the brick path. On the corner of the house. Hell, on a rock in the road. Who cares?"

"Why are the storm doors unlocked?" Jeff persisted.

"'Cause somebody unlocked them," Cormac shot back.

Austin took his sandwich back to the sofa, the better to hide the fact that he wasn't eating and wasn't likely to start anytime soon. The sheriffs would summon him any minute, and he could tell his story and get out of there. There was no reason to feel so nervous. No one could seriously think he had anything to do with this accident, or whatever it was.

Jeff believed it was murder.

Austin wasn't sure how he knew that, especially since he didn't know Jeff from Adam, but he could tell Jeff wasn't buying the theory of Dominic Williams's conveniently knocking himself out and then staggering into the Cashels' cellar to quietly die. And he wasn't sure the Cashels themselves bought that theory, although if they didn't, they seemed to take homicide in stride.

That was the only alternative, right? If Williams hadn't met with a fatal accident, someone in this house had killed him. Well, perhaps *not* in the house, but close enough that hiding him in the Cashels' cellar seemed a good plan. Austin couldn't fault the logic. In the normal course of things, Dominic Williams could probably have mummified down there with the oversize spiders and withered potatoes—no one the wiser.

But was that true? There was no reason to think Austin's visit was a secret. Didn't that support the idea of a tragic accident? Unless someone had wanted Williams's body to be discovered.

"Maybe the colonel killed him," Auntie Eudie remarked.

Carson giggled nervously.

"The colonel?" repeated Jeff.

"Colonel Sterling Cashel," Auntie Eudie said proudly. She gestured to the gold-framed oval painting on the wall of the Confederate officer in full regalia. "According to the family legend, the colonel will rise from his grave when the Cashels most have need of him."

"Where's he been the last fifteen years?" Cormac inquired sourly.

"I just can't see why anyone, including the colonel, would want to bash poor old Dom's head in," Carson said with what Austin thought was remarkable indifference for a former lover. "It's not like he ever did anyone any harm."

"He was a gambler, a womanizer, and a lousy driver," Cormac retorted.

"Oh, that's true. You did have that fender bender with him."

"He damn near took the front of my pickup off. And then he tried to claim I rear-ended *him*."

Austin felt someone's gaze. He looked up, and Jeff was studying him intently. Their gazes tangled, and Jeff looked away, his expression self-conscious. For some reason that awkward moment brought warmth to Austin's face and an unexpected stirring in his groin.

This was getting weirder and weirder. Given the little he knew about the South, he did not want to misinterpret curiosity for interest. That might get him lynched.

"The Williams women were always teched," Auntie Eudie commented. "But I never heard anything about the men."

"Well, if Henrietta was Dom's sister instead of his wife, I guess that would make sense," Carson said. "She's more than teched."

They fell silent at the sound of raised voices down the hall. A few seconds later Roark returned, flapping his arms impatiently, although no one appeared to be accompanying him. "I don't need any help!"

The rest of the Cashels observed him with polite interest.

Roark headed for his chair again. His bleary gaze fell on Austin. "They want to see you now."

Austin set his plate aside and went into the hallway. The young sheriff stood in an open doorway a few yards down. "This way, sir."

Austin followed him into what had once been a large ballroom. It was the length of three large rooms. The floors were of dark wood. Three huge pink-and-amber chandeliers studded the pale blue ceiling. The ceiling was decorated with ornate white plaster moldings and medallions of classical scenes: centaurs chased nymphs, nymphs chased centaurs, warriors battled warriors.

At the far end of the room, next to long windows covered by dark-blue draperies, sat Captain Thompson at a small writing desk. He looked up at Austin's approach.

"Sit down, Mr. Gillespie."

Austin sat on a fragile-looking, lyre-backed chair.

"How you doing?"

"Okay."

"You're probably wondering why we've kept you till the last to talk to."

"Sort of."

"Jeff Brady tells us you're a stranger to this house and this family, and we thought your observations as an outsider might be interesting." At Austin's blank look, Captain Thompson added, "Or maybe not. I guess we'll see." He studied his notes.

"Why don't we start with who you are and what you're doing here?"

Austin went quickly through the basics.

"And what exactly does a master of wine do?"

Short answer: masters of wine were the industry leaders in all aspects of the global wine business, but Austin could just imagine how that answer would go down. "It's a professional qualification. It basically means I've completed the Institute of Masters of Wine's two-year program."

"But what do you *do*? Do you just drink wine all day?"

This was starting to feel like one of those all-too-familiar family-dinner discussions. Austin was very proud of his master-of-wine status. He was not only one of the few American masters of wine; he was one of the youngest, period. It was a notable achievement, but to people outside the industry it probably seemed as useless as a degree in basket weaving.

"Masters of wine do a variety of things. Some are vintners, some are winemaking consultants, some work in the restaurant-and-hotel business, some are educators. I buy and auction wine for Martyn, North, & Compeau, which is one of the oldest and most respected wine shops in North America. I host wine tastings, I contribute articles to magazines, I write a weekly blog on wine and a syndicated monthly column for several newspapers…"

Thompson and the other sheriff looked singularly unimpressed.

"I do a lot of things," Austin finished lamely.

"And do you make money at that? Drinking wine and talking about it?"

"I…make enough. My family is…"

"Rich?" supplied Captain Thompson when Austin stalled out.

"Comfortable."

"Seems like a job for a rich man," Captain Thompson remarked. It wasn't particularly critical, just an observation. "So you came down here from DC to inventory old Dermot Cashel's wine cellar. Seems like a long way to travel. How come the Cashels didn't get someone local to do the job?"

Like Dominic Williams? Austin said carefully, "Martyn, North, & Compeau is very well known and very well respected within the industry. It's not like having someone from Bev Mo show up and count bottles."

"No need to take offense," Thompson said easily.

"I'm not offended. It's just… My job is more important than it sounds."

"Sure," Thompson said kindly. "We all like to think we're making a difference. I like to think what I do makes a difference." He looked at his notes again. "So why don't you tell me in your own words exactly what happened after you arrived at this house?"

It didn't take long to run through the events of the morning.

Thompson and the other sheriff exchanged a few glances but heard Austin out in silence.

"And did anyone do or say anything that seemed out of the ordinary to you?" Thompson inquired when Austin had wound down his recital.

"Uh…"

The young sheriff laughed. Thompson said easily, "I guess we Southerners all seem foreign to you Northerners. Let me phrase it this way: did anyone seem guilty or nervous?"

"No."

"Did anyone suggest you shouldn't work in the cellar?"

They had already been through this. "No. They had a work space set up for me. The butler, Faulkner, was downstairs spraying insecticide."

"Yeah, you mentioned that." The captain made a note on his pad. "What about these famous wine bottles? The ones that were supposed to belong to Robert E. Lee? Are they for real?"

"They could be. I didn't see them, but I didn't have very long to look. They were listed on the inventory sheets sent to us by the family. The list was pretty informal, but it is possible that the bottles are here."

"Really?" Thompson was politely disbelieving. "Wine bottles belonging to General Robert E. Lee?"

"It's possible. They're described correctly on the inventory list: hand-blown dark green glass and capped with a rough seal of thick red wax. The year 1822 is etched into the glass along with the initials R-E-L. The words *Blandy Madeira* can be read at the base of each bottle." Austin shrugged. "If they exist, they'll be easy to spot."

"And you think there's a chance they survived all this time? Survived the war between the states?"

"Madeira is a long-lived wine, so…yes. Barring some accident to the bottles. We know that Mrs. Lee moved the Arlington House wine cellar to the Ravensworth estate. There's evidence to support that the contents of the cellar were left at Ravensworth after she fled farther south. The house burned in 1926, but by then most of its contents had been dispersed among the Lee descendants."

Thompson nodded thoughtfully. "And if these Lee wine bottles had survived, what would they be worth?"

"The Lee connection makes them priceless."

"Worth killing for, would you say?"

Austin said reluctantly, "It's possible, I guess. Is that what you think happened? That Dominic Williams was murdered?"

"We don't know. That will be up to the forensics people to determine. It's possible Williams could have fallen, fractured his skull, but still climbed down into the cellar. That was one helluva rainstorm last night. A man disoriented by a blow to the head might simply grab on to the first door he came to. We can't say for sure yet. Of course, either way it doesn't explain what he was doing on the Ballineen grounds at night in the middle of a rainstorm."

"Did you find his car?" Austin wasn't sure why he asked that when he dearly wanted this all to go away so he could get back to inventorying the cellar, but Captain Thompson smiled approvingly.

"Nope. That's the trouble. We can't find Williams's car. Or his keys. So it looks like either he walked fifteen miles in the pouring rain at night in time to get knocked over the head, or someone drove him out to Ballineen, or someone took his keys after he was hit over the head, and drove his car away."

Austin sincerely wished he had not asked.

Captain Thompson continued to browse his notes and nod to himself. At last he looked up and smiled. "Thank you, Mr. Gillespie. You've been most helpful. You have a safe trip home now."

CHAPTER FOUR

$\mathbf{A}$ hot shower, a good meal with a better wine, and an early night—that was Austin's plan as he walked into the Stonewall Jackson Inn and went up to his room—named, as each room was in this lavishly appointed hotel, for one of the town's antebellum mansions. Anything more energetic than that was out. Never mind the seven-hundred-mile drive from DC; starting the day with finding a dead body and ending the afternoon with a police interview was guaranteed to wear anyone out.

Austin closed the hotel door, let his suitcase fall forward, and set his laptop case on the low table. The room was elegantly furnished in soothing tones of cream, fawn, cocoa, and sage. A bowl of hydrangeas sat on the fireplace mantel. Two plump and comfortable chairs and a small oval table were positioned in front. The bed was tall, and the fluffy, sand-hued duvet and pillows were down-filled. There was a bookshelf with offerings from a variety of Southern writers. The paintings were all originals by local artists. A small porch looked out over the park.

For a moment Austin stood unbuttoning his shirt, staring across the street at the tranquil view of huge shady trees, old-fashioned lampposts, and gazebos. A tall cast-iron fountain shot sparkling plumes into the soft blue sky.

On second thought, maybe he'd postpone calling Whitney. He'd rather talk to Peter anyway. Peter Compeau was the other half of Martyn, North, & Compeau. The Norths had died out in 1972, well before Austin's time, and it was just Whitney and Peter now. Unfortunately Peter was beginning to talk more and more seriously about retiring. Austin had always known his position was liable to become precarious after Peter left. He and Whitney had never been simpatico, and now that Whitney was engaged to the very ambitious Theresa...

But he didn't want to think about that now. Like Scarlett O'Hara, he'd think about it tomorrow. He'd had all the disappointment he needed for one day. In addition to the abrupt termination of the Cashel cellar appraisal and his failure to find the Lee bottles was the more puzzling sense of letdown that he wouldn't see Jeff Brady again. They'd said their casual good-byes when Austin had taken his leave of the Cashels, promising to return when the cellar was no longer a crime scene.

"You're not going now?" Cormac had exclaimed in open disappointment.

Carson had chimed in, inviting Austin to stay longer on the off chance that the sheriffs might reopen the cellar. Austin didn't know much about homicide investigations, but he knew enough to be confident he wasn't going to be allowed back into that cellar anytime soon.

He had declined as gracefully as he knew how, and then he'd turned to Jeff, who had smiled into his eyes and told him to drive safe.

It was just... Well, you could tell when someone was interested, and Jeff had most definitely given off that interested vibe. That was the hard-to-figure part because Jeff had really done nothing. It was just something in the way his gaze lingered on Austin's, a certain warmth to his smile, maybe something in the tone of his voice. Maybe it was just part of that automatic Southern charm. Or maybe it was pheromones? Whatever it had been, it was over now.

Besides, Jeff, in addition to appearing to be happily, vigorously heterosexual, really wasn't Austin's type. The ex-high-school quarterback and local lothario? Although maybe that was the point. There was nothing wrong with having an uncomplicated out-of-towner.

But it hadn't worked out, and that was probably for the best. Austin unbuttoned his cuffs, shrugged out of his shirt, and tossed it to the floor.

The bathroom was black-and-white tile with a roomy rain shower complete with teak stool. In case the whole bathing procedure proved too exhausting? Austin checked out the assortment of spa products and settled for shampoo and soap. There was as much dirt beneath his fingernails as if he'd spent the morning gardening.

After his shower he changed into jeans and a *Got Wine?* T-shirt, flopped down on the bed, sinking comfortably into the cloud of the duvet, and called Ernest.

"I don't see why I should have to stay there when they're located right here in Maryland." Ernest greeted him as though they had never ended their previous conversation.

"Because living on campus and forming those relationships with other kids is a big part of the school experience. You're all homesick. You're all going through all the same things, and it helps form bonds."

"I don't want to form bonds."

"Friendships."

"I don't like little kids."

"They won't always be little kids." Huh? Austin heard the echo of that and opened his eyes. He was too tired to do this right now.

"They won't like me. They'll think I'm weird."

Yes, they would most definitely think Ernest was weird. No way around that. They had thought Austin was weird, and Austin wasn't nearly as weird as Ernest. But Austin had survived. He had occasionally even thrived, and that had been under pretty much the worst possible circumstances: being shuffled off to boarding school after the death of his mother. Of course, in fairness to Harrison, what was he going to do with a grieving child around the house? Harrison had rarely been home in those days, always flying off to some war-torn corner of the world to report the death and disaster to the folks eating supper back home. The point being that if Austin could survive, Ernest, who was about a zillion times smarter and more self-possessed, could definitely do it.

"Listen, Ernesto, you can't live at home forever with just me and the girls for friends."

"Why?"

"Because it's not practical and it's not healthy." Not to mention the fact that Austin and his sisters were rarely at the house in Frederick.

"Why?"

"Because one day you're going to work and live in the world, and you need to know how to get along there."

Ernesto said coolly, "We're wealthy, Austin. We don't have to work. We choose to work. I can live at home forever and build my spacecraft."

Cue the *My Favorite Martian* theme.

Austin floundered briefly, coming up with, "There has to be more to your life than your work or even your family."

"I have Buzz and Armstrong."

Buzz was a springer spaniel, and Armstrong was a Chincoteague pony.

"You need more. You need... Well, you'll probably want a girlfriend one day." Yeah, good move. Maybe he should bring up marriage and kids now and go for the grand slam of totally inappropriate advice for a child.

"Maybe I'm gay."

"*Are* you?" Austin asked, startled.

Ernest gave one of his rare giggles. "No. I'm *nine*."

Austin reserved comment, but he had known at nine, although looking back he wasn't sure *how* he'd known. Crushes on playmates? Funny dreams? Somehow he'd known.

"Anyway, you goof, there isn't any point us debating it because it's going to happen. Once Dad's mind is made up—"

"You could talk to him."

Austin laughed and hoped Ernest didn't hear the trace of bitterness that slipped past. "Yeah, right. You'd have better luck talking to him yourself. You need to try and focus on the positives here."

"There aren't any!" Ernest's voice went high and shrill, a reminder that despite the mighty intellect, he was still a little kid with a little kid's emotional needs. "What will happen to Buzz and Armstrong?"

"Armstrong will go with you. And Buzz… We'll think of something for Buzz. I'll bring him out with me when I come to see you on weekends."

"Will you come?"

"Of course."

"Every weekend?"

Austin put the heel of his hand to the middle of his forehead and pushed hard, trying to inject some sense into his tired brain. "As often as I can."

"I'm not going," Ernest said and hung up.

Austin moaned and turned off his phone.

Food and sleep. That's what he needed. He rolled off the bed, hunting around for his Converse Chucks.

Right on schedule the phone rang again. He picked it up. "I can't promise to come every single weekend, but I'll come as often as I can."

There was a pause, and an adult male voice drawled, "That's a promise I'll take."

Austin swallowed hard, checked the cell phone display. Crap. Not Ernest, in case there was any doubt about that. There wasn't. His heart had sped up on hearing that deep, attractive voice on the phone because of course he'd recognized it instantly. In fact, Jeff's voice already seemed familiar to him. How could that be?

"Oh. Hi." He pictured it suddenly as a Lolcat caption: *Oh...hai!*

Jeff chuckled, and the husky, sexy sound seemed to go straight to Austin's cock.

"Hello, Austin. What are you doing for dinner tonight?"

Just like that. The direct approach. What a relief. What a relief to know he hadn't been imagining things. What a relief that this was dropping into his lap. Maybe literally. Hopefully literally.

"I was going to grab a sandwich downstairs, but I'm open to suggestion."

"I'll keep that in mind. Meanwhile, can I offer a little Southern hospitality and take you to dinner?"

"You could. In fact, I'd like that a lot."

"I'm at the office right now." The phone crackled as Jeff shuffled papers or maybe moved mountains. What exactly *did* Jeff do for a living? "How about we meet in the Magnolia Room around six thirty? We'll go on from there."

Austin glanced at the clock beside the bed. Five to five. "Great."

"I'll see you then."

Jeff clicked off. Austin glanced up and caught his reflection in the mirror over the fireplace. His cheeks were pink. His eyes were sparkling. "Don't," he warned. "Don't expect too much. You're probably going to hear football scores all evening."

* * * * *

The Magnolia Room was probably every bit as handsome as the rest of the Stonewall Jackson Inn, but Austin had only a fleeting impression of burgundy walls, gleaming brass fixtures, and comfortable rich dark wood. The nicest thing in the room was Jeff, who was already sitting at the bar chatting with another patron when Austin strolled in.

He smiled and raised his glass in greeting.

"You're early," Austin said, joining him. He was early too, but after he'd changed clothes and watched a few depressing minutes of news on the flat-screen TV, he'd decided to wait downstairs.

Jeff had showered and shaved. He wore khakis and a short-sleeved shirt in the exact same shade of green as his eyes. And whatever his cologne was, it was already driving Austin wild. God, what was that? Bergamot, citrus, basil, mint…and something else. Icelandic moss?

"I finished up earlier than I expected. What'll you have to drink? Or is that a silly question?"

Austin grinned and asked the bartender what they had available from local wineries.

Jeff lifted a hand in greeting to a couple who came in. They waved back and, to Austin's relief, took a table in the corner.

The bartender brought him a glass of Habersham Scarlett, a blend of Chambourcin, cabernet sauvignon, and white wine. Austin gently swirled the wine to release the bouquet. He breathed in the voluptuous aroma of moist earth and sun-drenched berries. He tilted the glass and checked the color. The light was all wrong in the bar, of course, but it looked like a hue with some heft. He sipped. Soft and fruity. A rich, ripe blackberry-blue-berry character. He nodded approval and turned back to Jeff.

Jeff was smiling at some private thought, but at Austin's inquiring look, he tipped his head at Austin's glass. "Not bad, I take it?"

"I'm pleasantly surprised."

"Your eyes light up when you're pleasantly surprised." That smooth, deliberate charm both excited Austin and made him uneasy. Jeff planned on seducing him, and Austin had no problem with that, but he couldn't help wondering if Jeff had some motive beyond the obvious. Things generally did not work like this for him. In fact, he couldn't remember a guy like Jeff ever pursuing him. Not that Austin didn't get hit on plenty, but he wasn't Jeff's normal type. He was pretty sure of that—even without taking into account that, from what he'd seen so far, Jeff's normal type was female.

"Tell the truth." Jeff sounded indulgent. "How often do you return wine?"

"Not often," Austin said seriously. "A lot of people misunderstand the purpose of tasting wine. It's not to decide whether you like the wine.

You're basically checking to see that it's the right wine and that it's not corked."

"Wine isn't supposed to be corked?"

"Corked as in corky. It means the wine has spoiled. The cork has been contaminated with TCA—trichloroanisole. Inevitably a certain percentage of wine is spoiled by bad corks. That's why companies are experimenting with screw caps and glass tops and plastic corks. Of course, most people can't tell if wine is corked unless it's in a high concentration."

"But you can?"

"Well, yeah."

Jeff offered a lopsided smile. "At the risk of looking like a total redneck, I admit I'm not much of a wine drinker. It gives me indigestion."

Austin glanced at Jeff's glass. "Jack Daniel's?"

"Predictable, huh?"

Sort of. But not in a bad way. Austin took another mouthful of wine, letting it roll across his taste buds, savoring it. "How were things at Ballineen when you left?" He pulled out his iPhone and texted himself a quick message with notes on the wine.

Jeff watched him, answering absently. "The sheriffs were still processing the crime scene."

"So no arrest is imminent?"

"Naw."

Naw. Funny how that drawl seemed to soften the negative.

Another couple entered the bar and greeted Jeff. Pleasantries were exchanged, and they moved away with surreptitious glances at Austin.

Seeing that he seemed to have lost Jeff's attention, Austin said, "I think the butler did it."

Jeff laughed. "Faulkner?"

"Why not? That's the way it works in books, isn't it? He's like a cross between Benson and Mr. E. Blackadder."

"I don't know who Mr. E. Blackadder is, but I remember *Benson*."

This led to a brief digression on television shows they'd watched growing up. Jeff had been a fan of *JAG* and *MADtv*. Austin confessed to *What a Cartoon! Show* and *NewsRadio*.

Austin returned to his original point. "I can't put my finger on it, but Faulkner's got this attitude. Like he's having a private laugh at them all. But yet he seems kind of fond of them too."

"Well, there you go." Jeff swallowed a mouthful of Jack Daniel's. "I don't think the sheriffs are looking at Faulkner."

"Who are they looking at?"

Jeff negligently lifted a broad shoulder. "I'm not in their confidence."

"It seemed like you were today."

Jeff's eyes were very green in the muted light. "Is that so?"

Austin nodded. His phone rang. He checked the number. Ernest. *Crap.*

"I've got to take this."

Jeff nodded politely.

Austin walked out to the polished hall with its marble pillars and glass-slick wooden floors and giant urns with floral arrangements.

"Hey, Ernesto."

"I could sue Harrison and Mother for mental cruelty."

Austin closed his eyes and counted to ten. That was too long, of course, because by four Ernest was detailing the grounds for his lawsuit and citing similar cases.

"Ernie…Ernest, stop." Austin finally made himself heard. He could hear Ernest's unsteady breathing in the silence between them. "You can't sue your parents."

"Article nine of the UN Convention on the Rights of the Child—"

"Snap out of it," Austin interrupted. "Have you considered how much that would hurt their feelings? Unless you're prepared to sever all ties but financial, you don't want to go in that direction."

"I'm prepared. I won't allow them to interfere with my work."

My kid brother, the mad scientist. "You're *not* prepared. Are you telling me you think you can sue Harrison—Dad—and then enjoy a jolly family Thanksgiving or Christmas? Are you planning to move out? What about your laboratory? What about Armstrong and Buzz?"

"I won't be able to use my laboratory while I'm at school anyway." He was doing that adenoidal breathing thing he did when he was trying not to cry. Austin's heart twisted, but sympathy was just going to encourage Ernest, and he was stubborn enough without encouragement.

"Ernie, I understand that you're upset, but if you think going to school is disruptive to your work, try suing your parents. And you'll still have to go to school of some kind."

"I could live with you."

"No, Ernesto, you can't. I'm sorry, but no. I can't take care of a child. That doesn't mean I don't love you, because I do."

"I could live with Shelia and study giraffes."

Sometimes the kid was refreshingly...kidlike.

"Then you wouldn't be working in your laboratory, would you?"

"I don't care."

"If that's the case, I think you should call Shelia right now." Good luck trying to locate Stepmother #1, currently somewhere in Kenya studying endangered giraffes. But anything that got Austin off the hook for a while was fine.

"I will." Ernest disconnected.

"Good-bye," Austin murmured to the dial tone.

He returned to the bar and said, "Sorry about that. My brother isn't happy about going to boarding school in the fall."

"I don't blame him."

"Yeah, but it's going to happen whether he likes it or not, so he needs to try to figure out how to make the best of it."

"Did you go to boarding school? Prep school?"

Austin nodded.

"Yeah, I thought so. You've got that way about you."

"What way is that?"

Jeff said immediately, "I'm not criticizing you. I like you, Austin. I just mean it's partly your way of talking—your accent—and it's partly—"

Austin grinned. "*My* accent?"

"You've got the look and the attitude, but inside you're different. Or you wouldn't be taking your brother's phone calls."

Austin smiled faintly. He picked up his wineglass.

"Yeah, you're not about the money or the position or the job in banking. What *are* you about?" Jeff seemed sincerely interested, and that openness and attention disarmed Austin. Before he knew it, he was explaining all about Ernest, who was, despite being a rocket-ship-building genius, a lonely little boy and close to his heart. Jeff listened. He was a very good listener. He kept eye contact, and he made all the right comments, while not interrupting Austin's train of thought.

"Holy shit," he said at the end of Austin's recital. "You spend your holidays with five stepmothers and four sisters? And today was the first time you were involved in a homicide investigation?"

Austin laughed. "I know how it sounds, but they all get along. Seriously. They're kind of like…sorority sisters."

Jeff snorted. "It sounds like a harem."

"Probably. I think being married to my dad must be like baptism by fire. I get the impression they're always burned-out and happy to move on when the time comes. Debra's the only one who has some issues with the family dynamic."

Jeff raised a hand in greeting to a newcomer who sat down at the bar. He appeared to know everyone in Madison. Or maybe he was just a regular in the hotel bar. "Debra is the current missus?"

"Ernest's mother, yeah."

"The documentary filmmaker."

"You really were listening."

"Sure I was." Jeff turned back to Austin and treated him to another of those intimate smiles. He glanced at Austin's wineglass. "Are you planning on finishing that? We should probably head over to the restaurant."

"Let's go. I'm ready." More than ready. It had occurred to Austin that as long as he and Jeff remained in the bar, Jeff would be too much in the public eye for anything interesting to develop between them. Not that anything was necessarily going to develop. Jeff might be one of those guys who flirted with his sexuality but had no intention of truly veering from the straight and narrow, but Austin remained hopeful.

Jeff paid for their drinks, and they walked out of the restaurant to where he had parked beneath the hundred-year-old trees. Austin had been privately betting that Jeff would either drive something small and sporty or a tricked-out pickup truck, but he was wrong. Jeff drove a perfectly sensible Honda Accord.

It was dark by then—darker still beneath the trees—and the evening smelled of sweet pecans and green shadows.

Jeff opened the sedan door. Austin started to get in, but Jeff put a light hand on his shoulder. Austin turned and, reading that smiling, wary look, it seemed very natural and easy to lean in and meet Jeff halfway.

What was it about a first kiss? That first brush of mouths, the first shared breath, the first taste of another person. So often it was just plain awkward. Too much too soon. Too much information. Or alternatively, a quick, clumsy bump with noses or chins or teeth in the wrong place at the wrong time.

Kissing Jeff was different. The first kiss was quiet, almost companionable, breath light and pleasantly scented of bourbon close against his face. A pleased-to-meet-you sort of kiss. Jeff's lips were warm, and there was the shape of a smile beneath the firm pressure. Partly, of course, it was simple biology. Jeff smelled good—Austin was falling in love with his cologne—and tasted good. An excellent vintage. Jeff kissed with just the right blend of assurance and sincerity. He kissed like he had spent a lifetime practicing—and maybe he had.

The second kiss was more urgent, less cautious, less practiced. Austin, not exactly inexperienced himself, felt the instant Jeff slipped gears and began to lose himself in the perfect combination of sweet heat and soft pressure. The sound Jeff made—a groan of distressed delight—sent excitement flashing to the base of Austin's spine and ricocheting up to his skull before zinging back down. He opened his mouth, and Jeff's tongue dipped in, exploring with a surprising delicacy. They were not going to make it to dinner if they kept on like this.

Which would be okay. Better than okay, except Austin wanted this evening to last. To his surprise, he wanted to get to know Jeff better. So... dinner.

He gathered his scattered wits, made a tremendous effort, and disengaged. Jeff released him reluctantly, their lips making a tiny popping sound as they pulled apart. A funny sound, but Austin, trying to catch his breath, didn't feel like laughing.

CHAPTER FIVE

They didn't speak until they were in the car and on their way. Jeff murmured, "I've been wanting to do that all day."

"All day?" As attractive as Jeff was, Austin had not been thinking about sex with a police investigation going on around him.

"Okay, all decade."

Austin said slowly, "All decade?"

Jeff chuckled. "It is you, right? You used to do those Calvin Klein ads? I recognized you the minute I saw you. You've got this way of standing with your head tipped, kind of looking up from under your lashes. It's... memorable. You've got distinct bone structure. And your eyes are... Well, let's just say I had a serious thing for you in college."

"Oh, crap."

Jeff threw Austin a quick, surprised look. "Is it supposed to be a secret?"

"No. Not a secret." *Hell yes, it was supposed to be a secret.* "It's just...a long time ago. I was in college myself."

"Why did you give it up?"

"Modeling? Are you kidding? It's not exactly..."

Jeff said with sudden perspicacity, "Oh. Right. I was forgetting the sister who's a social anthropologist, the sister who's a public defender, the sister who's a professor of political science, and the sister who writes biographies. I guess selling hair gel and underwear is out. How did you end up tasting wine for a living?"

Austin said shortly, "I don't just taste wine for a living."

He could feel Jeff trying to read his profile in the dusk. "Sorry. I didn't mean it that way."

"Nah. It's what most people think."

"How did you get into it?"

"I wish I had some great story to tell. I wanted to be a concert pianist."

"Really?"

"Yeah. I wasn't good enough, though. Not by any stretch. Anyway, I had this music professor, and he used to have us, his students, over for dinner once a month. He was really into the whole epicurean thing. He tried to teach us an appreciation of good food, good wine, good company. He was just a really interesting guy."

"Were you…?"

It took Austin a couple of seconds to understand what Jeff meant. "No. No, I don't even know if he was— He was very private. Anyway, I started getting interested in wine, and the more I studied, the more interested I became. And then it turned out I had a very good nose and an even better palate." Austin added derisively, "It's my God-given talent—to be able to tell a Viognier from a Torrontes at thirty paces."

Jeff smiled faintly.

They were driving through the beautiful historic heart of Madison, which according to legend was a town so pretty General Sherman had refused to burn it. It *was* pretty too. Very picturesque with its shady streets and gracious antebellum homes, elegant old gardens and parks, its shops and galleries and antique dealers.

The traffic was heavy on Main Street but thinned out once they turned off the central thoroughfare.

From the outside looking in, it certainly seemed charming and old-world. What would it be like to live in a place like this? A place where it was not impossible that everyone *did* know your name?

Shaking off his preoccupation, Austin asked, "What about you? I feel like I've been talking all evening."

"Not much to tell," Jeff said easily. "I grew up in Madison. Born and raised here. One set of parents. Two siblings, both younger—just as average-ordinary as me."

Average-ordinary? It was the first thing Jeff had said that sounded artificial. Austin remembered Auntie Eudie's story about Jeff's father committing suicide beneath a family portrait. Maybe Jeff was a better listener than talker.

Austin probed, "Where'd you go to college?"

"South University in Savannah."

"What did you study?"

He didn't imagine that hesitation, but then Jeff said in that same casual tone, "I've got a BS in criminal justice administration."

Austin absorbed that. "But you're not a cop?"

"I'm a private investigator."

"A private investigator. You mean like PI?"

Jeff did a bad impression of Humphrey Bogart. "Thash right, schweetheart."

"Now that's a day job."

"And nights and weekends and holidays."

"Do you mostly work for lawyers?"

"I mostly work for jealous spouses."

"It must give you a jaded view of relationships."

"Says the man with five stepmothers." Jeff added lightly, "Fortunately I had a jaded view to begin with."

"Ah."

"What's *ah* mean?" Jeff threw him another of those quick, almost wary looks.

"Mostly that I don't always think before I speak. You do seem sort of...smooth."

"Smooth?" Jeff laughed. "And you prefer rough?"

"No." No. Definitely not.

Jeff turned off a road lined with oaks. They passed through tall iron gates that led down a long tunnel of trees. He said with satisfaction, "Here we are. Hope you're hungry."

Old Plantation House. Why did that ring a bell?

The drive ended at the entrance to a crowded parking lot surrounded by tidy green lawns and meticulously kept flower beds. A few yards farther on, a small mansion in the Greek Revival style was illuminated by strategically placed spotlights.

"Old Plantation House? Isn't that where Dominic Williams was master sommelier?"

"Yep," Jeff replied. "It's also the best restaurant in town."

"I see. So you're actually working tonight?"

"Naw." Jeff turned off the engine, not meeting Austin's gaze. "They make the best fried green tomatoes you'll ever taste."

Austin smiled without humor and refrained from commenting that they were likely to be the *only* fried green tomatoes he'd ever taste.

Abruptly they seemed to be out of things to talk about. They strolled up the brick path to the house in silence. Jeff had made reservations, and they were taken immediately to their table in the long dining room with its eighteenth-century paintings and crisp white linens. The walls were the crimson that seemed so popular here in Georgia, and the tables and chairs were a dark wood that looked antique.

Once they were seated, Jeff made an effort to regain their former harmony. Austin studied the menu while Jeff advised him on such heirloom dishes as Southern panfried quail with country ham or St. Simons Island shrimp bog. Austin smiled and tried to respond normally, but his pleasure in the evening had dimmed.

The sommelier brought the wine menu.

"He's the expert," Jeff said, nodding at Austin.

The man started to hand the red leather book to Austin. He snatched it back and gasped. "Wait."

Austin looked up in inquiry.

"You're Austin Gillespie."

Austin assented cautiously.

"Only I read your column religiously. 'Message in a Bottle.' It's me. Corky. I'm one of the regular commenters on your blog."

Ordinarily Austin would have been pleased to put a face to the name, but his heart just wasn't in it right now. Still, he made an effort. "Sure. Of course. Nice to meet you, Corky." Austin offered a hand. They shook.

Corky spent the next half hour explaining the wine list and giving his opinions and tips. Austin consulted with Jeff as to his preferences and likes—which took about two seconds since when it came to wine, Jeff had none. When Corky at last departed with Austin's order for Domaine de la Pépière Clos des Briords 2007, Jeff said, "Whew. Does that happen every time you go out to dinner?"

"If I can perfectly match the wine to the meal, it makes for a better overall dining experience. And that makes for a better overall evening." He probably sounded slightly defensive.

"I meant do you often run into fans?"

"Oh. No. Almost never. More in DC." Austin buried himself in his menu once more, although he had already figured out he was going to try the lobster Savannah. He had been glad of the diversion offered by Corky. He was still bothered by the realization that Jeff either suspected him of something nefarious or was using him as cover for his investigation.

"Austin—" Jeff broke off as the waitress reappeared to take their order. "We need another minute, honey," he said, smiling but firm.

The waitress retreated.

Jeff leaned forward and said quietly, "I don't want there to be any misunderstanding. I am supposed to be working tonight. At least, that would be the smart thing. But you're leaving tomorrow, and I wanted to have dinner with you—take you someplace nice. Someplace they don't have in Washington DC. So I did think maybe I could kill two birds with one stone. It could be useful to see how the people Williams worked with are reacting to his death, but it won't be so useful that it'll make a big difference if you'd rather go somewhere else. If you're uncomfortable, we will."

Jeff seemed perfectly sincere. Austin was surprised by that—and by the fact that Jeff had picked up on his slight hurt. He relaxed. "No. It's okay. Unless you plan on working through dinner."

"No. I just wanted to get a feel for the mood here tonight." Jeff's smile was confident again. "I promise you'll have my complete and undivided attention for the night."

Austin found himself amused. Jeff clearly knew exactly how attractive he was and had no hesitation using his charm as necessary, but that was okay. Austin liked confidence as much as the next guy. He was reasonably confident himself. He glanced around the busy room. "I don't know what it's usually like, but it seems pretty much like business as usual to me."

"I agree. Nobody's cryin' in their soup over Dominic Williams."

"Maybe they don't know yet?"

"They know."

"Do you work for an agency, or are you a solo operation?"

"Solo." Jeff added rather darkly, "Which is just the way I like it."

"I can see the allure of self-employment." Austin was thinking of Whitney and his own imperiled position.

Jeff beckoned to the watchfully hovering waitress, and they gave her their orders.

When she departed, he said, "Two days ago Dominic Williams disappeared. His wife, Henrietta, hired me to find him. She believed he'd run off with a local girl he'd been having an affair with all winter."

"Carson Cashel?"

"Very good. Yeah, Carson. But when I did some checking around, I found out pretty quick that Carson hadn't run anywhere, so if Williams was with her, they were both staying out at Ballineen. Last night I followed Carson to the Blind Pig and…" Jeff shrugged.

"You seduced her?"

"She seduced me, actually. But I don't keep score."

"You take your job pretty seriously."

"Naw. I like sex."

Austin couldn't tell if it was a kind of bravado or not. At times Jeff seemed callous and shallow—even hard—but at other times he seemed unexpectedly sensitive and unexpectedly candid. Which was the real Jeff?

"With anyone?"

"I prefer attractive people." Now Jeff was laughing at him.

So…okay. This probably *was* the real Jeff. Good to know the ground rules before they got started. It wasn't a problem. Maybe a little disappointing to realize that Jeff was just your average, run-of-the-mill horndog, but the disappointment wasn't logical. It wasn't like this was the start of a relationship. They lived seven hundred miles—and a couple of universes— apart. They had absolutely nothing in common but lust. So why pretend it was anything else? Jeff had it right.

"You went home with Carson last night so you could look around for Dominic Williams?"

"That wasn't any hardship, let me tell you. Carson is one sweet peach of a gal. Anyway, it was obvious early on that she didn't have Williams stashed at the house. Her mind was on one thing and one thing only." Jeff's smile was smug, and logical or not, Austin began to get irritated.

Fortunately, Corky returned with the wine Austin had ordered, and they went through the ritual of uncorking and pouring and tasting.

The muscadet had a bright color and a scent of wet stone and warm citrus. Austin took a sip. Slightly bubbly, round, and...supple. Very nice. And a complex but sound structure: crisp, dry, but with a clean and fruity finish.

"Will you try it?" Austin asked Jeff. "I don't believe this will give you indigestion."

Jeff's hesitation was kind of amusing. You just didn't expect a big, tough private eye to be nervous of a little glass of wine. He nodded, though, and Corky poured a second glass of wine and withdrew.

"That's not bad," Jeff admitted after a swallow.

They sipped their wine for a few moments. Austin asked, "I'm just trying to understand. Are you bisexual? Or are you gay, and last night you were working undercover?"

The effect on Jeff was instantaneous. He set his glass down so hard the wine sloshed onto the tablecloth. He looked stricken and then furious. "Shut your mouth," he whispered harshly.

Shocked, Austin shut his mouth.

Jeff said, still with that quiet, furious intensity, "There is no *gay* here."

Austin managed to keep his mouth shut. Just.

A very long minute passed while they both struggled in silence to find a way through the stark, unbending awkwardness that had sprung up between them. Now Austin remembered why he didn't do this kind of thing, why the strangers-in-the-night scene was almost always more trouble than it was worth.

He sipped his wine and forced himself to analyze that and only that. High acid, a bit minerally... Aromatics of apple, citrus, and saline... Yeah, plenty of saline. He pulled out his iPhone and made some quick notes. Why not make it a business dinner all-around?

Jeff seemed to struggle inwardly. He made an effort. His tone was almost normal, though still low as he said, "Sorry. Sorry, Austin. That must have seemed… You have to understand. This is a small town. We've only got a population of about three thousand."

And bed checks every night. But Austin still kept his jaw clamped shut. He was not yet willing to write off the probability of getting laid. Even by this self-hating redneck jerk.

Jeff was still talking softly, urgently. "I have to live here and work here. It's not like the North. It's not even like Savannah. Hell, it's not even like *Athens*. You ever check the Web for a listing of gay nightlife in Georgia? There aren't fifty listings in the whole state."

"That can't be true."

Jeff didn't respond.

"So you're in the closet."

Jeff laughed, a short, hard laugh. "Yeah. That's one way of putting it."

What was another? Secret compartment? Hidden safe? Safety-deposit box? Austin struggled with himself and managed, "Then I'm flattered you invited me out tonight."

"No, you're not," Jeff said grimly. "You're appalled. And I apologize. Again. Maybe I shouldn't have asked you out. Maybe that's offensive to you. Maybe my whole situation is offensive. I don't know. I just know"—his voice dropped so low Austin could barely hear the words—"I want to be with you tonight more than I've wanted anything in years. And I assure you I will make certain it is the best you've ever had."

Austin couldn't seem to tear his gaze away from Jeff's intense stare. He swallowed, surprised to find his mouth dry with longing. It was so wrong, but he wanted it too.

Jeff added, "But…no pressure."

A splutter escaped Austin. He put his fist to his mouth to make it look like he was clearing his throat, but Jeff made a choked sound. Unbelievably, insanely, they were laughing. Maybe it was borderline hysteria, but Austin welcomed the release of nervous tension.

Their meals arrived then, and they turned with relief to that small diversion.

The lobster was excellent, and the wine perfectly complemented the undertones of butter and sherry and pimento. Austin realized he hadn't eaten all day and was genuinely starving. While they ate, Jeff took the conversational lead, offering a couple of amusing anecdotes about his early days in the private-eye business. He showed an engaging willingness to share stories where he looked anything but glamorous or heroic.

Granted, there was nothing of a revealing personal nature in these reminiscences—unless the fact that Jeff could laugh so easily at his mistakes was insight into his character. Sexually arrogant he might be, but in regard to the other facets of his life, he seemed totally without pretension. It was equally clear that despite the good-old-boy attitude, he was smart, worked hard, and took his job seriously.

"What sports did you play in school?" Jeff inquired when he had finished making fun of his early career.

He'd figured this was coming. "Cross-country, swimming, lacrosse." Austin had been a competent but not stellar athlete. He'd probably have enjoyed sports more if he hadn't always been competing against Harrison's record. He knew without asking that Jeff had excelled at sports. He'd be willing to bet Jeff could have given Harrison a run—literally—for his money.

"I always wanted to play lacrosse. Me? Football and cross-country." And sure enough, Jeff had been captain of every team he'd ever been on and, undoubtedly—though he was too modest to say so—had a shelf full of trophies he now used for doorstops or paperweights.

They exchanged a few cross-country war stories, and then Austin asked, "What was it like growing up in a Norman Rockwell painting?"

It was the wrong question, though he wasn't sure why. Jeff didn't exactly freeze, but the guarded look was back, despite the fact that he was still smiling.

"It's got its pluses and minuses. It's a slower pace, and that's not necessarily a bad thing. You walk down the street in Madison, and people say hello. People look out for each other. There's a sense of community. Everybody knows everybody else."

They don't know you. But Austin didn't say that. "You've lived here your whole life?"

"Yep. Well, not counting the years at college. The Bradys have lived in these parts since the Revolutionary War."

"Did you ever consider living anywhere else?"

Jeff's smile was odd. "In college. It didn't work out that way." He changed the subject, turning the conversation away from himself and back to Austin.

Austin recognized the maneuver for what it was, but he went with it. He liked Jeff too much to want to risk making him uncomfortable, and it was clear Jeff had a number of "no trespassing" areas posted. Even so, Jeff was very easy to talk to. Partly it was his skill as a listener—his private-investigator training maybe?—and partly it was knowing that this night would be the entire extent of their affair that gave Austin the rare freedom to be completely honest. It was like talking to a stranger on a plane. That was what Austin told himself, anyway. The fact was, he was talking more openly and honestly with Jeff over the course of two hours than he'd talked to Richard in two years. Austin even found himself opening up about the situation with Whitney at work—and then, unbelievably—about his need to prove himself to his family. Especially to his father.

"Who *is* your father?" Jeff asked finally.

Now that was almost funny. He'd been talking to Jeff steadily for half an hour, revealing his greatest hopes and deepest fears, but had managed to skip right over that essential information. "Harrison Gillespie."

"*The* Harrison Gillespie? The news commentator?" Jeff looked impressed—but then everyone always did. "You're kidding. That's like having Dan Rather for your daddy."

"Tell me about it."

"We used to watch him on TV every night when I was growing up."

"Everyone did." Except Austin. They hadn't watched much TV at his boarding school.

Jeff studied him thoughtfully. "I see."

"What do you see?" Austin asked, afraid that Jeff probably did see only too clearly.

"That's quite a pedigree."

"And I modeled underwear in college and drink wine for a living."

"You didn't just model underwear, and you don't just drink wine." Jeff was studying him. "You're good at what you do. You're successful, right?"

Austin nodded.

"And you like what you do?"

"I love what I do."

"Well, there you go." Jeff seemed to think he had made some point, but if he had, it was lost on Austin. Lifting his glass in acknowledgment, Jeff added, "For the record, you were totally right about this wine."

"Thanks. The Pépière Clos des Briords are kind of a legend with wine geeks." Austin suddenly remembered the Lee bottles. Another failure. Not his fault, but that wasn't the point. Had he found those bottles, had they been the real thing, it would have bulletproofed his career. Good luck Whitney's getting rid of him then.

Once again Jeff seemed to read his mind because he said, "What do you think of the chances those antique wine bottles are in that cellar?"

"I'd barely got started looking. I still don't know how much on those original inventory sheets is really down there. I did come across some nice vintage wines, and I'll cross-reference those I had time to list. It was such a mess down there I'd decided I could move faster and be more accurate if I tackled the shelves one by one." Austin admitted, "I should have just searched for the Lee bottles, I guess, but I was caught between wanting to know if they were really there and avoiding the disappointment of finding out for sure that they weren't."

"If they were there, how much would those bottles be worth?"

"The sheriffs asked the same thing. There are supposed to be four of them. If they do exist, if they are the real thing, well, the minimum I'd expect to see each bottle go for at auction would be around five hundred grand."

Jeff whistled. "You're talking two million dollars worth of wine?"

"It's the Lee affiliation that makes them close to priceless."

"And how did old Dermot Cashel get his hands on them?"

"That's the tricky part. He's not here to ask, and no one seems to know. Roark collected the old man's notes on his wine purchases and sent them on to us. I think he had only the vaguest idea of the value of those bottles alone. But really the whole cellar—just the little I saw—was thrilling."

"Thrilling, huh?" Jeff's smile was teasing but not unkind. "Well, in a couple of weeks the Cashels will have their cellar back, and you can finish your inventory."

Austin nodded, unconvinced.

"No?"

"It depends on what else is going on at the shop by then. Whitney might send someone else." Like Theresa. Hopefully not, but it was a possibility. "On the bright side, at least the cellar will be sealed off for a time. They keep it unlocked."

"Those storm doors should have been locked. They're usually locked, but it's spring and there's a lot of gardening and repair work going on, folks looking for tools, going in and out… It happens." Jeff tilted his head, appraising Austin. "So this might be your only trip down this way?"

"Yeah."

Jeff said softly, "Then unless you're just dying to try the key lime pie, why don't I pay the bill and we get out of here and go someplace private?"

Austin's heart skipped a beat, and the sneaking fatigue born of a long day, a rich meal, and more than enough wine vanished. He'd enjoyed the evening even more than he'd expected to, and he felt pleasantly confident that the best was still to come.

Jeff signaled to the waitress.

They ended up going back to Austin's hotel. He had wondered if Jeff would prefer somewhere off the beaten track—*Motel 6 in Atlanta?*—but he made no objection when Austin suggested returning to the Stonewall Jackson Inn. If he wasn't relaxed, he was doing a damn good imitation of it.

"That was an amazing dinner. Thank you," Austin said as the Honda sped down the quiet streets past the stately, old homes limned in moonlight. It *had* been an amazing dinner, but not because of the food or drink. Austin had plenty of wonderful meals in his line of work. No, the difference tonight had been the company. Whatever else Jeff might be, he was unnervingly easy to talk to. It had been a long time since Austin had felt this kind of connection with another man.

Jeff said, "It was my pleasure," and, without taking his gaze from the road, lifted Austin's hand, pressing it briefly to his mouth. It was about as old-fashioned and courtly a gesture as you could ask for, but Jeff did it so lightly, so naturally, Austin barely blinked, though his mouth was suddenly dry at the sensation of unexpectedly soft lips against his bare skin.

Jeff, still not looking at him, was smiling. Austin felt his mouth curve too.

CHAPTER SIX

Austin's hotel room was softly lit, the polished tabletops glowing, the books and paintings and flower vases lustrous. The bedding had been turned down.

"Uh-oh," Jeff murmured. "Is it a school night?"

Austin laughed. It had a breathless sound to it. He turned, and Jeff was right behind him, almost stepping on his heels. It was startling, but it made it easy to reach out, each moving to steady the other and somehow winding up in a hug.

Not a clinch. A hug.

It was unanticipated and surprisingly sweet to simply be held in strong arms. No demand, not even a request—just an ordinary hug. Which somehow, in these circumstances, seemed anything but ordinary. Austin could feel Jeff's heart pounding against his own chest, and he picked up the fragrance of Jeff's cologne, now diffused with wine and his own light male scent. Jeff smelled warm and alive in the pristine perfection of the hotel room's recycled air.

He rubbed his smoothly shaven cheek against Austin's. "Hello," he murmured.

"Hello," Austin whispered back.

Jeff's mouth sought his, and there was an artless misjudging of lips and distances before they were kissing again, sharing breaths, laughing.

Austin found both the fumble and the laughter reassuring. He didn't particularly want to go to bed with a porn star.

The kiss moved from companionable to dizzying in a couple of thudding heartbeats. Jeff's mouth pressed harder against Austin's, parting his lips with a delicate tongue, tasting him in a long, fluid kiss. Jeff tasted sweet, structured, and muscular. An earthy Barolo perhaps. Colorful with complex, focused flavors and a long, mellow finish.

"What would you like?" Jeff asked after a bit. "Anything. Just ask."

"I…" What exactly was on offer? Another of Austin's preconceptions toppled. He hadn't expected quite this…generosity.

"Let me suck you off."

Austin's breath caught in his throat. "Are you sure?" His voice came out sounding thin and ragged, because if Jeff meant something else—for example, the more likely, *I want you to suck me off*—the disappointment was going to kill him.

"Hell yeah, I'm sure." Jeff's hands went to Austin's zipper at the same instant Austin's hands went for his own waistband. Austin laughed again, although it felt slightly hysterical, this mutual desperation to get him out of his clothes. His trousers were down around his ankles in a couple of beats. His briefs followed, once he'd navigated them around the flagpole of his cock. Jeff gave him a gentle push, and he sat down, knees weak, on the foot of the bed. Jeff knelt before him.

"Oh yeah. That's what I'm talking about," Jeff said softly, and it seemed touchingly heartfelt.

Austin closed his eyes, sucking in a deep breath at the trails of lightning flashing through his skin as Jeff's hands closed on his hips, Jeff's breath warm against his belly.

Austin's cock was erect and straining; his nerves felt as dangerously exposed as bare wires as Jeff's fingers moved to stroke his thighs. All his body hair seemed to stand up crackling in a storm of static electricity as Jeff bent, closing his mouth over the sensitive head of Austin's cock.

The noise—naked and uninhibited—that tore out of Austin's throat filled him with distant astonishment.

The next sound he uttered was more of a squeak as the hotel-room door jumped beneath a sudden knock. Jeff's fingers dug into his thighs as he steadied himself, and that wonderful mouth stopped working its magic.

"You expecting someone?" Jeff asked in an urgent undertone.

"No." Austin expelled a long, rattled breath. "Maybe they've got the wrong room?"

They listened tensely.

The knocking began again, this time with more energy.

"Crap." Austin rose, scrabbling to drag up his pants without doing himself injury. He started for the door on shaky legs. "Hold that thought."

Jeff didn't respond. His pose was wary, intent. Austin wondered if he'd run out and hide on the balcony if someone walked into the room. He felt a flicker of sadness. It was a shame because he really liked Jeff, but where could you go from that?

He raked his hair out of his eyes, flipped the security bar over, and dragged the door open.

It took a second for his eyes to adjust after the muted light of the bedroom. Cormac Cashel stood in the brightly lit hallway. He wore black jeans, a black sweatshirt with a skull-and-crossbones logo, and his perpetual scowl.

"Hi," Austin said, surprised.

"I wanted to see you."

Austin spared a quick look over his shoulder, but Jeff was standing out of sight behind the corner. "About wha—" The rest of that was lost as Cormac pushed into the room and wrapped his arms around Austin, hugging him tightly.

"I want to be with you tonight," he panted in Austin's ear. He smelled of pot and Irish Spring and nervous perspiration.

"Huh?"

"I…want to…be…with…you," Cormac gasped out as they wrestled. Austin freed his right arm and tried to push him away, but Cormac was strong and agile, and he kept enfolding Austin while trying to cover his mouth with his own.

It seemed to be his night for hugs, but the intent here was clearly different from Jeff's earlier embrace.

"What *are* you doing?" Austin demanded, finally wriggling out of that human straitjacket. The question was mostly rhetorical. He could hardly fail to understand what Cormac was doing—or at least attempting to do.

Cormac reached for him again, the hammer hit the wrestling bell, and it was round two. Austin tried to bat Cormac's clutching hands away as Cormac gulped out, "I feel like a wet seed wild in the hot blind earth."

"You feel *what*?"

"Faulkner said that."

"Faulkner said *that*?"

"William Faulkner. The greatest American novelist who ever lived."

Someday this was going to be funny, but all Austin could think about was Jeff standing a few feet away listening to this—and the fact that Cormac must not discover Jeff's presence in Austin's room. Not least for the sake of Cormac's own dignity.

Losing patience, he stiff-armed the younger man, who gave an *oof.*

"Knock it off!"

Cormac gasped, "You can't say you don't feel it too. I knew the minute I saw you. It's like I've known you all my life. You're exactly how I pictured. Exactly. Well, except for your awful accent."

Oh, great. Another guy who'd spent his formative years pawing through magazines and daydreaming.

"I *don't* feel it. I don't even know you."

"That's why I'm here." Cormac tried to wrap his arms around Austin again, despite Austin's squirming determination to keep a respectable distance. "We're going to get to know each other. That's what I'm aiming for."

Oh, *that's* what he was aiming for. Because it felt like Cormac had trained his sights significantly lower. Austin pushed him back again. "It doesn't work like that!"

"Well, how does it work?" Cormac was starting to sound irritated too. "I know you're gay."

"That doesn't mean… Look, I'm just not…" Austin tempered the truth at the last instant as it occurred to him how lonely and desperate Cormac must be to brave what he had to know was almost certain rejection. "I'm in a relationship. I can't do this with you."

"He wouldn't have to know."

"*I* would know."

Cormac continued to clutch him, breathing unevenly, but at last his breaths slowed. His hands loosened their grasp. "I don't understand. The second I saw you, I knew you were the one."

"I'm sorry." Austin *was* sorry. Cormac was so very genuinely puzzled that the feeling wasn't mutual.

"Are you sure you don't want to?"

"I'm sure." Despite the physical evidence to the contrary. That was more about Jeff standing two feet away, his silhouette half-merged in the other shadows, than the friction supplied by wrestling around with Cormac.

"Well, all right, then." Cormac reluctantly turned away. Austin grabbed the door for him.

"Good-bye," Cormac said disconsolately.

"Good-bye."

"Maybe when you come back to catalog the cellar next time?"

"I… Probably not."

Cormac went out.

Austin closed the door and leaned against it.

Jeff came around the corner. "You okay?" He looked serious—*too* serious.

Austin said, "Hey, it's not funny."

"It was pretty funny from where I was standing."

Someone pounded on the door.

"Oh shit," Jeff muttered, drawing back.

Austin waited till Jeff was out of sight before yanking the door open. Cormac was rearranging his T-shirt with one hand and offering a sheaf of papers with the other.

"Will you at least read my stories?"

Austin took the stack of papers automatically. Where exactly had Cormac stored them? Probably better not to think too much about it.

"Uh, yes, if you'd like me to. I don't write fiction, though."

"I want you to read them."

"Okay."

Crestfallen, Cormac nodded and turned away. Austin closed the door, locked it, set the papers on the table, and moved into Jeff's obliging arms.

"Let's try this again," Jeff said.

Yes. *This.* These muscular arms, this hard, taut body, that warm, smiling mouth.

Jeff murmured, "Did you put out the DO NOT DISTURB sign?"

"Do you think it'll do any good?"

Jeff laughed. "Not in this town."

* * * * *

Velvety, vibrant, voluptuous pulses of pleasure… There was a reason so many of the attributes used in describing wine were sexual. A very good reason. Austin threw his head back on the pillow, gulping for air, shuddering head to toe with the exquisite sensation of Jeff sucking his cock. Once again that crazy, nearly unrecognizable sound tore out of his throat as Jeff's tongue pressed and lapped where he was most sensitive. Was it something unique to Jeff, or was it just some temporary chemical imbalance? He was sort of hoping for chemical imbalance, because falling for Jeff would be such a foolish thing to do.

Round, rich, red… Lights were flashing behind his eyelids, and nerve shocks of colors were tingling through every fiber in his body. Austin felt like he was lighting up, incandescent and luminous with feeling. So much feeling it didn't seem possible to contain it in a human shell. Jeff took him deeper still, that incredible hot, wet mouth moving on him, his breath rolling down the sensitive skin of Austin's inner thighs, and Austin flung his arm across his face to keep himself from yelling. Or to smother the sounds, because there was no corking them completely.

He'd been in a state of partial arousal for most of the evening, and that skillful dredge and drag, the combination of pressure and pull, had every muscle in his body clenching tight, hips jerking as the tight, soft, warm lips brought him so relentlessly, lovingly to the breaking point.

Come the vintage. Where had he heard that phrase? Was it biblical? Was it…?

Austin's teeth closed on the back of his wrist as the explosion tore through him, flash fire racing, spiraling through the amaranthine harvest.

He swung out into a sparkling blue-black darkness and dropped like a star falling out of the sky.

Seasons later he was aware of Jeff settling beside him, running a lazy, appreciative hand down his torso. Austin wanted to say something, acknowledge what Jeff had done for him, assure him that it truly *had* been the best he'd ever had, but he was so beautifully relaxed. His cock rested against his thigh, spent, and the rest of his body felt as soft and boneless. He settled for a long, heartfelt sigh.

Jeff stroked his chest again. He smiled faintly, enjoying Austin's last involuntary shudder of pleasure.

"And I was afraid this was going to be a wasted trip," Austin mumbled.

"And I was thinking this morning was going to be just another ordinary day."

This morning Jeff had woken in Carson's bed. Austin preferred not to think about that.

Jeff lowered his head and licked Austin's nearer nipple. Austin caught his breath.

"Was that true about having a boyfriend?" Jeff asked after a time.

Austin shook his head. "We broke up three months ago."

"Yeah? How long were you together?"

Were they really going to talk about Richard? They were.

"Two years."

"What happened?"

Austin often wondered himself. "It wasn't anything dramatic. One day I realized I'd be happier on my own."

"Just like that?"

"No. I hadn't been happy for a long time, but I hadn't been unhappy enough to do anything about it."

"Why were you unhappy?"

"Maybe I expected too much."

"Like what?" In the moonlight, Jeff's face was so handsome, so perfect, it resembled a mask.

"It's hard to explain. The sex was good, and we had a lot in common, so I kept thinking we'd get there eventually."

"Get where?"

Jeff was beginning to remind Austin of Ernest at his most persistent. He said reluctantly, knowing how sappy he was going to sound, "To…love, I guess."

Jeff said with genuine astonishment, "You kept thinking you'd fall in love with someone you didn't love after two years of being together?"

"Well, how long should it take?"

"Five seconds. Give or take a second." Jeff's eyes, gleaming in the darkness, seemed to hold Austin's for what felt like a very long moment.

Austin swallowed hard.

"Was he in love with you?"

"Who?" Austin asked.

"Your boyfriend. The one you kept waiting to fall in love with."

"Richard. No. I doubt it. He moved in with a guy from his office six weeks after we split up." He reached for the hand that was lightly caressing him, lifted it to his mouth, and kissed it. "Did I even thank you? Thank you. You're the nicest thing that's happened to me in a long time."

He sensed Jeff's smile. The hand he held gave his own a friendly squeeze.

"Where'd you learn to do that?"

"College." Jeff added lazily, "I majored in criminal justice and minored in blowjobs."

Austin considered this while the moonlight glancing through the balcony grillwork strewed wavering cutouts of vines and leaves across the ceiling. It seemed a pretty crass statement from someone who professed to believe in love at first sight. But maybe the five-second rule was more of a guideline. Maybe it was a line, period.

"How do you do this, Jeff?" he asked at last.

Jeff taunted gently, "You need another demonstration?"

"You know what I mean."

Silence.

Jeff pulled his hand away and rolled onto his back. "Sex is sex. It's all good."

"It's not, though. We both know that."

"I don't know any such thing. And you don't know anything about me, Austin."

"I know you're in the closet, and I know you like sucking cock. It seems to me there's a conflict there."

"It seems to me there's a conflict there," Jeff mimicked. "The fact is, you don't know fuck-all about me or my life."

Austin clamped down on his impatience, his anger. He had no right to be angry. Jeff was right. He didn't know fuck-all about him or his life, and just because he didn't understand Jeff didn't mean Jeff's feelings weren't valid. Maybe Jeff did believe that sex was sex and it was all good and it didn't matter if you spent your life denying yourself everything you most needed and wanted. Who was to say what Jeff most needed and wanted, if not Jeff?

"So you never have sex with men? This is unusual?"

The pause lasted so long he gave up on Jeff answering, but at last Jeff gave a long, weary sigh. "I have sex with men. It's nothing like this, all right? You don't want to hear about it. Tonight was… This was something different. Special. One in a million."

The awful part was Austin felt the same way.

Jeff added quietly, "But part of why it's special tonight is because we both know this is a one time only."

Was that true? Was it special only because it was unique? It didn't seem that way to Austin, but he didn't have a lot of experience with one-night stands.

He was shocked to hear himself say, "Is it? Because I feel…like there could be something more here. Or is that just me?"

There was a frozen silence.

"Don't." Jeff's voice was tight. All the mockery, all the joking vanished. "Don't say it. Don't try to turn this into something it's not."

Austin laughed awkwardly, trying to pretend he didn't feel that slow, hot flush of embarrassment washing over him. "I know. I must be overtired or something. It's not like I don't know how this works. That was just… Maybe it's something in the air." He shut up because if he kept talking, he was going to make it worse. He was going to drive Jeff right out of this hotel room. He had already pulled away and was sitting on the edge of the bed, his back to Austin.

Austin thought of and discarded a dozen possible comments. In the end, silence seemed safest.

"Listen." Jeff's voice was muffled. He kept his back to Austin. "It's not just you. But that doesn't change anything. This isn't...going anywhere."

"I know," Austin said quickly, relieved to back away from it. Appalled at how much he had risked—and without justification.

"If you want me to leave—"

"No. God no. I'm not kidding about being overtired. I'm starting to babble."

Jeff lay down again and reached for Austin. "You are," he agreed and covered Austin's mouth with his own.

If it wasn't making love, it was certainly a reasonable facsimile, but Austin was not letting himself think in that direction anymore. He told himself that it was simply sex, passionate, beautiful sex, and there was nothing wrong with it. No need for it to be anything more. Jeff was inventive and experienced, but he was sensitive too, attuned to Austin, seeming to anticipate everything Austin desired before Austin was more than half-aware himself.

Austin shivered beneath a delightful assault of kissing, nipping, caressing. Jeff straddled his body, and Austin could just make out the sheen of his pale hair, the gleam of eyes and his smile in the darkness. His palms stroked Austin's chest, grazing his nipples. That brush of callous hands on sensitive nubs started a restless ache within Austin. He moved uneasily, thrusting up under Jeff.

"We can do that if you want," Jeff whispered, shocking Austin rigid.

More rigid.

Oh, he wanted it, all right. He wanted a lot more than this, but this felt unsafe enough. Not physically unsafe—they were taking reasonable precautions—but emotionally unsafe. He was off-kilter tonight, knocked off balance by Jeff's unpredictable and varied charms.

When he didn't answer immediately, Jeff shifted, finding Austin's cock and pressing into it, grinding against him with a deliberate and slow sensuality. Austin's cock seemed to pulse in time with Jeff's.

"You like that?"

"Yeah," Austin said hoarsely.

"Me too." Jeff's hips rolled with that lazy, sexy rhythm. He rubbed their cocks together. "I used to dream about doing this with you—to you…" He leaned forward, braced on one muscular arm so he could bend down and kiss Austin's eyelids…and the bridge of his nose…and the jut of his chin…his mouth…

Austin couldn't hold back any longer. He began to thrust, rocking his hips in fierce upward motion. Jeff drove back at him. They lost the rhythm, regained it, lost it again, and snapped all restraints, each of them going hell for broke.

Long, fraught minutes passed in a haze.

Jeff went perfectly still. Austin, sweating, trembling, still fighting for his own release, felt the ripples of Jeff's coming extending further and further out like shining water or shock waves. Hot, sharp-scented release burst against his damp skin.

Groaning, Jeff rolled over, pulling Austin on top of him, and Austin thrust violently between Jeff's sinewy and accommodating thighs. There it was—Austin was flying, soaring up and up, not caring as his wings began to melt in bursts of salty, singed white, and he plummeted earthward, dimly surprised when he landed safely in the cradle of Jeff's arms.

He woke to a warm mouth moving on his with gentle insistence.

Smiling, his lips parted in welcome; he reached up to hook an arm around Jeff's broad shoulders and draw him closer. Jeff's mouth smiled against his. He tasted…robust, full-bodied. Sleepy and warm and human.

The last twenty-four hours came back in all their astonishing detail. Austin remembered thinking that nothing must be allowed to go wrong with the Cashel appraisal—shortly before everything that could possibly go wrong had gone wrong. It didn't seem to matter much just now.

He lifted his lashes. Morning. A soft, rosy daylight filtered through the open drapes. Jeff's eyes looked impossibly green in the vernal luminance. There was a faint gold bristle on his jaw, and his hair was sexily mussed.

"Thank you for last night." The whispered words were commonplace enough, but Jeff's expression transformed them into something more.

Or maybe that's what Austin wanted to see. He said, equally unoriginal, "I had a really nice time."

"I wish I could stay, but it's already six o'clock."

Austin wished Jeff could stay too. If Jeff changed his mind, he'd reschedule his own leaving. He couldn't say it, though. He'd said far too much the night before. It had to be Jeff's idea, Jeff's choice, and Austin already knew that wasn't going to happen.

Part of why it's special tonight is because we know this is a one time only.

But for a few sweet heartbeats, it seemed like maybe Jeff would decide to at least postpone his leave-taking.

"You really are something, you know?"

"Naw," Austin mimicked gently.

Jeff laughed. He rested his hand against the side of Austin's face as though trying to memorize him in the soft uncertainty of the morning light.

Austin gazed unblinkingly up at him. *Stay. Please.*

Jeff's face seemed to close. He drew back, rolled lithely off the bed, and reached for his underwear and khakis.

He dressed quickly, efficiently.

Austin enjoyed the view for a few seconds. There was no point rising until Jeff left. He planned to shower and then dress and then hit the road. He'd grab coffee and breakfast on the way, fill the gas tank at that station on the corner... He forced himself to think only of the day ahead, concentrate on the practicalities of his trip home. He must not—*must not*—be stupid about this. Indulging in a one-night stand had been stupid enough. Trying to make it into something more than it was would not only be stupid, it would be pathetic.

Interrupting his thoughts, Jeff said suddenly, "If they do send you back this way, you could give me a call."

Was that supposed to be some grand concession? Judging by the guarded look on Jeff's face, it was.

Austin said neutrally, "Sure."

Jeff swiftly buttoned his shirt.

Austin knew it was a mistake, but he couldn't seem to stop the words. "Do you ever get to DC? Or—"

"No."

Jeff didn't look at him. He reached for his wallet, automatically checking its contents.

Austin opened his mouth, then closed it. What was the matter with him? It wasn't like he couldn't take a hint. Or like Jeff didn't understand what he was saying.

He threw back the bedclothes, and the scent of warm linen and recent sex wafted through the room. He walked to the window and gazed down at the park.

He felt Jeff come up behind him even before warm hands fastened on his biceps.

Jeff said huskily, "Austin. I won't ever forget last night."

Austin said over the tightness in his throat, "The pleasure was all mine."

He could feel Jeff's uncertainty, his hesitation, and it was ridiculous that he found himself unable to make this easy on them both. It was crazy. Crazy to react like this. It wasn't like he hadn't understood the rules of engagement. Or hadn't had them explained to him in words of one syllable.

He hadn't had enough sleep; that was all. And yesterday had been stressful by anyone's standards. Naturally, after all that had happened, the evening with Jeff seemed to take on a greater, almost symbolic importance. Once he was home and everything got back to normal, he was going to wonder what the fuck his problem had been.

Maybe he was coming down with the flu or something.

"Are you…?" Jeff stopped. "Austin?"

He could hear the uneasy question in Jeff's tone, and he nodded tightly to show he was listening. He hoped Jeff didn't say anything that required a verbal response because that was going to be hard to pull off without embarrassing them both.

"You take care of yourself, you hear?" Jeff said at last. He dropped one quick, final kiss on Austin's shoulder and turned away.

Austin was counting the leaves on the tree across the way when he heard the door close.

CHAPTER SEVEN

"It looks like the situation in Madison has finally been resolved," Whitney announced to Austin in passing on the wrought-iron spiral staircase that led from the staff offices.

Austin, heading downstairs on his way to the Martyn, North, & Compeau showroom on Connecticut Avenue, paused. "So it wasn't murder?"

"I have no idea. I suppose not."

Whitney Martyn was a tall and lean forty-something. He had recently started touching up his thinning hair and goatee with hair color and taken to wearing polka-dot shirts. Austin attributed the dye job to Whitney's engagement to Theresa, but what polka-dot shirts signified was beyond him. Today's offering was white with navy blue dots.

Whitney added, "All I know for sure is the daughter phoned yesterday to say that the police had signed off on the cellar, so the appraisal can proceed." He added meaningfully, "She asked to speak to you."

"Who?"

"The girl. Miss Cashel." He said it as though there was some significance to it, but if there was, it escaped Austin. "We'd like you to leave tomorrow if you can arrange it. There've been too many delays already."

"But I can't leave tomorrow," Austin said, startled. "I've got the 1990 champagne cocktail party at Café Milano. In fact, I can't leave this week. Thursday is part four in the wine workshop, and this weekend is the Margaux versus Palmer dinner at Maestro."

"There are no auctions this week. Theresa can handle all the rest of it," Whitney said breezily.

"*Theresa?*" Surprise gave way to alarm. "I host the Maestro dinner. I've hosted it for the last four years."

"Martyn, North, & Compeau hosts the Maestro dinner," Whitney shot back immediately, which was a pretty good hint that he'd been ready for Austin's reaction. "After four years it's probably time to mix things up."

"What's that supposed to mean?"

Whitney's eyebrows arched. "I'm sorry?"

"Is there something I should be aware of?"

Whitney responded in true asshole fashion. "I'm sure there are many things you should be aware of, Austin. Did you have something particular in mind?"

This was not the strategic moment to tackle this, but Austin felt backed into a corner by the news he was being sent back to Georgia in what felt like a deliberate move to shut him out of three major store events. Besides, the idea of returning to Madison filled him with nervous anxiety. It had taken him two weeks to stop hoping every time the phone rang that Jeff might be on the other end. In fact, it had taken a month to stop thinking about Jeff on a daily basis. For some reason he could not make sense of, Austin's brief encounter with Jeff Brady had affected him deeply. The last thing he needed was reexposure to the virus. Even getting another chance at the Lee bottles didn't feel like enough inducement.

"Is there some reason you're not sending Theresa to do this inventory?" It was a mistake to let even a hint of his antagonism show. Austin knew that, and yet he was so rattled, he couldn't help it.

"Theresa doesn't have your experience at this kind of thing."

"She doesn't have my experience at teaching workshops or hosting dinners."

"All the more reason for her to tackle it."

Austin's stomach felt like it rolled onto its side and began its slow descent to the bottom of the sea. "Why would that be?"

Whitney gave him a look that said as clearly as words, *I didn't want to do this now, but since you're insisting...* "Peter and I have made our decision regarding the new position." He drew a deep breath, so maybe he wasn't as calm as he seemed. "We're appointing Theresa senior director."

"Theresa," Austin parroted. *"Theresa?"* Somehow he managed not to say all the undiplomatic things that immediately leaped into his mind—starting with the fact that if Theresa wasn't leading Whitney around by his peanut-sized balls, there was no way she'd be regarded as a serious candidate. She had maybe a third of Austin's qualifications for this job.

Perhaps Whitney knew what he was thinking—maybe because it was what everyone would be thinking. He said sharply, "Certainly Theresa. She's eminently qualified."

Austin had known this was coming, but he still couldn't believe it. It was so blatantly, flagrantly unjust. He had worked so goddamned hard over the past years, and his efforts had paid off. Martyn, North, & Compeau's stodgy, conservative rep had been replaced by a new hip, edgy image. These days they were DC's number one wine shop, and a large part of that was due to Austin's efforts and the following he was building. It wasn't any secret either. Whitney knew it as well as anyone. Knew that everyone internally and externally believed the new job would be—should be—Austin's.

"You don't think you'll be accused of nepotism?" Austin inquired as politely as he could manage. "I mean, she is your fiancée. And the least experienced or qualified person on staff."

Whitney's face went red and then white. "That's a matter of opinion."

"Oh, she's not your fiancée?"

Whitney swallowed. "Be careful, Austin. In case you've failed to get the message, you're not by any means irreplaceable. You work for *us*, not, as everyone here seems to believe, the other way around. Your continued employment following our restructure is contingent on your willingness to work under your new boss." He added, "And speaking of nepotism, let's not forget that you originally landed your position here because Peter and your old man are good friends."

"I was a credentialed master of wine when I was hired. Theresa is one step from a restaurant hostess."

Okay, that wasn't quite fair, but neither was this.

"One more goddamned word," Whitney said, starting to shake, "and you're fired. And if Peter has a problem with it, he can talk to me."

Austin opened his mouth to say the one more goddamned word—two goddamned words, actually—but he remembered he was driving out to the house in Frederick for his father's birthday party that evening. Having to admit to the entire family that he had failed yet again was unbearable. He couldn't do it.

But how the hell could he stay? To roll over and accept this—accept being passed over in favor of Whitney's fiancée—was humiliating. It was insulting. It was demeaning. And given his years of enthusiastic hard work, it was plain old hurtful.

He couldn't stay.

He couldn't leave. This was his world. His life.

But he *couldn't* stay.

Whitney was glaring at him, waiting for him to say it, quivering with anticipated righteous indignation.

In the end, that was what saved Austin: knowing how badly Whitney wanted him to quit. "Excuse me," he managed. "I'm expected downstairs."

* * * * *

"Haaaaapy birthday, dear Harrison, haaaaapy birthday tooo yooooou!"

The exuberant, off-key singing trailed to a straggling stop as Harrison Gillespie drew a deep breath, leaned forward, and efficiently blew out every one of the sixty candles on his birthday cake.

There was a noisy round of applause, and Harrison looked around, smiling broadly as he accepted his dues. He reached out to Ernest, who reluctantly left Austin's side to stand self-consciously within the ring of his father's arm.

"That's my boy," Harrison said.

Ernest coughed and politely covered his mouth.

Though Ernest was small for his age and a deceptively fragile-looking child, there was a marked resemblance between father and son. They had the same fierce, dark eyes, sallow complexion, and aquiline features. Harrison had been a puny, sickly child with a powerful imagination and a will of steel. He had not let anything stand in the way of his desire to become an investigative journalist, and against the odds, he had succeeded beyond even his own dreams. According to all the biographies Austin had read, anyway.

"Presents!" Debra was a petite, pretty, and energetic woman just a couple of years older than Austin. Viv, Austin's public-prosecutor sister, referred to Debra as the "Nazi cruise director." Debra did have a tendency to try to manage people who were getting along fine without her help, but Harrison seemed to take it all in stride. But then there was no question about who wore the pants in Harrison's home.

"Here you are, Harry." Bella, Stepmother #2, offered a square, flat parcel in recycled paper.

The parcel turned out—unsurprisingly, as Bella always gave books— to be a biography of Norman Podhoretz. This was the signal, and everyone pushed their presents forward. Harrison exclaimed at their generosity and accepted his due with the placidity of baby Jesus receiving the wise men. The gifts ranged from a vintage Rolex watch (Rebecca, Stepmother #3) to an exercise video (Bryant, Stepsister #1). Harrison exclaimed graciously over each and every gift.

Austin's offering was a Kindle wireless reading device.

"Well, well," Harrison mused, holding the box up. "Electronic books, eh? That's very thoughtful, Austin."

Ernest's gift was a computer game called NIER. Harrison chuckled and hugged him. "You'll have to teach me how to play this, son."

After the presents came the cake and ice cream and the annual speech from Harrison about his real legacy being his family. His legacy patted him on the back and kissed the top of his head and urged him to hurry up and cut the cake.

Austin listened and ate cake and watched his smiling stepmothers and sisters and brother—and felt like a stranger staring through a window. This was his family. He loved them. And yet he didn't think he could feel more alien if he had been one of those white-haired, angular-faced characters in Ernest's video game.

What was wrong with him tonight?

Partly it was his anxiety at the idea of returning to Ballineen. As much as he'd love to know if the Lee bottles were in that dusty dungeon of a cellar, he dreaded the possibility of running into Jeff again. He was embarrassed when he remembered how worked up he'd gotten over the one night they'd spent together. Sure, the sex had been terrific, but…Austin had carried on like it was love at first sight. He went cold every time he remembered the things he'd blurted to Jeff. Clearly he was not cut out for casual flings. Clearly he was a lot more romantic than he realized. Clearly he was a lot lonelier than he realized.

No, he definitely didn't want to risk running into Jeff again.

Forefront, though, was the worry about what to do over the situation at the wine shop. The more Austin considered the blatant dis of Theresa's promotion over him, the more convinced he was that he needed to do something, needed to react strongly, decisively. React as Harrison would if Harrison had elected to spend his life pursuing something as peripheral as wine consulting—and someone had the balls to challenge him. But the only something left open to Austin was to leave Martyn, North, & Compeau, and the idea of that scared him silly.

Without the clout of MN&C behind him, he was just another guy with a blog and an opinion. And who would care about his opinions if he didn't work for MN&C?

He could try for another position at another wine shop, of course. Start over somewhere. Or he could try for a job at a winery. Or a restaurant.

Or even go for something completely different.

He didn't want to go for something different, though. He loved his work. He loved wine. He was proud of his achievements, even if they didn't feel like much compared to those of his family.

Every time one of his sisters or stepmothers asked him in that tactful way about how his job was going, he was deeply relieved that he hadn't resigned that afternoon. Having to try to explain why he had quit... No.

So maybe he should just accept Theresa's promotion with good grace and be grateful he still had a job.

"I've decided not to sue Mother and Harrison," Ernest informed him when Austin went upstairs to say good night.

"I think that's a wise decision."

Ernest wore green pajamas with dinosaurs. He was brushing his teeth, and he let the toothpaste boil out and spill over his chin and spatter his pajama top. Austin sat on Ernest's bed and watched, fascinated. Ernest didn't give a damn what anyone thought of him, and Austin envied him that. He'd been a neurotic mess of insecurities at Ernest's age. He was probably still a neurotic mess of insecurities compared to Ernest.

"Not because I wouldn't win," Ernest said, foaming at the mouth. "I would. But you were right about my birthday and Christmas. I don't think Mother and Father will let me build a reflecting telescope in the attic if I sue them."

"You're all heart, Ernesto."

Ernest made an *ar-ar-ar* sound like a laughing sea lion. "Humor, earthling!" He nearly choked on toothpaste and had to retreat to the bathroom, where he was wasting gallons of water running the taps at full blast.

Austin was still chuckling when Ernest returned, dripping but foam free.

"I'm going to make them let me come home on weekends."

"Oh?" Austin said noncommittally.

"Harrison will do that for me," Ernest said, supremely confident. Maybe he was right. Harrison wasn't traveling much these days, and it wasn't like Ernest was a child who required a lot of parental interaction.

Ernest's small, wet hands locked on Austin's shoulders, and he gave Austin a quick, damp kiss on his forehead. "I'm going to bed now. Good night."

Amused at his clear dismissal, Austin rose. "Right. Night." He dropped a quick kiss on Ernest's spiky, little-boy-smelling hair and went to the door. "Lights on or off?"

"On. I'm going to read." Ernest picked up a copy of *An Introduction to Modern Astrophysics* and crawled between sheets featuring *The Jetsons*. The sheets were Debra's choice. Ernest disapproved of *The Jetsons*.

"Nighty-night," Austin said and left him there surrounded by his mobiles of distant galaxies and assorted glow-in-the-dark models of planets and stars.

"Your father wants to speak to you," Debra said when Austin arrived downstairs. "He's in his study."

Austin nodded, ignoring that flare of foreboding, and headed for Harrison's study, where he found his father reclining in the big leather chair behind his desk, enjoying his habitual after-dinner cigar and brandy.

"Help yourself, Austin," Harrison instructed.

Austin loathed cigars—few things were more effective at spoiling palate and nose—but he poured himself a brandy and took the chair on the other side of his father's desk. Now that he thought about it, most of his meetings with his father took place either across this desk or meal tables. He could count on one hand the number of hugs he remembered receiving—even including when he was younger than Ernest. But Harrison had mellowed with age. He was more sentimental these days.

"You're very quiet tonight," Harrison said, studying the tip of his cigar. "Everything all right?"

"Yes. Everything's fine, Dad."

Harrison's dark gaze moved to Austin's face, scrutinizing him. "How's the job?"

"Fine." More than ever, Austin was glad he had not quit in a fury that afternoon. Peter was liable to phone Harrison with the news. No way would Austin's resignation have gone unnoticed. He had an uneasy feeling not even his recent run-in with Whitney had gone unnoticed.

"I see." Harrison was silent. Austin felt his nerves tighten. "You know, Austin," Harrison said at last, "you're getting to an age when it's time to make some decisions about the future."

Austin sipped his brandy and waited, nerves on edge.

"You rejected the idea of journalism, even though that's what you majored in and that's what you've got a degree in. You wanted to try music and then modeling. Well, your mother was a model, so I guess that's not as strange as it might otherwise have been."

"I did the modeling for spending money. It wasn't ever a career choice."

"I'm relieved to hear it. Or would be, except for the fact that you don't seem to have ever settled on *any* career choice. At nine, Ernest has a better idea of what he wants to do with his life than you do at twenty-nine."

Austin could feel the blood draining from his face. It had been a long time since they'd had one of these father-son chats. He'd have been happy to go the rest of his life without another one. "I have settled on a choice. I'm a master of wine—"

"Oh, for Christ's sake," Harrison burst out. "That's a hobby. That's not a career. What the hell kind of job is that for a grown man? Master of wine. That's one step from claiming you want to be a Jedi knight when you grow up." Harrison broke off and seemed to struggle for a more reasonable tone. "I understand you have some resentments, but it's time to pull yourself together. I can get you a starting position at the *Washington Post* the minute you say the word."

"I don't want to be a journalist." Like it wasn't hard enough living up to the legend? Try competing in the same field.

"Then why the hell did you study journalism in college?"

"Because *you* wanted me to."

That took Harrison aback for a moment, but he recovered quickly. "You didn't know what you wanted to do with your life then, and you still don't. Sometimes I even think this whole matter of your sexual orientation is just…" Harrison let that go.

Austin asked evenly, "Is just what?"

Harrison's eyes were as black and hard as jet. "I'm not sure. Fear of competition? A bid for attention? Adolescent rebellion?"

Well, he'd asked. Now he knew. He should probably be furious. Oddly, he just felt numb. Numb and more depressed than he'd ever felt in his life. Austin set his brandy snifter on the desk and rose.

"I'm not an adolescent, and I'm not aware of any particular resentment. I've always been proud to be your son." Harrison's face changed. He moved as though to speak, but Austin made himself finish. "My sexuality doesn't have to do with anything but me. It's not a choice. I'm sorry the choices I *have* made with my life disappoint you, but better you than me."

"Austin—"

"Night, Dad. Happy birthday."

CHAPTER EIGHT

It was already unseasonably hot and sultry at ten o'clock in the morning. The scent of roses and rust drifted on the restless breeze along with the *scrape, scrape, scrape* of a rake on stone. The same young black man Austin had seen working in the front garden of Ballineen was still at it. He didn't seem to have made much progress against the encroaching jungle during the past month.

One of the green shutters had fallen to the grass, giving the face of the house a bare, lopsided look, like a woman missing one of her false eyelashes.

The peeling front door opened, and Carson Cashel, dressed in tight white jeans and a black-and-white-polka-dot midriff top that revealed her flat tummy and emphasized her small, perky breasts, drawled with friendly mockery, "Why, Mr. Gillespie, I do declare."

Remembering his last trip to Ballineen, Austin said, "How was your party?"

She looked blank, then laughed. "It was a lot of fun till Cormac got thrown out for fighting."

"What was the fight over?"

"I don't remember now. Something to do with whether Carson McCullers was as fine a writer as Mr. Faulkner. Did you read Cormac's stories?"

Did she know under what circumstances those stories had been delivered to him? Austin wondered, meeting her bright, mischievous eyes.

"I did, yeah."

"Lucky thing, because I know Cormac is looking forward to talking to you." Yes, she was definitely laughing at him. "I told that boss of yours that he was to send you and no one else."

"Thanks."

Austin followed her into the house. Buckets had been strategically placed down the front hallway to catch leaks near the window casements. His nostrils twitched. The place smelled strongly of dampness, cooking turnips, and ham.

"Corrie said he didn't believe you would come back, but I knew you would."

"How did you know that?"

"I just had that feeling." As Carson led him down the dark hallways, she added, "I checked the cellar myself this morning, and everything seems normal. For this house. They never did figure out how poor Dom ended up down here."

"It's only been a month. The investigation must still be ongoing?"

"I suppose so. It sure is a mystery."

"I hope you don't mind my saying so," Austin remarked, "but you seem to take Williams's death pretty much in stride."

"Ballineen is a very old house. A lot of people have died here." Carson added, "Any old how, there's no use me pretending to feel something I don't feel. It was all over between Dom and me long before crazy Henry started threatening to kill us."

"Crazy Henry. You mean Williams's wife?"

"That's right. But in fairness to Henry, I'm sure a lot of people were happy to see the last of Dom. He did have a tendency to get on your nerves. Although, *personally*, I think it was probably just an unfortunate accident, his landing in our cellar."

"Is that what the sheriffs say?"

"Oh, they don't tell us anything."

"But it *is* all right for me to work in the cellar? The sheriffs have okayed it?" Austin couldn't help that flash of suspicion. The Cashels seemed to have peculiar notions of law and order.

He wasn't reassured when Carson chortled without answering.

A thin voice wafted from the parlor as they passed. "Is that him, honey? Is that Mr. Gillespie?"

Carson whispered, "You better look in and say hello to Auntie Eudie."

Austin followed her into the parlor. Auntie Eudie sat in her accustomed place on the moth-eaten sofa. She wore wire spectacles and was industriously knitting what appeared to be some kind of fox-fur stole complete with merino-wool paws.

She bestowed as friendly a smile as if Austin was a longtime friend, and Austin found himself bending down to kiss her dry, wrinkled cheek. She smelled comfortably of apple-blossom talc and gingerbread. "Why, you sit down here and tell me all the news, Mr. Gillespie."

Austin had that familiar sense of being caught in a social riptide. There was something so…alternate universe about the Cashels. It seemed easier to go with the flow than to try to fight.

He gave a brief and probably uninformative account of the weeks since he'd left Madison. Auntie Eudie listened, her bright eyes fixed politely on his face while her fingers nimbly maneuvered the glinting needles.

"You poor boy," she said disconcertingly at the end of his dull recital. "You're plumb tuckered out. You need a nice long vacation."

"You do look interestingly pale," Carson put in mischievously, leaning over the back of the sofa so that her cheek nearly brushed Austin's.

"It's been a long week." Austin did his best to change the subject, but the only thing he could think of was the unfortunate topic of Dominic Williams.

Auntie Eudie's cheeks turned pink with indignation. "It's perfectly clear to me that the colonel struck down Mr. Williams for sticking his nose where he had no business."

Austin vaguely remembered her saying something along those lines the last time. "You mean you think some supernatural force killed Mr. Williams?"

Auntie Eudie looked at him over her spectacles. "Ballineen is haunted. Don't ever doubt that, Mr. Gillespie."

"I won't."

"Well, Mr. Gillespie has a mighty big job ahead of him," Carson interjected brightly.

"That's right," Auntie Eudie said. "You go right ahead and start counting those bottles, Mr. Gillespie, but don't forget to come upstairs for your meals. We're having a proper Southern dinner for you today."

Austin assented, thanked her, and escaped.

"Did you really read Cormac's stories, Mr. Gillespie?" Carson inquired as they headed down the first flight of stairs to the cellar.

"I did."

"Well, don't you worry about telling Cormac the truth. He doesn't mind what people say about *his* work, so long as they don't disrespect Mr. Faulkner."

By which, Austin was quite sure, she didn't mean the faithful family retainer. He began to feel increasingly nervous about those stories.

At last they reached the cellar, which was remarkably cool despite the heat of the day and smelled blessedly free of dead bodies and bug spray both. Austin saw no sign of crime-scene tape or anything to indicate an investigation was still in progress, so perhaps Williams's death *had* been an accident.

The card table and chair were back in position beneath the giant spiderweb. Austin set his laptop case down and unzipped it.

"What *did* you think of Cormac's stories?" Carson asked with sudden seriousness.

Austin glanced around. "I thought they were really well written, but I don't know a lot about publishing or selling fiction."

"Oh, Corrie doesn't care about *that*. He means for the stories to be published *after* he's gone."

"Gone where?"

She giggled. "*Dead*, silly."

"Oh." Considering that four out of ten protagonists in Cormac's stories had killed themselves, Austin wondered if departure was imminent. Anything he might have added was forgotten as muffled voices floated down from above.

"One more time and you won't have to worry about your parole officer. I'll ring your scrawny neck and feed you to the dogs."

Parole officer? Austin stared ceilingward. "What's that?"

Carson widened her eyes and said in a spooky voice, "Why, that's the colonel, Austin. He doesn't like people fooling around his wine cellar."

"Very funny."

Another voice, lower and indistinct, answered the first. The words weren't clear, but the defensive tone filtered through the bricks, wood, and termites.

Carson laughed. "Naw, that's Faulkner. And Tyrone, it sounds like. Tyrone's Faulkner's nephew. Great-nephew. As a matter of fact, Tyrone is going to help you out today. We thought it would go faster that way, and you won't have to get your hands dirty."

"I'm not afraid to get my hands dirty." Austin spent a part of every year backpacking in places like South America and Australia, checking out remote wine-growing areas.

"No, I guess you're not." She gave him an oddly shrewd look. "Tyrone is Auntie Eudie's project. You might have noticed him when you drove up. He's supposed to be trimming the boxwood, although that's always a risk because he likes to make the hedges into shapes. Animals and such. What do you call that?

"Topiaries?"

"Topiaries. That's right."

"You're kidding."

"No. No, Ty's very artistic. But that doesn't cut any ice with Faulkner. So it's always kind of…tense when Tyrone is staying with us because Auntie Eudie and Faulkner butt heads over his…administration."

"His what?"

"I guess I'll leave you to it," Carson announced with one of those bewildering changes of subject. She headed for the staircase. "Now don't forget about lunch. Jeff is coming."

Austin froze. "Jeff?" he repeated as though the concept of Jeff was utterly foreign. In some ways that was probably true.

"Sure! You remember Jeff?" She chuckled. "He remembers you."

What the hell did that mean?

Austin must have had a peculiar expression because Carson confided, "When I told him you were back, he insisted on coming to lunch. I think he's partial to Auntie Eudie's greens. What do you think?"

"So you and Jeff are still seeing each other?"

Carson giggled. "Oh Lordy. I think we've seen all there is to see of each other."

Austin opened his laptop, turned it on. He was angry with himself for asking such a question—and for caring about the answer. One night. That's all it had been. And he thought *these* people were crazy?

"Jeff is a PI. Did you know that? Henry Williams hired him to find Dom." Carson seemed enormously amused at the idea that Jeff had been poking around Ballineen—literally—on a job. Or maybe it still hadn't occurred to her that Jeff had been using her. Austin swallowed all the things he would have liked to say.

Carson continued up the rickety staircase, calling cheerfully, "I'll send Tyrone down to you. You just tell him what you want him to do."

"I honestly don't need any help."

"Don't be silly."

She trotted away up the stairs.

Overhead, Tyrone the Possible Jailbird Artist and Faulkner the Faithful Family Retainer continued to exchange loud pleasantries. Austin brought up the file with the Ballineen inventory.

He stared unseeingly at the list before him.

It hadn't totally escaped him that he might run into Jeff, but he'd been fairly sure Ballineen would be a Jeff-free zone since Jeff's purported main interest in Carson had been her connection to Dom Williams. Austin had even assumed that once that connection was revealed, Jeff wouldn't be welcome at Ballineen. But he'd got it wrong. Jeff, it seemed, was a regular fixture at the old homestead.

What was up with that he-remembers-you business? Had Jeff told Carson what had passed between them?

No. No, if only because Jeff would never reveal that he'd been to bed with another man.

Austin rubbed his forehead tiredly. He couldn't deal with this right now. Could not deal with Jeff. It felt as if his whole life was coming apart. If he had to run into Jeff again, he wanted it to be when he was feeling strong and successful and in control, not when he felt like a loser professionally and personally—and with the memory of this last romantic failure vivid in his mind.

Resting his face in his hands, Austin breathed quietly, trying to gather himself for the job ahead. He'd been on the move ever since he walked out of the house in Maryland. Suddenly he was exhausted.

Where do I go from here? For years he'd convinced himself he was building something, achieving something: excelling at a career he found satisfying and rewarding—and maybe even, eventually, earning the respect of the people he loved. Now he discovered that the people he loved didn't even believe in the validity of his sexual orientation, let alone his career choice. His job was hanging by a thread. In fact, if he had any guts, he'd cut the thread himself. He had failed with Richard; he had failed professionally—

He caught motion out of the corner of his eye. A spider had dropped from the web above him and was crawling over his keyboard. Austin brushed it away, rose, and moved the card table out from under the web. He decided to postpone his breakdown for the comforts of the hotel bar that evening.

A short while later Tyrone arrived downstairs. He was about twenty, tall, and strikingly good-looking, despite the tattoos that covered both arms. He wore baggy, distressed jeans and a white-and-purple WAR GOING ON T-shirt.

"Miz Carson says you need some help down here?"

"I honestly don't have anything for you to do," Austin told him. The last thing he wanted was help. He wanted to stay so busy he didn't have one spare second to think about the all-too-swiftly-approaching lunchtime and the inevitable encounter with Jeff.

Tyrone's face fell. He'd probably been looking forward to escaping yard work in that humid heat for a while. "I could be a big help to you. I'm a hard worker, sir."

Austin wasn't sure he bought the puppy-dog eyes and humble expression, but he relented anyway. It was a huge task, and whether he wanted to admit it or not, he could use help—unless he wanted to spend the next month in the spider-festooned bowels of Ballineen.

"All right. You read me the labels, and I'll check for them on the inventory list. If they're not on the main list, we'll add them to a separate tally sheet."

"Thank you, *suh*!" Tyrone said, sounding for an instant like Faulkner at his most ironic.

In the end, Austin's decision to accept Tyrone's help was a good move. Not only did it halve the work involved in moving from table to shelves, but Tyrone turned out to be surprisingly charming. He asked a lot of well-founded questions about wine and winemaking, which kept Austin's mind blessedly occupied.

"You're an artist. Is that right?" he asked during a rare lull.

Tyrone gave him a cheeky grin. "That's what Miz Eudie say. She should know."

"Did you grow up around here?"

Tyrone's smile faded. "I grew up in Atlanta. My mama used to send me to stay here to keep me out of trouble."

"Can't you get into trouble in Madison?"

Tyrone's smile returned—momentarily sharkish. "If you know where to look, you can." He picked up the next bottle and read the label.

Austin considered this as he checked the inventory list. He could see Madison might not be the first choice for a streetwise kid from Atlanta, and something told him Faulkner was probably not the most patient guardian for a teenage screwup. Not that Tyrone was a teenager anymore.

"Do you miss Atlanta?"

Tyrone offered another of those wide grins and declined to comment.

Eventually one o'clock rolled around, and Austin's stomach began to knot with nervous dread. He wondered what would happen if he just kept working and didn't go upstairs? They couldn't *force* him to eat lunch, after all.

"What about this bottle?" Tyrone inquired, holding up a 1959 Hermitage La Chapelle. "Is this a valuable one?"

"That's about a ten-thousand-dollar bottle of wine," Austin said carefully. "Don't drop it."

"Wow! Ten thousand dollars for a bottle of wine. Looks like the Crazy Cashels are going to be swimming in bread." Tyrone replaced the bottle with exaggerated care.

"The Crazy Cashels?" Austin inquired curiously. "Is that how people around here think of them?"

"Yeah, but they're not so bad. You just gotta know how to handle them." He watched Austin click on the inventory sheet. "You going upstairs?"

"Eventually." Austin checked the time on his desktop. One twenty. His palms started to perspire. He wiped them on his jeans. Really, what the hell *was* his problem? He and Jeff had had a nice time together, and that was that. So, okay, yes, he would have liked to see Jeff again, and Jeff had not been averse to that. He had said Austin should call if he was ever in town again.

Yeah, that was the part that hurt. Because Jeff was also not averse to never seeing Austin again.

"When do you think you're going upstairs?" Tyrone asked a few minutes later. At Austin's look of inquiry, he said, "I want to know when I should take my dinner break."

"Sorry, I didn't think about that. You can go now." Austin glanced at his desktop. One thirty-five. His heart sank. "I'll see you when you get back."

Footsteps thumped down the stairs. Cormac appeared, scowling as usual. "Were you coming up to dinner?" Austin hesitated. Cormac put in, "Or we could just have ours down here and talk?"

Austin glanced at Tyrone, who was smiling to himself as he pulled a comb out of his pocket and ran it across his stick-straight hair.

"I think we'd better go up," Austin said, pretending not to notice Cormac's disappointment.

* * * * *

"There you are." Auntie Eudie greeted them as they entered the dining room. "Mr. Gillespie, you sit right here between me and Cormac."

Austin self-consciously took his seat next to Cormac and across from Carson. A quick glance placed Jeff on the other side of the table and down one. Jeff looked absolutely unchanged, but then how changed could he be in the space of a month? His green gaze met Austin's across the brown-and-white china. He offered his heartbreaker smile.

"Hi, Austin. So they sent you back after all."

"Hi. Yes."

Auntie Eudie handed Austin a large bowl of some really revolting-looking green mush she referred to as collard greens, and he was able to turn away. He made sure he stayed busy passing salt and pepper and butter and biscuits and anything else he could lay his hands on. But eventually he ran out of busywork, and when he risked a look down the table, Jeff was staring at his plate with a somber expression.

Austin's phone rang. He apologized, checked it, and saw that the call was from Ernest. The temptation to leave the table and take the call was great, but Austin resisted.

When he glanced up again, Jeff was smiling his way. It was an oddly tentative smile.

Austin smiled politely back.

Roark, who had been eating since Austin entered the room, put his fork down and said grimly, "How much longer is this inventory supposed to take?"

"It's going to take at least a week merely to count everything," Austin answered. "Longer to authenticate."

"Why?"

"You've probably got a thousand bottles down there. Everything from two-dollar Charles Shaw to 1959 Hermitage La Chapelle. And not shelved in any particular order that I can see. This isn't a job you want me to rush through."

Roark looked unconvinced on that point as he picked up his fork and resumed eating. He glowered at Austin.

A bare foot brushed lightly over Austin's ankle. He sat up straight. Carson winked at him from across the table.

Faulkner entered the room carrying a carved ham on a platter. He lowered it carefully to the table.

"My, my, doesn't that smell delicious?" Auntie Eudie murmured. "You're in for some real down-home Southern cooking, Mr. Gillespie."

"It smells great." Austin was confident no morsel of food could possibly wind its way through his digestive tract, given the knots his stomach was in every time he looked at Jeff. Nonetheless, he bravely took some of everything and shoveled it in, washing it down with swallows of tooth-achingly sweet iced tea.

Afterward he remembered almost nothing of the meal itself or the conversation, although everyone seemed to eat and talk continuously. All his awareness seemed centered on Jeff, who, as far as Austin could tell, was doing his level best to charm the birds off the trees—or more likely, the moths out of the draperies.

At the end of the meal, Roark pushed his chair back and, weaving slightly, announced he had work to do.

Hopefully it was nothing that involved heavy machinery. Austin waited till Roark safely cleared the doorway before saying, "Same here. That was a wonderful lunch, though."

Carson asked, "Is Tyrone making himself useful?"

"Yes, he is. He's very helpful."

"That's nice. Maybe his last...stay in Atlanta did him some good, bless his heart."

"That boy is badly misunderstood," Auntie Eudie murmured, helping herself to another slice of cobbler. "You know, he's a very talented artist."

Cormac snorted. "I guess you can call forgery 'art.'"

"Any sign of the Lee bottles?" Jeff asked, speaking directly to Austin for the first time since he'd greeted him.

"No. Nothing so far." Austin's gaze seemed to tangle up in Jeff's before he was able to look away.

"More iced tea?" Auntie Eudie asked of no one in particular.

Austin shook his head.

* * * * *

Back downstairs, Austin found himself on his own, Tyrone still on lunch break.

He picked up the legal pad and studied it, then walked over to the shelf where they had left off. He picked up the next bottle. A 2008 Sutter Home chenin blanc. From the sublime to the ridiculous. He sighed.

From up above, the cellar-door hinges squeaked loudly, followed by the quick, light tread of someone coming downstairs. Instantly Austin's neck muscles went so tight he thought he was going to throw his back out. He knew who it was without having to turn, but he turned anyway.

Jeff reached the bottom step, glanced casually around the cellar, and walked up to Austin. He was smiling and seemed perfectly relaxed.

"You didn't call me."

"Sorry?"

"When you got in last night. You should have given me a call. I would have made time to get together."

"I'm flattered."

Jeff's blond brows drew together. "Why's that?"

Austin let it go. "I got in pretty late last night."

"Oh. Well. What time do you think you'll be wrapping it up today?"

Illogically, as much as Austin did not want a confrontation, his anger mounted at Jeff's easy acceptance of the situation between them. He, on the other hand, didn't even know what the situation *was*. He said shortly, "I don't know. I'm going to try and work as late as I can tonight. I want this job done as fast as possible."

Jeff's smile faltered, recovered. "How's the boy genius?"

"What?"

"Your kid brother. Has he adjusted to the idea of boarding school yet?"

"He's getting there." Austin stared determinedly at the shelf of wine in front of him.

There was a fresh X on the dusty label of the 1959 Hermitage La Chapelle. Had Tyrone marked the bottle for some reason?

Austin scanned the shelves he and Tyrone had inventoried. There were several bottles with those small X's. He moved to the shelves they hadn't got to yet. No X's in the grime and dust. Were these marked bottles wines Tyrone wanted to learn more about? Was it a coincidence that all the bottles Tyrone had marked were very valuable?

He became aware that the pause following his reply to Jeff was beginning to stretch too long.

Jeff said quietly, "You riled at me about something?"

Riled? No, Deputy Dawg, I'm not riled. Why would I be riled? Austin gave him a steady, direct look. "Me? No."

Jeff stared at him for a long moment. "Yeah, you are. What's wrong?"

"Nothing." He made himself add, "I've got a lot to do. That's all."

After an astonished second, Jeff said, "Pardon me for taking up your valuable time."

Austin opened his mouth, but Jeff had already turned and was vanishing back up the stairs.

CHAPTER NINE

The thunderstorm started around three.

The feeble light overhead flickered, went out, and as Austin reached blindly to steady himself in the inky darkness, flared back on while the old house shook in the wake of a long, booming roll of thunder. The bottles rattled musically on their shelves.

"Crap," Austin muttered. The power was probably going to go for good any minute, and he was going to have to crawl out of the cellar on his hands and knees.

He waited grimly. The lightbulb swung gently back and forth, throwing eerie shadows.

Austin returned to work, and though the house shook and groaned beneath the storm's onslaught, the power did not go off for more than a few seconds at a time.

Tyrone finally returned around three o'clock carrying a ghetto blaster. He apologized for taking so long to get back. "Womenfolk," he said with a wink.

Womenfolk? Did people really still say that? Not in Austin's neck of the woods. Did people still say *neck of the woods*?

"I noticed you marked some of the bottles," Austin commented. "Did you have questions about them?"

Tyrone looked startled and guilty. "No."

He hadn't denied marking the bottles, Austin noted. Surely he would have if he was up to something?

They resumed work, picking up where Austin had left off. Tyrone's ghetto blaster pumped out a frenetic song about bombs over Baghdad.

Tyrone said, "I guess I was just fooling around, not paying attention."

"Hmmm?"

"When I drew in the dust."

"Oh sure."

Tyrone was smiling at him, a bright, guileless grin, but Austin couldn't help thinking that it had taken him a long time to come up with an explanation. In fact, Austin had forgotten about the *X*'s until then. He began to puzzle uneasily over Tyrone's earlier questions and interest.

He was guiltily aware that he might be suspicious simply because he knew Tyrone had a criminal past. And that, of course, could explain why Tyrone was still worrying about the *X*'s. He was probably used to being everyone's favorite suspect the minute anything remotely suspicious happened.

Around five o'clock they reached a long line of Madeira. Austin's heart sped up. This might be it. The wine in the Lee bottles was Madeira. His gaze fell on four empty spaces in a row on the rack.

Four. Just like the Lee bottles.

"Something wrong?" Tyrone asked from right behind him.

"This is odd." Austin glanced back. Tyrone was staring at him with peculiar intensity. Austin pointed out the four empty slots.

Tyrone shrugged. Austin could smell his perspiration and his musky aftershave. Both of them were very strong up this close. Nerves. Tyrone was nervous. Why?

"The Crazy Cashels like wine with their supper. So what?"

A dead leaf crackled under the sole of Austin's high-tops. No. Not a dead leaf. A brown and dry cherry blossom. He knelt to pick it up. The cherry blossoms were long gone. This had been tracked inside a month or so ago. The papery petals crumbled in his hand.

Tyrone stared at the blossom and then at Austin. Something flickered in his eyes. Austin's scalp prickled. He rose quickly, telling himself he wasn't seeing what he thought he was seeing—it was too unbelievable.

They both jumped at footsteps coming down the stairs. Tyrone was suddenly smiling again, showing that big, wide, goofy smile. He winked at Austin.

"You got company."

Cormac appeared, looking sleepy and smelling of pot. "You can go," he told Tyrone arrogantly.

Tyrone glanced at Austin, inviting him to share the joke. He drawled, "Yes, *suh, Mistah* Cashel, *suh*!" He sauntered past Cormac and up the stairs.

Cormac glared after him. He turned back to Austin and smiled. "I haven't had a chance to really talk to you."

"It's been a busy day."

Cormac was still smiling. "But you're working for us, so we get to say when you can take a break."

"It's not quite like that."

Cormac walked toward him, smiling with foolish affection, his eyes slightly unfocused. He held his arms out as though to hug Austin.

"Not this again," Austin protested, backing up into the wine racks.

"But why not?"

"Because I'm here to *work*."

Cormac stuck his bottom lip out in a boyish pout, reminding Austin briefly of Ernest, though Ernest didn't pout much. He was more about world domination. "So what? You can do both, can't you?"

"I don't want to do both," Austin said, losing patience.

Cormac stopped and placed his hands on his hips. "I don't understand you!" It was obvious that he was telling the simple truth.

"I thought there was no gay in Georgia," Austin said bitterly.

Cormac blinked his long lashes, looking more confused than ever.

"Look, I like you," Austin said patiently, "but I'm not in the mood right now. Why don't we talk about your stories?"

"How can you not be in the mood?" Cormac confided, "I'm always in the mood. Carson's always in the mood."

Uh-oh. "That's nice, but I really have a lot to do. See all these shelves? Let's talk about your stories, and then I have to get back to work."

Cormac wrapped his arms around Austin and thrust gently against him. "Just a quickie."

"Will you knock it off?" Austin freed himself with less patience. "*No.* Read my lips."

Cormac stared at Austin's mouth intensely and then plastered his own to it.

Somewhere in the distance, Austin heard footsteps pounding down the stairs again.

He pinched Cormac's arm hard, and Cormac broke contact and yowled into his face like a startled cat.

"Sorry to break this up," Jeff said coldly, "but there's a tornado warning."

"There's always a tornado warning," Cormac said irritably.

Jeff was staring at Austin as though Austin had crawled out from behind the shelves with the other insects.

Austin stared stonily back. Jeff had one hell of a nerve disapproving of anything *he* did.

"Why are you here all the time, anyway?" Cormac demanded of Jeff.

Jeff gave him a level look and said nothing.

A few seconds later Auntie Eudie and Carson came trooping downstairs, followed by Faulkner. They carried blankets, pillows, and an assortment of books, flashlights, and candles. Faulkner, freighting a picnic basket, closed the door behind them.

It began to look like they were preparing for a state of siege, seeming to take the tornado warning seriously. That was a surprise. Maybe Ballineen was truly in the twister's path. That was pretty much the way Austin's luck was running these days. In fact, at this point, getting blown away by a tornado might be an improvement.

"Isn't Mr. Cashel coming downstairs?" Austin asked.

"Daddy won't come down to the cellar," Carson told him. "He says a true Southern gentleman never acknowledges fear."

Cormac put in sardonically, "Plus he'd be in more danger trying to negotiate the stairs than he is up there."

Faulkner switched the CD player on Tyrone's ghetto blaster to the radio. A newscaster announced, "If you can hear my voice, you are in the tornado-warning area."

"Tyrone just left here about ten minutes ago," Austin said.

Faulkner said stiffly, "Tyrone can look after himself."

"Don't you worry. We'll hear him if he bangs on the storm doors," Auntie Eudie reassured him.

Austin watched them find folding chairs and set them up. Faulkner dug out a cobwebbed kerosene lantern and lit it. They seemed to have it down to a science.

"How long is the tornado warning likely to last?"

"Just depends." Carson pulled out a deck of cards and began to shuffle them. "Strip poker?" she suggested to Jeff.

Jeff grinned lazily and joined her at the card table.

"Want to play cards, Mr. Gillespie?" Carson inquired.

"I'm going to try to work as long the light holds out." He added doubtfully, "*Will* the light hold out?"

"Sure it will," Jeff said. "Unless we actually get hit by the tornado." His gaze glittered wickedly in the gloomy light.

Auntie Eudie took out her knitting, and Faulkner fiddled with the dials on the ghetto blaster. Austin continued to work, trying to ignore the flirtatious background conversation between Jeff and Carson. He was unhappily aware that beneath the teasing banter, Jeff was angry—angry with him—and that there was an underlying message for Austin in many of his comments. Even if Austin couldn't figure out what the message was.

"You want your laptop turned off?" Jeff asked Austin as Carson began to deal cards. "You don't want to take a chance of it getting zapped or knocked off this table. Your whole life is in there."

"Just what do you plan on doing on this table, Jefferson?" Carson murmured.

Austin crossed to the table and powered down his laptop, acutely conscious of Jeff—the fine blond hairs on his tanned forearm, the gold-tipped eyelashes concealing his gaze, the hint of men's fragrance—bergamot, citrus, basil, mint, and something else. Something intrinsically Jeff.

Jeff ignored him. With the lid closed on his laptop, Austin moved back to the safety of the wine racks.

If he looked at the situation dispassionately, it was sort of strange how much…energy and emotion there was between him and Jeff. They had only spent one night together, after all. Yet he had spent a month trying not to think about Jeff and getting angry because Jeff could apparently not think about him—and here Jeff was angry because Austin didn't want to pick up where they had left off.

Cormac came to join him. "Can I help you?"

"Sure. If you read the labels, I'll write them down on this pad."

For a time they worked together, and Austin was able to tune out Jeff and Carson's chatter.

"What's so special about wine, anyway?" Cormac asked. "It's just booze."

"It's not just booze," Austin argued. "From the beginning, wine has possessed symbolic and spiritual significance. It's a communion between man and nature. It links centuries and generations."

"How many wines do you taste in a wine tasting?" Carson asked from the table.

"Usually not more than fifty. It's hard to keep clarity of palate after that."

"Clarity of anything, I'd say. You must get drunk as a skunk!"

"He doesn't inhale," Jeff drawled, and Carson giggled.

"What's the best wine you ever had?" Cormac asked.

"I can't really say. It's not like that. Every wine is different and... mutable."

Austin fully expected Cormac to guffaw, but he continued to watch him with that intense, scowling expression. "Wine changes all the time. Every day makes a difference in the life of a grape. Once the wine is bottled, it continues to mature. Even after it's opened, it continues to interact with air and sunlight and glass. Seven different glasses means seven different tastes of wine."

"So some of these old wines are still good to drink? They wouldn't just be for collecting?"

"Some of these wines would be *great* to drink," Austin told him. "I would love to drink some of these old wines. I had an 1864 Angelica a few years back that was produced during the Civil War, and it was amazing. Very aromatic. It tasted of raisins and walnuts. Very sweet with a long and flavorful finish. One of the best wines I can remember was an 1870 Château Montrose. I don't know how to explain it. It's like drinking history."

"I'd rather create history. That's what writing is." Cormac was regarding him with that severe, blazing look that always made Austin uncomfortable.

"Corrie, honey, why don't you come over here and tell us one of your stories to help while away the time," Auntie Eudie instructed.

Cormac replaced the bottle he was holding and walked over to sit on the stairs. Without any self-consciousness, he began to recite a story about a boy who set out to build a secret campfire to roast marshmallows and accidentally burned down the family barn.

Listening, Austin remembered that he still needed to talk to Cormac about his stories. He wasn't sure Cormac was going to like what he had to say, but it needed to be said nonetheless. He glanced around the cellar. Auntie Eudie was smiling contentedly to herself as she knit her fake fox fur. Faulkner had found some sweet potatoes, and he was peeling them. The sharp penknife he used scraped steadily, the small sound lost beneath the static of the radio and the creaking timbers overhead. Faulkner's rather ascetic face was without expression, but every so often his dark gaze would rest on Cormac.

Austin tried to analyze the complex emotions he read in the old man's face. There was a gleam of satirical amusement, but there was tolerance too and what appeared to be genuine affection. It seemed strange that Faulkner might truly care for the Cashels. Might be able to find tolerant affection for them, when he seemed to have scant for his own great-nephew. People were confusing and contradictory.

Austin's gaze roved to Carson, who was now playing solitaire. He liked Carson. She was a kook, but there was something direct and uncomplicated about her. In a weird way he found her more attractive than Cormac, even though Cormac was male. But then for all her flirtatiousness, there was something about Carson that reminded Austin of a playful boy.

He thought about Jeff's comment that sex was sex. He couldn't believe Jeff really meant that. Granted, Austin had never been with a woman. Never had any desire that he could recall. Inevitably that reminded him of his father's charge that he'd chosen to be gay.

That was still too raw to examine closely. Instead he looked around for Jeff. He had finished playing cards, it seemed, and was leaning against the wall, watching Austin.

Meeting Austin's eyes seemed to be his cue. He pushed away from the wall and joined Austin by the shelves.

"Any sign of those Lee bottles?" He kept his voice low so as to not disturb Cormac's storytelling.

Austin discovered that he was relieved with a cessation in hostilities. He didn't really want to fight with Jeff. For one thing, it wasn't going to solve anything, and it wasn't going to heal the pain of rejection. So why not accept what Jeff could offer, which was a very casual friendship with benefits?

"Not exactly. I did find something I wanted to show you." In the excitement of the tornado watch, Austin had briefly forgotten those bizarre moments when he had thought Tyrone might not at all be who he seemed. When Tyrone had seemed almost...dangerous.

He showed Jeff the rack with the four empty cradles and the surrounding bottles of Madeira.

"Not that there's any rhyme or reason to the way this cellar is organized, but it would make sense to store the Madeiras together. And there's this." He pulled what was left of the dried cherry blossom out of his pocket.

Jeff's brows rose. "I'm deeply flattered you want to share your crushed potato chips with me, but—"

"They're not potato chips. It's what's left of a cherry blossom. When I was here in March, the cherry blossoms were still covering the ground. It's possible that this gives a reference point for when these four bottles were removed."

Jeff considered this. He said neutrally, "Maybe. That doesn't mean the four bottles that were here were the Lee bottles. It doesn't mean that the four bottles that were here weren't removed and drunk at dinner one night. The fact that someone tracked a cherry blossom inside isn't exactly conclusive."

He took the crumpled blossom from Austin, his fingers warm against Austin's bare skin. Jeff glanced at the Cashels. "All the same, keep this quiet for now."

"There's something else."

Jeff's gaze seemed to linger on Austin's face, but his words were matter-of-fact. "Go on."

"Tyrone, Faulkner's nephew, was marking some of the more expensive bottles we inventoried this morning. I was with him when I found this, and for a couple of seconds…"

"What?"

"I'm not sure. I thought he—this is going to sound ridiculous—I thought he was going to hit me. Or maybe…worse."

Jeff stood motionless. He could have been turned to stone. "That kid's got a rap sheet longer than US 80—including assault and battery."

Assault and battery? Maybe he hadn't imagined the menace in Tyrone's eyes. Austin asked uneasily, "*Was* Williams's death an accident?"

"Hell no." Jeff's voice was almost inaudible. "His car was found with the keys in it in the parking lot at Old Plantation House. No way did he walk out here on his own."

"What was he doing out here at all?"

Jeff smiled wryly. "Personally? I think he was looking for your Lee bottles."

"But how would he know they were here?"

"Because I think he sold them to old Dermot Cashel in the first place. Henrietta Williams asked me to investigate her husband's death, and one of the first things I found out was Williams was involved in buying and selling vintage wines—and not, according to some people—always the real deal."

Wine fraud. It was increasingly rampant. Some experts believed as much as 5 percent of wine sold in secondary markets was counterfeit.

Austin gazed at the towering shelves, the racks of green and amber bottles with their gilded and ornate labels beneath the velvety veil of dust. "Do you have proof of that?"

"Yeah. I do. Now we're trying to figure out who would have been Williams's partner in that lucrative sideline."

"You think this partner killed Williams?"

"It's one possibility."

"Could this partner be one of the Cashels?"

"That's also a possibility."

Austin's gaze got caught up in Jeff's. He couldn't seem to look away.

"What are you two whispering about over there?" Carson called.

Jeff turned away abruptly. Austin felt a jab of disappointment. But that was how it was always going to be with Jeff—assuming there was anything with Jeff at all—so he needed to get used to it.

"We could open a bottle of wine," Cormac said, having finished his storytelling stint.

Austin kept his mouth shut, but it wasn't easy.

Jeff said easily, "I believe Austin would fight to protect this wine to his last breath."

The others laughed.

"Some things are worth fighting for," Austin said.

The lights flickered again and went out.

Austin had that tilting sense of disorientation. On the other side of the cellar, he could hear Faulkner soothing the Cashels. Jeff put his hands on Austin's shoulders, turning him. Austin went with it. Just the feel of Jeff's hands resting lightly on him sent a blaze of awareness through him, as though his longing for Jeff were something constant, often banked down but always smoldering.

Unerringly, despite the almost complete absence of light, Jeff's mouth landed on Austin's. Until that instant Austin hadn't realized how desperately he had wanted it, wanted to taste Jeff again, wanted his kisses. One of the major erogenous zones, lips; and no wonder, because there was something indescribably satisfying about the soft pressure of a man's hard mouth moving on his own.

"Austin." Jeff sounded like he was in pain.

Their mouths lingered dangerously, parted a split second before the faded light winked on.

Jeff was walking back to the card table before Austin had regained his balance.

* * * * *

At nine o'clock the radio announcer cheerfully conveyed the all clear.

"It's too late to drive back to Madison now," Auntie Eudie told Austin kindly. "You stay the night, honey. We got plenty of room."

No way in hell—no way in *God's Little Acre*—was he spending the night. Never mind the hours he'd already spent listening to tornado horror stories and histories of the Cashels' and their friends' and neighbors' most gruesome illnesses, and the insanity that was these people's political opinions. No way could he spend the night under the same roof as Jeff, knowing how Jeff and Carson would be passing the time.

"Thanks so much, but I've really got to get back." Austin clutched his belongings as though he feared they would be forcibly taken from him as he headed for the front door. He could hear the Cashels protesting behind him. "I'll be back tomorrow first thing," he called without slowing down.

He opened the door and saw a fantasy landscape of trees bent nearly in half and rain coming down in glinting sheets. A large empty plastic bag for topsoil swooped past like a grubby ghost in the deluge of rain and wind. He wouldn't have been surprised to see Margaret Hamilton fly by pedaling her bicycle.

"You can't drive in this," Carson protested, joining him at the door. "Even if you knew these roads, it would be crazy dangerous. Sleep here tonight. You may as well. Look at it this way: you can get an earlier start tomorrow."

He shook his head stubbornly, although even he knew she was right. There was no way he was driving anywhere tonight.

"Why, I'm beginning to think you're afraid of us, Austin," Carson teased. "Now you come back in here, and I promise I'll keep the colonel from interrupting your sweet dreams tonight."

Fifteen minutes later he was in a large room on the second floor, holding a stack of much laundered towels and an extra wool blanket to "help keep the drafts out."

The room had old-fashioned green-and-blue wallpaper. Two of the windows were missing blinds. There was a rummage sale's worth of broken antiques, including a shaving stand with a cracked mirror and a small butter churn. Whatever the heck the Cashels did with butter in the bedroom, he did not want to know.

The lock on the bedroom door was broken.

Austin sat on the edge of the bed, sinking about a foot into the swamp of a mattress, and checked his phone messages.

In addition to Ernest's earlier message, there were four messages from the direct house line in Frederick. It was hard to believe Harrison would be calling. For one thing, he didn't believe in apologizing; and for another, he would not believe himself in the wrong. Austin pressed to retrieve the messages and got a low-battery warning. And his phone charger was in the rental car.

The windows rattled in a blast of wet wind.

Whatever Ernest or whoever was calling him wanted, it was just going to have to wait till morning.

He put his phone away and spread the extra wool blanket over the bed. He hoped the sheets had been washed in the last decade. He hoped he would not be sharing a bunk with spiders.

There was a tap on the bedroom door.

Jeff stood in the hallway. His face was grim.

"I want to talk to you."

Austin stepped back, and Jeff entered, closing the door behind him. "I *know* there are things worth fighting for." He kept his voice down, but he was angry all the same. "You don't have the right to stand in judgment."

"Fine. Agreed. I don't have the right." Austin reached for the door handle. "Was that it?"

Jeff's eyes were dark with emotion. "What is the *matter* with you?"

"You know what the matter is with me."

Jeff's gaze fell. "Naw. Now you're being... It doesn't work like this, Austin."

"I know," Austin said tersely. "I get it. For you, it was just sex. For me, I don't know why, but somehow it turned into something different. I don't *know* why, but...it did."

"Naw." Jeff tried to take him into his arms. "Don't do this. It doesn't have to be like this."

"How does it have to be, Jeff?"

A muscle jerked in Jeff's jaw. "You're asking for something I can't give you."

"Am I?"

"Yes, you goddamned well are."

"Jeff, what do you want me to say? I understand it was just sex for you, and I'm *not* asking for anything—except that you leave me alone so I can get over it."

"Get over it," Jeff repeated in amazement. "What are you getting over? You can't seriously think you're—"

"Jeff. Will you please leave me a little dignity here? Go away."

"Austin." Jeff looked stricken. He pulled Austin closer, and Austin remembered that first shared hug in his hotel room. The comfort of simply being held, of being genuinely cared for. But that was an illusion. Even if Jeff did care for him on some level, no way was he going to acknowledge, let alone act on those feelings. He had made that just as clear as he could.

Jeff was talking, his voice rough and uneven. "I don't mean to hurt you, sweetheart. I didn't want this."

Sweetheart. Well, at least it was an improvement over the *honeys* they all bestowed indiscriminately on each other. Jeff's lips brushed his temple. So gentle. Almost cherishingly. Austin closed his eyes. Who was he kidding? Of course he wanted this. Want blazed through his bloodstream like a high fever, something that would either run its course and leave him wrung out and empty, but once more cool and sane—or kill him. Either way, there wasn't any denying how urgently he wanted Jeff.

One last time.

The door swung open. Jeff dropped Austin like a hot potato.

"What's going on here?" Cormac demanded, looking from Jeff to Austin.

"Did you ever hear of knocking?" Jeff blustered.

Cormac bristled. "It's my house."

"It's his guest room." Jeff jerked his head Austin's way.

"Would you both go away?" Austin requested wearily. "It's been a really long day."

Jeff hesitated.

"You heard him," Cormac said imperiously.

Jeff shook his head, clearly longing to pop Cormac, but in the end he settled for shooting Austin a long, unreadable look before walking out.

"What was he up to?" Cormac asked suspiciously, closing the door behind Jeff.

"Nothing. Look, I wanted to talk to you." As Cormac brightened, Austin amended quickly, "About your stories."

"Oh." Cormac looked watchful.

"They weren't exactly my kind of thing, to tell you the truth, but I still thought they were really well written and...powerful. So—and here's the part that you might not like—I asked a friend of mine in publishing to take a look at them."

Cormac seemed to draw himself up to his full height. His scowl went blacker than ever. "I didn't give you permission to do that. I don't care what any damn publisher thinks of my work."

"I know. I apologize. But my opinion isn't worth a lot. I thought it would be better to show them to someone who knows books and writing. If Gary had said they were no good, I wouldn't have said anything, but he thinks they're excellent. He thinks they're publishable."

The rage drained out of Cormac's face. He said faintly, "He does?"

"He does, yeah. And if you give me permission to let him have your contact information, he's going to discuss it with you himself."

"He's going to publish me?"

"You have to talk to him yourself, but...that's how it sounds to me."

Cormac was smiling with an unlikely, startled sweetness. "Really?"

"Really. So I guess I can give him your information?"

"Hell yeah!"

Austin grinned wearily. "Then that's turned out okay. Thank God." He swallowed a yawn. "No offense, but I've got to get some sleep or I'm going to start hallucinating. In fact, I think I may already be hallucinating."

A calculating look came over Cormac's face. "I was just thinking—"

"No. No. No."

"But you don't know what I'm going to say."

"You're going to say you want to have sex with me."

Cormac smiled again. "*See?* You're thinking it too!"

Austin laughed and held open the door. "Good night, Cormac. Sweet dreams."

He shut the door and looked for a likely chair to prop beneath the handle, but the room's only chair was too short. Anyway, who was left? Carson would be occupied with Jeff, and Auntie Eudie was unlikely to be feeling *that* frisky.

Austin gave it up and climbed into the raised bed, not putting up a fight as the sagging mattress tried to swallow him whole.

He was dozing, dreamily counting wine bottles while ably assisted by the colonel, when the bedroom door opened quickly and shut again.

Austin's eyes flashed open. He raised his head. Even in the darkness he recognized Jeff, but his nostrils twitched at a second presence. Green-apple shampoo and...Carson.

"Crap." He sat up as a weight lowered next to his feet. The other side of the lumpy mattress dipped, and a slender, warm someone snuggled next to him. Austin scooted away, reaching for the lamp.

"Surprise!" Carson smiled broadly in the green-gold glow of the Tiffany lamp. Jeff was positioned at the foot of the bed. Austin thought his expression watchful.

"What is the matter with you people?" Austin demanded, and it wasn't a rhetorical question.

"Awww." Carson pouted. "Jeff said you needed cheering up, honey."

"Oh, did he?"

Meeting Austin's hostile gaze, Jeff said silkily, "Don't knock it till you've tried it."

"I don't need to try it to know it's not for me."

"What are you afraid of?"

"What are *you* afraid of?"

"Now don't be like that, Austin honey," Carson said, nestling closer still. Her breasts pressed softly against his arm. "Jeff's trying to do a nice thing for you."

Austin snorted.

"Don't you like me?" Carson asked, genuinely curious.

"Yeah, I like you." He put his arm around her shoulders. "That doesn't have anything to do with it."

"Well, it ought to." She nibbled delicately on his ear; there was no denying the response that shot right to his groin.

Jeff said, "Come on. You can't tell me you're not curious."

No, he couldn't tell Jeff that. He was curious. Not to experience it himself so much—although there was no question that Harrison's suggestion that Austin's sexuality was preference and not orientation was in play—but to see, to understand what Jeff got out of it. Jeff was smiling at him, teasing and affectionate, as though it were no big deal, just a bit of harmless fun. And the terrible part was Austin wanted Jeff badly enough one last time to take him any way he could get him, even if it meant something as outlandish as ménage à trois, or whatever they called it down South.

Jeff continued to smile that killer smile, but Austin thought there was a dangerous glitter in those green eyes.

"What's the worst that can happen? You might find you like it?" Jeff's voice went lower, rougher. "I dare you."

Carson kissed his shoulder, looking from one man to the other.

Jeff held out his hand. After a tense moment, Austin reached to lace fingers and let himself be drawn forward.

CHAPTER TEN

"**O**h, Jeff, *honey…*"

The surprise—the thing Austin had not expected—was that it was a turn-on to watch Jeff with Carson. Kneeling next to the headboard, Austin found his hand going to his aching groin as Carson moaned, undulating her hips, and Jeff thrust up beneath her. That too had surprised Austin— that Jeff let Carson set the pace. He had expected Jeff to have some very old-fashioned notions there, but no. Jeff was smiling and relaxed as Carson climbed on top. They were beautiful to see: Jeff, all lean and sun-gilded muscle, and Carson slim and lithe as a boy, except for those plump, dove-like breasts that Jeff took such pains to squeeze and stroke while he shoved his hips up in a smooth rolling motion.

It was a turn-on, but it was a lonely titillation, like watching a well-made porn flick—possibly one in a foreign language.

Carson's head fell back, her black curls tumbling down her back and over her shoulders as she mewled her pleasure. She was quite lovely in her lack of inhibition, her frank enjoyment and freedom from self-consciousness. Austin was by far the most self-conscious person in that sinking raft of a bed. Huck Finn on a sexual odyssey. But it was all right; they seemed to have forgotten he was there anyway. He was glad of that. He was ashamed for having given in to what amounted to peer pressure. At his age too.

Austin bit his lip as his hand closed around his painfully stiff cock. He gave himself a comforting couple of tugs, unable to tear his eyes away. Jeff's blond head thrust back on the pillow. His muscular chest arched up, and he flung out his arm, his hand landing on Austin's thigh. Austin nearly jumped out of his skin, but then he stilled as Jeff began to caress him, gently kneading Austin's rigid muscles. He was thinking that perhaps it was unconscious on Jeff's part, just an automatic reflex, but Jeff's gold-tipped lashes lifted, and he shot Austin a strange gleaming look.

What did that look mean?

"Still there?" Jeff asked huskily.

Austin made a noise that was part assent and part denial. He was there in body certainly. His hand worked more urgently on his cock while Jeff's fingers stroked him, soothed as though he knew that pained and unwilling excitement too well.

With his free hand, Jeff reached up and rubbed the pad of his thumb against the nub of Carson's clitoris. She cried out and came with a convulsive shudder. Austin pumped himself frantically while Jeff told her what a great girl she was and murmured a lot of sweet nonsense, and then he said, "Now it's Austin's turn."

Carson raised her head and smiled at Austin, and every muscle in Austin's body locked so tight he actually banged against the headboard. Astonishingly, the other two didn't laugh. Carson raised off Jeff's still-massive erection and padded on hands and knees toward him like a friendly lioness. Jeff sat up too, reaching out a welcoming hand.

Austin's mouth opened, but the words seemed to have dried in his throat. What could he have said? *I don't want this?* The now-painful erection between his legs gave the lie to that. But that was sex, and in that Jeff had been correct. Sex was sex. Which didn't change the fact that Austin's aching heart did not want this, no matter how much his aching body did.

The body won, as the body generally did. He let himself be coaxed from the safety of his vantage point, let them draw him into the nest of pillows and bedding, settling him in a comfortable tangle of stroking hands and tender mouths.

He'd never experienced anything remotely like it. It was bewilderingly, terrifyingly intense. He felt overwhelmed. He couldn't keep track of who was doing what to him. Someone lightly squeezed the fragile sac of his testicles, someone else gently, gently bit on his nipple, and he was shocked at how much he wanted both to be Jeff. What did it matter who it was if the sensation was sufficiently enjoyable?

Somehow it did, so he kept his eyes closed and believed it was Jeff flicking the tip of his tongue against the point of Austin's nipple and Jeff's square hand cupping his balls.

"Shhh, shhh," Carson was murmuring, maybe misreading the fact that he was shivering—or maybe reading it correctly, because Austin felt like he was experiencing some kind of sensory overload. Her small mouth closed over the head of his cock. She was practiced and committed, and it felt very good—not like it had when Jeff had sucked him, but still very good. Austin let his thighs fall wide and instinctively pushed up into the sweet, tight warmth of her. He heard himself moaning, and he opened his eyes in surprise in time to see Jeff climbing into position behind her.

Jeff's eyes were fastened on his, his face absorbed, serious.

Austin swallowed hard, unable to read that look, unable to think past the distracting pleasure delivered by Carson's inspired mouth.

Still holding Austin's gaze, Jeff began to fuck Carson from behind, slow and deliberate. It was startling to see her face, to see the mobile, fleeting expressions, and it was a disappointment because for all that he liked her and appreciated what she was trying to do for him, Austin didn't want to watch Jeff fucking Carson.

He closed his eyes again, focusing only on the physical feelings, and he heard Carson panting and felt the luscious slide as she sucked all the harder and more lovingly on his cock, and the sweet feeling surged through him. Carson's body acted as a lightning rod between them. The flash point.

Lost in sensation though he was, he felt the moment that her second orgasm caught her, felt her throat contract, felt her shudder. Austin shuddered in instinctive response.

"Austin," Jeff said urgently. "Open your eyes." Austin recognized distantly that Jeff felt himself shut out, that he needed the connection between them, but if that had been the case, why had he brought Carson into their bed? Jeff had set the parameters.

Hazily, beneath half-closed eyelids, Austin saw Carson master herself, saw her thrust her middle finger into her mouth, withdraw it wet and shining, and feel for the place between his ass cheeks.

"Wait." He gasped.

The next instant she slipped into his anus, pushed and pressed with unholy knowledge. Something fluttered wildly inside Austin and tore apart. The orgasm that ripped through him was more like a convulsion or a seizure than recognizable pleasure. The sound bursting out of him was close to a shriek of pain, although he was not hurt. It was a pleasure so intense and unexpected it was almost sickening, like the sudden dip of a roller coaster. Too fast, too hard. He was shaking. Through blurred eyes, he saw Jeff reach past Carson, offering his hands.

"It's all right. You're all right."

Austin curled away, ignoring him. He was on his own in this; he always had been.

However oblivious Jeff was, he seemed to understand finally that this had been too much. He was climbing over Carson, gathering Austin close, his own erection wilting as he settled them together.

He was whispering something. "Sorry. Sorry, sweetheart. I didn't mean for it to happen like that." A near-inaudible thread of apology.

Carson was murmuring her confusion. "Doesn't he like it? But everybody likes it..."

Austin shoved Jeff away, but he hadn't heart or energy to fight, and Jeff was determined to hang on until the last throb and twitch of electricity faded out and went dark. Gradually Austin caught his breath. It was sticky and uncomfortable, and there were too many people in his bed. Maybe he could find an empty sofa and spend the rest of the night there. In a minute. He closed his eyes.

After a time, he was aware the lights were out and that Jeff was dragging blankets up and tucking them around him.

He closed his eyes and let the darkness take him.

* * * * *

He woke warmly cocooned in blankets. Alone.

That was the good news: alone.

For a few minutes Austin lay blinking at the ceiling. It was raining. He could hear the whisper of water on glass, feel the draft from the weakened window seals, smell the rising damp and mildew.

Depression unlike anything he'd known in his adult life swamped him. He thought he would sink beneath it.

Instead, he rose and began to dress.

Someone tapped on his door. He ignored it. The door inched open. Jeff poked his head in. His eyes narrowed when he saw Austin was awake and nearly dressed.

"I didn't think you'd be awake so early."

"Yeah. Well." Austin's voice was husky. It was an effort to get the two words out.

"How're you feeling?"

Austin looked at Jeff. On the nightstand he found his watch and snapped it onto his wrist.

Jeff slipped inside the room, then closed the door behind him. For a few moments he watched Austin. Austin ignored him.

"Okay. I'm sorry." Jeff's voice was edged. "It was a bad idea. You can't tell me you didn't enjoy any of it, though. I was here, remember?"

"I remember."

Austin turned away, and Jeff crossed the room and grabbed his shoulders, turning him. "All right. Go on. Say it. I know what you're thinking, and you're right. I'm a shit."

"Then I don't need to say it, do I?"

Jeff let him go. He looked like Austin had slapped him. "That's it?"

Austin said dryly, "Did you want to talk about it?"

Jeff seemed at a loss for words. He said at last, "What I want is to apologize. I'm sorry, Austin. Very sorry."

"You said that. I believe you."

"I don't understand. What is it that you want?"

"Not a thing."

"You enjoyed it," Jeff insisted. "Why the hell *wouldn't* you enjoy it? Can't you concede that much?"

Wearily, Austin said, "I can concede that some of it felt good. I can concede that you're right. Sex is sex. We're talking about two different things, Jeff. You're talking about sex, and I was talking about...a connection. An emotional connection."

Reading Jeff's instantly closed expression, Austin added, "And that's what last night was really about: ending the possibility of anything between us."

"That wasn't—" Jeff's voice gave out. Or maybe not, because he finished steadily enough. "No. You're wrong about that. I don't want that. But it's not realistic—what you want."

"You don't know what I want. Hell, you don't know what *you* want."

Jeff seemed to struggle inwardly. He said at last, "I know that I don't want to hurt you. And I swear to God that was not my intention last night. I wanted to make a point, I admit that. You pissed me off with that holier-than-thou attitude."

Austin opened his mouth. Jeff cut in. "But it was an idiot point, and I'm an idiot for trying to make it. Can we... I don't know. Can we..." Jeff drew a deep breath. "Can we maybe start over?"

It was the last thing he'd expected to hear. Austin pressed the heels of his hands to his eyes. After a few seconds, he lowered his hands. "Has anything changed? I mean, other than the fact that you're sorry about last night?"

The confusion on Jeff's face was almost painful to see. "I...care about you. I can't... I don't know that I can do what you want. You're asking... I don't think you realize what you're asking. But I can try to... We could try it one step at a time."

"How?"

Jeff continued to stare at him with that hungry, frustrated look.

"Maybe if we didn't live seven hundred miles apart," Austin said. "But it's going to be hard for me to keep coming up with excuses for flying down here just to see my good fishing buddy. Even if I fished."

Austin waited, but Jeff seemed to have no answer, so eventually he moved past him and went out, leaving the door to the bedroom standing open.

* * * * *

Back at his hotel, Austin plugged his phone into the charger, showered, and changed into clean jeans and a fresh T-shirt.

He sat down to check his e-mail, knowing he should probably use the time to try to grab some breakfast. He really wasn't hungry, and the sooner he got back to Ballineen and finished the appraisal, the sooner he could get home and start putting the memory of Jeff behind him.

That was the only option he could see. As much as it was going to hurt, it would hurt about a thousand times worse if he let this thing go any further. Regardless of what Jeff told himself, he was not ready to compromise, and there was no way the tentative relationship budding between them could survive without Jeff making the first concession.

Besides, if he was honest, Austin was still angry about the night before. He accepted that Jeff was sorry, but he resented the fact that he'd been manipulated, used. It would be one thing if he could convince himself that last night had been about Jeff merely, misguidedly, trying to share a sexual adventure. But they both knew that wasn't true. Last night, first and foremost, Jeff had been trying to prove something to Jeff.

What?

That sex with Austin had been meaningless? That it had meant no more and no less than sex with Carson?

That all sex was essentially the same?

That if Austin could experience sex the way Jeff did, Austin would give up his foolish and disturbing notion that something special had happened between them?

All of the above?

None of the above?

It took a while for the knocking on his door to register. Austin went to answer the peremptory summons, and Jeff pushed into the room. His eyes looked almost black in his white face.

"Okay, that didn't go so well. Let me try this again."

Austin had not anticipated this; he wasn't happy about it either. "Jeff—"

Jeff shook his head, negating whatever Austin was trying to say. "Why don't we do it like this: what do you want from me?"

"Nothing. I've already told you. *Nothing.*"

Jeff said shortly, "Now *you're* not being honest."

Austin started to speak, but Jeff was right. Besides, what did he have to lose at this point? He said slowly, "I have feelings for you. I'd like a chance to explore them. See if there's a chance that there could be more."

"Me too."

"You know what I think," Austin said as the memory of the night before came rushing back. "I think you resent the fact that I've made you consider—seriously consider—that you're closing yourself off from what you really want and what you really need."

Jeff interrupted forcefully. "I *said* me too!"

Austin stared as Jeff's words registered. Jeff *agreed*? Now that he had truly not seen coming. "What? You think we could have some kind of long-distance relationship?"

"I don't know."

"You think you could just pick up and move to Washington DC?"

"Yeah, right!" Jeff glared. "My family has lived in these parts for over two hundred and fifty years."

But wasn't that the point? That Jeff could never live openly as a gay man in the town where generations of Bradys had been born and died? What compromise would be possible? Yet to his astonishment, Austin heard himself say, "What if I moved here?"

Jeff said, "Would you do that?"

"I...don't know. I may be leaving my job. It's a possibility."

Jeff just stared. Longing and apprehension seemed to war in his eyes.

Austin's hope died. "It wouldn't work, would it? It would be the same problem we have now. You don't want to accept or even acknowledge that you're gay."

The *G* word. For an instant he thought Jeff was going to tell him to shut up again, but though a muscle jerked in Jeff's jaw, he said nothing.

The phone rang. Not his cell phone, the hotel phone. Austin automatically picked it up. Jeff went to the window and stared out at the rain-wet park, the line of his wide shoulders uncompromising and tense.

"Where have you been?" Debra cried. "We've been trying to reach you since last night! Why haven't you picked up your messages?"

"There was a storm. I—"

"Austin..." He realized then that she was crying. "Harrison's gone."

"Gone?" he repeated stupidly.

"It happened last night. We tried to call you. We called and called."

"But he can't be. He was fine." Dimly, he was aware that Jeff had turned, was coming over to him. "That can't be right."

"It was a massive heart attack."

"No."

"They tried to resuscitate him at the hospital, but..." Debra's voice died out, and he thought she was crying again.

Austin protested, "But that can't be right. He just had his birthday. He was fine."

Debra was still talking. He tried to make himself concentrate on the words. He kept thinking that he must be dreaming. "You have to come back. Now," she said at last.

"Yes. I'm on my way."

Numbly, he replaced the handset. He stared blankly at Jeff's face. What had they been talking about? Jeff looked so serious and concerned. He took Austin into his arms as though it was the most natural thing in the world, and for some reason that was the last straw.

Jeff held him while he cried. He stroked Austin and squeezed the back of his neck and didn't try to hush him or tell him it would be all right. He didn't say much of anything at all except an occasional murmured "Austin."

Afterward, when Austin had control of himself again, Jeff was helpful and businesslike, getting Austin booked on a small plane out of Madison Municipal and then rearranging his flight to and from Atlanta. He helped Austin pack and promised to let the Cashels know what was going on.

He drove Austin to the airport and saw him safely to the airfield.

"Fly safe," he told Austin and hugged him—albeit briefly—right there in the bright Georgia sunlight.

Austin nodded. He felt nothing. He felt instinctively that it was the last time they would meet, but even that pain felt removed, remote. One more weight on a heart that already felt like lead. "Bye, Jeff. Take care of yourself."

He turned away, but Jeff said urgently, "When you come back, we'll work it out. I promise you."

Work it out? He remembered their conversation in the hotel room. It seemed a thousand years ago. Nothing to do with real life. In any case, he wasn't coming back. Not ever. Someone else could do the appraisal, or the fucking cellar could rot. He just didn't care anymore. Austin smiled politely and went up the portable stairs.

As the plane lifted, he could see Jeff's figure grow smaller and smaller, a white dot on the green of the landing field that eventually blended in with the other dots and vanished.

CHAPTER ELEVEN

The lilacs were in bloom.

Austin could smell their cool fragrance as he came down the brick steps of the house in Frederick. He'd spent the afternoon with Ernest—or maybe Ernest had spent the afternoon with him. Sometimes Austin wasn't sure who was supposed to be comforting whom during these long, terrible three weeks since Harrison's death. Either way, leaving Martyn, North, & Compeau had given Austin time to spend with his little brother—time they both needed.

It had also given him a chance to figure out what he wanted to be when he grew up. Not a journalist. He had toyed with the idea briefly, but Bella was the one who'd reminded him that he already had a career that he loved and was very good at and that trying to live your life for someone else was an exercise in futility. Especially when that someone else was no longer around.

Parked in the square brick courtyard was a silver Honda Accord with mud-splashed tires and fender. There was something familiar about the vehicle, although it wasn't until Austin registered the lean, sun-browned man leaning against it that he realized what.

His heart, in hibernation these past weeks, stirred, and Austin walked quickly down the remaining steps, suddenly aware of the scent of flowers and the feel of sunlight on his face.

"Hey. Hi."

"Hello." Jeff, in jeans and a dark green shirt, straightened as Austin came to meet him.

"This is a surprise. Were you just going to wait out in the driveway all afternoon?" Austin asked, puzzled.

"I didn't want to intrude," Jeff said, "but I needed to see you."

"How did you find me?"

"I'm a PI, remember?"

"Right." Austin smiled uncertainly. Jeff seemed so grave and polite. They were standing close enough to hug, but Jeff made no move to hug him. Hell, they weren't even shaking hands. Maybe he was only there to tell Austin he was required to testify at an inquest or something like that. Not knowing what to say, he settled on the truth. "It's really good to see you." It was. Like seeing the sun come out after a month of rain.

He didn't ask—he was afraid to hear the answer—*why are you here?* But maybe the question was on his face.

"You didn't come back," Jeff said abruptly. "To Madison. You never came back. Not to finish the appraisal. Not for anything. It's been three weeks, and I haven't heard a word from you."

Three weeks. It felt both much longer and much shorter than that. Austin had thought about Jeff a lot during that time—nearly as much as he had avoided thinking about Jeff. Because while thinking about Jeff was comforting in some respects, it was equally painful. He just couldn't see Jeff disappointing all those generations of dead Bradys. And emotionally, Austin was at a place where he couldn't have handled knowing for sure that it was over.

"I left the wine shop. I ended up resigning."

If anything, Jeff's face went sterner. "Yeah, that's what the woman they sent to replace you said. She said you decided to write a book instead."

Austin gave a disbelieving laugh. "Not exactly. That friend of mine who's publishing Cormac's stories suggested that collecting some of the wine blogs I've done over the years would make an entertaining book."

"Congratulations."

He wasn't imagining it; Jeff seemed different. Older. Serious—almost subdued.

"How are they? The Cashels?"

"Fine. Enjoying spending all that money they don't have yet."

The silence that followed Jeff's sardonic comment felt final.

Austin broke it awkwardly. "I've been meaning to phone you. I just..."

"Yeah?" Jeff's smile was crooked.

It hadn't occurred to Austin that Jeff might be hurt by his lack of communication. In fact, in his darkest moments, he had figured Jeff would probably be relieved to be let off the hook.

"I...was waiting till I knew what to tell you."

Jeff said levelly, "I thought maybe that would be something we'd figure out together."

Austin's lips parted, but he really had no answer to that.

Jeff looked around. "Is there someplace we can talk?"

Austin also looked around vaguely. The gazebo? He didn't want to bring Jeff into the house if Jeff was only here to officially tell him good-bye. There were enough painful memories in that house without adding that one. Which reminded him.

"How did the appraisal turn out? Were the Lee bottles ever found?"

"That's kind of what I wanted to talk to you about."

Right. Of course. "Let's try the gazebo," Austin said.

"Wait," Jeff said suddenly. "I brought you something." He dived back in the car and carefully lifted out a brown-wrapped package. He handed it to Austin, who took it automatically. A bottle of wine. Well, not the most imaginative gift he'd ever received, but then again, maybe it was a vintage bottle from the Cashels' cellar. Or a bottle of champagne. Maybe they were going to have something to celebrate?

"What's this for?"

"I guess you'd better open it and find out."

"Is it from you?"

"It's from me. From me to you. Personal delivery."

Austin felt a smile starting.

As they walked to the gazebo, Jeff asked, "How are you doing?"

"I'm okay. I never thanked you for—"

"Yeah." Jeff sounded dry. "I'd be just as happy if you forgot most of that morning."

Oh.

"How's the boy genius doing?" Jeff asked into his silence.

"Better than me. He's just dealing with grief. It's painful, but it's uncomplicated."

To his surprise, Jeff slung an arm about his shoulders and gave him a hard, affectionate hug. "He loved you, Austin."

"I know. But I disappointed him too. I don't think we ever really got a chance to know each other. Really know each other. And I always thought we would. That one day…"

When Jeff didn't reply, Austin said, "The hardest part is not having any warning, you know? Not having a chance to say good-bye. The last time I spoke to him, we were arguing."

Jeff had an odd expression. He said, "I only knew your daddy like most people did, through the things he wrote and the things he said on television, but there is nothing about you that could have disappointed that man. You're honest and kind and conscientious and intelligent. You're a good man."

It was Austin's turn to color. "Thanks."

Jeff added teasingly, "And sexy as hell."

Austin laughed, looked away over the lawn. "Thanks again. Especially for that last one, although somehow I don't think that mattered a lot to my dad."

They walked up into the large open-air gazebo that looked over the roses and hedges. Austin leaned against the white railing. "Do I open this now?"

Jeff nodded curtly. "Sure. I thought if nothing else, you'd want to know how it all turned out."

Austin could feel Jeff's sudden tension, and it affected his own nerves. He tore off the wrapping. He gazed in amazement at the dark, dusty bottle with the date 1822 etched in white above the letters R-E-L. The words *Blandy Madeira* were printed at the base of each bottle.

"Wait a minute..." He stared bewilderedly at Jeff.

"They were buried beneath the cherry trees at Ballineen."

"Oh my God. But...they can't be the real thing."

"You're right. They're not."

"They're not?" Although Austin had just said so, he lifted the bottle, scrutinizing it closely in the dappled sunlight. "How do you know?"

"Because none of the vintage wines Dominic Williams sold Dermot were the real thing."

"According to whom?"

"According to Henrietta Williams, his wife and partner in crime."

"Wine fraud?" Austin stared down at the dark bottle, the mysterious liquid sloshing inside it. It was a letdown, no doubt about it, but definitely less of a letdown because Jeff had taken the time and trouble to break the news himself. "Crap. So what's in here?"

"Hundred-year-old Madeira. The booze is real enough. It just didn't belong to Robert E. Lee. The bottle was doctored to make it look like it came from Lee's cellar."

"So *all* that vintage wine is counterfeit?"

"Anything supplied by Dom Williams is counterfeit."

Austin stared, perplexed. "You seem awfully pleased about it."

"I wouldn't say pleased, but I'm certainly glad that the Martyn, North, & Compeau representative who vouched for all that vintage wine being the real deal was some woman named Theresa Bloch and not you."

At last Austin said faintly, "Theresa authenticated the cellar—the *entire* cellar?" Appraised *and* authenticated in the space of a few weeks? What had been the rush? Had she been in such a hurry to establish her position following Austin's departure?

Jeff was nodding. "I thought you'd enjoy that."

"I don't know about *enjoy*. There but for the grace of God, if you know what I mean."

"Anyway, that's what I've been doing these last few weeks. Working with the sheriffs to uncover Dom's partner in his counterfeiting scheme. It turned out to be Henry all along. We cracked the case the day before yesterday." He added, "Or I'd have been here sooner."

Austin found it hard to look away from that bright green gaze. When Jeff looked at him that way, he couldn't help thinking maybe everything was going to be okay. "Who killed Williams? His wife?"

"Bingo. She claims it was an accident, but it's hard to accidentally hit someone over the head with a bottle of Madeira."

"She used—" Austin stared at the bottle in his hand.

Jeff gave an abrupt laugh. "Different bottle. She broke the one she used. It turns out Faulkner cleared it up."

"Hold on," Austin said. "I'm getting confused. Henrietta killed her husband. Why? And why did she hire you to find him in that case?"

"Henry hired me to throw suspicion off herself once Dom's death was discovered. As for why she killed him, well, I have a suspicion that had to do with jealousy over Carson, but Henry's not talking on that point. She claims it was an accident, but everyone knows she had a terrible temper and was jealous as hell. What she does admit is that when she and Dom heard there was going to be an appraisal of the Cashels' cellar by such a noted expert, they panicked and went to the house, trying to recover the

Lee bottles as the most likely counterfeit to fail close inspection. At some point they quarreled, and Henry whacked her husband over the head. Then she panicked and fled."

"And Faulkner covered for her?"

"Faulkner covered for Tyrone, who he believed had killed Dom."

"I'm lost. Where does *Tyrone* fit in?"

"It would be nice to ask him one of these days, but he split the afternoon he was helping you with the appraisal and hasn't been seen since. From what we can get out of Faulkner, it sounds like Tyrone had either figured out the wine fraud or was hoping to lift a couple of vintage bottles to sell. We think he must have seen Henrietta conk Dom because Faulkner saw him bury the remaining Lee bottles beneath the cherry trees. I guess Tyrone was planning to dig them up again once things cooled down, but when it looked like he might end up taking the rap for murder, he skipped."

"I can't believe it."

"You can believe it," Jeff said. "It's taken us three weeks to put together the evidence to charge Henrietta."

Austin stared down at the bottle.

"And that's why you're here? To tell me how it all worked out?"

"I'm here," Jeff said, "because you never came back, and I'm not about to let this…this relationship go without a fight."

Relationship, not affair. That sounded great, but what did it really mean? Had anything really changed between them?

Austin turned the bottle over absently, thinking.

Jeff said suddenly, "Don't make the mistake of thinking that because he had trouble talking about his feelings, he didn't care."

"Who?"

"Your daddy."

"He made his living talking about his feelings."

"About big political issues. It's not the same thing. You're good at putting your thoughts and your feelings into words. Not everyone is." Was Jeff still talking about Harrison, or was he talking about himself?

Austin was still thinking it over, warning himself not to assume, when Jeff said calmly, "When my daddy found out I was gay, he shot himself."

Austin nearly dropped the bottle of Madeira. *"What?"*

Jeff smiled faintly—presumably at Austin's patent horror and not his own remembrance. "I'm not saying he didn't have some other...issues. He'd tried to kill himself once before. He battled with depression a lot of his life. That's another thing we don't have in the South. Southern gentlemen do *not* get depressed."

Reading Austin's expression, Jeff said, "I'm not trying to blame my dear old daddy for all my hang-ups. The truth is, I was happy enough with the way things were until you came along. I'd given up all those dreams and ideals I'd had in college, and I was doing fine. I thought. Then you showed up."

It was impossible to read his profile.

Jeff expelled a long breath and said, "You were right. About all of it. Mostly, I didn't want to feel what I was feeling—didn't believe it could be true—and I guess a part of me thought that if I could make you acknowledge... Hell. I don't know what I wanted. I was safe before you came along."

"And now?"

"And now I realize that being safe isn't the same as being happy. And that it's hard to be happy without love. And if I let fear keep me from loving someone like you..." Jeff's voice strengthened. "Which is funny, because I never thought I was one for settling down. I've hardly known you any time at all, but this last month I've missed you like I've never missed anyone in my life. I knew when you didn't call after the second week that you probably weren't going to, and I could go back to the way things were and nobody would be any the wiser. You know what? It didn't feel safe. It felt lonely. I miss you all the time." Jeff's voice sounded strained. "I don't know why you didn't give up in the first five minutes, Austin, but since you didn't, I'm going to ask you to give me another chance. This time I won't let you down."

Austin's heart jumped. He said very carefully, "What exactly are you saying? What are you asking?"

"I'm saying that together we can work this out." Jeff's smile was wry, but the depth of feeling in his eyes was something Austin had all but given up on ever seeing. "I don't know how we'll do that, but I know I want to try. And I hope you still do too. I don't know if that means me moving here or you moving there or us finding someplace midway. I don't know. I just know...I can't lose you now."

Austin looked down at the bottle he was holding. "Is this evidence in a court case?"

"Yeah, well, this piece of evidence was conveniently lost. I thought you might want to drown your sorrows or..."

"Or?"

"Toast to a new beginning."

Austin nodded gravely. "Kind of a BYOB proposal?"

"Yep." Jeff's gaze never wavered.

Austin held up the bottle. "How do we get it open?"

Jeff pulled out a Swiss Army Knife with a corkscrew. He opened the bottle and handed it to Austin. "It might be vinegar, you know. It might be... What do you call it? Corked. I probably wouldn't know the difference, but you will."

Austin grinned. "If it's vinegar, we'll have a really terrific salad."

"If you say so. Just don't...send it back."

Austin took the bottle, swirled it gently to release the rich, earthy bouquet: nutty and sweet in the spring afternoon. He took the first sip and handed the bottle to Jeff, leaning forward, smiling into his eyes. "Naw. I know my wines. This is an excellent vintage."

BLOOD RED BUTTERFLY

Blood Red Butterfly *was another exercise in blending literary traditions, but this time I was exploring the tropes of Japanese yaoi (boy love) manga. The challenge was trying to meld a fairly restrictive—and largely visual—art form with a contemporary crime story. The result wasn't exactly what I expected, but the real point was to experiment, push the boundaries a bit, and see if an entertaining story could come out of it.*

CHAPTER ONE

"**B**ad news," Hernandez said. "Your homicide suspect's alibi just turned up."

"No way." Ryo grabbed a paper towel and dabbed at the fleck of mustard on his navy silk tie. He shot Hernandez a look in the mirror over the bank of sinks in the john. "You're kidding me."

Hernandez shook his head. He was not a kidder.

"No. Way." Now Ryo was angry. Still watching Hernandez in the mirror, he scrubbed ferociously at his tie. "Torres is not walking away from this. He popped the Martinez woman, and he's going down for it. And no little *chiquita*—"

Hernandez' sour grin stopped him. "The alibi is male."

"Male?" Ryo stopped rubbing his tie. "You mean…?"

"I mean *you* might even know him." This was not a dig. Hernandez had been Ryo's partner for a couple of years back when they were both street cops, and he knew a thing or two about Ryo's personal life that Ryo didn't generally share. "Might be something you can use. I don't think the Sotels are an equal opportunity employer, you know what I mean?"

Yeah, Ryo knew what he meant. As badly as he wanted Torres, he wasn't sure he liked that idea. He'd prefer to break Torres' alibi, which should be easy enough to do because Torres *had* murdered that old woman in cold blood. Nothing and nobody was going to convince Ryo otherwise. "You believe this punk's credible?"

Hernandez shrugged. "Torres used his one phone call to get this guy over here. See what you think. He's sitting at your desk, biting his nails as we speak."

Ryo curled his lip, double-checking he didn't have a piece of lettuce between his teeth. He ignored the derisive sound Hernandez made. It wasn't about looking good, though Ryo knew he looked good—on a scale of Asian Hawtness, Russell Wong to Dean Cain, he fell comfortably in the middle of Yeah Baby!—it was about conveying bulletproof confidence and unassailable assurance. *Attitude*. It was half the game.

He straightened his tie. "I don't think this is going to take long."

Hernandez cocked an eyebrow and said nothing.

The punk was still sitting in front of Ryo's desk, though he had stopped biting his nails. Ryo had a quick impression of a slight and slouching boyish figure clad in jeans, a pair of chucks, and a gray hoodie. Across the noisy bullpen someone slammed a file drawer and the kid flinched. Ryo smiled inwardly. Yeah, he'd smash this bogus alibi in less than twenty minutes and get back to building his slam dunk case against Mickey Torres. And this time Torres would not be getting off lightly because of his tender age and deprived childhood. This time he was going away forever. Or what counted as forever in the screwed up Los Angeles County judicial system.

The punk raised his head, and Ryo almost walked into a chair. A pale, pointed, delicately boned face, chestnut hair, wide light eyes like a faun— assuming a faun was what Ryo thought it was.

The Ice Princess.

No fucking way.

Mickey Torres' alibi was the same guy who had three times blown off Ryo at Fubar, a gay club he used to frequent. In fact, the Ice Princess was the main reason Ryo had quit going to Fubar. A guy could only take so much rejection.

So this little stuck-up femme dude had cold-shouldered Ryo but was willing to offer his bony ass to Mickey Torres? Willing to supply gang banger Mickey Torres with an alibi for homicide?

Ryo smiled unpleasantly, noisily dragging his chair out from behind his desk. "I'm Detective Miller. You have information for me Mr....?"

The Ice Princess jerked straight. His face went whiter, his eyes went wider, but there was no recognition in his turquoise eyes. Just fear. Maybe the fear a lot of honest citizens seemed to feel dealing with the law. Maybe the fear of someone about to perjure himself to the police.

"Tashiro. Kai Tashiro." His voice was light and husky. A young voice. A young man. But not as young as Ryo had originally thought. Probably in his mid-twenties. Twenty-three or twenty-four.

"How can I help you, Mr. Tashiro?" Tashiro looked about as Japanese as the big-eyed androgynous figures in the manga Ryo's little nieces loved so much. A poser. It was another point against him, though Ryo knew that wasn't fair.

Murder wasn't fair.

"I got a call from a fr—Mickey Torres. He said he'd been arrested, and he needed me to"—a nervous swallow—"verify where he was three nights ago."

Ryo opened the long desk drawer, removed a file, and slammed the drawer closed, harder than he had to. Tashiro gave another one of those little jumps. Ryo opened the file, read for a moment, and then studied the man on the other side of his desk.

"Did Torres tell you what he was arrested for?"

"Homicide." Tashiro's voice was almost inaudible.

"That's right." Ryo shoved the file with the Martinez crime scene photos across the desk. "He killed a seventy-year-old woman by the name of Esther Martinez. Take a look at what he did to her. Take a good look."

Tashiro looked—he couldn't avoid it—and closed his eyes. He opened them almost at once. "Mickey didn't do that."

"Yep, he sure did. He strangled her and then, for good measure—and because he's a fucking animal with no conscience or self-control—he beat her head in." Ryo kept his tone cool and cordial; hoping nobody at the surrounding desks was listening too closely.

Tashiro gave a shake of his head. "He *was* with me, Detective Miller."

Ryo took the file back. He considered his strategy. There were a couple of ways to play this. He hadn't missed Tashiro's hesitation using the word "friend" in regard to Torres.

"Okay," he said easily. "He was with you. From when to when exactly?"

Tashiro was still wearing the hood of his sweatshirt. It gave him a strangely monkish look. "From about eleven thirty to seven thirty the next morning."

"*About* eleven thirty? So is that eleven fifteen, eleven twenty, a quarter to twelve? You're going to have to be precise about the time when you stand up in court and swear to it in front of a jury."

Tashiro's eyes flickered, but he said, "When we left the bar, the clock on my car dashboard said eleven twenty-eight."

"And what bar was that?" Ryo pulled out his notebook and jotted down the times.

"Fubar."

"Fubar. Hmm. I think I've heard of it. Where's that located, exactly?"

"Santa Monica Boulevard."

"That's a gay bar, right?"

Tashiro nodded, not meeting his eyes.

Ryo put his pencil down. "Do you really not recognize me?"

Tashiro looked across, and his eyes went wider still. "Huh?"

Ryo picked up his pencil. Made a sharp notation. "So you and Torres leave Fubar together at eleven twenty-eight on Tuesday night. Then what happens?"

"We drive—drove—to my place."

"Which is where?"

"14159 Armacost Ave."

Ryo grunted. "Nice." Very nice. Half a million nice. What the hell had the neighbors made of street scum Mickey Torres? And what the hell did Kai Tashiro do for a living that he could afford that kind of prime real estate? Nothing legal probably. "Then, what? You guys sat around and played checkers all night?"

Tashiro turned a shade of pink that would require some serious cross-hatching in manga. "No. We had another drink, and then we...went to bed."

"Went to bed? Yeah? Did you watch Letterman? Eat animal crackers? Tell spooky stories? I bet Torres has a few of those. Has he shared with you how he wound up in prison the first time?"

Tashiro shook his head. "We...had sex."

"I didn't catch that."

"We had sex."

"You fucked. Is that what you mean?"

Tashiro's look was murderous. Ryo smiled. He had a very white and charming smile, and he knew how to use it for maximum annoyance. "So you're gay?"

"Obviously."

"No, no. We try not to make insensitive assumptions on the police force. So you're gay and I guess Torres is gay?"

"I..."

"That news is going to cause quite a stir with the home boys. Homosexuality is not popular with Torres' gang. And I use the word *gang* deliberately."

"Is that it?" Tashiro demanded. "Are we done? Mickey was with me. I'll swear to it in court if I have to. Can I go?"

"You don't want to wait around for Torres to be released?"

Tashiro's brows drew together in confusion that was at least partly dismay.

"I'm kidding you," Ryo said. "It'll be hours before he's out. Lots of paperwork involved. In the meantime, we need to get a little more background on *you*, Kai."

CHAPTER TWO

His name was Kai Tashiro; he was twenty-four, single, gay, and self-employed as an illustrator.

"Huh. What do you illustrate?" Ryo asked, momentarily distracted.

"Books." Tashiro was terse.

"What kind of books?"

"How is that relevant?"

Ryo was very polite. "To what?"

"To your case!"

"It's hard to know. I'm still building my case. Everything could be relevant." Ryo paused. "Or nothing."

Tashiro gritted his jaw. Ryo repressed a smirk and went back to making notes.

Tashiro lived in a stylish, luxury condo, drove a Tesla Roadster, and claimed to possess a sizable trust fund. No wants, warrants, or priors.

And no matter how hard Ryo pressed, he did not waver in his story. Mickey Torres had spent Tuesday night from eleven twenty-eight to seven thirty in the Wednesday a.m. when they said their fond farewells over Kashi cereal.

"How often do you and Torres get together for your slumber parties?" Ryo was running out of angles, but he kept trying.

"We don't. That is, this was the third time."

"You're practically going steady."

Tashiro's mouth tightened.

"Well, take a piece of friendly advice. Don't make a habit of it. People around Mickey Torres have a way of turning up dead."

Tashiro said wearily, "May I please go now?"

"You can go." Ryo waited until Tashiro was on his feet and starting to turn away before he added, "We'll be in touch."

"Why?" Tashiro demanded. "I've told you everything I know. Everything there is to tell."

Ryo took his time answering, deliberately looking the other man up and down, from his cowled face to the badly bitten fingernails. "Because you're lying," he replied. "I *know* Torres did it. I'm going to prove it. I'm going to break this bullshit alibi and, if I have to, you with it."

He could see Tashiro struggling with that, struggling with anger and resentment, and fear. He controlled himself though, throwing a bitter, "Knock yourself out!" to Ryo before walking away.

Yeah, Tashiro was scared and angry, and that's the way Ryo wanted him.

The problem was…Tashiro was not lying. Not as far as Ryo could tell, and Ryo was a damn good judge of such things. If he did say so himself.

"**W**e can't hold Torres," Captain Louden said. He opened the bag of Taco Bell on his desk, groped inside, and fished out an orange and purple wrapped triangle. "Don't ask. How did Mayer do in court today?"

"I don't know. I haven't talked to Mayer."

"He's your partner. Why haven't you talked to him?"

Ryo ignored this feeble effort at distraction. "Torres did it, Captain. We've got the perp in custody. I'd stake my career on this one."

Louden, middle-aged, paunchy, balding, perpetually irritable, thanks to perpetual indigestion, replied, "Miller, has it ever occurred to you that maybe you're obsessed? There are other bad guys out there. They deserve a little of your attention too."

"Torres killed the Martinez woman. He throttled that old lady, and he beat her brains in."

"We don't have a motive!"

"The motive is revenge. The testimony Martinez gave at the Revelez trial was responsible for putting Torres behind bars for a decade."

"Revenge!" Louden gave a hoot of derision. "Don't go all Korean drama on me, Detective."

Ryo swallowed his irritation with a wide smile. "I'm not. Even if I was Korean, which I'm not." Louden waved that off. "I'm talking machismo. I'm talking the psychological profile of a gang banger. I'm talking a freaking psychopath."

Through a mouthful of tortilla and shredded lettuce, Louden said thickly, "What you *ain't* talkin' is anything resembling evidence."

"Let me talk to Torres. Let me interrogate him."

"He's got an alibi."

"That's another thing. Why didn't he say the first time we interviewed him that he had an alibi?"

"I'm thinking you could answer that more easily than me, Miller."

Being a Korean drama queen and all? Before Ryo had a chance to respond, Louden continued, "We've got no grounds to hold him. And what I do *not* need is the public defender's office—"

"Please. Fifteen minutes. Just give me fifteen minutes."

Loudon shoved the rest of the taco in his mouth, chewed rapidly, and said at last, "I don't know what good you think fifteen minutes is going to do, but you better make every second count."

* * * * *

Torres sat in the interrogation room, arms folded on the scratched table. He stared at the ceiling, whistling soundlessly. When Ryo stepped inside the room, closing the door behind him, Torres smiled at the ceiling.

"I know you did it. I don't care how many boy toys you trot out to vouch for you. I *know* you did it."

Torres made a kissing noise. "Kai came through, huh? That little queer *loooves* me."

"Yeah," Ryo drawled. "Why not. You're such a lovable guy. When you aren't murdering old ladies and teenagers."

Torres continued to smile. He was twenty-seven, medium height, muscular and tattooed. His head was shaved; his eyes were dark and long-lashed. Maybe he was good-looking, if you had no taste. To Ryo he was just another ugly face in Ugly Town.

"You can't prove nothing, *popo*. I got an alibi. I got a solid citizen to speak out for me."

"Yep, you do, amigo. But I don't know what the boys in the barrio are going to say when they find out you're swag."

Torres' eyes flattened. "Swag?"

Ryo offered his biggest and most annoying grin. "Secretly Walking Around Gay."

Torres jumped to his feet, and Ryo braced for assault. Welcomed it, in fact. But Torres was vicious, not stupid. He stopped mid-step and held up his cuffed hands. "I know what you about. You can't get me legally, so you want me to jack you, jack a police officer. Then you can hold me." He laughed at the disappointment he must have read in Ryo's expression and did a couple of double-handed karate chops in thin air. "Not going to happen. I'm walking out of here a free man."

"Not for long. Why'd you do it, anyway? Why'd you kill that old lady? You've only been out of Chino a month. Can't adjust to life on the outside?"

"I have an ALIBI, *marrano*. You have to let me go. This is false arrest!"

"Sure. Go. *Via con Dios*." Ryo smiled. He opened the door to the interrogation room. "Officer Smith will escort you back to your cell while we finish your paperwork."

"It's *vaya*, dumbshit."

"Yes, it is. And yes, you will." As Torres sauntered past—as much of a saunter as he could manage with leg irons—Ryo added, "Say hi to the boyfriend."

* * * * *

It was all two-for-one drinks and cray cray good times at Fubar on Friday night.

The Ice Princess was having his usual, a Japanese Cocktail. Cognac, orgeat syrup, and Angostura bitters. It was the drink that had first caught Ryo's attention. He'd been lazily flirting with a new bartender when the order popped up. The bartender had asked if Ryo knew what the hell a Japanese Cocktail was. He had no clue. But he'd been interested in checking out whoever had ordered it. Apparently a *gaijin* with a taste for the mysterious Orient.

Not that strong of a taste, because he'd turned down Ryo three times running with barely a glance. But then the Ice Princess turned everyone down. Almost everyone.

It was no different that night. Kai Tashiro sipped his blood-colored cocktail and stared through the sweating, shifting crowd like he was surrounded by ghosts. He wore his usual skinny black jeans and black shirt. Unimaginative but effective with his coloring. The fingers of one hand tapped idly to the beat of the music. "Titanium" by David Guetta. Seriously. Who came to Friday Nights Dance Bitch to listen to the music?

Ryo pushed through the crowd and squeezed into the seat next to Tashiro. He had to shout to be heard over the music. "Hey there! Remember me now?"

He'd hoped to catch Tashiro off guard, but no such luck. Tashiro must have spotted him when he came in. He stared at Ryo with hostility and shouted back, "Sure. You're the asshole cop who wants to frame Mickey for murder."

"Sorry to be such a hard-ass." Ryo offered his big white smile. "Nothing personal. It's just my job. You know, good cop bad cop? Today was bad cop."

"I hear every day is bad cop with you."

"That what your boyfriend Torres says?"

Tashiro looked pained. "He's not my boyfriend."

"He's the closest thing you got to a boyfriend, right? You went home with him four times."

"Three."

"But who's counting."

Tashiro's gaze held Ryo's as he swallowed the last of his drink. He had painted his bitten fingernails black. The nail polish gave Ryo a weird hungry feeling. His cock stirred. Something about femme guys turned him on. Always had. And Tashiro, with his long hair and those huge, jewel-colored eyes and ethereal features, with his tall, willowy body...Ryo had wanted him from the minute he'd laid eyes on him.

"Can I get you another drink?" he asked brusquely.

"No," Tashiro answered, equally brusque.

Ryo ignored that and fought his way back to the bar. He ordered another Japanese Cocktail and a vodka martini for himself. When he returned to the table, he found Tashiro busy rebuffing another would-be suitor with that laser-beam stare of his. The guy retreated, tail between his legs, and Ryo reclaimed his chair, placing the drinks on the table.

"Just my way of saying sorry for earlier."

Tashiro grimaced, but he took the drink and sipped it.

"You waiting for Torres to turn up here?"

Tashiro shook his head.

"Not really his kind of scene, I guess," Ryo said. "Unless he comes for the karaoke on Tuesday."

"I wouldn't know. I don't know him that well."

"Well enough to take him home with you. Well enough to alibi him for murder."

Maybe it was the funky lighting, but Tashiro's eyes seemed to glitter. "I don't need to know him to take him home. I gave him an alibi because it's the truth. He was with me."

"Okay. Okay. Just checking." Ryo winked at Tashiro.

Tashiro scowled.

"If you're telling the truth, you've got nothing to worry about. If you're *not* telling the truth...well, I wouldn't want to be in your shoes. That's all. I'm not talking about perjury or being an accessory after the fact. I'm talking about the danger you present to Torres."

Tashiro's elegant eyebrows drew together. "What danger?"

"Think about it. You're the only one who can prove where he was that night. I mean, either way. Seeing you supplied him with an alibi, he might not want to take a chance on you changing your story."

Tashiro put down his drink. He shoved back his chair, rose, and turned to walk away. Ryo caught his wrist. It was a slender wrist, but a man's wrist, with a tensile, wiry masculine strength.

"Dude, I'm trying to help you."

"No, you're not. You're trying to build your case. You don't care about me. And you don't care about the truth." Tashiro yanked his hand away and disappeared through the wall of drunken, dancing bodies.

Ryo swore and went after him. He wasn't sure why. It wasn't part of the plan. Not part of his strategy. He had no plan. No strategy. But there he was, on his feet and in pursuit of Tashiro, who moved with unhurried grace through the writhing, many-tentacled crowd toward the entrance.

Ryo caught him on the street, bathed in the sickly, jaundiced glow of the street lamps as he unlocked the carelessly parked Tesla Roadster. Who the hell left a vehicle like that unattended? It was an open invitation to be car-jacked.

Ryo put a hand on Tashiro's shoulder, and Tashiro jumped a foot, whirling to face him.

"Sorry." Ryo raised his hands to show he was harmless. "It's just me."

"What is your *problem*?" Tashiro yelled. "I told you the truth. Why are you harassing me?"

"I'm not. I didn't mean to—sometimes I get a little carried away. What can I say? I'm a cop. I take my job seriously. That's why I come here. I need to unwind once in a while."

"You come here because you're gay and you want to get laid!"

"That too," Ryo admitted. The thump of music from Fubar filled the silence between them. He couldn't help asking, "Are you sure you don't remember me?"

"What is it with you? Remember you from *where*?"

"From here."

If possible, Tashiro looked even more bewildered.

"Forget it," Ryo said. "I just…believe it or not, I don't want to see you get hurt. It's not all about my case, okay?"

"You're full of shit. This is totally about your case."

Probably. Ryo hoped so. He wasn't sure, though. "No. Let me prove it."

Tashiro asked warily, "Prove it how?"

And to his shock, Ryo said exactly what he was thinking—though maybe *thinking* wasn't the word because this was simply what he wanted, had wanted since the first time he'd seen Kai Tashiro sitting in the corner of that funky little club. "Let me take you home."

"I've got a home."

Ryo leaned in and said softly, "Let me make love to you."

That was probably spreading the Cheez Whiz way too thick. Because that's all this was, Ryo was just doing whatever he could, whatever he had to, to get to the truth, to break this bogus alibi, to put Mickey Torres back in the zoo with all the other wild animals. And anyway, *lemme fuck you through the floor* just didn't have the same ring to it. Right? But his mouth dried the minute the words left it.

He fully expected Tashiro to burst out laughing. He would have in Tashiro's place.

But maybe Tashiro was more naïve than he looked. More gullible. Because he just stood there frowning away like Aya from *Weiss Kreuz* or somebody else from the dimly remembered cartoons of Ryo's youth.

"Isn't that illegal?" Tashiro asked, at last.

"Not since 1976."

"Huh?"

"You didn't say no," Ryo observed. "Does that mean you're saying yes?"

"Aren't I a suspect?"

"You're an accessory after the fact, assuming you're lying about being with Torres. But you're not lying, right? I have your word of honor."

"Honor?" Tashiro repeated the word like it wouldn't translate into any language he spoke. Which was probably correct. Ryo didn't care by then.

"Sure. You've alibied Torres. You're willing to testify in court. I have to take your word, right? Why not? We're two sons of Japan." He teased, "Two *rising* sons."

Tashiro laughed. It had a rusty sound to it. His eyes were still wary.

"What do you say?" Ryo pressed. "Your place or mine?"

Tashiro's humor faded. He eyed Ryo skeptically, but he said finally, briefly, "Mine."

He drove like a bat out of hell. Ryo had to keep pedal to the metal in order not to lose him. In fact, if he hadn't had designs on Tashiro's dubious virtue, he'd have arrested him for speeding or driving under the influence, or all of the above.

Fourteen minutes of palm trees and light trails and billboards flashing by in a neon blur. Ryo stayed right on Tashiro's tail, but that was more to make a statement. He knew where Tashiro lived. He could have taken his time; hell, he could have stopped for doughnuts and coffee. Instead Ryo rode Tashiro's ass every mile of the southbound CA-2. Pushing Tashiro. Crowding Tashiro.

Why? What was he doing?

Aside from risking his job?

Never in his entire professional life had he done anything like this.

But Ryo didn't want to think about it. Couldn't think about it. So he ignored the appalled voice in the back of his mind and swung a right on Armacost Avenue.

This was the heart of West L.A. Plenty of money, but plenty of diversity too, including a large Japanese-American community. In fact, a part of Sawtelle, from Santa Monica Boulevard to Olympic Boulevard, was known as "Little Osaka." Not to be confused with Little Tokyo, which was in downtown Los Angeles.

This wasn't Sawtelle, though; this was the ritzy stretch of Armacost with vaguely Mediterranean high-priced condos and luxury apartments, discreetly tucked behind fancy street lights and ornamental trees.

Ryo parked his unmarked Ford Taurus in the back and followed Tashiro through the security gate and into the elevator that carried them to the fourth floor. Tashiro didn't speak, didn't look at Ryo. Ryo never took his gaze from Tashiro's pale, withdrawn profile, though he didn't speak either. He figured Tashiro was already regretting the impulse to bring Ryo here—Ryo was—and yet he didn't want to take the chance of saying something that might tip the scales the wrong way.

The elevator doors opened onto an exterior walkway with four-foot stucco walls and a view of the sparkling carpet of city lights. The night was mild and smelled of smog, fast-food, hot engines, and other unhealthy things. It smelled alive. Exciting. The orange and brown tile beneath their feet pounded with the beat of another tenant's overtaxed sound system, a dull bass thump that kept time with Ryo's heart as he watched Tashiro's straight, slender form stalking ahead of him.

Oh yeah. Tonight you're mine.

Tashiro reached the door of his condo and unlocked it. "Wait here a second." He kicked off his shoes and disappeared inside. Before Ryo could respond, the door closed. He had time to remove his own shoes and start wondering whether Tashiro had just played him for the fool he was, when the door opened again.

"Putting the wife and kiddies to bed?" Ryo inquired.

"Disarming the security system." Tashiro's mouth curved in a malicious smile at Ryo's surprise. "That's right. I have my own security system. So, yeah, I'd know if Mickey had left anytime during Tuesday night."

"Hey, did I say a word?" The minute Ryo had learned of Torres' supposed alibi he had requested the building's security camera tapes. Unfortunately they were erased every forty-eight hours, and he had narrowly missed his window of opportunity. In fact, he half suspected that might have been one reason Torres had delayed mentioning an alibi. Now Ryo would have to requisition Tashiro's alarm company—maybe ultimately subpoena them, if they wouldn't cooperate. But no need to break the mood by mentioning that now.

Tashiro crooked an arm behind his head and leaned against the door frame. He tilted his head provocatively. "Was that what you came here to find out?"

Ryo reached for him, guiding him back inside the condo, and kicking the door shut behind them. "No. I came here to find out how you get those jeans off without throwing your back out." Tashiro felt light and supple in his arms, insubstantial, and yet as immediate and active as electricity. His eyes, those unnatural turquoise eyes, were almost level with Ryo's. They seemed to laugh silently into his own.

If there was one thing Ryo hated, it was being laughed at. He yanked Tashiro closer, letting him feel how aroused he was, and getting more aroused in turn by the size of Tashiro's erection through his jeans. He covered Tashiro's mouth with his own.

Tashiro's mouth was not soft and receptive. He kissed back with punishing fierceness, a forceful, hungry heat that met and matched Ryo's. It surprised Ryo and daunted him. That wasn't his style. He didn't want a real fight, didn't want to hurt or be hurt. Instinctively he gentled, turning his grip into a caress and his kiss into a coaxing, and, gratifyingly, Tashiro seemed to melt in his arms. His lips parted sweetly, he murmured something that could have been enjoining or supplication, but either way was totally exciting.

His hands went to Ryo's zipper and Ryo went for Tashiro's waistband, but that was awkward. Tashiro knocked Ryo's hands away and wriggled out of his jeans with the agility of an eel. Even Ryo, occupied now with shedding his own garments as fast as possible, had to spare an admiring glance for those moves.

Tashiro kicked his jeans aside and punched his fists into Ryo's broad shoulders, sending him back against the flat surface of the door. Ryo laughed. This kind of playful wrestling, he didn't mind. He enjoyed it. He yanked Tashiro to him and they roughly rubbed against each other. *Oh God.* Hot, moist friction, soft skin, hard muscle…

It wasn't enough, not by a long shot, but if they kept at it—

Tashiro pulled free, turning his back, and settling his ass into Ryo's groin, grinding back in invitation. Ryo groaned and wrapped his arms around Tashiro's slim waist, drawing him closer, pressing his cock against Tashiro's ass, seeking entrance. Not *that* entrance. He wasn't so far gone he didn't remember where he was, and who he was doing this with. He was aiming for that shadowy divide halving the white globes of Tashiro's buttocks.

There. There it was. Not what he wanted, not tight enough or hot enough, but time being of the essence…he thrust up. "Good. That's good."

"More!" Tashiro urged, thickly.

Ryo bent his head, nuzzled Tashiro's bony shoulder, tasting perfumed soap and bare skin. His own cock was rigid and ready, pearling in anticipation. He reached down with his right hand, found Tashiro's cock as stiff as his own, feeling the pulse of Tashiro's heartbeat in that hot, hard length.

Tashiro moaned in answer to that first tug. "Do it."

"Yeah?" Ryo gave a rolling upward thrust, and Tashiro's muscles clenched tight. Oh, this was sweet. *Sweet.*

Tashiro rose on his toes, offering better access. Home run. Ryo's cock grazed past that tight, hot center. It required superhuman effort not to push right in.

"Come on," Tashiro gasped between thrusts. "Come on. Fuck me."

"...am..."

"For...real..."

Ryo panted, "Not...like this."

"Then...how?"

"Not...bare...back."

"I...don't...*care.*" Kai's voice cracked.

Ryo gulped, "I do!"

Tashiro's muscles clenched tight, and he shifted on the balls of his feet. Ryo rocked his hips and barely managed to avoid penetrating him. A well-fucked young ass, this, with the minimum prep needed. So easy to just give in and take what Tashiro was offering, so easy...but no. God, no. Ryo wasn't completely stupid. He didn't trust Tashiro, and even if he had trusted him, well, he'd have to be crazy to trust him. So leave it at that.

That was the extent of Ryo's thinking. The rest of his gray matter was preoccupied with sensation. The sounds of the creaking door and floor, the flowery smell of Tashiro's hair, the feel of his sleek, hot body gripping Ryo's, the taste of his flushed skin.

There was an enormous red-lacquered cabinet covering half the wall of the entrance hall. Chinese, not Japanese. Maybe Tashiro didn't know the difference. What did they call that color? Cinnabar? When Ryo closed his eyes he could still see that red blazing behind his eyelids.

Tashiro knew exactly how to move to intensify the experience for both of them. He knew the sounds to make, the sounds that cued Ryo, that drove him on. Winded, wounded, wanton sounds, as though Tashiro were helpless with excitement and pleasure.

It was a turn-on, no question.

Ryo jerked his hips in counter tempo to the hand briskly working Tashiro's cock. Tashiro shoved his ass back in meter, and in far less time than it took to describe, they were both coming in molten and messy tandem.

Ryo slumped back against the door, loosening his grip of Tashiro, who fell to his knees. Neither spoke. Their ragged breathing was the only sound.

CHAPTER THREE

"That was…wow," Ryo managed, when he could form words again.

He had sort of been counting on their encounter lasting more than seven minutes. What now? Was he supposed to pull up his pants and say good night?

Tashiro was still trembling on his hands and knees, flame-colored hair tumbled over his skinny shoulders.

"Not that I didn't enjoy that," Ryo said, "but I was hoping for a drink first."

Tashiro's face jerked his way. He stared at Ryo. Ryo shrugged. "You know, get to know each other a little."

It could have gone either way. Clearly Tashiro had a hair-trigger temper. Ryo watched him deciding whether he was offended or not. Then Tashiro laughed, a startled snap of sound, and jumped to his feet in a quick, lithe movement. "What do you want to drink?"

He seemed unconcerned with his nakedness. But then he was beautiful, so where was the ground for concern?

Ryo resisted the urge to reach for his own clothes. He was in great shape. There was no need for self-consciousness, right? "Martini?"

"Get out of here. Do I look like a bartender?"

"You look gorgeous," Ryo admitted.

Tashiro stared at him in disbelief.

"Anything with vodka," Ryo prompted, finally.

Tashiro's eyes widened; then he smiled a quirky, pointed grin. Ryo liked that, liked that Tashiro had a sense of humor, a sense of the ridiculous. Because this *was* ridiculous.

But ridiculous or not, he had every intention of spending the night with Kai Tashiro. He wanted to see for himself whether there was some way Torres could have duped Tashiro into covering for him. It wasn't very likely, and the fact that one quick fuck had him trying to see Tashiro as an innocent bystander was bad news, but…Ryo liked to think of himself as a guy who dotted his i's and crossed his t's. So it was kind of his job to stay and see if he could punch holes in Torres' alibi.

"Anything with vodka," Tashiro repeated. "Doable."

He disappeared into the kitchen, and Ryo took a quick look around the condo. There were three bedrooms, one of which had been turned into an art studio. There was only a single long and very high window, and clearly no one had climbed out that way. It was a serious work space: oversize drafting table, meticulously organized shelves, compartments for art supplies, and carefully planned lighting. Framed posters of luscious manga-style artwork lined the walls. *Something Red Something* read the kanji. At least, Ryo thought so. He was more familiar with *hiragana*.

The guest bedroom also offered no egress, but the master suite had double doors leading out onto a small balcony. Ryo checked out the balcony, but unless Torres had set up a trampoline in the pool courtyard or had sprouted wings like the gargoyle he was, he wouldn't have had any way down from this fourth-story apartment. Let alone a way up again.

Ryo spared a quick look at the rest of the room and raised his brows at the sight of a black wood canopy bed sitting on a framed platform in the middle of the room. Technically, Tashiro's bed was on a stage. Swathes of white gauze draped tastefully over the raised framework. The remaining pieces of furniture were equally stylish and impractical. Off the bedroom was a sumptuous bathroom complete with a black marble sunken tub. A large walk-in closet was mostly empty. A few pairs of skinny jeans, boots, and hoodies. Ryo had more suits than this guy had entire wardrobe pieces.

The living areas offered pale wood floors, stark black walls, crisp white crown moldings and discreet recessed lights. The furniture was oversize sectionals, chairs and couch, upholstered in a smooth, gray fabric that looked like silk. There was a white fireplace that looked unused and a giant mural of girls in kimonos gettin' jiggy with it. Not the peel and stick kind of mural you bought for two hundred bucks. This thing looked hand-painted, old, and extremely valuable.

Possibly even more valuable was the massive aquarium built into the wall opposite the bank of picture windows. Several pale blue koi, *taki asagi*, swam languidly in their giant tank. A fortune in fish. Maybe that's what Tashiro spent his wardrobe money on. How the hell would you clean such a tank?

That reminded Ryo. He looked over at the front door, but the polished floor was immaculate once more. His clothes had been retrieved and draped over a low stool next to a flower arrangement that seemed to consist of green sticks in a white vase.

Tashiro appeared at that point, drinks in hand, and Ryo went to meet him. He took his drink in one hand, wrapped his fist around the ponytail of Tashiro's hair and dragged Tashiro's face to his for a kiss. Tashiro's lashes went down submissively, and he opened his mouth to Ryo's kiss—then nipped him.

"Ow!" Ryo let go and drew back, touching his lip. He checked his fingers for blood. "What was that for?"

"If I wanted to be pawed, I'd get a dog."

"Jeez, dude!"

Tashiro was smirking at him, untroubled, unworried. He had put his jeans back on, which seemed unfair to Ryo, who wasn't exactly sure how to rectify the situation without looking like he felt at a disadvantage—which he naturally did. Tashiro held out his drink, and Ryo automatically touched his glass to it. The rims rang with crystal cheer. *"Kanpai."*

"Mazel tov." Ryo sipped. Vodka soda. Unimaginative but reliable, and it was a good vodka. Kai was drinking pale green liquid from a martini glass.

"What's that? Absinthe?"

Tashiro's brows rose. "I guess you've never seen absinthe before."

"Nah. I'm not an absinthe kinda guy."

"No, you're not."

"Meaning you are?"

"Er…no." Tashiro gave him that quirky, three-cornered smile again.

"So what *are* you drinking?"

"Shochu and Midori."

"What's shochu?"

Tashiro offered his glass to Ryo. "I thought you were Japanese."

"Is that a turn-on for you?"

Tashiro shrugged. "Depends who's wearing it."

"I'm American," Ryo said, a little testily. But he sipped the cocktail. Mostly he tasted the sweet melon flavor of the Midori. He shook his head. "Doesn't do it for me."

"I don't know why not. They call it the Japanese vodka."

"Too sweet for me."

Tashiro laughed. It was a mocking little laugh. Ryo liked his sense of humor less that time.

"So what's the point of all this?" He gestured at the geisha mural, the bowls of smooth black stones, and spartan orchid arrangements. "You have some kind of Asian fetish?"

Tashiro flung himself down on one of the low couches. "What's wrong with embracing your heritage?"

"What heritage are you supposed to be?" Ryo tugged on a long red strand of hair.

Tashiro gave him a level look. "I'm fifth generation. *Gosei.*"

Ryo grunted. He was third generation. *Sansei.* Not that his family paid attention to that kind of thing. The Millers were as American as apple pie and baseball. Okay, apple pie. "Did you grow up in L.A.?"

"Is this part two of the interrogation?"

"No."

"I was born in Montana. My parents died when I was eleven, and I moved back here to live with my grandfather."

"What happened to your parents?"

Ryo was standing behind the sofa so he couldn't really see Tashiro's expression, just the angle of his mutinous mouth and lowered lashes. "They died in a house fire. Before you ask, no. I wasn't there. I was spending the night at a friend's."

That was horrifying. Ryo didn't know what to say. "I'm sorry."

Tashiro shrugged.

Part of being a cop was you got hardened to other people's tragedies. You tried, anyway, because it was the only way to survive the job. Even so…being orphaned at eleven… Still, if Kai Tashiro wasn't crying over it, it sure wasn't Ryo's place. He twined a silky strand of Tashiro's hair around his finger. "So you grew up around here? Where did you go to school?"

Tashiro shook his head briefly, impatiently, freeing his hair.

"Did you go to *hoshu ko*?" *Hoshu ko* were supplemental classes, typically weekend or after-school courses, to teach *Sansei* kids to read, write, and speak Japanese.

Tashiro looked up, his expression sardonic. "Try *Nihonjin gakko.*"

"You're kidding." *Nihonjin gakko* was the kind of schooling the children of wealthy Japanese nationals received while they were living in the States. To send an American-born kid like Tashiro to *Nihonjin gakko* was, in Ryo's opinion, bizarre.

"You have no clue. I trained in everything from kendo to *chaji.*"

"Tea ceremony!"

"Hey, if it was good enough for the samurai…"

Samurai? Tashiro was offering that funny, mocking smile again. It dawned on Ryo that maybe the person Tashiro was really mocking was himself. He said boldly, "Yeah? Well, I learned *ikebana.*"

Tashiro blinked. "Flower arranging?"

Ryo grinned sheepishly. "It was my mom's idea. I was the only kid, well, the only boy, in the entire class. It was mostly all these older ladies."

"No shit!" Tashiro chuckled and all at once, unexpectedly, they were laughing together, in something like harmony.

Never in his entire life had Ryo expected to share that bit of personal history with another dude. Of course, in his case Japanese school had only amounted to Saturday classes at the cultural center, and as soon as he'd been old enough to make his feelings properly known, they'd been replaced with Little League practice.

"So your grandfather was pretty traditional?"

"You could say that." Tashiro's tone was dry. He said, "My turn. What made you become a cop?"

"Instead of a math professor?" It was Ryo's turn to be dry.

"No. I'm not a math professor."

"My mom is. My old man was a cop."

Tashiro snorted. "Let me guess. He was killed in the line of duty."

"Dude, you have a nasty tongue. No. As a matter of fact, he put his back out golfing and took early retirement. He lives in Florida now with his second wife."

Tashiro laughed and finished his drink. "What's your first name?"

"Randall. Randy. Ryo to my family and friends."

"Well, I'm neither, Randall, but if you want to put that drink down, I'll show you just how nasty my tongue can be."

One thing about Kai Tashiro. He was a man of his word.

Ryo'd had plenty of blowjobs in his life, but they seemed like dull exercises in spit and sucking compared to the wet-hot miracle of Kai's beautiful mouth wrapped around his cock. Kai gave head with consummate skill. Such discipline and delicacy. Ryo found himself wondering if he'd had training in that too. How the hell did a guy learn to do that? Ryo had always thought tying knots in maraschino cherry stems was pretty cool. He'd have to rethink his party tricks.

And then, just as he was dangling there on the razor's edge of orgasm, Kai spat him out, sat up, and said, "Now *fuck* me."

Ryo's eyes flew open as a foil packet landed on his groin. He fumbled the condom on, rolled onto his knees, reaching for the proffered bottle of oil. His hand was shaking, whether from the immediate disappointment or the anticipation of what was promised, he wasn't sure.

"Massage into lather, rinse, repeat as necessary," Kai remarked.

Smart-ass. But the sarcasm somehow added to his appeal, or at least to the desire to fuck him into mewling submission. Ryo wanted nothing more than to bury himself to his balls in that long, lithe body. He slicked his stiff cock with a couple of quick swipes of oiled hand and leaned over Kai. Kai bent his knee and shoved his ass up. Not the most dignified position in the world, and yet somehow he did it with grace and efficiency. He reached behind himself with one black-tipped hand and spread himself for Ryo's viewing pleasure.

Ryo's throat moved in a sound that was close to a gulp. Probably inaudible given the boom of his heart in the ō-*daiko* drum of his chest.

"You're..." Beautiful? Strange? Unique? Words failed him. English or Japanese.

"You talk too much." Kai's voice came out squeezed and breathless.

And talking made it personal? Okay. Maybe Kai was right. Maybe personal wasn't a good idea.

Ryo guided himself toward that sweet little target, the pink bull's-eye, and Kai shoved back to meet him. Ryo's stiff cock penetrated the ring of muscle and slid home like a foot shoving into winged sandals. Contact. He was already taking flight.

Kai gave a long, lush moan—an X-rated sound if there ever was one—and made a sinuous kind of wriggle so that Ryo was indeed buried to his balls.

"Oh, yeah," Kai breathed. "Oh, that's it. That's *so* good. Oh, yeah. Move like that."

Ryo obliged, feeling gratified when Kai sucked in a sharp breath. "*Oh. Oh, yeah. Again.*"

Ryo gave a couple of tentative thrusts.

Kai made a keening sound. "You're so big, Ryo. So big, so hard, so hot..." And then another of those gasps.

Ryo was on top, but was he in control? Kind of doubtful.

Did it matter? Even more doubtful.

"Oh."

God. Was there ever such a fucking hot little word? Was it even a word? Or was it just the craziest, fuckingest, hottest, littlest sound ever yanked out of a pair of laboring lungs?

Ryo jerked his hips spasmodically, losing restraint, losing his rhythm, and with each thrust Kai made that broken *oh* sound.

"Oh. *Oh.* Oh. Ry*Oh...*"

It excited Ryo beyond control. He began to shove and strain, ramming into Kai over and over, without style, without skill, just wanting to possess, to own, to be part of this sleek, beautiful weirdo.

And all the while in a dim, shadowy recess of his brain was the knowledge that Kai had done this before, done it many times, done it with Mickey Torres.

Good thing Ryo wasn't a guy who believed in happy-ever-afters.

Ryo opened his eyes.

Something white and filmy was floating above him. A ghost? Probably not. Although if Captain Louden found out what Detective Miller had been up to this night, he'd probably kill him.

Did that make sense?

Probably not.

How drunk *was* he?

Drunk enough, obviously.

The white drapes above him swept languorously out and in, like giant moth wings. No, butterfly wings.

Ryo turned his head. Moonlight through the glass doors illuminated the other half of the mattress. He was alone in this big empty raft of a bed.

He looked for a clock, but there didn't seem to be one. He sat up. There was a glass of water on the low table beside Kai's half of the bed. He picked it up and drained it in a couple of fuzzy-mouthed gulps. That was better. His head was still pounding, but it was a more manageable thump.

Where the hell were his clothes?

Oh yeah. On that stool thing near the kitchen.

There was a bar of light beneath the door. Ryo rose and went to the door, opening it a crack. Every other light in the condo seemed to be on. He winced at the brightness, listening.

Silence.

Was he alone here?

No. There. An impatient mutter and a noise like crumpling paper. Ryo followed the sounds down the hall.

Kai was working in his studio beneath the painted gazes of the sharp-featured men in samurai and kabuki costumes. He had donned his jeans again, but he was barefoot and bare-chested. His hair was pulled back in a ponytail, and he had a glint of red stubble on his jaw. Lost in his work, he looked older and serious. For a few seconds Ryo watched him thoughtfully in the harsh, white light of the swing-arm lamp. Kai worked on, oblivious, frowning at the drawing, making quick adjustments and then frowning again.

Ryo leaned on the door frame. "It's late." He swallowed a yawn.

Kai's head jerked, and he stared blindly past the glaring light. He cleared his throat. "What time is it?"

Ryo peered at his watch. "Three. Thereabouts. What are you doing?"

"Working."

"Now?"

Kai shrugged. "Why not now?"

"Because now is time for sleep."

Kai made a derisive noise. "I don't sleep."

"You mean you sleep in the day?"

"Sometimes, I guess."

"You have…what's it called? Insomnia?"

"I don't need a lot of sleep."

In other words, insomnia. Or maybe a guilty conscience.

Ryo sauntered over to Kai's drafting table, aware that Kai tensed, unhappy with the intrusion, but so what? Kai Tashiro had too many secrets. It wasn't healthy to have that many secrets.

Ryo stared down at the pencil drawing. It was a cartoon of an androgynous figure dressed in period costume, though what period would be hard to say. The figure had long white hair and long white fangs. The cartoon was done in the manga style. Or at least what Ryo thought of as manga style. He was no expert, though he'd bought enough copies of *Vampire Knight* for his young nieces. It was also similar in style to the framed paintings on the wall.

"I think I arrested that guy last week."

Kai snorted. Then he frowned and erased a wayward strand of the figure's hair.

"Is he supposed to be a vampire?"

Kai sighed, then nodded. "Vampire ninja."

"Ah. How's that pay?"

"Better than manga-ka." Kai put a hand to the small of his back and arched, stretching his spine.

"You didn't mention you were a manga-ka when I asked what you did for a living."

Kai curled his lip. "I get tired of explaining what manga is to people who don't know the difference anyway."

Ryo hooked a thumb at the framed portraits. "Those are your work?" Now that he had time to examine them, he could see they all featured the same two impossibly handsome, sharp-featured characters. Each poster represented the cover of a different volume. There were seven altogether.

Kai threw a dismissive look at the row of scowling samurais and haughty kabuki actors. "Yeah."

Ryo squinted at the kanji. *"Blood Red...Butterfly?"*

Kai nodded curtly.

"What is it, a series? Like *Vampire Knight*?"

Kai made a strangling sound. *"Vampire Knight?* Seriously?"

"Hey." Ryo spread his hands. "So? What is *Blood Red Butterfly*?"

"What does it look like?"

"Manga."

Kai sighed long and loudly in the manner of one who was once again going to have to explain himself to people who didn't know the difference anyway. "It's *Shōnen-ai. Yaoi.* You know what that is?"

"Nope."

"What they call Boy Love or BL now."

"Boy Love?"

Kai grimaced. "Don't worry, Mr. Police Man. They're not boys, as you can see. Oniji Zenji is a Seventeenth Century actor in the *yarō-kabuki*. He's *onnagata*. I suppose you don't know what that is either?"

"You lost me at kabuki."

"I wouldn't be so proud of it. Anyway, he falls in love with Kato Kiyomori, a famous samurai."

Ryo eyed the two scowling figures in the nearest poster. Zenji was pointing his fan at Kiyomori who had him at sword point. It didn't look like it was going to be much of a duel. "And they live happily ever after?"

"Oh, hell yeah. They take out a mortgage and adopt three adorable kids and a puppy."

Ryo laughed. He was thinking. If Kai was habitually sleepless, there went another theory—the theory that Torres had figured out the security code and somehow sneaked out while Kai was in Dreamland—and then sneaked back, in time for breakfast. "Sounds like heaven. Come on back to bed."

"No point. I don't like lying there staring at the ceiling, waiting for the sun to come up."

"We don't have to lay there."

Kai gave him a withering look. "It's going to take me a day or two to get over what we already did."

Ryo blushed. "I guess I got kinda—"

"I liked it," Kai cut across coolly. "It hit the spot. In every way. But that's enough for one night. You should go now."

It was kind of surprising the way his heart sank at those words— what was he expecting? Kashi cereal at the least. Damn. But Ryo was not a guy who gave up easily. He rested his hand on the back of Kai's neck and squeezed gently, feeling the network of overstrung nerves and muscles draw tighter still. A *lot* of tension there.

"Come to bed," he coaxed. "I'll help you sleep."

Kai tossed his pencil down. "I said no—"

"Dude, I'm offering you a backrub, that's all."

Kai's expression changed, irritation giving way to wary curiosity. "A backrub?"

"Cross my heart." Ryo held his hands out and flexed them for Kai's inspection. Kai's strange blue eyes studied him. "Permit the maestro to work his magic."

Kai shook his head, but it wasn't refusal, more like he thought Ryo was crazy. Probably true.

They padded back into the bedroom. Kai stepped out of his jeans and flung himself face down on the bed. Ryo sat on the edge of the mattress, gazing down. Kai's skin was pale and mostly smooth, with the usual amount of nicks and scars. Nothing to indicate a particularly tough life. He was built as lightly as a kid, but he wasn't a kid. There was nothing innocent here.

Ryo rested his hands on Kai's shoulders and squeezed lightly. Bare, warm, supple skin. Kai was nice to touch. He smelled nice, too, an exotic blend of sex and flowers.

"Go ahead," Kai said shortly. "Ask your questions."

"About what?"

"Come on. That's what this is about, right? Get me relaxed and comfortable and then start in again."

"No." Ryo dug his thumbs in, kneaded the tight shoulders. He *had* kind of been thinking vaguely along those lines, but Kai seemed so vulnerable like this. Such a slight, flimsy body to contain all that energy and tension. Unexpectedly, Ryo found he really did just want to help him wind down, relax.

"Yeah, right."

"I do have one question."

Kai sounded bored. "I figured."

"Are your eyes really blue?"

Kai gave a smothered-sounding laugh. His head moved in negation. "No. I wear contacts."

"Ah." Ryo had figured. According to his DMV records, Kai had brown eyes. Ryo continued to squeeze and ply Kai's shoulders. He couldn't get too enthusiastic in his ministrations given that there was no meat on Kai's bones. Even so, Kai had decent musculature for a guy who clearly didn't take very good care of himself. Maybe he swam. Maybe he jogged. Maybe he still practiced kendo. He stopped himself from asking.

"Next question?"

"This would work better if you'd shut up."

There was silence, and then Kai gave a huffy laugh. Some of the rigidity went out of his shoulders.

Ryo continued to work over him using long, slow, relaxing strokes. He'd dated a masseuse for a few weeks, and he'd learned a few tricks along the way. The surprising thing was that it was actually kind of relaxing to give massage. Not as relaxing as getting one, true, but it was pleasant to touch and caress, especially when the body being touched and caressed was as attractive as this one.

Kai's flanks rose and fell in slow rhythm as he breathed more deeply and evenly.

Ryo was nonplussed to hear himself say aloud, "My *obaachan* used to give us backrubs when we were little and couldn't sleep."

Kai chuckled, sleepily. "That's sexy. Talking about your grandma."

"I'm not trying to be sexy. I'm trying to give you a peaceful night."

Another one of those abrupt silences. Kai lifted and turned his head to stare at Ryo, though it was doubtful he could see much in the gloom.

After a moment, he lowered himself to the mattress again. He did not speak. In time, Ryo knew Kai was sleeping. He rose, went around to the far side of the bed, and lay down, careful not to disturb the other man.

CHAPTER FOUR

Kai Tashiro and Esther Martinez lived on different planets.

Or at least that's how it seemed. Remembering the crystal glasses and pale blue koi and veils of white gauze, comparing all that to the shabby cleanliness of his crime scene, Ryo found himself wondering if he had dreamed the night before.

For forty-five years, the Martinez woman had lived in the little Spanish-style house on Nebraska Avenue. She had raised her children and buried a husband and grown old in this house, and though she had been well into her seventies, everyone who knew her agreed Esther was still as spry and sharp as a tack.

Oh, yeah. They had interviewed everyone on this block and the next one over. For all the good it had done. But that was the job. You spent hours and days just talking to people, collecting and then sifting through all the bits and pieces of information that might eventually form the picture— though usually the bits and pieces amounted to a lot of funny shapes that never quite fit together. Jigsaw puzzles were the same the world over.

The only thing Ryo and his partner Eddie Mayer had gleaned from Esther's neighbors was that she didn't miss much and that everybody had thought she'd be good for another seventy years.

It was that sprightly sharp-eyed quality that had made Esther such an excellent witness in the Revelez case eleven years earlier. One ordinary June morning she'd been walking back from the grocery store. She had to pass Stoner Park, which in those days had been located in a much worse neighborhood than it was now. Back then the park had been a hangout for gangs, home turf to the Sotels. You could still read fifty years of gang graffiti on the surrounding sidewalk. As Esther had marched along, toting her brown grocery bags, she'd looked across what was now the skate plaza in time to see sixteen-year-old Mickey Torres march up to fifteen-year-old Humberto Revelez, who happened to be dating Torres' sister without Torres' permission, and shoot him five times in the chest.

There had been other witnesses, but none of them had been willing to come forward, let alone testify. Only Esther had had the guts—despite living in such close proximity to the park and the Sotels—to ignore the advice of family and friends, and speak out. And her testimony had been key in putting Torres away. Not forever, sadly, because Torres was a juvenile offender and this was L.A., home to bleeding hearts and misguided social activists. But for over a decade Torres had been safely locked up, and the streets of West Los Angeles had been a little less mean and a lot prettier.

But all good things come to an end, and last month Torres had been released from prison. And apparently, once on the outside, the sick bastard had nothing better to do than even old scores, including murdering elderly ladies.

Ryo walked slowly from room to room of the dark, silent house.

The kitchen was due for a remodel. The appliances were all that scary avocado color so popular in the seventies. The table was set for one. A box of cornflakes sat next to a small vase with artificial daisies.

Ryo thought about his own breakfast that morning—an English muffin eaten over Kai Tashiro's sink in the condo's large kitchen with its quartz counters and stainless-steel appliances. Kai was already back in his studio working when Ryo had stumbled out of bed. It was Saturday, and Ryo had the day off, though technically he was on call. That didn't mean he would get called in. He'd have been willing to hang around for a while if Kai had been interested.

But Kai had told Ryo to help himself to a shower and whatever he could find for breakfast. And that had been that. Not so much as a good-bye kiss. Hell, he hadn't stopped long enough to take off his headphones.

The fact that Ryo even noticed made him uneasy. He'd gotten exactly what he had wanted—a night with the Ice Princess. And yeah, it had been better than he'd imagined, given that he'd previously pretty well convinced himself Tashiro was just a prick tease.

But, no. Wrong there. Tashiro clearly had his issues, but not putting out wasn't one of them.

So what was Ryo's problem? It wasn't like he was looking for a relationship. It was his experience that cops and relationships were not a good fit. In fact, the only happily married cop Ryo knew was his partner, Mayer, and in his opinion, Mayer was in the wrong line of work. And even if Ryo *had* been looking for a relationship, Kai Tashiro was not the kind of guy you brought home to meet Mother. Or, as Kai would no doubt call her, *kaachan*.

Anyway, back to the job at hand. He opened Esther's fridge and studied the rapidly spoiling contents. He had been through this house, combed the processed crime scene a couple of times already, but if Torres' alibi couldn't be broken, then maybe he needed to take another look.

Maybe his contempt for gang bangers like Torres was clouding his perspective. He doubted it, but…it never hurt to take another look.

It wasn't like there were no other possible suspects. Esther had left fifty thousand dollars worth of CDs and stocks to her daughter, Graciela. She had left the house to her son, Oscar. Fifty grand wasn't a fortune, but like a lot of people these days, Graciela was drowning in credit card debt. As was brother Oscar, who was trying to put his own kids through college. The house wasn't large, but it was now sitting on prime real estate.

Money was always a motive. No question. But in his initial interview with Graciela and Oscar, Ryo hadn't caught a glimmer of anything but the shock and grief you would expect from the recently bereaved. Both Graciela and Oscar had separately brought up Mickey Torres and the threats he'd made a decade ago. In fact, those accusations were what put Ryo on Torres' trail, but once he'd read the case files, done a little background checking on Torres, and finally personally interviewed Torres, he'd had no doubt he was talking to the perp.

Not that Esther, a bit of a busybody and the kind of old lady who turned the sprinklers on people who cut across her lawn, hadn't managed to make her fair share of enemies. Well, enemies was a strong word, but everybody had people they rubbed the wrong way, people whose hearts wouldn't break if you fell off the planet, who might even give you a push if it seemed safe enough. A lot of people liked Esther, a few people loved her, but it was safe to assume a couple of people hated her. Everybody made enemies.

It was the violence of the crime that caused Ryo to zero in on Torres.

Strangling was personal. It required strength—or at least know-how—and in this case it had required being the special kind of person who could look your victim in the face as you choked the life out of her. And then lifting that heavy statue of the Virgin Mary that had formerly sat on the dining room credenza and bashing it over the old lady's head a few times. That wasn't your average every day citizen. Or even your average every day burglar.

And while it was always possible that money-hungry offspring might commission a murder, this hadn't been a professional hit. There had been nothing professional about it. This was animal-like rage and brutality.

The killer had come in through the dining room window during the wee hours of the morning. The other windows were secured by iron grille, but this particular window was ornamental. It had been high and round and made of stained glass. At one time it had probably been inaccessible, but the trees in the front yard had grown tall over the years, and if you were lean and agile and determined, it was your access into the house.

It hadn't been quiet though, and the noise of the breaking glass had woken Esther who had come trucking out wearing her yellow, quilted bath-robe and carrying her baseball bat.

And that had been that.

It made Ryo angry. It made him sick. But mostly it made him determined to see Mickey Torres back behind bars where he belonged. So, yeah, maybe he did have a one-track mind, but you needed a one-track mind in his business, because it wasn't a business for the faint of heart or infirm of purpose.

Ryo moved over to the boarded window. He didn't need to be able to look out to know the vantage point offered a scenic view of treetops and beyond, the pale citadel-like towers of the condos on Armacost Avenue.

* * * * *

"Food before romance, *Ryo-chan,*" Ryo's grandmother told him over dinner when he dropped by his mother's house that evening.

"That's why I'm here, *Obaachan.* I could be out on the town, but I'm here with my best girls."

Dove and Raven, Ryo's nieces, looked at each other and giggled. They were at the mysterious age where they giggled at pretty much everything. But *Obaachan* wasn't letting Ryo wriggle off the hook. "Time you were getting married. That's what I am saying."

"If Ryo gets married, we'll never see him again." Ryo's mother smiled, serving him another helping of vegetarian lasagna.

Ryo shook his head. "Not true. Not fair." He winked at his grandmother. She winked back at him. They both knew he was the apple of her eye.

"We never see him now unless he's looking for a hot meal," his sister Cheryl—Cherry to her family—observed. Cherry was four years older than Ryo and still felt it was her bounden duty to make sure he didn't get too big for his britches.

Ryo ignored her and said to his nieces, "Tell me everything you know about being a manga artist."

"I'm going to be a manga artist one day," Raven informed him. She was fourteen and favored motorcycle boots and frilly dresses. Dove was twelve. Her hair was chopped like a boy's, and she wore skinny jeans and T-shirts with anime characters. Tonight's shirt featured Alphonse and Edward Elric from *Fullmetal Alchemist*.

"I know. So what does that mean?"

"Manga-ka," Dove corrected through a mouthful of lasagna.

"Don't talk with your mouth full, Dove," Ryo's mom said. "You girls can be whatever you like *after* you graduate from college."

Raven and Dove exchanged another of those enigmatic giggles.

"Not every career requires a college education, Mom," Cherry put in.

"But you're glad you have one, aren't you?" Ryo's mother returned without heat. "Ryo's glad *he* has a college education."

This was covering old, old ground. Cherry, a graphic artist, and her girls had been living with Ryo's mother since Cherry's boyfriend, a potter, had split seven years earlier. In a household of five women it was only natural there would be the occasional difference of opinion. Most of the disagreements revolved around Cherry's girls and all the possible scenarios for their future.

"Leave me out of this one," Ryo said. "So how do you get to be a manga artist?" Partly, he really wanted to know; partly, he really wanted to change the subject.

Raven said airily, "You start drawing, and you put your stories online, and then you get a lot of fans and a publisher puts your pictures in a book."

Right. Even Ryo knew it couldn't be that easy.

"A Japanese publisher?"

"Maybe."

Dove said, "Sometimes one person draws and one person writes the story. Like in *Bakuman*."

"Yep," Raven agreed.

"Have you ever heard of a manga-ka named Kai Tashiro?"

Raven's dark brows drew together. She shook her head.

"He draws samurais and that kind of thing."

Dove and Raven seemed to find this comical. "Lots of people draw samurais!"

Dove put in, "There aren't many boy manga-kas."

Ryo grunted. It belatedly occurred to him that Kai probably did not draw the kind of stories his teenage nieces were—or should be—reading.

"Why all the interest in manga?" Cherry asked.

"It has to do with a case."

"I figured. You're about as artistic as a sledgehammer."

"We have enough artists in the family, right?" To his nieces he said, "Do manga-ka make a lot of money?"

This, too, the girls found funny. "You don't do it for the *money*," Raven informed him.

Well, that put him in his place. Ryo devoted the rest of the meal to his food, listening absently to his mother and sister and grandmother chitchat, the girls speak in the coded language of sisters. It would have seemed like a strange coincidence, his grandmother bringing up the subject of Ryo's marital status, except lately *Obaachan* was always bringing up the subject of Ryo's marital status. Ryo was thirty-two and, in *Obaachan's* opinion, it was high time he settled down. Of course, *Obaachan* had no idea that if Ryo did decide to settle it would not be with a lovely young girl from a good Japanese family. Then again, maybe she did know. Just because Ryo had never discussed his sexuality didn't mean his loved ones hadn't had plenty of time to draw their own conclusions.

He had never really considered it before. He wasn't sure he wanted to consider it now.

And yet…what would it be like if he *could* bring someone here to meet his family, be part of his family? What would it be like to have someone to come home to? To fall asleep beside the same person every night? Wake up to the same face every morning? Be able to have all the sex he wanted whenever he want—well, anyway, what would that be like?

Some people made it work. Not his sister, not his parents, not most of the guys and gals he worked with, but some people had whatever it took to make love last a lifetime.

Maybe it was just luck. Or maybe it was stubbornness.

Ryo hung around until about seven and then headed back to his own apartment on Carmelina Avenue. But once home, he realized he was too restless to call it a night. He dressed again and headed over to Akbar in Silver Lake. Strong drinks, lousy DJ, and most to the point, no Kai Tashiro.

He spent the rest of the evening drinking, dancing, and flirting, until some time after one when his cell phone rang and he was called out to investigate a floater found beneath Santa Monica pier.

It was five o'clock in the morning when he finally handed the case off to Detectives Hart and Ruiz and started home. But somehow as he was driving along Santa Monica Boulevard he ended bypassing Centinela and speeding straight on 'til he came to Armacost.

"You're out of your fucking mind," he muttered, but he still made the left turn. He was too tired and tightly wound to sleep, and Kai didn't sleep anyway, so what harm would it do to see if he was on his own?

But when Ryo pulled into the parking lot in the back he immediately spotted Mickey Torres' ride, a black Cherokee with the license plate RUBUOUT. The Cherokee actually belonged to Torres' kid brother, but Torres had been driving it ever since his release from Chino.

Ryo parked and got out to examine the vehicle. The hood was cold, so it had been parked for a couple of hours. Meaning Torres was planted for the night and not there to…what? Do bodily harm to Kai? Or at least not any bodily harm Kai didn't welcome.

Ryo got back in his Taurus before he was tempted to do something really stupid. Like what? Break in and arrest Torres for daring to sleep with the guy Ryo wanted to sleep with? That wasn't just stupid, it was pathetic.

He had no grounds for hassling Torres. As a matter of fact, he should be grateful for the reminder of where Kai Tashiro's loyalties lay.

Ryo gazed at the dark windows of Tashiro's condo. Finally he turned the key in the ignition, started the engine, and drove home.

* * * * *

The Tashiro Nurseries opened in 1930. The first nursery was started by three Japanese brothers newly immigrated to the States. Two of the brothers had returned to Japan right before the outbreak of World War II. The third and youngest brother, Akira, had remained behind and continued running the nursery until his incarceration in the Manzanar Internment Camp. Akira had remained in Manzanar for the duration of the War, but when the War ended, he had returned to Sawtelle and the nursery. Business had boomed, and by the '60s, there were three Tashiro Nurseries in Southern California, and Akira was a very wealthy man. A pillar of the Asian community.

He had married twice and had seven children, including three sons. One son had died in the Korean War, one son had died in Viet Nam, and one son had drowned surfing off Malibu. That, it seemed, was how Kai had eventually ended as Akira's heir. None of the remaining daughters had managed to provide sons. In fact, two of them had not produced children at all. Kai was the first and only surviving male child in two generations. The fact that he was only one-eighth Japanese and had been born Kevin Cole was apparently irrelevant.

Ryo learned all that and more on Sunday, which he spent further investigating the principals of his case—although now and then it felt uncomfortably like stalking an ex-boyfriend. Not that Ryo had ever stalked an ex, and he hoped he wasn't laying the groundwork now, but there was no question he was fascinated by Kai Tashiro.

His investigation yielded little, and what he did learn was not remotely sinister. Tashiro owned his condo and car. He paid his bills on time. He lived debt-free. He bought his groceries with an American Express card, but paid off the card at the end of each month. That eliminated a lot of paper trail right there.

Tashiro paid his taxes on time, and the numbers all added up. More money did not go out than came in.

He had attended Cal Arts for a couple of years but had dropped out despite excellent grades. He did not have student loans.

Eighteen months ago he'd gotten a speeding ticket. That was the closest Kai Tashiro had come to a brush with the law.

Mickey Torres on the other hand... There was a wealth of information all confirming what Ryo already knew.

Torres was the product of a broken home. He had three siblings, each the result of a different father, none of whom had stuck around longer than it took to conceive the little bastards. Despite her lousy taste in men, Mama Torres was a mostly decent, hardworking woman who had somehow raised three gang bangers and a nun. Yep, after Mickey had capped her fifteen-year-old boyfriend, Maria Torres had opted for a spiritual life. She had taken her first vows when she was nineteen. Mickey's older brother was on death row at San Quentin, but since he'd been there since 1998, it didn't look like he was going anywhere anytime soon. Like Mickey, the youngest Torres brother had been in and out of trouble since he was twelve. Unlike Mickey, he'd so far managed to avoid anything more serious than a handful of misdemeanors. But with Mickey home to serve as an example, that would probably change.

And then there was Mickey.

His earliest teachers described him as bright, even gifted, with an extraordinary aptitude for art. In fact, his first arrest had been for tagging the abandoned Exposition right-of-way train line. It had been all downhill from there.

So, yeah, very sad what the lack of opportunity and options could do to a kid. But so what? Ryo had seen hundreds, maybe thousands of similar cases during his years on the force. He wasn't a social worker or a time traveler. He couldn't undo the past, couldn't change one minute of it. Plenty of other people had similar lack of opportunity and options, and they didn't turn out to be criminals, let alone murderers. It wasn't his job to fix the system, just keep it up and running.

Torres was what he was—and that was too dangerous to let run free. Where he fit into Kai's life, Ryo couldn't quite see. Maybe he didn't want to see. But given what he knew of Kai, Torres spending four nights at the condo on Armacost was significant. And worrying. Because apart from his case and—sure, admit it, sexual jealousy—Ryo didn't want Kai to be hurt. In fact, he was made uneasy by how much the idea disturbed him.

Whether Kai thought he was slumming or whether he was genuinely infatuated with Torres or whether it was something entirely different, however Kai was reading this situation, Ryo knew Kai didn't begin to understand what he was dealing with. It was like watching a butterfly go up against a hawk. Kai was going to end up in pieces.

Ryo couldn't let that happen.

But how did he prevent Kai from jumping back into the fire? Nothing he said was going to stop Kai.

On impulse he contacted Akira Tashiro at his home and asked for an interview. His request was granted for that afternoon.

The house was built in the Craftsman style, a graceful structure of natural wood and smoky windows. It sat back from the street, surrounded by Japanese maples and roses. In fact, as attractive as the house was, the real beauty was the garden with its symmetrical walkways and artfully grouped large stones. Chimes tinkled soothingly in the warm breeze as Ryo reached the front door.

Ryo rang the bell. The door opened, and a very pretty twenty-something Japanese woman dressed in jeans and a pink flowered smock stood before him.

"Good afternoon." Ryo flashed his tin. "I'm Detective Miller. I'm here to see Mr. Tashiro."

It wasn't that the woman's face tightened. If anything her expression went more smooth, more blank. But Ryo sensed her bracing herself. "You're here about Kai?"

Ryo raised his eyebrows. "What makes you think so?"

Her smile was polite and unamused. "Familiarity. I know Kai very well. Better than anyone."

"And you are?"

"Laurel Tashiro." Laurel added, "Kai's wife."

"Wife?" Ryo reddened at his own obvious shock, but how had he overlooked that information? He couldn't have. Not that he never missed anything, but he wouldn't have missed *that*.

"That's right." Laurel's expression was a strange mixture of satisfaction and mockery. "If you're investigating Kai, I don't blame you for being surprised."

"I am surprised. There's no record of his marriage."

"We were seventeen. The marriage was annulled."

If that was supposed to clarify things…fail. If the marriage had been annulled, why was she still calling herself Kai's wife—and what was she doing here at Kai's grandfather's home? Ryo was attempting to make sense of Laurel's information while still trying to wrap his mind around the idea of a teenaged Kai marrying another seventeen-year-old. Had they run away together? Who had pushed for the annulment?

"Are you, er, on good terms with your ex-husband?" Ryo asked.

Laurel laughed. "We're not on bad terms. Kai is what he is. We don't have anything to do with each other, really."

That was clear as mud. Ryo said, "I think I'd better speak to Mr. Tashiro," although he was already thinking better of the impulse that had brought him here. It was hard to imagine that anything he might learn in this house would tie in with his investigation, and it was suddenly clear to him that Kai would take a very bleak view of this particular digging into his past. But it was too late now. A detective had to be part psychologist, part diplomat, part…well, whatever was needed when it was needed. Sometimes that something was rude, intrusive bastard. Knowing how to handle different types of personalities, people coming from all walks of life—getting them to feel comfortable enough to open up. And then being able to assess the quality of information, and from all that, filter through all the possibilities to figure out a lead or even a suspect…it was all part of the job.

Ryo removed his shoes and followed Laurel through several beautiful, immaculate rooms that looked like no human had ever set foot in them, out shoji-style doors into a surprisingly large and lush garden.

The sound of running water and a child's laughter greeted them as they walked down a graceful path of pale crushed stone.

"Did Kai grow up here?" Ryo questioned.

"Yes."

"Do you live here?"

"Yes."

At the end of the garden was a pond with a small ornamental bridge. A very old man stood on the bridge feeding koi. He wore dark *monpe* work pants and a baggy blue denim shirt. He had the kind of beard that was usually reserved for fairytales of ancient Japan. A small boy of about four, dressed in jeans and a Gap Kids sweatshirt, knelt beside the pond, peering down into the water.

"Please excuse the interruption, *ojiisama*," Laurel said softly, formally. "This detective wishes to speak to you about *Kai-san*."

The old man turned and stared at Ryo, who found himself automatically bowing. It seemed natural in this setting. In fact, it seemed mandatory. "Thank you for agreeing to see me, Mr. Tashiro."

"Mama, the koi are eating cantaloupe!" The kid began to babble about the fish. Laurel smiled and the old man's dark gaze dropped to the animated little face and softened.

Laurel held out her hand. "Come on, *Kenji-chan*. *Ojiisan* has to talk to this man."

Kenji jumped up and ran across the bridge, his small feet drumming lightly. He took Laurel's hand and grinned with cheeky shyness up at Ryo.

Ryo nodded at him. "Hi."

Kenji hid his face against his mother's thigh. She ruffled his hair and led him away, giving Ryo a meaningful look. What meaning that look was supposed to convey, Ryo had no idea. *Don't upset the old man?* Probably too late for that.

"You wished to speak to me about Kai?" Tashiro had a deep and vigorous voice, startling for one so very old. How old *was* he? Ryo did some quick calculating and guessed Tashiro must be close to a hundred years old.

"Your grandson's name turned up in one of my cases. I'm trying to get some background information on him."

"Is Kai suspected of a crime?" Tashiro threw the last of the cantaloupe into the pond. The koi, dark red *Goshiki*, darted to the surface, hungry mouths sucking at the pale chunks of melon.

"Would that come as a surprise to you?"

The old man seemed to struggle internally. He shook his head and looked away from Ryo to the swarming fish. Ryo wasn't sure the head shake meant Tashiro wouldn't be surprised or if it meant a refusal to answer.

At last Tashiro said, "I know nothing of Kai's life."

That was pretty sweeping. Nothing in Ryo's background research had indicated that state of affairs. He reconsidered his original plan of attack. While he couldn't let Kai's strained family relationships side rail his investigation, he didn't want to aggravate the existing tensions more than he had to. "What can you tell me about Kai's friends or business associates?"

Tashiro repeated, "I know nothing of Kai's life."

"Would it be correct to say there's a-a family estrangement?"

"*Hai.*"

"Do you support Kai financially?"

"An arrangement exists."

"What kind of arrangement?"

Tashiro turned his dark gaze back to Ryo. "The matter can have nothing to do with your investigation."

"It depends. Could someone place financial pressure on your grandson?"

"No." An almost rueful expression crossed Tashiro's weathered face. "Kai's temperament is not amenable to duress."

"When was the last time you saw your grandson?"

"Three years ago."

Estrangement was the right word. "His ex-wife lives with you?"

"My grandson's wife and child live with me."

Ryo had the feeling the ground was shifting beneath his feet. "But... Kai...that is, the marriage was annulled, according to your..."

Tashiro stared steadily at Ryo. It was pretty damned intimidating, but Ryo reminded himself he was a grown-up LAPD Homicide Detective and not Kenji's age. "According to your daughter-in-law, the marriage was annulled. You're saying Kenji is Kai's son?"

"Hai."

Kai did not pay child support. That would have turned up in Ryo's background check. Furthermore, Kenji couldn't be more than four, five at the most, and though no expert on the topic, Ryo was pretty sure if you had children, you couldn't get an annulment except in extraordinary circum- stances—and those extraordinary circumstances would have turned up in his investigation.

Tashiro continued to stare at him, stony and unblinking.

Clearly, this line of inquiry was going nowhere fast. Ryo asked slowly, "Are you of the opinion your grandson would lie to protect a friend?"

Tashiro said bluntly, "My grandson's entire life is a lie."

CHAPTER FIVE

Ryo's cell phone rang while he was in Starbucks getting coffee. The number was unfamiliar. He scowled at it and gave the ponytailed girl behind the counter his second most charming smile as she handed over his order and narrowly avoided spilling coffee down his shirt. He pressed his phone. "Miller."

"Who the fuck do you think you are?" a youngish male voice snarled.

"Detective Randall Miller, LAPD. Who the fuck do you think YOU are?"

He assumed he was intimidating some asshole wrong number into better manners, but the voice yelled back, "How fucking dare you go to my grandfather with those lies?"

Unexpectedly, Ryo's mood did a one-eighty as he recognized the ranting voice as Kai Tashiro's.

Ryo paused to hold the glass door open for a woman with a stroller and a whining toddler. The woman glared at him, and he recalled that dropping the F-bomb in Suburbia was generally frowned on. He hung around with too many cops and robbers these days.

On the other end of the line, Kai was still giving him an earful. The words "police harassment" figured prominently.

Ryo let the door swing shut and strode across to his Taurus, pressing the key fob to unlock the driver door. "Are you finished?" he asked Tashiro, who had been forced to pause for breath.

Kai got his wind back. "I haven't even started!" he raged.

"Look, I don't know what you think I said to your grandfather, but—"

It was doubtful Kai even heard him.

Ryo busied himself securing the coffees, buckling up, starting the engine, backing out of the narrow parking slot. When there was another lull on the phone, he inquired politely, "Still there?"

"Oh, fuck you," Kai said bitterly and rang off.

Ryo pressed call back, and the phone rang a couple of times before it was answered and Kai said fiercely, "Don't ever contact me again."

"Don't hang up," Ryo told him.

Gratifyingly, Kai did not hang up, though from the harsh sound of his breathing, that could change any second.

"I categorically deny that I ever said or implied that you were involved in anything illegal," Ryo stated. "If someone drew that conclusion, I'm very sorry." That last part was the truth. He didn't want to do anything to hurt Kai. But he had a murder to solve, he needed cooperation, and he wasn't getting it from Kai.

"Why would you do that? Why would you go to my grandfather? I've cooperated with you, haven't I? Why would you tell *Ojiisan* about Mickey?" Kai sounded aggrieved now, which meant he was starting to wind down. "I *told* you we're not involved."

"Then what was he doing at your place Saturday night?"

There was a pause that lasted no longer than the time it took Ryo to wince at his own dumbness.

Kai said in a very different tone, "Are you *stalking* me?"

"Of course not. Torres is under surveillance."

Kai hung up.

This time Ryo didn't call him back. That "stalking" comment had stung. He recognized uneasily that there might be a finer line than he had realized—and that he might have crossed it. He knew he was obsessed with Torres. That didn't worry him. The obsession—no, call it concerned interest—in Kai...that was different.

He hoped.

He picked up his partner at Mayer's home in Silver Lake. Mayer had been out with the flu since last Wednesday though he'd managed to testify on another case in court on Friday. Ryo had nothing against Mayer, but he preferred to work alone. However, LAPD policy was everyone got partnered, so...Mayer.

As usual Mayer was late. He came running out of the house, shrugging into his suit jacket, and flung himself into the car. "Let's roll!"

It was the same routine every morning with Mayer. Ryo sighed and released the brake. "How'd your testimony go with the Halpern thing?"

"Halpern's going to walk. How's the Martinez case building?" Mayer waved briefly to his youngest daughter peeking out from behind the front window drapes.

"It's building. I've been looking for a way to punch holes in Torres' alibi."

"I heard." Mayer slurped his coffee. "You're stepping on toes."

"Whose?"

"Toes in general."

"Yeah, well, some people shouldn't go barefoot."

Mayer chortled. "Some people shouldn't wear *zōris*." Meeting Ryo's blank look, he said, "What? It's a Japanese joke."

"Oh. I thought it was a *lame* joke."

"No, that would be a *pedi-phile* joke. Get it? Pedi—"

"What kind of a joke is it if I ram this car into that truck and kill us both?"

"A not funny joke." Mayer swallowed another giant mouthful of coffee. "I've been thinking."

"That's new."

"About the Martinez kids."

Ryo grunted.

"Follow the money trail, Miller."

Ryo shook his head. "It's not the kids. I thought we agreed on that?"

"It was somebody."

Mayer was a good detective, but he was preoccupied with his—admittedly high—clearance rate.

"I know exactly who it was. So do you."

Mayer made a pained noise. "You've got Mickey Torres on the brain."

"He did it. You *know* he did it."

"We have to be able to prove he did it. It has to hold up in court."

Ryo threw Mayer an impatient look. Ryo's own clearance rate was nothing to sneeze at.

"We need a different angle." Mayer dreamily contemplated a billboard with a seven-foot-tall, half-nude girl kissing a bottle of vodka. "I think we should step back. Look at it from another direction."

The money trail, in other words. "Fine by me," Ryo said. He knew to pick his battles.

They spent most of the morning doing the never-ending paperwork that made up so much of the job, reviewing notes, making calls, and surfing the web in the interests of research.

Blood Red Butterfly Ryo keyed into his laptop. His search results included a song by an unsigned Irish grunge band, a reader of fan fiction, and first and foremost, a Wikipedia article.

Blood Red Butterfly (血 赤 鮮血蝶 Buraddo Reddo Batafurai) is a yaoi manga series written by Tashi. The series premiered in the January 2005 issue of *LaLa* magazine and ran for a total of seven volumes. In North America, the series was released in English by Be Beautiful between September 2007 and August 2009 when the company filed for bankruptcy. Digital Manga Publishing later acquired the license and condensed the entire series into three volumes, published from September 2010 to May 2012. The series is regarded as a cult favorite.

PLOT:

(See also: List of Blood Red Butterfly characters)

In 17th Century feudal Japan, Oniji Zenji is a much-adored actor in the yarō-kabuki. Zenji is an onnagata, a male actor who impersonates women. Known as the "Blood Red Butterfly," he is also the protégé and lover of powerful Lord Hishikawa Hino. A rift comes between the two men when Zenji witnesses Hino's murder of his rival Lord Sayama. Later he meets and falls in love with the legendary samurai Kato Kiyomori who has sworn to avenge the murder of his master, Lord Sayama. Kiyomori uses Zenji to gain access to Lord Hishikawa even though he has fallen in love with the young actor. The plot fails and Zenji turns against Kiyomori. Eventually the lovers are reunited, but circumstances arise to separate them again. Through the course of the seven volumes Zenji and the out-lawed Kiyomori are often lovers and usually enemies as dramatic political events revolve around them. In the final pages of the last volume the two men write death poems pledging their eternal love for each other and commit ritual suicide.

"Holy shit," Ryo muttered.

"You say something?" Mayer looked away from his laptop.

"Uh…no." Ryo stared at the webpage before him. Disturbing much? Surely the fact that Kai could come up with a plot this melodramatic and tragic indicated a not so healthy psyche. Did he maybe imagine himself and Torres inextricably bound in a doomed Romeo and Julio scenario whereby they both ended in a blaze of gunfire or a drive off a rooftop?

Whatever happened to just writing about high school vampires?

Mayer, now buzzing from his third cup of coffee, said, "I say we go talk to Graciela. She's not married. No steady boyfriend. She doesn't have any kind of alibi for the night of her mother's murder."

"Who the hell *would* have an alibi for three o'clock in the morning? In my opinion, having an alibi is suspicious. I say we go roust Torres again and see what shakes out."

Mayer gave him a narrow look. "Is this some kind of an Asians versus Latinos thing?"

"Excuse me?"

"If I didn't know better, I might think it's personal with you and Torres."

"What can I say? I take strangling little old ladies personally."

"Come on, Miller." Mayer shook his head.

"She stood up to that thug," Ryo said shortly. "She had the guts when no one else did. And she died for it. No way am I letting Torres walk."

"I know, but you can't let it get to you. We can only do what we can do. We've got other cases sitting here. This isn't like you."

Ryo muttered, "Maybe she reminds me of somebody." Yeah. He hadn't really considered it before, but maybe that was part of it. Not that Esther had been in any obvious way like *Obaachan,* except in that surprisingly stern moral fortitude, that spine of titanium that made backing down from the truth a physical impossibility. The world needed more people willing to do the right thing, not fewer.

Mayer cleared his throat. "Okay, well… But there's still such a thing as innocent until proven guilty. Remember due process? We don't have anything on Torres. So for now we have to focus our energy on the other players."

"How about this? You go talk to the son and daughter, and I'll go pound on Torres' door. Just so he knows we haven't forgotten him."

"Yeah, I don't think so, Mr. Personality," Mayer said. "If anything, I go talk to Torres and you talk to Gracie and Oscar. But I say we stick together. The last thing the department needs is another harassment charge."

Ryo closed his laptop. He felt unsettled and worried after reading the Wikipedia article. Maybe it was silly, but he had an almost superstitious feeling that time was running out. Not for him, not for his case. For Kai. He pushed his chair back from his desk. "Then saddle up, amigo, because I'm going calling on Torres."

* * * * *

They tracked Torres down to the Taco Bell on Pico where he and his compadres were enjoying the fine cuisine while scaring the shit out of the middleclass clientele by their mere raggedy-ass presence. Counting Torres, there were five youths—maybe Sotels, more likely just wannabe Sotels— and two *chicas*. The girls looked borderline underage, though it was hard to tell beneath the glitter eye shadow and weirdly outlined lips. Torres was the oldest of the bunch, which Ryo figured told a tale. Why wasn't he hanging with the real hombres? Didn't the wolf pack want him back?

The girls were talking too loud and laughing too much, the boys offered the usual swaggering sideshow of obscenities and raucous laughter. That all died away to sullen mutters when Ryo, flanked by Mayer, walked over to the center tables they had commandeered.

"Hey, look who's here!" Ryo said to Mayer.

"Mr. Torres. And friends," Mayer responded. "How's the food?"

"Not so good, now that you're stinking up the place," a chubby youth in a camo T-shirt and red bandanna responded.

Close up, Ryo could see that Torres looked like he'd been in a fight. There was a cut above his right eye, a bruise on his cheekbone, and one of his eyes was swollen shut.

"What happened to you? Another welcome home party?"

Torres lifted his lip in a contemptuous curl and said nothing.

"You can't just hassle us for no reason," one of the girls piped.

"I don't know. Assault and battery seems like a good reason," Mayer replied. He looked at Ryo, waiting for Ryo to take lead in the questioning.

"Nobody filed a complaint," Torres growled. He picked up his super-size Pepsi and pursed his lips around the straw. There was something about a bad guy drinking soda pop through a straw that sorta defused the menace.

But Ryo's smirk was wiped away by the sight of the fresh ink on Torres' hand. A large red butterfly, still crusted with the dots of Torres' blood.

Ryo stared at the tat and a bad feeling spread in the pit of his stomach. "Or maybe your boyfriend said no?" he suggested, silkily.

As insults went, it was really pretty routine. Inflammatory, provocative, sure. But nothing out of the ordinary in the exchange of civilities between cops and crooks. No, what changed it from routine to dangerous was the fact that it was true—at least the part about Torres having a boyfriend. What changed it from routine to dangerous was Torres' reaction. It was too raw, too revealing. He shoved the table back, sending the *chicas* and *chalupas* flying. The girls squealed as the drinks spilled across the table. The boys began swearing and squaring up.

"Don't do it. Don't be stupid," Mayer warned them.

Ryo never took his eyes from Torres. Torres was the color of old ivory. His eyes were black with rage. His hands twitched by his sides like a gunslinger in the Old West. If he'd been packing, he'd have pulled his weapon. The fact that he wasn't packing was a surprise.

It surprised everyone, including his home boys. But that was the least of their surprises, because Torres had given himself away with that naked reaction. Torres knew it too, belatedly. Ryo wasn't the only one observing shocked realization dawn in that fraught, frayed pause, wasn't the only one who saw it in the hard, young faces watching Torres struggle not to betray himself.

If there was ever a moment when Ryo felt sorry for Torres, it was then.

Torres managed a laugh. "I know what you want, *chapete*." His voice was thick. "It's not going to happen. You're not busting me on a two four three."

"Don't worry," Ryo told him. "When I bust your ass it won't be for assaulting a police officer. And when we lock you away this time, you'll stay locked away."

Torres was still and silent, leaving it to his sidekicks to bluster and posture as Ryo and Mayer walked out of the restaurant into the parking lot.

"Are you out of your goddamned *mind*?" Mayer said furiously, as the glass doors swung shut behind them. He threw a quick look back at the building. "I thought we were going to *question* him."

"What question do you think there's left to ask?"

"Great! So what *were* you trying to do there? Start World War III? What do you think would have happened if they'd thrown down on us?"

"Who? Those wankstas? No way."

"You don't know that."

Ryo shrugged. Yeah, he did know that. Unlike Mayer, he'd grown up in this town. He knew the cowboys from the Indians. But Mayer was right. Ryo could have handled that better. He'd been knocked off balance, his guts in knots the instant he'd spotted that red butterfly tat. He wasn't even sure why. So Torres had a butterfly tattoo? He was covered in tattoos. What was one more?

But that tattooed butterfly mattered. Ryo knew it did.

Mayer was still fuming. Seeing the shrug, he said, "You're too damned cocky, Ryo. You keep pushing buttons, and someday you're going to open a fucking trap door!"

CHAPTER SIX

In an effort to drum up business on what was typically the slowest night of the week, Fubar was advertising Dirty 30 with Sigma Alpha Spank! Ryo felt old just reading the lineup of festivities. Beer pong! Flip Cup! Dart board! Spank! Shots!

Did they do anything in this place that didn't involve exclamation points?

But then he saw Kai sitting in his usual corner, and everything was good again.

Unaware of his approach, Kai sipped his crimson cocktail and, with a small flourish, added an embellishment to the napkin he was drawing on.

Ryo reached the table and rested his hand on the back of the chair across from Kai.

"Can I join you?"

Kai glanced up. He didn't look surprised to see Ryo. He didn't look pleased either. "Oh. It's you."

Ryo jiggled the chair. "May I?"

"Why so polite? You know you'll sit down whatever I say."

Ryo pulled out the chair and sat down. He leaned forward so he could be heard over the music. "Why wouldn't you take my calls? I tried calling you four times today." It had been closer to seven, but the last few times he'd hung up when he heard Kai's message come on.

"I didn't have anything to say to you." Kai's gaze was cool and direct.

"Maybe I had something to say to you."

"Maybe I didn't want to hear it."

Ryo drew the napkin Kai had been doodling on toward himself. The sketch was of a pig in a police uniform. His face warmed, although maybe that was the alcohol. He'd had a couple of drinks at the bar before he'd noticed Kai. No. Before he'd had the nerve to even let himself *look* for Kai.

"Nice," he said thickly.

Kai's mouth curved into that three-point smile. He laughed silently at Ryo. Ryo's temper flared, but then he got his first clear look at Kai. Kai had a black eye.

Ryo's jaw dropped. "What happened to you?"

Kai's face grew solemn. "Somebody punched me."

"Who?" Ryo was angry and ready to return the favor. Then comprehension took shape. "Torres?"

A malicious spark lit Kai's eyes. The good one, anyway. "Maybe *you* did, Detective Miller. Maybe you tried to beat me into saying Mickey's alibi was false."

Ryo drew back in his chair. He stuttered, "I-I never touched you!"

"How soon they forget!"

"You know what I mean. I never— I wouldn't ever—"

"Yes?"

Ryo swallowed and half whispered, "Hurt you."

"All you've done is hurt me."

Ryo didn't know what to say.

Kai said, "Who would believe you? Your fingerprints are all over my place. It would be your word against mine."

Ryo couldn't seem to tear his stricken gaze from Kai's glinting one.

"Maybe I should report you for police brutality? What do you think?"

Ryo's lips parted, but no words came to him.

Kai seemed to find that funny. He leaned back in his chair, laughing.

He was crazy. Ryo could see that now. Kai was out of his head. He had probably planned this trap with Torres.

The whole thing played out in his mind's eye like the last reel in a film noir with himself in the role of patsy.

Kai righted his chair before it tipped over. He gulped. "You should see your face."

"Why would you do this to me?" Ryo asked. "I didn't—"

Kai stopped laughing. He said in a low, furious voice, "Why would you go to my grandfather? Why would you tell him all that shit about me and Mickey?"

"I didn't."

"Don't lie to me!"

"I'm not lying. I asked questions, yes. And I guess, yes, from those questions, it's possible your grandfather could infer—but I didn't give him any details. If he got details, he got them from you. You filled in the blanks yourself."

"Right. It's *my* fault!"

"I'm not saying that. Of course I'm not saying that. I'm only saying—"

"You think Akira Tashiro doesn't have the means to find out anything about me or anything about your case he wants to?"

It wasn't something Ryo had given a lot of thought to. But he hadn't seen Kai's grandfather as an enemy. "Look, I know you don't want to hear this, probably won't listen to me, but you're in a dangerous situation. I thought maybe your grandfather could...I don't know. Apply pressure."

"Pressure." Kai's face twisted. "Nice. You mean blackmail. Bribery. Coercion. But you see, I don't need my grandfather's money."

"There are different kinds of pressure."

"There sure are." Kai spoke with contempt.

Ryo reached across the table to cover Kai's tensed hand with his own. "Believe it or not, I'm trying to help you."

Kai stared at their joined hands and then raised his gaze to Ryo's. "Yeah, well, I *don't* believe it."

"It's true." Ryo dropped his voice. Not that their conversation could be heard over the wall of noise surrounding them. "I guess it sounds crazy. I don't know what it is about you, but from the first time I saw you, I wanted to—"

Kai laughed, a short, unfriendly sound. "*That* I believe."

"It's not just that, though yeah. I do want that. All the time."

Kai's lashes swept down demurely. When they rose again, his eyes seemed to shine with an unholy light. "You want it right now?"

God help him, he did. Kai Tashiro scared the hell out of him, but it didn't change wanting him. Ryo nodded as though hypnotized.

Kai looked pleasantly interested. "Want to trade seats? You sit here in the corner and I'll sit on your lap. You can do me right now."

"I…"

"No one will see. No one will know. This chair is well in the shadows." Kai gave an inviting wiggle on the chair, and Ryo had to close his eyes. He was terrified he was going to disgrace himself right there in public. He was terrified at how badly he wanted to accept Kai's insane challenge.

"It would feel *so* good."

Somehow, despite the music, the voices, the general noise, he could hear Kai's soft voice. Hear him quietly chuckling. Ryo burned with shame and anger. It was humiliating to want someone like this, humiliating to be laughed at, humiliating to *deserve* being laughed at.

"No? Too shy?" Kai's voice was derisive. "How about the men's toilet?"

Ryo shook his head sharply.

"I didn't hear that. No?"

"Shut up," Ryo whispered.

"Okay. How about out back?" Kai's chair scraped.

Ryo opened his eyes.

Kai stood over him. He wore a short black leather jacket. He was leaving. His smile slanted as he studied Ryo. He shook his head sadly. "No?"

Ryo motioned negative. He had no words left.

Kai said, "Then I guess you better just come home with me."

* * * * *

They barely managed to get the door locked before they were ripping each other's clothes off and falling to the plush runner on the shining hardwood floor.

When it was over they lay on their backs, not speaking, their harsh breaths the only sound in the room.

At last Ryo turned his head. Kai's eyes were closed, his expression withdrawn, remote. "I think I..."

Kai opened his eyes, turned his head to face Ryo. He raised his eyebrows.

"I can't keep doing this," Ryo said, instead.

Kai made an expression of distaste. "Of course you can. Of course you will. Until you get bored and move on to the next piece of ass."

Ryo shook his head. His heart felt heavy. He had handled this wrong from the first. Was it possible to fix something that had gotten off to such a bad start?

"You can't think that's all this is to me?"

Kai made a contemptuous sound. He trilled in a falsetto, "Because for the first time in your life you're *soooo* in *luuuurve!*"

There were only a few inches between them, but it felt to Ryo like reaching across a vast distance. He rested his hand against Kai's cheek, tracing his thumb with feather lightness along the brow bone above Kai's badly bruised eye. "Does it frighten you so much that someone might really care for you?"

Kai's eyes squinched shut. He jerked his head away. Ryo viewed his averted face, the quick, rough rise and fall of his chest. Kai said roughly, "Then what should I think?"

"Kai." A strange warmth flooded Ryo's chest, an emotion that seemed to crowd out everything else, all the fear and insecurity and anger. There was no room for it in the wake of so much tenderness and compassion and…love.

Yes. Love.

He opened his mouth, but Kai said suddenly, "I earn my own way. Every penny. The trust fund is…something else."

"Of course." Now Ryo was not sure what they were talking about.

"I don't need it. I *want* it." Kai turned back to face Ryo. His eyes glittered. Tears? Ryo's gut tightened. He didn't understand, but the thought of Kai's tears moved him almost past bearing.

He nodded, not daring to speak.

"I'm Tashiro's heir. And I will stay Tashiro's heir."

"Sure." Ryo couldn't help asking, "What does that have to do with anything?"

Kai threw him a quick, furious look and was on his feet and moving down the hall.

"Okay," Ryo said to no one in particular. He sat up. His jeans were tangled around his ankles. He pulled them up, zipped them, got to his feet, and shrugged back into his shirt.

He looked down the hall. Still no sign of Kai.

Ryo walked into the kitchen, found the liquor cabinet. An impressive selection, but no vodka. He checked the stainless-steel freezer and found a bottle of Belvedere. He splashed a couple of ounces in a short glass and drank it down. He poured a second drink.

Kai appeared, dressed in navy sweatpants and a flannel shirt. His hair was knotted in a loose ponytail, and he wore glasses. "Pour me one."

Ryo complied. As he handed the glass to Kai, Kai's gaze flicked to his. Behind the scholarly looking spectacles, his eyes were a warm and lovely red-brown, like fox fur.

"You took your contacts out."

"They were bothering my eyes. I've been wearing them too much lately," Kai admitted.

Ryo was smiling. "You have eyes like a *kitsune*."

Kai laughed. He took a swallow of vodka and choked. "It tastes like poison. How can you drink it straight?"

"I like the taste. If it's the real thing. If it's good quality."

Kai made a face, drained his glass. For a moment he stood looking at his empty glass.

With this recognition of his true feelings, Ryo seemed to have gained insight into the object of those feelings, and he recognized that Kai was self-conscious and unsure of what to say or do next. Because? Because he still didn't believe or understand what Ryo was trying to say to him? Or because he didn't want to hear it?

Ryo said, "I asked you out three times before you finally said yes."

"Oh. That." Kai's smile was rueful. "I think maybe I do sort of remember you. I thought you were too…I don't know. Arrogant. Conceited. Slick. I don't like slick guys."

"Oh." Ouch. "I'm not that slick."

"I know, dude." Kai was laughing at him again, but without meanness. "You try to be, though. I don't need that."

"What do you need?"

Kai gave him an uncertain look. "I don't know. What everybody needs, I guess."

"Mickey Torres?"

It was like a door slamming shut. Kai said flatly, "You know what I believe? I believe you want what you think Mickey has. That's about as deep as it goes with you."

"Not true. Not fair." Kai was turning away, and Ryo caught his arm. "Three times, remember? I quit going to Fubar because I couldn't take seeing you there night after night and knowing I wasn't ever going to get any closer than across the room."

Behind the spectacles, Kai's eyes went wide and soft and vulnerable. The pulse at the base of his neck beat visibly. But when he spoke, he said, "I have an arrangement with my grandfather. As long as I don't bring disgrace, dishonor, to the Tashiro name, I remain his heir. If I fail in that, I lose everything. All of it goes to Kenji. So, you see, any kind of a real relationship, an open relationship, is out of the question while *Ojiisan*..."

Back to *Ojiisan* and the trust fund. Were they really walking in circles, or did it just feel that way thanks to how much Ryo had had to drink that night? He said painstakingly, "Got it. But you said you don't need his money."

"And I said that I *wanted* it. That I intend to have it. Every penny of it. And then, you know what I'll do?" Kai's face flushed with the intensity of his emotions. "I'm going to divide the Tashiro fortune between my aunts. They'll have it all. Every cent." He gave a shaky, furious laugh.

"Why?"

"Because nothing would make *him* more unhappy."

Or you, Ryo thought. He didn't say that, though. Instead he said gently, "Okay. So you don't want Kenji to have the money."

"It's nothing to do with Kenji!"

Kai was glaring at him again, and Ryo said, "I'm lost. Or drunk. Or both. Can we sit down? I feel like this may take a while."

"I love Kenji. Or I would if they would let me see him. He doesn't know me. I don't know him." Kai's face worked. "My son is growing up without his father." There was no question the pain that accompanied those words was real.

Ryo fastened on the piece he could make sense of. "So Kenji *is* your son?"

"Of course."

"And you're married or you're not married?"

"Of course I'm not married." Kai's expression changed. "*Oh.* I thought you knew the whole story. No wonder you're looking at me like I'm crazy." He pushed his glasses up and rubbed his eyes. "No. Kenji happened when Laurel and I tried to get back together. It didn't last very long. Getting back together, I mean. But...there was Kenji."

"You didn't remarry?"

"No. I won't do that."

"He's your kid, dude."

Kai resettled his glasses. "I know that. I've acknowledged my paternity. As much as they'll let me."

"Your grandfather and your—Laurel?"

Kai nodded.

"Okay. I think I get it now. We'll be careful. It's not like I go around advertising my private life."

"Huh?" Kai looked confused, taken aback. "What are you saying?"

Ryo said, "What I've been saying for the last hour. I care for you. I want to keep seeing you. You can set the conditions."

Kai's lips parted, but no words came out.

Ryo looked past him to the clock in the stainless-steel microwave over the blue-brown quartz counter. "I'm saying it's late and we should probably try to get some sleep. I have to be at work early."

"I won't be able to sleep."

Ryo grinned. "Well, we don't *have* to sleep."

"But..." Kai continued to stare at him with wary uncertainty. He said finally, "You know, you're a very strange guy, Ryo."

"Strange is better than slick, right? Anyway, have you looked in a mirror lately? It takes one to know one." Ryo summoned his old smirk.

Maybe attitude wasn't half the game, but it still counted for a lot. "Look, we both know I wouldn't be here if you didn't have some feeling for me."

"I like sex," Kai shot back.

"Yes, you do, you little horndog. But that's not why I'm here tonight, so can we not pretend anymore?"

Ryo spoke with all his old confidence, but it was a relief when Kai, still looking mostly bemused, turned and led the way back to the bedroom. Through the double doors leading onto the balcony, Ryo could see the black outline of swaying palm trees. The wind had picked up. A ghostly breeze moved the white veils of the bed's canopy.

Kai hit a switch and soft amber accent lights lit the room.

The lights changed everything, turned the room familiar and ordinary, turned it into a space where they might simply hold each other and talk, where they might indeed sleep together—and was there anything more trusting than allowing yourself to fall into a deep sleep beside a lover who was still a stranger?

But they would not stay strangers. Ryo was sure of that now.

Kai removed his glasses and began to unbutton his shirt.

"Okay if I take a shower?" Ryo asked.

"Sure." Kai added politely, "There are clean towels in the tall cupboard."

Ryo nodded, then turned back to Kai as someone pounded on the front door. Kai's brows drew together.

"Expecting company?" Ryo asked.

"No."

Kai dropped his shirt on the foot of the bed and left the room. Ryo went to the doorway to watch. Kai reached the door, slid the bolt, and opened the door. Not wide enough that Ryo could see who stood on the other side, but he had an idea.

He could tell from the way Kai's back straightened, his shoulders squared, that he had guessed right.

Torres.

"The fuck," said Kai. "Didn't we go through this last night?"

Ryo left his post at the bedroom door and stepped quietly down the hall, making sure he stayed out of view of the open door. Judging by his own jealousy of Torres, it was only too easy to picture what Torres might do if he realized Kai was sleeping with him, sleeping with any cop, but Ryo in particular.

He couldn't make out the words of Torres' answer, but he was plainly not happy. Ryo reached automatically for his shoulder holster, but he wasn't wearing a weapon. He didn't carry when he was out drinking and dancing in a club. His backup Beretta was in the locked glove compartment of his Taurus.

"No," Kai said, "I'm not going through this every night, Mickey. Last night was it. Last night was good-bye."

The door shoved inward, sliding Kai back a few inches. "You got someone in there, *maricón*?" Torres demanded. He sounded drunk. "You bring someone here behind my back?" His hand, marked with the butterfly tattoo, shot around the edge of the door, tangling in Kai's hair, yanking it loose from its ponytail.

Kai knocked Torres' hand away. "It's none of your goddamned business who I bring home." He rammed the heel of his hand through the door opening, Torres abruptly let go of his hair, and Kai put his shoulder to the door. Ryo jumped to join him, still trying to stay out of view.

Torres' voice rose in shouted obscenities. His flailing arm withdrew just before the door slammed shut. He began to rain blows and kicks on the door.

"I'm warning you, you asshole," Kai yelled. "Get out of here before I call the cops."

Ryo threw him a quick, alarmed look.

Torres delivered a final couple of hard kicks to the door, and then there was the sound of his retreating footsteps.

Ryo went to the window looking over the parking structure. Standing to the side, he watched, and at last Torres appeared below. Torres flung himself into his illegally parked SUV. For a few seconds he sat revving the engine, the angry snarl rising through the night air. Finally the white Cherokee tore out of the lot, tires screeching as they hit the street.

Ryo turned to Kai who was leaning back against the door with his eyes closed. Ryo went to him, putting his arms around Kai. Kai leaned into him, wearily. His hair, soft and silky, spilled over Ryo's hands. "I don't know what the hell he wants from me."

Yeah, for all his worldliness, Kai was pretty naïve. Ryo said, "Torres gave you that black eye, didn't he?"

Kai gave a short laugh, muffled against Ryo's shoulder. "Believe me, he got the worst of it."

"Yeah." Ryo was thinking. "You have to watch what you say to him, though. Don't antagonize him. Don't threaten him with the cops."

"What?" Kai lifted his head and stared at Ryo. "Why the hell shouldn't I? I'm not putting up with this shit. If he'd gotten in here tonight—"

"That's not what I'm saying. I'll deal with Torres."

Kai's eyes narrowed. "What's that mean?"

"It means there are ways to deal with him—legally—that don't involve you setting yourself up as the focus of his rage."

"He nearly kicked down my door. You want me to be diplomatic with him?"

"Listen. Pedestrians have the right of way, but if some jackass runs a red light and mows you down, you're still dead. Do you get what I'm saying? It doesn't matter that you're in the right. You have to be smart and stay safe. Which includes not threatening him with going to the cops again. You do not want him to see you as a threat."

Kai scowled. "Mickey's not going to do anything to me. I'm his alibi, remember?"

"It doesn't work the way you think it does. If he thinks you've become a liability, well, he's got nothing to lose. Without your alibi, he's looking at first degree murder."

"I'm not going back on my word," Kai said impatiently. "I didn't give him an alibi because we fucked. I gave him an alibi because he was here that night."

"Kai, you're not looking at this clearly."

"If he kills me, he loses my alibi. So what's the difference?"

"The difference is, Torres is a psychopath. He's not going to weigh this logically. If he thinks he's fucked either way, he'll kill you. Besides that, did you hear him? It isn't just about his alibi. He's..."

Obsessed.

Ryo didn't want to say the word. It hit too close to home. But if Torres was coming here night after night, risking the Sotels finding out he was gay, it wasn't casual with him. Ryo had recognized that from the instant he'd seen the butterfly tattoo on Torres' hand. Torres was risking his life to be with Kai. That wasn't casual. And he wasn't going to forgive his feelings not being reciprocated.

"If you have to deal with him again, try to be tactful. Without opening the door or letting him inside."

"You're serious?"

"Hell, yes, I'm serious."

"Well, in that case, maybe I should just let him in here. What could be more tactful than letting him fuck me when he wants?"

"That's right. Bust my balls, if you have to, but I'm on your side." Ryo dug in his pockets for his keys. "I'm going to run downstairs to my car. Lock the door after me."

"What? Why?"

"Just lock the door. I'll be right back."

"Ryo—"

Ryo slipped out the door and sprinted down the walkway to the stairs. He took them two at time. Reaching the parking lot, he ran across the warm asphalt to his car, flinching when he stepped on a piece of gravel. A faded flyer for a local club scraped past in a gust of wind. Glancing upward, Ryo spotted Kai's silhouette watching him from the top story. He raised his hand in brief greeting, but Kai did not respond.

Ryo unlocked his car, slid inside, and unlocked the glove compartment. He felt silly getting his Beretta out, but better safe than sorry. He felt naked without a gun at hand, that was the sad truth of being in law enforcement. Not carrying a firearm felt much the same as not carrying his wallet or his keys. He closed the compartment and slid back out of the car.

He pressed the fob to lock the door. Headlights swept the driveway, and a white SUV turned into the parking area. A white Jeep Cherokee.

"Shit."

Torres was back.

Ryo stood motionless, ready but waiting. He was hoping that Torres, cruising silently past, would miss him in the rows of parked cars. He couldn't see through the tinted windows, but he was pretty sure Torres would be focused on Kai's apartment. Especially since Kai was still standing there, outlined by the light behind him.

The Cherokee rolled past, tires sighing, engine growling; then suddenly Torres accelerated and hurtled down the driveway at the other end. The Cherokee's taillights vanished around the corner.

CHAPTER SEVEN

"**I**'ll talk to him," Kai said. "It's going to make it worse if I act like I'm afraid of him. Like I'm afraid to face him."

Now that he had calmed down, Kai was in a more forgiving frame of mind. In fact, he seemed almost melancholy as they lay on their sides, facing each other, talking quietly in the wide bed. If the talk had not been about Mickey Torres, it would have been a lovely thing to lie together in the darkness and simply talk and touch each other. Ryo could not remember ever sharing this kind of quiet intimacy with another man.

"What is it you think you could say that would get through to him?"

"I don't know. Something. Let him know that it's not..." Kai's voice drifted away.

Ryo reached out, brushing the shimmer of hair back from the pale oval of Kai's face. Kai's hair crackled with static electricity, clung to Ryo's fingers. "What?" Ryo asked.

After a second or two, Kai said, "It's being treated like a nothing, like you don't exist, that kills you."

The quiet revelation closed Ryo's throat. It took him a moment to be able to say, "He's not like you, *Kai-chan*."

"He's like me in that. Everyone is like me in that."

Yeah. Maybe. But you didn't patch the cracks in the Mickey Torreses of the world by applying a little sympathetic validation. It was a nice thought, but what Mickey wanted was... Ryo thought of Saturday night when he'd sat in his own car, staring up at Kai's dark windows. The last thing he wanted was to feel sorry—or akin—to Torres, but he couldn't easily forget the hell of being on the outside. Fearing that he would always be on the outside.

The difference was, he would have taken no for an answer. Torres wouldn't.

Ryo leaned forward and kissed Kai's forehead. "Don't worry. Tomorrow I'm going to my captain. I'm going to tell him everything."

"You can't. Sex with a suspect? You know you can't."

"You're not a suspect. You're a witness."

"Sex with a witness is just as bad. You'll lose your job."

"It's not *just* as bad." But yeah, he probably would lose his job. Best case scenario was he was going to get a reprimand and demotion. It didn't matter. Well, yeah, it did matter. He loved his job, loved being a cop, was proud as hell of making detective. And he was a good detective. But tonight everything had changed. Now his first concern was Kai. And he couldn't protect Kai if he didn't come clean. It wasn't so complicated.

"If anyone goes to your captain, it'll have to be me," Kai said. "I'll tell him I need a restraining order or whatever it is. If I'm a witness, he'll have to see that I get protection."

"You're a witness for the defense," Ryo said, amused despite himself. "Anyway, you're not in any better position. You can't have any scandal or disgrace without jeopardizing your inheritance, right? Think about the kind of publicity that move would bring down on you."

Actually, from that perspective, Kai had shown real courage in coming forward the first time to give Torres an alibi. Until now, Ryo hadn't appreciated what Kai had been willing to risk. No wonder he had been scared and angry and reluctant talking to Ryo that first day.

Kai was quiet. "Okay," he said at last. "So we're back to Plan A. I talk to Mickey."

Ryo sighed. "And tell him what? That you'd still like to be friends?"

"We weren't friends," Kai said, reflectively. "I did like him, though." He made a sound of amusement at some memory. "He's smart and he can be funny."

"I'm sure he's a great guy."

"Maybe not, but he's not a waste of space, which is what you think. He can draw. He designed his own body art. Did you know that? He got most of his ink when he was thirteen. His English class read *The Illustrated Man*, and he was inspired by the cover illustration."

Ryo restrained himself from saying something unkind.

"I can let him know that it wasn't just…"

Ryo wished he could see in the dark. "Wasn't just what?"

"You know what I'm saying. If things had been different, I could have cared for him. He isn't like you think he is."

Yeah. Right. Was there any statement more useless than *if things had been different*? Wasn't that pretty much true of everything? But Ryo restrained himself. Kai was not nearly as hard or cynical as he had first believed. He thought of the badly bitten fingernails and the insomnia, and he said only, *"Blood Red Butterfly."*

Kai raised his head. "Huh?"

"Blood Red Butterfly. Your story. Two men who can't be together and can't be apart. They hate each other and love each other and end up killing each other."

"Oh. Yeah." Kai made a faint sound, not quite a laugh. "That's not what I meant, though."

"Did you notice Torres got a red butterfly tattoo on his hand?"

Kai was perfectly still. Ryo could practically see the thought balloon over his head. At last he lowered his head to the pillow again and said, "I was seventeen when I wrote the first story."

It was kind of a relief to hear it. Ryo said, "You mean you don't want to be with a dude who would commit murder for you?"

Kai said quietly, seriously, "I think I'd rather be with a dude who would risk his job to keep me from being murdered."

"Smart choice." His spirits lifted when Kai wound his arms around him and nestled his head against Ryo's heart.

"Hai."

Ryo laughed. He could feel Kai's face crease in a faint answering smile.

For a time they lay in silence, breathing in peaceful unison. Ryo's head was throbbing. Too much vodka and too much worry. He dreaded the thought of tomorrow, and at the same time, the sun couldn't rise fast enough.

Kai's breaths grew deep and slow. Was he sleeping? Now there was timing for you. Then Kai sighed.

"Want a backrub?" Ryo asked.

"Hm?"

"It'll relax me too."

"I could give *you* a backrub." Kai sounded sleepy.

"Yeah?"

"Oh, yeah. I have *many* bedroom skills." Kai still sounded more sleepy than seductive.

"You don't have to convince me. Actually, do you have something for a headache?"

"Bathroom cupboard. Top shelf. There's water here." Kai rolled over and sat up. Ryo heard the *plash* of water pouring into a glass.

Ryo padded into the master bath, blinking as he switched on the lights and opened the cabinet. Aspirin and Tylenol both on the top shelf, as described. He dry swallowed two aspirin, absently scanning the other shelves. There was a small pharmacy here. The usual cold and flu remedies along with prescriptions for anxiety, indigestion, heartburn, acid reflux, and insomnia.

Okay. Well, at least he knew what he was getting into.

He closed the cabinet. His fingers froze on the light switch. He opened the cabinet again and picked out the vial of Restoril.

"Couldn't find it?" Kai's voice asked behind him.

Ryo turned holding the vial. "Sleeping pills?"

"What about them?"

"Did you take them the night Torres killed that old woman?"

Kai frowned. "Of course not. If you'll notice, I *don't* take them. Which is why we're standing here having this conversation."

"But you had them here." Ryo examined the label for the date of the prescription. "This bottle was here that night?"

Kai's face tightened into older, harder lines. "You can't stop snooping, can you? You pretend it's me you want. You don't want me. You just want answers." He grabbed the vial from Ryo and threw the pills in the cupboard. The mirrored image of their angry faces swung past as he slammed the door shut.

Ryo ignored Kai's display of temper. "Tell me the truth. Did you take sleeping pills that night?"

"Yeah. Of course. I palmed a mouthful. I thought Mickey might like to fuck a corpse. What the hell are you *talking* about? Of course I didn't take sleeping pills that night!"

Even as the words left Kai's mouth, his expression altered. It was infinitesimal, but Ryo caught it.

He grabbed Kai's shoulders. "But you slept?"

Kai's mouth opened, but he didn't answer. His eyes were dark and guarded.

"You slept, didn't you?"

"I-I'm not sure. Maybe."

"He drugged you!"

Kai shook him off. "You're crazy, Ryo."

But Ryo was sure now. He said calmly, with conviction, "You know he did. If you didn't take them yourself, he slipped them to you."

"No. He didn't!" Kai looked frightened. And no wonder. "How could he, without me knowing? I'm telling you, I don't even remember if I slept or not. You're running away with this insane, ridiculous theory."

"How can you not remember?"

Kai stared at him, shaking his head in disbelief. "I do sleep some-times, you know. I was nearly asleep five minutes ago—until you started asking if I wanted a backrub."

"Think back to that night. Did he give you something to drink?"

"He didn't give me *anything*." Kai fell silent, thinking. He shook his head. "Yes, we probably drank. But if there were drinks, I fixed them."

Ryo was thinking too. "How hard would it be for him to use the john and grab a handful of your pills? Hell, he could have brought sleeping pills with him."

"I think I would have noticed him pouring a handful of pills into my glass!"

"Maybe he—"

"Do I have to spell it out? We didn't sit around sipping cocktails and making small talk."

Ryo ignored that. "You keep a carafe of water beside your bed. He could have dumped the pills into that."

"And then what? He poured the carafe down my throat when I wasn't paying attention?"

"You drink a lot of water. You've poured yourself water twice tonight. He could have noticed that the first night he was here. And when he saw the drugstore in your bathroom—"

"You're. Out. Of. Your. Mind."

Ryo shook his head. "The only person you're fooling is yourself."

"You know what, Ryo?" Kai pointed toward the front room. "Just go. I've had enough of you for one night. Get the hell out of my home."

"Sure, I'll go," Ryo said. "But before you start feeling too sorry for Torres, keep in mind he was willing to risk giving you an overdose just so he could go bash an old lady's brains in."

"Get OUT of here!" Kai yelled.

"Don't worry, I'm going." Ryo brushed past Kai and went into the bedroom. He found his jeans on the floor beside the bed, retrieved his gun from the bedside table, and jammed it in his waistband. He went into the brightly lit living room and found his socks and boots.

Kai, dressed in sweatpants, came out of the bedroom. He folded his arms across his chest, watching silently.

"I'm still going to my captain first thing tomorrow," Ryo told him. "So don't do anything stupid."

"You mean as stupid as letting you in here so you could search through my things?"

Ryo stared right back at him until Kai looked away.

As victories went, it was pretty hollow. Ryo was still getting tossed out on his ear, and all the hopeful promise and quiet intimacy of the previous hours felt like a dream. How was it possible to feel so much disappointment over something that had never really been much more than a wish?

"This isn't about me breaking your trust. We both know what this is really about," Ryo burst out. "This is you scared to death at the idea of the morning after. Anything is easier than that. Hell, *suicide* is easier than having an actual relationship with a guy who might get to know you without your fake blue eyes."

Kai's eyes were dark with fury. He strode down the hall and punched the security code into the pad before yanking the door open. "Don't worry about losing your job, Ryo. You can always become a mental health expert. You're such a natural."

Ryo made sure he had his keys and took a final glance around the room double-checking he wasn't leaving anything behind. He stepped outside. "Sayonara, sweetheart," Ryo told Kai. "Don't forget to lock the door behind me."

It was pretty good as exit lines went, but the end result was he was still standing on the wrong side of a slammed door.

The deadbolt slid home with a smooth finality.

Ryo sighed and started down the walkway. The wind whistled a hollow, empty tune down the open corridor. He stopped, bracing himself with one hand on the low wall and pulling his boot on with the other. The windblown palm trees made a flapping sound, like broken birds. All around, the lights of West Hollywood glowed and glittered, like an overturned treasure chest.

Well, he wasn't going to sleep tonight anyway. He might as well go get a drink somewhere. A raging hangover might help dull the pain of tomorrow. He'd meant what he said. Regardless of how things had ended with Kai, Ryo was going to Captain Louden first thing. Kai was too stubborn or too scared to see his danger, and if protecting him required the sacrifice of Ryo's career, well, it wasn't like Ryo hadn't understood the risk of getting involved with the Ice Princess.

He pulled on his second boot, glancing down as motion in the driveway below caught his eye. A silver monster truck, headlights dimmed, glided to a stop in the fire lane. The doors flew open, and three males in black jackets and ski masks piled out of the truck cab.

What the hell?

Ryo leaned over the wall, trying to get a clear view. As the figures vanished around the corner of the building, the cadaverous lights of the parking structure picked out the gleam of the assault rifles they carried.

Ryo's heart went into overdrive. He raced back down the walkway, hammering his fist on Kai's door. *"Kai! Open the door. Open the door. Kai, open the door. Now. Kai! Open the—"*

The door swung open. "Okay," Kai said. "Maybe I did overreact a little."

Ryo pushed him inside, slamming the door and sliding the lock. "Help me shove this cabinet in front of the door." Ryo was already at the other end of the giant lacquered cinnabar cabinet, giving it a test push. It didn't budge. "Come on. *Move.*"

"What? What's go—" Kai broke off at the unmistakable and ear-shattering drawn out *cra-a-a-a-a-k* of AK-47s from below.

"They're coming for you," Ryo told him. "That's the security doors going down."

Color drained from Kai's face, his eyes going wide with terror. He leaped to help Ryo drag and push the huge cabinet across the slick floor. Ryo swore and sweated and strained. The thing weighed a ton. Maybe literally. It felt like trying to shift a house. Thirty seconds felt like an eternity, but at last they got the cabinet positioned in front of the door.

"It won't hold," Kai told him breathlessly.

From below the floorboards came more bursts of gunfire and crashing sounds.

"It'll slow them down." Ryo fumbled for his phone. His hands were shaking as he hit speed dial, calling Dispatch. Had he made a terrible mistake in choosing to stay with Kai? Kai was the target, but it was Ryo's job to protect everyone in this building. What if some innocent citizen got in the way? Shouldn't he be out there seeing that didn't happen?

"Dispatch," came a laconic voice on the other end of the phone.

"Officer Needs Help." With his free hand, Ryo pushed Kai toward the bedroom, still talking to dispatch, giving their address, his badge number, the number of shooters, the make of their vehicle, Torres' name, giving everything he could think of to facilitate rescue or—if they didn't make it out of this alive, which sickeningly felt like a real possibility—apprehension.

Kai stumbled into the bedroom, and Ryo slammed the door behind them. It took Kai two tries to lock the door while Ryo plastered his back to the low bureau, scooting it noisily across the room. Kai joined him, and together they shifted the bureau the last few feet in front of the locked door.

Kai's teeth were chattering. "Th-this isn't going to stop th-them. None of th-this will help." He hugged himself, as though physically restraining himself from coming apart. Ryo sympathized with the feeling. He was trained to respond to mortal threat and even *he* was afraid. Afraid that nothing he did would be enough and that in a matter of minutes he would see Kai die.

"We just have to slow them down enough." Ryo dropped his phone in his pocket. Help was coming. Maybe it would arrive in time.

Kai wiped at his eyes and nodded. Ryo put his arms around him. He didn't try to reassure Kai. They listened tautly to the fast approaching pop and crack of automatic gunfire.

Kai's arms were locked around Ryo's waist. His face pressed against Ryo's. His breath was moist; his damp lashes flickered in butterfly kisses against Ryo's eyes.

"Sorry," he said unsteadily. "Sorry for this. Sorry for all of it."

Ryo shook his head. From down the hall came the splintering sound of the front door being shot to pieces. "Let's go out on the balcony."

Kai drew a breath, stepped away from him. They walked out onto the narrow balcony. Lights were blazing on all around them. Buildings coming to life. Windows and doors opening—*the wrong response to gunfire, people*—tenants calling out to each other.

Ryo stared down at the courtyard below. The pool was a glowing aqua square framed by lazily swaying palm trees. Four stories down. They had a much better chance of hitting the surrounding pavement than the pool itself.

He raised his head at a faint keening sound carried on the breeze. Sirens. They sounded a million miles away.

The balcony—in fact, the whole complex—bounced. That would be the lacquer cabinet blocking the front door tipping over.

"We could climb," Kai said suddenly, grabbing Ryo's arm. "We could climb onto the roof."

Ryo leaned back, staring upward. About ten feet above them, the tile roof jutted out like a black wing. "Yes! Great. Go for it."

Kai hopped onto the ledge of the stucco balcony, slowly straightening to his full height. He was a couple of inches too short to reach the overhang.

"Stand on my shoulders." Ryo's eyes jerked back toward the bedroom at the deep sporadic bursts of *cra-a-a-a-a-k, cra-a-a-a-a-k.* Bullets tore through the door and wooden chest and opposite wall. "Steady." He reached up a hand and Kai took it, stepping onto his shoulders. He was light, but not *that* light. Ryo managed to stay upright and solid. He gripped Kai's wrists tightly.

Kai let go of Ryo's hands, his weight shifted and then swung off Ryo's shoulders. He clambered onto the roof and then leaned over the edge. His hair tumbled around his bloodless face. With his enormous eyes and wild hair he reminded Ryo of pictures of dying or crazed samurais he'd seen all those years ago in *hoshu ko.*

"Hurry," Kai told him. "Now you, Ryo. You're taller. You can make it standing on the ledge."

"Go," Ryo told him. "I'm right behind you." He scrambled onto the narrow ledge of the balcony as the bedroom door gave with a crash, followed by the second crash of the bureau sliding across the room.

Ryo jumped. He was taller then Kai, but still not quite tall enough. His fingers brushed rough tile, and he had a sickening moment when he realized there was nothing to grip, he was sliding back down. Kai's hand clamped down on his forearm with an unexpectedly powerful grip. Kai's other hand locked on Ryo's collar. Ryo dangled, kicking his legs in open space, and then Kai hauled him up, hanging on until Ryo managed to throw a leg over the parapet and wriggle over onto the roof. Kai dragged him farther back from the edge.

"Run," Ryo gasped as their pursuers spilled onto the balcony below.

Kai was on his feet and bounding away like a gazelle, gravel dusting up from beneath his bare feet. Ryo was right on his heels, but as they passed one of the large air compressors, he dropped down behind it and pulled his weapon. His heart was pounding so hard he wasn't sure he could keep his hands steady enough to hit anything. He had never shot anyone. In fact, he'd only pulled his weapon a handful of times in his entire time on the force.

The first masked shooter swung over the edge of the rooftop. Ryo fired. The man shouted and fell back.

Ryo closed his eyes. He had shot someone. Maybe killed him. Numbly he listened to the sirens floating in the distance. Ryo opened his eyes. Bullets stitched through the air compressor, and he flattened himself to the ground. He threw a quick look back at Kai. He could just make out the pale outline of him crouched at the far edge of the rooftop.

"Can you make it across to the next building?" Ryo called hoarsely. At least if Kai survived, there would be some point to this, some good out of it.

Kai looked, judged the width, gave Ryo a thumbs-up. Ryo gave him thumbs-up in return and risked a look around the air compressor which was making mortally wounded noises.

It took a few vital seconds to pinpoint one shadowy figure climbing over the parapet. Movement to his right sent Ryo's heart rocketing into warp speed. The remaining gunman was already on the roof and nearly on top of him. Ryo fired off a round, and the gunman dived behind the concealment of a water tank closet.

Fuck. That had been too fucking close. Ryo sucked in a shaky breath.

Ryo risked another glance back and saw that Kai had successfully made the jump to the next rooftop. He expelled a breath. Thank God. At least Kai was safe. All he had to do was keep his head down and keep moving. *Please keep your head down. Please keep moving. Please be safe.*

Now all Ryo had to do was manage to stay alive for the next...how long? How long 'til help reached him?

Another stream of bullets ploughed through the shattered air compressor. Ryo tried his best to become as one with the roof. He swore quietly, fervently. What the hell was the matter with these suicidal freaks that they didn't give up and try to get away? They couldn't miss that the police sirens were right beneath them now. They couldn't miss the red and blue strobe lights cutting swaths through the nighttime.

Ryo breathed quietly, keeping his eyes on the water tank closet where he knew the other gunman was still hiding.

The night smelled of gun powder and burnt oil. Above the crackle of police radios, the buzz of voices, came a pulsing thrum of sound. Ryo raised his eyes. Across a stretch of starry sky he could see fast approaching lights and hear the droning beat of helicopter blades.

"You hear that?" he called out. "It's over."

The response was another fusillade of bullets.

It *was* over. But was it over if the bad guys didn't know it was over?

The first gunman must have reloaded because he was advancing, firing steadily, bullets chewing stucco and tile and everything else in its way. Ryo looked desperately for new cover. He couldn't get a clean shot off under that steady bombardment.

He inched to the other side of the compressor and risked a blind shot. He missed, but the gunman ducked down behind another compressor.

Footsteps pounded past Ryo. He fired, thought he hit his target, but the shadow ran on. Ryo fired again, missed, and then was under fire himself from the first gunman.

The second shooter was going for the next rooftop and Kai. Ryo ignored the man advancing once more on him and fired again at the second shooter, but he sailed across the divide and landed on the rooftop where Kai was hiding.

Fuck. Fuck. Fuck. "Where *are* you, you sons of bitches?" Ryo cried out. He meant his fellow cops. He was talking to Mayer and Hernandez and Louden and every other cop he knew. He couldn't do this by himself. He had nine rounds left.

The advancing gunman laughed.

The laughter cut through Ryo's rising panic. He ducked back, took a couple of deep breaths, and then threw himself forward, rolling to his side and firing off three quick rounds. One shot went wide, but the other two hit the gunman dead center, plowing into his torso. He cried out, firing his AK-47 straight into the sky, and then fell backward and lay twitching.

Ryo flipped over and jumped to his feet, running for the edge of the roof. To his horror he saw Kai and the second gunman caught in the spotlight of the hovering police chopper as they struggled on the brink of the apartment roof opposite. Why the gunman hadn't simply shot Kai was a mystery. It seemed unlikely Kai could have managed to get the drop on his pursuer. But he was still standing, still struggling.

Ryo brought his weapon up, training it on the entwined figures, but he didn't dare fire for fear of hitting Kai.

His heart stopped as the grappling figures stumbled and fell. They continued to fight, rolling closer to the edge, seeming unaware of their danger. And then one man went over. Ryo's eyes closed instinctively, but not knowing was worse than knowing. He opened his eyes. Kai's red hair blew wildly around him as he stretched out on the roof, offering his hand to the man who dangled from the edge.

Kai's mouth was moving, but Ryo couldn't hear the words over the whirring beat of the helicopter blades, he could only see the urgency in Kai's face.

The man reached up, but instead of taking Kai's hand, he caught a strand of his hair, winding it in his fist. Ryo leveled his weapon, sure the masked figure would drag Kai over the edge with him. But the man only held on for an instant before his fingers loosened, and he let go, let go of Kai, let go of the roof, let go entirely, falling into the darkness.

CHAPTER EIGHT

Fubar on a Friday Night. Cheap, strong drinks poured by the best bartenders in town; prim dudes and hot cowboys in assless chaps all dancing to Gotye's "Somebody That I Used to Know"; crowded photo booth; darkside-of-the-moon lighting; and glitter on the floor. The never-ending boy party. Some things never changed.

Ryo smiled faintly. The bartender, catching his eye, smiled back. Ryo nodded yes to another drink and casually glanced over his shoulder.

Yep. There, in the shadowy corner, sat a willowy figure dressed in black. A riot of chestnut hair curled and tumbled around his pointed face, reminding Ryo of one of those Renaissance Madonnas. Or maybe he was thinking of the Dark Ages? Anyway, wild hair and scholarly specs and an untouched blood-red cocktail sitting in front of him.

Ryo turned his back and sipped his vodka martini. Maybe he would go over and speak to Kai. Maybe he wouldn't. Probably he wouldn't. A year was a long time—and this had been a particularly long year.

But that was love and it's an ache I still remember...

It hadn't been love, though. Maybe something that might, in different circumstances, eventually have turned into love. A silk worm that never got the chance to be a butterfly. Ryo shook his head at himself and lifted his drink.

He would finish this drink and go. The fact was, he felt a little...old for this scene. He'd only stopped by out of curiosity. And because it was

Friday night and he had nowhere he had to be—which was sometimes a lonely feeling.

But I'll admit that I was glad it was over...

Someone crowded in on his right, jostling Ryo's arm. "Dude," Ryo said, turning.

He found himself confronting Cousin Itt. Okay, more like a thicket, scented of Japanese Flowers. The thicket turned its head, and Ryo's heart skipped a beat as he found himself gazing into a pair of wide brown eyes behind severe-seeming spectacles.

"Sorry. I wanted to buy you a drink," Kai said.

For a second or two Ryo couldn't think of a response. He was surprised and flattered and, yes, thrilled that the Ice Princess should have defrosted to such a degree as to come and say hi. There was a time when—but that time was passed, and Ryo didn't have the same fondness for games.

"Two's my limit," he said. "I'm driving."

Kai didn't respond, and Ryo couldn't seem to look away. Kai's eyes were outlined in purple-black, and he seemed to be wearing false eyelashes. He fluttered them coquettishly. Ryo felt a smile pulling at his mouth.

"How've you been?" Kai asked. A small black star sparkled in his earlobe.

"Okay. Good."

"I heard you lost your job."

"I got a new one," Ryo said. He could say it now without a pang.

"I'm okay too. In case you're wondering."

Ryo had wondered. Many times. He said reluctantly, "I heard you lost your inheritance."

"Yeah." Kai's lashes swept down and then up again. "I thought you would probably call me, but you never did." Kai caught the bartender's eye.

"I've got it," Ryo said to the bartender. The bartender nodded.

"Thank you." Kai propped his elbow on the bar. They were pretty much standing chest to chest, and it turned out to be harder than Ryo had thought to be this close to Kai and not touch him. The sultry eyes and velvety lashes were a turn-on, no question. He liked the shining mane of hair, the winking jewel in his ear.

Was anything about Kai Tashiro not a turn-on? Oh yeah. The mile-wide streak of crazy.

"What are you doing now?" Kai asked. "For a living, I mean."

"I work for a firm of private investigators."

Kai raised his eyebrows. He turned to sip his drink.

Ryo slid his card to the bartender. "Close me out." The bartender assented.

Kai said, "Why didn't you call, Ryo?"

The simple directness of that caught Ryo off guard. "Why didn't *you* call?"

"Because you lost your job because of me. Because I nearly got you killed. Because you were walking out on me that night and the only reason you came back was to save my life."

"Now you know why I didn't call."

Kai gazed at him gravely. He nodded, picked up his drink, drained it, and turned away from the bar. He walked with remarkable steadiness through the mash of laughing, talking, dancing men.

Ryo shook his head. He was still shaking his head as he hurriedly signed his bill, pocketed his card, and followed Kai out of the club.

The sidewalk was empty. Ryo looked up and down the street. There was no sign of Kai. Well…hell.

Cigarette and voices drifted from the patio. He turned and saw Kai standing in the shadow of the building, watching him.

"Practicing your ninja skills?"

Kai said, "I was wondering how serious you were about catching me."

"I'm willing to meet you halfway, but I'm not going to chase after you again."

Kai said slowly, "But you just did."

"Because what I said to you wasn't true. Or fair. I lost my job because I deserved to lose my job. I did that without any help from you. Just like I nearly got myself killed. That wasn't your fault. I made a lot of mistakes last year. I didn't read Torres correctly. Not completely, anyway. So it would be just as fair to say I nearly got you killed. And as for the reason I left that night…"

"I was stupid."

"I left because I didn't want to turn into another Torres, forcing my way into your life, hurting you—"

"You weren't. You didn't. Ryo." Kai sounded like he was in pain.

Ryo said with a flicker of humor, "If I'd realized how fast you were going to open that door, I wouldn't have waited for gang bangers to show up."

Kai crossed the pavement so that he was within arms' reach again. "Ryo, can't we go somewhere and talk?"

"Talk?" Ryo said doubtfully.

Kai, mimicking Ryo all those months ago, said, "Well, we don't *have* to talk." He tilted his head back. His smile was challenging, but it was wistful too.

Ryo wanted to kiss him, but that was probably not wise. Instead he laughed. "Maybe we do, after all."

"Good. You'd better drive. I'm a little drunk."

"Where am I driving us?" Ryo wished the idea of driving somewhere, anywhere, with Kai didn't make him so happy. But it was no use pretending. The stars suddenly seemed brighter, the night less dark.

"To your place."

"Okay," Ryo said slowly, "but it's not what you're used to."

"Oh, Ry*Oh*." Kai sighed.

That was the last thing he said. He was quiet as they walked to Ryo's car. Quiet on the short drive. Quiet when Ryo let them into his apartment.

Fortunately the place wasn't too much of a mess. There were breakfast dishes in the sink and a stack of newspapers on the coffee table and a few extra pairs of shoes scattered around, but it wasn't too bad.

Kai moved around the front room, studying the framed photos on the shelves, checking out Ryo's CDs and his Netflix rentals. *"Harakiri?"*

Ryo smiled self-consciously. "Yeah."

"Did you like it?"

"I haven't watched it yet. I work a lot of hours."

Kai nodded absently and continued to prowl. "I'm living in Westwood now."

"I'd heard." No surprise there. The surprise would have been if he'd gone on living on Armacost Avenue.

Kai moved on to the dining alcove, stopping to examine the silk painting *Obaachan* had given Ryo when he was a little boy. Plum blossoms with Mount Fuji in the background.

"Have you been to Japan?" Kai asked.

"Not yet. You?"

"Oh, yeah. Lots of times. I was there in December for Comiket. We should go sometime."

"Sure." Ryo laughed. Kai looked surprised. "Er...would you like something?" Ryo asked. "Coffee? Water? Alka-Seltzer?"

"Jasmine tea?"

"Seriously, dude?"

"Water," Kai said. Adding with a flash of his old imperiousness, "With a slice of lemon if you have it."

"I don't." But God help him, he'd be stocking lemons and jasmine tea from now on in case Kai ever decided to drop by again. So much for his resolve not to reopen these old wounds. Ryo poured water and ice in a glass and brought it to Kai who was now sitting on the sofa. Kai drank half the glass of water and then leaned back. He had taken his glasses off. His eyes looked huge and shadowy.

"This will work better if you sit beside me."

"Whatever you say." Ryo sat down on the sofa.

Kai moved closer to him. "And if you put your arms around me."

Ryo snorted, but he complied. He was happy to comply, happy to put his arms around Kai again. It felt good to hold him, cradle that lanky length. Kai moved still closer and wrapped his arms around Ryo, putting his head on Ryo's shoulder. Burying his head, in fact.

When he didn't move, didn't speak, Ryo's smile faded and he put his lips to Kai's ear. "All right, *Kai-chan*?"

Kai nodded. After a minute he asked in a muffled voice, "You're not seeing anyone, are you?"

"No. Of course not."

Of course not? Really? What was sadder, the fact that it was true or that he admitted it so easily? Ryo shook his head inwardly, but sitting here with his arms full of the bundle of bones and hank of hair that was Kai, he was happy again for the first time in a year.

"Me neither," Kai muttered. "I haven't been with anyone since you."

"That's hard to believe," Ryo said, but he said it gently because it was clear that it had been a tough year for Kai too.

Kai swallowed and his whole back moved. He was *so* thin. Of course, he was always thin. One of Kai's hands rested on his shoulder. Ryo scrutinized the plum-painted nails. Kai wasn't biting his nails anymore, so that was a good sign, right?

Kai said, "I thought you meant those things you said that night. I thought if I gave you time. Gave you space."

"I...couldn't," Ryo said. He didn't know how to explain it without further hurting Kai. For months he had lived those terrible life and death minutes on the rooftop over and over again. He'd questioned his every thought, every action in the days leading up to the gun battle. And long before the official inquiry was over or even the proceedings for his dismissal from LAPD, Ryo knew he'd fucked up. Fucked up about as badly as you could.

The only comfort was he hadn't gotten Kai killed. Maybe he'd even kept Kai alive. But two other men, Mickey Torres and his younger brother, had died on that rooftop. And the third shooter had wound up paralyzed. Ryo had done that. The responsibility was his. Maybe not all his, but he had a lion's share of the blame.

And even if he could have somehow shrugged aside his guilt, he was never going to forget those final moments, watching a mortally wounded Mickey Torres lifting his hand up and caressing Kai's hair before letting himself fall to his death. *Blood Red Butterfly*. How the hell did anyone compete with that? And who would want to? Ryo was just an ordinary guy. He could only offer an ordinary love. The From This Day Forward In Sickness And In Health Would You Like Takeout Tonight? kind of love. And he didn't have a lot of experience at that either.

Kai said, "And then I thought maybe if I wrote you."

Ryo angled his head to try and see Kai's face. He brushed down the cloud of hair. "Did you write me?"

"Lots of times. But I could never get it right, the things I needed to say to you."

"What did you need to say to me?"

Kai slanted a sideways look beneath those ridiculous lashes. "I love you."

Ryo felt winded. That was almost too much. Certainly more than he'd let himself hope for. On the occasions he'd let himself fantasize, he'd always pictured himself wooing Kai, courting him, and never getting any further than the occasional *I think I'd rather be with a dude who would risk his job to keep me from being murdered.*

It wouldn't have been enough, and it was one more reason he hadn't tried to contact Kai. He didn't have energy for or interest in those kinds of games anymore.

He had been silent too long because Kai's expression changed, grew remote. "You don't feel the same now."

"It isn't… I never expected…"

Kai shielded his face against Ryo's shoulder. One day, when he looked back on this moment, was this going to be funny or unbearably sad? Ryo didn't know. His stomach was knotted in a way that had not been familiar for twelve months.

"I didn't know my grandfather when I came to live with him," Kai said suddenly. He was still not facing Ryo. Ryo could hear the hard, fast beat of his heart and realized that Kai was scared to death and talking before he had a chance to change his mind. "I'd never met him. I didn't know any of my mother's family. But I tried to be what he wanted. He was all I had left. My only family. I wanted him to…"

"That's natural," Ryo said.

"I wanted him to love me," Kai said more clearly. "I wanted to be worthy."

Ryo's eyes prickled. He closed them tight. "You are worthy."

Kai was still speaking in that quick, rough way. "Everything he asked, I did. Everything. I changed my name. I gave up my father's name so that I could make *Ojiisan* happy. He wanted me to be Japanese and so did I want it, if that would make him love me. I thought he *did* love me in his own way."

Ryo nearly said, "You don't have to tell me any more." But he realized in time, the point was not his hearing it. The point was Kai saying it.

"Everything was okay. Mostly. But then…when I turned seventeen, I realized that something really was wrong with me. Different, I mean. Not wrong. But I thought it was wrong."

Now they were getting to it. Ryo had figured it must be something like this. "You realized you were gay."

"And I thought I would find a way to change that. So. So Laurel and I ran away and got married." Kai shuddered. "It was horrible. Not Laurel, but the whole…thing. It was a mistake. It was such a bad mistake. And I knew I wasn't going to change. That I couldn't change. It was a relief when they found out. *Ojiisan* and Laurel's parents. They annulled the marriage."

"And around that time you wrote *Blood Red Butterfly*?"

Kai sat up and looked at Ryo in surprise. "That's right. How did you know that?"

"You told me you wrote the first volume when you were seventeen."

"Oh. Yes, that's right. I began writing the stories and putting them online. And people liked them. I got a contract with a publisher. And that gave me the courage to tell him...tell *Ojiisan* that I was gay."

"I bet that didn't go well."

"No." Kai was silent for so long Ryo thought perhaps that was the end of the story. That was okay. He felt he had heard what he needed to. He understood now why it was hard for Kai to trust anyone, including Kai.

Kai drew a deep breath and said briskly, "So I tried again to be what he wanted. And I kept trying. And then finally I wondered why he couldn't love me as I was. And why I did love *him* when he wanted me to be everything I wasn't."

"And somewhere in there you tried to get back together with Laurel."

Kai's smile was wry. "Yes. Can you believe that? After that...after that crashed and burned, I knew I couldn't be anything but what I was. And *Ojiisan* and I made our agreement. Which I did try to keep, though he'll never see it that way."

"And now that's all over?"

Kai nodded slowly.

"And how do you feel about that?"

"Like the fever broke." Kai's smile was rueful. "All I wanted for so long was to win the war between us. To beat him at his own game. Make him give me what he promised. But now I see he can't change who he is anymore than I can. Anyway, the thing I really wanted from him wasn't the money. So I made a deal with Laurel. When...the time comes, I won't contest *Ojiisan*'s will provided she gives me visitation rights to Kenji."

"And she agreed to that?"

Kai nodded. He gave Ryo a sideways look. "I've been seeing him a couple of days a week for the last six months."

"That's...wow. I don't know what to say. I think it's great, though."

"Yeah." Kai sighed. "But I can see why maybe you're not so sure how you feel about me. I come with baggage."

"Yeah," Ryo said. "I'm thinking the full set of luggage complete with carry-on containers. You know what, this time you're not scaring me off."

"I don't want to scare you off. That's the last thing I want. That's why I thought if I explained, maybe you'd remember what you liked about me."

Ryo brushed the curls back from Kai's forehead. "I remember exactly what I liked about you. The same things I love about you."

Kai flushed. His mouth quivered. He said earnestly, "I know you think there was more between Mickey and me, but you're wrong." His eyes gazed steadily, solemnly into Ryo's. "I knew right from the start you were the one for me, *Ryo-chan*. I knew the night you told me your darkest secret."

"What darkest secret?" Ryo said, uncertainly.

Kai leaned forward and, breath warm against Ryo's ear, whispered, "Your early training in the art of *ikebana*."

Ryo laughed. He was still laughing as his mouth found Kai's. Kai's lips parted sweetly, smiling beneath his own.

It was a tentative kiss at first; shared laughter, shared breath, shared wonder. It warmed, strengthened, and love swelled, stretched, spread between them like a butterfly unfurling gossamer wings.

ACKNOWLEDGMENTS

Sincere thank you to the editors throughout the years who worked on these various projects: Judith David, Sasha Knight and Keren Reed.

Sincere thank you to—among others—Amanda, Aki Fuyuto, L.B. Gregg, Rhys Ford, Eve Lo, and Janet Sidelinger for their help with *Blood Red Butterfly*.

About the Author

Author of over sixty titles of classic Male/Male fiction featuring twisty mystery, kickass adventure, and unapologetic man-on-man romance, JOSH LANYON'S work has been translated into twelve languages. Her FBI thriller *Fair Game* was the first Male/Male title to be published by Harlequin Mondadori, then the largest romance publisher in Italy. *Stranger on the Shore* (Harper Collins Italia) was the first M/M title to be published in print. In 2016 *Fatal Shadows* placed #5 in Japan's annual Boy Love novel list (the first and only title by a foreign author to place on the list). The Adrien English series was awarded the All Time Favorite Couple by the Goodreads M/M Romance Group. In 2019, *Fatal Shadows* became the first LGBTQ mobile game created by Moments: Choose Your Story.

She is an Eppie Award winner, a four-time Lambda Literary Award finalist (twice for Gay Mystery), An Edgar nominee, and the first ever recipient of the Goodreads All Time Favorite M/M Author award.

Josh is married and lives in Southern California.

Find other Josh Lanyon titles at www.joshlanyon.com, and follow Josh on Twitter, Facebook, Goodreads, Instagram and Tumblr.

For extras and exclusives, join Josh on Patreon.

Also by Josh Lanyon

NOVELS

The ADRIEN ENGLISH Mysteries

Fatal Shadows • A Dangerous Thing • The Hell You Say
Death of a Pirate King • The Dark Tide
So This is Christmas • Stranger Things Have Happened

The HOLMES & MORIARITY Mysteries

Somebody Killed His Editor • All She Wrote
The Boy with the Painful Tattoo • In Other Words...Murder

The ALL'S FAIR Series

Fair Game • Fair Play • Fair Chance

The ART OF MURDER Series

The Mermaid Murders •The Monet Murders
The Magician Murders • The Monuments Men Murders

OTHER NOVELS

The Ghost Wore Yellow Socks
Mexican Heat (with Laura Baumbach)
Strange Fortune • Come Unto These Yellow Sands
This Rough Magic • Stranger on the Shore • Winter Kill
Murder in Pastel • Jefferson Blythe, Esquire
The Curse of the Blue Scarab • Murder Takes the High Road
Séance on a Summer's Night
The Ghost Had an Early Check-Out

NOVELLAS

The DANGEROUS GROUND Series

Dangerous Ground • Old Poison • Blood Heat
Dead Run • Kick Start

The I SPY Series

I Spy Something Bloody • I Spy Something Wicked
I Spy Something Christmas

The IN A DARK WOOD Series

In a Dark Wood • The Parting Glass

The DARK HORSE Series

The Dark Horse • The White Knight

The DOYLE & SPAIN Series

Snowball in Hell

The HAUNTED HEART Series

Haunted Heart Winter

The XOXO FILES Series

Mummie Dearest

OTHER NOVELLAS

Cards on the Table • The Dark Farewell •The Darkling Thrush
The Dickens with Love • Don't Look Back • A Ghost of a Chance
Lovers and Other Strangers • Out of the Blue
A Vintage Affair • Lone Star (in Men Under the Mistletoe)
Green Glass Beads (in Irregulars) • Blood Red Butterfly
Everything I Know • Baby, It's Cold • A Case of Christmas
Murder Between the Pages • Slay Ride

SHORT STORIES

A Limited Engagement • The French Have a Word for It
In Sunshine or In Shadow • Until We Meet Once More
Icecapade (in His for the Holidays) • Perfect Day
Heart Trouble • In Plain Sight • Wedding Favors
Wizard's Moon • Fade to Black • Night Watch
Plenty of Fish • The Boy Next Door
Halloween is Murder

COLLECTIONS

Stories (Vol. 1) • Sweet Spot (the Petit Morts)
Merry Christmas, Darling (Holiday Codas)
Christmas Waltz (Holiday Codas 2)
I Spy...Three Novellas
Point Blank (Five Dangerous Ground Novellas)
Dark Horse, White Knight (Two Novellas)
The Adrien English Mysteries
The Adrien English Mysteries 2